From the author whom *Romantic Times* hails as "the reigning queen of Americana romance"

# LINDA LAEL MILLER

The three brothers who began it all

## THE McKETTRICK COWBOYS

McKettrick land. McKettrick pride. The foundation of a dynasty.

### Rafe McKettrick

Proud, passionate, and hot-tempered, he's determined to win his inheritance, but he never dreamed that the cost would be his heart.

### Kade McKettrick

He's determined not to lose to his brother in the marriage stakes—but he hadn't counted on falling in love.

### Jeb McKettrick

He thought proposing marriage would be the hardest thing he ever did. That was before his new bride's secret past wounded his pride.

**These titles are also available as eBooks.**

**And praise for more McKettrick stories by**

# *LINDA LAEL MILLER*

"Highly enjoyable. . . . Strong characterization and a vivid western setting make for a fine historical romance."

> —*Publishers Weekly* on *McKettrick's Choice*

"Engrossing western romance. . . . Miller has created unforgettable characters and woven a many-faceted yet coherent and lovingly told tale."

> —*Booklist* (starred review) on *McKettrick's Choice*

"There's just something about those McKettricks . . . that makes you want to jump right into the pages and stay for a while."

> —*Romantic Times* on *McKettricks of Texas: Garrett*

"Fast-moving, emotional."

> —*Booklist* on *McKettricks of Texas: Garrett*

"A passionate love too long denied drives the action in this multifaceted, emotionally rich reunion story that overflows with breathtaking sexual chemistry."

> —*Library Journal* on *McKettricks of Texas: Tate*

"High drama, spiked with intense romance."

> —*Publishers Weekly* on *McKettrick's Heart*

"Love and blazing sex ensue in this satisfying romance."

> —*Booklist* on *McKettrick's Heart*

"Heartwarming and heartbreakingly poignant."

> —*Romantic Times* on *McKettrick's Heart*

## ALSO BY LINDA LAEL MILLER

# Linda Lael Miller

## High Country Bride

**POCKET BOOKS**

New York  London  Toronto  Sydney

A Pocket Book published by
POCKET BOOKS, a division of Simon & Schuster, Inc.
1230 Avenue of the Americas, New York, NY 10020

Copyright © 2002 by Linda Lael Miller

First Pocket Books printing December 2002

20   19   18   17   16   15   14   13

POCKET BOOKS and colophon are registered trademarks of Simon & Schuster, Inc.

For information regarding special discounts for bulk purchases, please contact Simon & Schuster Special Sales at 1-800-506-1949 or business@simonandschuster.com.

The Simon & Schuster Speakers Bureau can bring authors to your live event. For more information or to book an event contact the Simon & Schuster Speakers Bureau at 1-866-248-3049 or visit our website at www.simonspeakers.com.

Cover illustration by Aleta Rafton

Manufactured in the United States of America

ISBN 978-0-7434-2273-4
ISBN 978-0-7434-2457-8 (ebook)

*For my nieces:*

*Kelly Lael,*
*Angela Lang,*
*Samantha Lang,*
*Jenni Readman,*
*And great niece*
*Courtney Lael*

*With much love*

# High Country Bride

# ❧ *Prologue* ❧

*Early Winter 1884*

*Arizona Territory*

ANGUS MCKETTRICK hated every thorn and cactus, every sprig of sagebrush, every juniper tree and jackrabbit, and hunk of red rock for fifty miles in all directions, and if he could have scorched the land bare as a pig's hide at rendering time, he'd have done it, yes, sir. He'd have laughed while the flames roared from one end of that ranch to the other, consuming it all.

He stood high on a hilltop, gazing now at Georgia's marker, a snow-white angel, chiseled from the finest Italian marble and big as a full-grown woman. He'd ordered it a week after his wife passed over, had it sent all the way from New Orleans, Louisiana. Georgia's people hailed from that godforsaken country, with its swamps and alligators and wet heat, and seemed to favor fine stonework, not just on their graves but in their gardens, too. Angus reckoned it was because so many of them had French in their blood and were thus inclined toward frippery and fuss.

"Georgia," he said, right out loud, since they were alone there, the two of them, in that high, windswept place. "I turned ~~fifty~~ seventy-five today." She'd know that, of course; she surely kept track of him, even from the other side. Had she been among the living, she'd have built him one of her brown sugar and molasses cakes to mark the occasion. "Far as I'm concerned, that's plum old enough for anybody, but I guess the good Lord doesn't see it that way." The good Lord, in Angus's experience, was a contrary sort, slow to act and as likely to be cussed as to be kind when He did, but real just the same.

Angus extended a hoary finger, traced her name and the carefully chosen words of remembrance carved into the white stone pedestal, atop which the angel stood on one bare and delicate foot, trumpet raised, eyes set upon the heavens, ready to take flight.

GEORGIA BEAUDREAUX McKETTRICK
CHERISHED WIFE, BELOVED MOTHER
TAKEN TOO SOON

Beneath were the dates that enclosed her life like brackets: BORN SEPTEMBER 13, 1824, DIED JUNE 17, 1870. It seemed a travesty to Angus, the mere attempt to confine so much beauty, so much love and laughter and vitality—all the vast configuration of traits that had been his Georgia—to a handful of vanished years.

If only he could have gone in her place. It was a coward's wish, he knew, but he'd made it often since her passing. It wouldn't have served, his passing over first, though, because as strong as she was, as smart as she was, Georgia probably couldn't have held on to the ranch all this time, a woman on her own, and the boys, the eldest just fifteen when she died, would have been more hindrance than help.

Hell, they were *still* more hindrance than help, all three of them.

Angus laid a hand on the angel's foot, ruminating. "It's past time those lads of ours had done with their carousing and got themselves settled down, I'm thinking," he said, when he'd gotten all his maverick thoughts rounded up and herded in the same direction. "Our Rafe, he's going to turn thirty this June, and he's nothing but a rascal, brawling in the saloons and chasing women. Thinks there's one opinion in all the world that matters, and that's his own. Why, he spent half the winter in and out of jail. And Kade's no better, he just plays his cards closer to his vest, that's all. As for Jeb—" He paused, shook his head. "That young'un is good-lookin' as the devil before the fall, wild as a mustang, and ornery as a three-legged mule. I was too easy on 'em, Georgia. I listened to you, and never laid a hand on one of them, but I see now that I should have taken a strap to their hides once in a while. Yes, indeed. They might have been worth something today if I'd hauled them off to the woodshed now and again, the way my pa did me."

He turned his head, looked out over the land that had soaked up so much of his blood and sweat and spit since he first came there from Texas, way back in 1853. He'd been a young man then, torn asunder, in some deep and private region of the soul, by the loss of his first wife, Ellie, who'd perished giving birth to their son. Overwhelmed, he'd left the infant behind, for Ellie's people to raise; maybe that was the greatest regret of his life, the secret sin that prickled his conscience like a burr, even after all these years.

The plain, unflattering truth was that he'd blamed that little baby for Ellie's being gone, turned his back on his own flesh and blood. It was wrongheaded of him——he'd acted like a damn fool jackass and he knew it——and still he'd never been able to get past that feeling of quiet, unreasoning rage. He'd walked away from Florence and Dill's place, Dill being Ellie's favorite brother, not daring to look back, and joined up with a big cattle outfit, helping to drive a herd of longhorns north to Kansas City.

He'd had a few letters from Florence over the years, telling him Holt was a fine, sturdy boy with a good head on his shoulders, and Angus had sent a few dollars their way whenever he could, scratching out a terse reply if he had writing paper handy. Flo never once asked him for anything, would have died first, but she and Dill ran a hardscrabble farm, and raising a son was a costly process.

Gradually, the letter writing ceased. On the day Holt turned twenty-one, Angus arranged for a bank in Denver to wire the boy his legacy, a thousand dollars for every year of his young life. Holt, stiff-necked as any McKettrick before him, had turned right around and wired it back, every cent.

Stubborn himself, Angus had put the funds aside, still earmarked for Holt, and they'd been gathering interest ever since.

Now, Angus had nearly thirty thousand acres, grass enough for a sizable herd of cattle and almost as many horses, though he'd started with just a half section, a broken-down horse, and an old ox. He smiled, remembering those early days. There had been a great deal of sorrow and hardship, and yet, in many ways, that had been the best part of his life, because his years with Georgia, the loving years, the healing years, had still been ahead of him, waiting to be lived.

He chuckled rawly and shook his head. She'd lasted one term as the schoolmarm in Indian Rock, Georgia had, and then, worn out by his dogged style of courtship, she'd finally thrown up her hands, laughing, and said she'd marry him.

Looking out over the land, he turned somber again. He squared his shoulders and jutted out his strong Scottish-Irish chin. "Georgia," he said, in the tone of a man expecting an argument, "it's time those sons of ours learned some responsibility, got themselves married off proper, gave you and me some grandchildren. I'm laying down the law. They've run hog wild long enough, and now, by God, they're going to start acting like men!"

The only answer was the sweet spring breeze, ruffling his white hair.

Angus breathed it in, as if it bore some wordless message from Georgia, and put his hat back on. He whistled for his horse, a venerable black and white gelding named Navajo, and swung up into the saddle with only slightly less ease than usual. Though Angus had the rheumatism in all his joints, he'd been on horseback most every day of his life, and he mounted and dismounted with no more bother than if he'd spat or scratched his head. The reins resting lightly in the palm of his left hand, Angus tugged at his hat brim with the other, in a gesture of farewell, and headed down the steep hillside toward home.

When he reached the barn, after a quarter of an hour of hard traveling, he turned Navajo over to Finn Williams, one of the hands, and set off in the direction of the house, spurs jingling a deceptively merry tune as he went. He came into the kitchen through the back door, by way of the porch, and almost forgot to take off his hat.

"You don't walk on my floors with spurs on your boots, Mr. McKettrick," said Concepcion, who'd been keeping house for him ever since her husband, Manuel, a sheepherder, had gotten himself cut up and then hanged by a bunch of outlaw cowpunchers, some twenty years back. She was kneading bread dough at the big plank worktable next to the fireplace, her face and the bodice of her calico dress smudged with flour. "How many times must I tell you?"

He flung the woman a narrow look, but he backtracked to the threshold, unfastened his spurs, and tossed them out onto the porch with a resounding clang. Then he hung up his hat and coat on their allotted pegs next to the door.

"Where," he began, with portent, "are my sons?"

Concepcion arched her eyebrows, shrugged her shoulders. "How should I know?" she asked, she who knew everything about everybody, not only in the McKettrick household but for miles around, too.

Angus figured her nose was still a little out of joint because that morning, at breakfast, he'd told her straight out that she was getting a little beefy and ought to cut back some on her vittles. Now, he favored her with a glower, and she didn't even pretend to be cowed. She could be almost as fierce as old Geronimo himself, and just as likely to stake a man out on an anthill if he crossed her once too often.

"All right, then," she said. "Rafe went to town day before yesterday, which you would know already if you ever listened to a word I say, and Kade left the house this morning, right after you did—something about a horse. Jeb is still in bed."

Angus glared up at the ceiling. "Is the boy ailing?"

Concepcion smiled fondly. She'd fussed over those three scoundrels like an old hen, ever since Georgia had passed away, taken their part against him, their own pa, separated them when they got to tussling fit to kill one another. Oh, yes, she loved them, loved them like they were her own, and she made no secret of it, either. "He's just tired, I think," she said.

Angus went to the base of the rear stairway and clasped

the newel post with such force that it snapped off in his hand. "Jeb!" he yelled, his thunderous voice echoing. "Roll your hind end out of that bed and get down here, pronto!"

The boy appeared on the upper landing just about the time Angus was ready to head up there and drag him out by the hair. He was blinking, Jeb was, wearing a pair of misbuttoned trousers and nothing else, and he looked affronted at being disturbed.

He was twenty years old, dammit. Why, at Jeb's age, Angus had been earning a living for the better part of five years.

"What is it, Pa?" he asked.

"It's ten in the morning," Angus bellowed in reply, pounding the newel post back into place with the side of one fist. "What do you think you're doing, lolling around in bed like some old whore after a big night? We've got a ranch to run here!"

Jeb flushed, and his eyes—McKettrick blue, Georgia had called them—flashed. "I know that, Pa," he said. "I just spent a week running the fence lines in a buckboard, remember?"

So he had. The reminder took some of the edge off Angus's bluster, but not much. "Get dressed," he said. "I want you to find your brothers, both of them, and make sure they're here at dinnertime." Dinner, on the Triple M, was the midday meal, not just another word for supper, like in some places, where folks didn't know what was what. "I've got something to say to all of you."

Jeb muttered an imprecation that would probably have

gotten him horsewhipped if Angus had heard it clearly, but he staggered back to his room, got himself dressed, and rode out within twenty minutes, in search of Rafe and Kade.

The mantel clock was striking two when the family sat down at the long table in the kitchen, and all the boys were there, cleaned up, too, though Rafe looked some the worse for wear, with a big green and purple shiner practically obliterating his right eye. He'd been talking politics again, it would seem; if that young fellow didn't start a range war all on his own, it would be a miracle.

Kade clearly wanted to be elsewhere, and Jeb was still riled because he'd had to roust himself out of bed before noon.

"I've come to a decision," Angus told them.

They waited.

Angus cleared his throat. "I'm an old man. Seventy-five, in fact. Ready to hang up my riggin' and take it easy for a while. Maybe even turn my toes up for good." He stopped, drew a deep breath, and released it. "But before I do that, dammit, I want a grandchild. An heir."

The boys looked at one another, then at him, but no one spoke.

Angus went on. "So here's what I decided. First one of you gets himself married and produces a child—son or daughter, it doesn't matter to me—will have this house, a pile of my money, three-quarters of the herd, and all the mineral and water rights."

That got a rise out of them, as he'd known it would.

Rafe nearly overturned the bench he was sitting on. Kade scowled, and Jeb looked like he was ready to yank down the oil lamp suspended over the table and take a bite out of it.

"Wait a minute, Pa," Rafe said, testy-like. "You always said you were going to divide everything evenly, ~~between~~ *among* the three of us. Now, it's all going to one. What I want to know is, where does this fine plan leave the other two?"

Angus smiled. "Why, it leaves them sucking hind tit, of course," he said. "Taking their orders from whoever had the good sense to take me seriously and get himself a wife and baby. Now, pass me those mashed potatoes."

Kade slid the big crockery bowl, heaped with steaming spuds, to his father. His expression was grim. He had Georgia's deep brown hair, with glints of red, along with her green eyes, and a generous measure of her stubborn nature, too. "You want us to go out and get married. Just like that."

"That's right," Angus said, gesturing. "Pass that platter of fried chicken down here, if you're just going to sit there looking at it." He paused, favored each of his sons with a benign glance. "But getting hitched isn't enough. There's got to be a babe, too. I trust you wasters know how *that's* done?"

Jeb was red from the neck up. A vein jumped under his right temple. "Where are we supposed to find these women?" he asked.

Angus speared the best pieces of chicken—after all, it was his birthday—and shoved the denuded platter back into the center of the long table. "I reckon that would be *your* problem," he said, "not mine."

The silence that followed was stony and sullen.

Angus ate with good appetite, and at the end of the meal Concepcion brought a cake from the pantry, complete with icing and a candle burning in the middle, and then she commenced to singing the birthday song.

Nobody else joined in.

# CHAPTER

## 1

RAFE MCKETTRICK PEERED at the small, tasteful advertisement in the back of the *Cattleman's Journal,* dog-eared the page, and then slammed the magazine against the edge of the desk in his father's study. It was a desperate measure, sending away for a bride, the way a person might send away for a book, or a custom-made belt buckle, but then, Rafe was a desperate man.

He had no doubt whatsoever that his father had meant precisely what he'd said that day at dinner; Angus was not the sort to make idle threats. Rafe neither knew nor wanted any other life than the one he had, right there on the Triple M, and he'd be damned if he'd spend the rest of his days dancing to whatever tune Kade or Jeb chose to play. That meant he needed a wife, pronto, and if he got her in the family way on the way home from the church, so much the better.

Pushing back the big leather-upholstered chair, he

jerked open a desk drawer and took out a sheet of the fancy vellum stationery his pa used for business correspondence. With great ceremony, he selected a pen, opened a bottle of India ink, and ordered his thoughts. Some moments had passed when he began to write.

> *To Whom It May Concern,*
>     *Please send one wife. Healthy, with good teeth. Able to read and write. And cook. Must want children. Soon.*
>                         *Rafe McKettrick*
>                         *Triple M Ranch,*
>                         *near Indian Rock, Arizona Territory*

Rafe read the note over a couple of times, decided it could not be improved upon in any significant way, folded the page, and jammed it into an envelope, along with a draft drawn on the bank in town. Nothing to do but slap on a stamp and get the letter onto a stagecoach headed east.

He frowned as he copied out the address. The few times he'd had occasion to send a letter, he'd simply entrusted it to whoever happened to be heading into town next, but this was different. For one thing, it said "Happy Home Matrimonial Service" right there on the front of the envelope, for everybody to see, and that alone was fodder enough for a merciless ribbing from every other man on the ranch. For another, he didn't want either of his brothers to beat him to the punch by swiping his letter, copying his idea, or both.

No, sir, Rafe reflected, leaning back in the chair, tucking the missive into his vest pocket, he'd post it himself, personally. Ride all the way down to Indian Rock and meet the outgoing stagecoach.

He sighed, closed his eyes, and kicked his feet up onto the desk.

He reckoned it wouldn't be so bad, having a wife. He'd have a woman right there handy, on a cold night, and that was no mean blessing in a place as isolated and lonesome as the Triple M. He'd get her to expecting before the ink dried in the family Bible, and that would be that. The ranch would be his, when the time came, and Kade and Jeb would either have to do his bidding or saddle up and ride.

He knew they'd never leave—the place was in their blood, the way it was in his—and he smiled at the thought of working them like a pair of field horses. He'd have them dig a new hole for the privy first, then shovel lime into the old one. The bunkhouse roof needed replacing come spring—they'd be damned lucky if it held up through the coming winter—and of course he and the missus would want an addition built on to the main house, so they could have a little privacy. While Jeb had been working to repair the boundary fences, many of them needed to be replaced, and up on the northern boundary there was timber to be cut. While his brothers were sweating over the chores he would outline for them, he would ride out looking for the fine roan stallion he'd seen haunting the red canyons like a ghost, but never gotten close to, and the capture of that horse would mark the beginning of his own herd.

Somebody slapped his feet off the desk, and he sat bolt upright, with a sputtered curse, startled half out of his skin and ready to fight.

Kade, two years younger at twenty-seven, was gazing down at him. "What were you thinking about just then, Big Brother?" he asked in a slow drawl. He perched on the edge of the desk and folded his arms, eyes narrowed. "Why, from the look on your face, I'd say you were up to no good."

Rafe was glad he'd slipped the letter into his vest pocket, where it was out of sight. He laid splayed fingers to his chest and feigned an injured expression. "What's this? You don't trust me, Little Brother?"

"Not unless he's stupid, he doesn't," put in Jeb, from the doorway, his mouth curved into one of those wry grins that always made Rafe want to slap the holy bejiggers out of him. "Me, I'd sooner trust a polecat." He stepped into the study, closed the door behind him. The large room seemed to shrink, with all of them there; Rafe considered getting up to open a window, but he wasn't about to risk losing the chair he already thought of as his own.

He did sit up straight, though, planting his boots squarely on the floor.

Kade turned, watched their youngest brother approach, drag up a chair of his own. Sit. He moved languidly, Jeb did, as if his bones were fitted loosely at the joints. He was the best broncobuster on the ranch—Rafe and Kade had seen their little brother thrown from many a horse, and most of the time he landed on his feet.

"What are we going to do?" Jeb asked, serious now, resting one foot on the opposite knee. "This isn't just another of his tangents, you know. Pa meant what he said out there."

Kade nodded grimly, arms still folded. He was the quiet, mannerly brother, the thoughtful one, the reader and resident quoter of poetry, the one you had to watch like a ring-tailed snake. "I believe he did," he agreed. "It's got to do with his birthday. He's feeling old."

"Hell," Rafe said, "he *is* old."

Jeb chuckled, shook his head. "Tell that to that ranch hand he caught beating one of the mares with a switch last week," he said. "The fella's still laid up over there at Daisy's rooming house. Doc says it might be spring before the poor bastard can hit the trail."

Kade grinned. "Daisy," he said. "Now there's a prospective bride. Why don't you go sparking her, Rafe?"

"I'd sooner take up with an old sow bear," Rafe answered, and he was serious as a Montana winter. Daisy Pert was a dainty six-foot-five, in her stocking feet. She weighed more than a loaded hay wagon and had two teeth in her head, both of them bad. She chewed snoose, and anyway, she was sweet on the circuit preacher's cross-eyed brother, Lemuel, who feared her more than the devil himself.

"I think Rafe's got something up his sleeve," Kade

speculated smoothly. The cadence of his voice was light, but there was a quiet, brotherly menace in it that you had to listen hard to hear. He leaned in a little. "Don't you, Rafe?"

Rafe did his damnedest to look innocent. He hadn't polished the skill over the years, so it didn't come easy, the way fighting, shooting, and riding did. "What makes you say a thing like that?" he asked.

"Just a feeling," Kade answered evenly, taking in the splotches of fresh ink drying on the blotter. "And twenty-seven years of experience."

Just then, the double doors of the study burst open, and Concepcion blew in like a storm cloud coming over the rise, burdened with bad weather and bristling with lightning bolts. Rafe, who had been expecting their father, was only slightly relieved; this didn't look like much of a reprieve to him.

Concepcion turned with immeasurable dignity, latched the two doors, and when she faced them again, her dark eyes were blazing. "How could you?" she seethed. "How could you forget such an important day?"

Jeb stood, if belatedly, his blue eyes dancing with mischief, and gestured for Concepcion to take his chair. "I can't speak for my brothers," he said, "but it just so happens that I *did* remember."

Kade and Rafe glared at him.

"Like hell you did," Rafe said.

"I've got a book upstairs, wrapped up fancy and tied with a ribbon, just for Pa," Jeb told them.

"You bought that for that new hurdy-gurdy girl that just hired on at the saloon," Kade accused.

Concepcion plopped into the chair, singed the short hairs on Kade and Rafe with a single scorching glance. The look she gave Jeb was only slightly less incendiary; clearly, she was skeptical about his story, but willing to give him the benefit of a doubt. Females were always inclined to give that rascal the benefit of a doubt, it seemed to Rafe.

Jeb's smile became a smirk, and he gave a cocky shrug. "Think what you like," he told his brothers.

"Sit down," Concepcion told him smartly, "and shut your mouth."

Jeb grimaced and sat on the raised hearth, his hands loosely clasped and dangling between his knees. Kade shifted his attention from the ceiling to the floor, and Rafe fixed his eyes on a point just above Concepcion's left shoulder.

"Do you know what I think?" she rattled on, shaking that familiar finger, taking them all in. Rafe figured they were about to get some clarification on what she thought, whether they already knew or not. "Your father is right. It's time you were settled down, all of you, with homes and families of your own."

Kade was the first to break. He gave a long sigh. "I forgot that it was Pa's birthday," he admitted. "All the same, I don't see what that has to do with—"

Concepcion turned huffy. "If you thought about something besides books, bad women, and horses," she accused, "you would realize that you are wasting your life." When Jeb and Rafe grinned, enjoying Kade's discomfort, she turned on them, fierce as a she-wolf. "You think you are any better, either of you?" She made a spitting sound, purely Latin and very expressive. "You, Rafe, with your temper and your brawling? You, Jeb, with your card-playing?"

Kade raised both hands, palms out, in a gesture of surrender.

Rafe set his jaw and tried to stare Concepcion down, knowing all the while that he'd never succeed.

"I guess," Jeb said meekly, breaking the ominous silence, "I'll just go and give Pa the birthday present I got him."

"You set one foot out of this room," Kade warned, in a furious undertone, "and I'll take a layer of hide off you, right here and right now."

Jeb flushed and shot to his feet, fists clenched, always ready for a fight. Concepcion was quick, though, due to long practice, and she got between him and Kade before either of them could throw a punch. Being the youngest, Jeb usually got himself whupped in these little set-tos, but he kept trying anyhow.

"That is enough," Concepcion said, in a tone no one could have mistaken for anything but utter sincerity.

Jeb laid his hands on her shoulders, turned her around, and made calf eyes at her. "Concepcion," he said, sweet as pie, "will you marry me, and be the mother of my children?"

For a moment, there was silence, reminiscent of those few seconds of shock that come just after a wasp's sting and right before the venom starts to spread. A cracking sound followed, and Jeb's face glowed red where Concepcion had slapped him.

"*No more*," she fumed, all fury and fire.

Rafe and Kade looked at each other, stifling their laughter, and just as quickly looked away.

"You have broken that fine man's heart," Concepcion went on, after pausing to gather herself up like a chicken settling its ruffled feathers. "You are a disappointment, a disgrace. All of you."

They all stared at her. None of them had ever seen her in such a fine dither, and given some of the pranks they'd pulled over the years, both independently and in cahoots with one another, that was saying something.

"Until you start treating your father with the respect he deserves," she said, straightening her spine and smoothing her flour-splotched skirts, "I will not cook another bite of food for any of you. I will not sew buttons or make beds or wash clothes. For once in your lives, you can do for yourselves." With that, she turned, chin at a regal angle, eyes bright with conviction, and swept to the study doors. She worked the latch, flung the doors wide, and stepped through without looking back.

"Do you think she meant all that?" Jeb asked, not so cocksure now.

Kade rolled his eyes. "Oh, yeah," he said, resigned. "She meant it, all right."

Rafe stared at the ceiling, wondering how long it would be before his bride arrived. He didn't fancy cooking his own meals, and he'd never done a lick of laundry in his life. He'd best get himself down to Indian Rock and send off that letter.

"Pa will never allow it," Jeb said, grasping at straws. "He pays her to cook and clean."

"For him," Kade pointed out. "Not us."

Jeb pondered that, looking pained. "Oh."

"We'd better figure out how to get back on her good side," Kade speculated. "It's that or eat in the bunkhouse, and you know what Red's cooking is like—scorched beans for breakfast, dinner, supper, and dessert."

"What do you suggest?" Rafe asked, without opening his eyes. He was doing his best to keep his spirits up by imagining himself with a wife by his side. In the meantime, he'd just make do with meals in town. That Chinese fella, Kwan Somebody-or-other, could do his wash once a month. A man just had to be resourceful, that was all.

"I'd suggest," Kade said, "that we do what Pa wants. We do that, and our problems will be over."

"That goes for one of us," Jeb said, and something in his tone indicated that he figured on being that one. "The other two are pretty well screwed."

Rafe didn't comment.

"I plan on getting myself married to the first decent woman I can find," Kade said confidently. "You two needn't worry too much, though. I won't make you salute or wear uniforms. You can put in a ten-hour day, like all the other hands, and take off one Sunday a month."

Rafe opened his eyes. "Just who do you figure on marrying?" he asked, suspicious and more than a little alarmed. Of the three of them, Kade was the craftiest. A fellow never knew what might be going on in that clockwork mind of his.

Kade smiled; butter wouldn't have melted in his mouth. "Do you really think I'd be fool enough to tell you?" he asked. Then, just like that, he strolled out without another word. You'd have thought he had a wife upstairs at that moment, in the throes of childbirth, he was so damn sure of himself.

Rafe slammed to his feet to follow, and Jeb was right behind him.

Out in the large entryway, Kade was buckling on his gunbelt. He took his round-brimmed hat down from the usual hook on the hall tree, stuck it on his head, and reached for his three-quarter-length coat, the one Concepcion said made him look like a drifter and an outlaw.

"You headed for town?" Rafe demanded, brows lowered.

Kade straightened his collar, checked the angle of his hat in the wall mirror next to the long-case clock, and offered not a single word in reply.

Jeb, meanwhile, was sprinting up the stairs, taking them two at a time. Probably going to get the present he'd bought for that saloon girl and go toadying to their father, acting like he'd remembered all along what day it was.

Rafe was downright disgusted. His brothers were deceitful men, both of them.

He reached for his own hat, his coat, and the gun belt and pistol he kept in the top drawer of the hall bureau. Yes, sir, he'd just ride on over to Indian Rock, meet the stage, and send out his letter. Before he could say "Shivaree," his bride would be arriving, ready to set up housekeeping and start a baby.

Hell, with a little luck, she might even be halfway presentable.

## Kansas City, Missouri

Emmeline Harding closed the second-story window of Miss Becky's Boardinghouse with a bang, barely muffling the dusty din of bawling cattle and shouting cowboys choking the street below. Another herd, probably driven up from Texas, headed for the stockyards. Within an hour, the drovers would be streaming in, wanting hot baths, whiskey, and women, though not necessarily in that order. With the help of her "girls," Becky, Emmeline's aunt, would see that they were all accommodated. For a price, of course.

Emmeline sighed. From a social standpoint—essentially the only standpoint that mattered to her at the time, since she was just a week shy of nineteen—she was neither fish nor fowl. Becky had sent her to the best finishing school in the city and kept her well away from the customers—and for what? With all her splendid manners, lovely clothes, and book learning, she was still a pariah, unwelcome in the respectable homes of her former class-mates.

Life, it seemed to Emmeline, was one big party, and she wasn't invited.

Standing on the other side of the upstairs parlor, with its bead-trimmed lampshades and velvet drapes, Becky rolled a black fishnet stocking up over one slender leg. She was a beauty, Becky was, with a real head for busi-ness, and she'd been unfailingly kind to Emmeline, pro-tecting her and providing for her ever since infancy, when she'd been orphaned. Now, Becky watched her niece thoughtfully.

"You spinning day dreams again?" she asked.

"No," Emmeline lied. Often bored and always lonely, she liked to take refuge within the broad borders of her imagination. There, she'd constructed a lovely little cot-tage for herself, and a morally upright husband, too, though he was unknown to her as yet, several rosy-cheeked, golden-haired children, and two rotund cats. The place boasted shutters on the windows and flowers in the yard, and at the base of the walk there was a white gate that creaked a little, when the weather was dry. There were other scenarios, too, to fit her different moods; in one, she was held captive by Indians, the mate of a pas-sionate brave called Snow Wolf, who touched her in ways that made her blood heat.

Becky didn't look in Emmeline's direction right away, as she was busy examining her reflection in the ornate full-length mirror next to the door. Becky was tall and voluptuous, with clouds of dark hair, flawless white skin, and amazing green eyes, and even taking her reputation into consideration, half the ranchers and businessmen in Missouri would probably have married her and put her up in a fine house if she so much as crooked a finger at them. Apparently satisfied with her appearance, she turned to her niece.

"I don't reckon I need to tell you to stay clear of the downstairs parlor until things quiet down a little. You know how cowboys are when they've been on the trail awhile."

Emmeline pulled a face. "I know," she said. She had no desire to "entertain" men, the way her aunt did, but she'd surely been restless lately. She'd read every interesting book in the public library, seen every play that came to town, and stitched up enough samplers to carpet the path to perdition. She was tired of marking time, keeping up appearances, and waiting for her life to begin. If something didn't happen, and soon, well, there was no telling what she'd do.

One by one, the other women who lived at the boardinghouse began to straggle in, most of them yawning, all in various states of charming dishabille. Some greeted Emmeline with a waggle of their fingers, others smiled sleepily. It was one in the afternoon, by the clock on the mantel—the crack of dawn from their point of view.

Becky, who never hesitated to take charge, promptly began to give instructions, a general in silk and gauze, and dispatched her troops to their rooms, there to make themselves fetching, before taking up their battle stations in the downstairs parlor. That sumptuous room had always fascinated Emmeline, though she was seldom allowed to set foot inside it. There were paintings of bare-naked women on the walls, Turkish carpets on the floor, and the heavy draperies were fringed in gold. Cigar smoking was permitted, and whiskey was discreetly served, for though Becky had no license to sell spirits, neither did she fear the law. The marshal and his deputies were regular customers, and due to the pitiful salaries they received from the city counsel, they always got a special rate.

Today, the pull of that mysterious room was all but irresistible.

Emmeline tried to curb her adventurous nature—it was this same reckless bent, after all, that had nearly gotten her arrested for swimming naked in the mill pond, one moonlit night, with one or two "wild" girls, and caused her to break an arm climbing a tree on still another occasion—but the hours ahead were too long and too dull and, quite simply, she succumbed.

Becky had been gone an hour when, moving like a genie summoned from a bottle after a long, long sleep, Emmeline sneaked into her aunt's sumptuous bed chamber and opened the massive wardrobe across from the fireplace. The interior swelled with clouds of colorful silk, satin, velvet, and lace—such a delicious contrast to her practical brown crinoline dress—and a wondrous disarray of feathers, bangles, and beads. After due deliberation, she selected a daring red gown of shiny fabric, with an edging of black lace, scrambled out of her own clothes, and put it on. She stood spellbound in front of Becky's mirror, adjusting the shoulder straps.

Emmeline barely recognized herself. She loosened her nearly blond hair, caught up in a prim coronet at her nape, and pinched her cheeks. Her gray-green eyes, usually calm, sparkled with spirit, and she struck a provocative pose, putting her hands on her hips and jutting out her bosom. She smiled a saucy smile, the way she'd seen the other girls do, countless times, and whirled around once, admiring herself.

She loved the sensation of being someone quite apart from her ordinary self, someone entirely new, someone bold and even a little brazen, and she was reluctant to return to her normal drab personage.

What harm could possibly be done, she wondered, if she crept downstairs, just for a very few minutes, and mingled? The place was already crowded; the noise from below told her that. If she kept to the far edges of the gathering, she could avoid Becky's notice and indulge in a little harmless playacting. Flirt with a cowboy or two, play at being a lady of the evening, and then slip back upstairs without ever being discovered.

The plan nearly unfolded in precisely that fashion.

Nearly.

Emmeline put a little extra sway in her hips as she descended the stairs, keeping an eye out for her aunt all the while. As she'd hoped, Becky was busy holding court in a far corner of the room, surrounded by spruced-up wranglers swilling liquor. The other women were equally occupied, chatting, pretending to tell fortunes, serving drinks.

Her gaze went unerringly to the biggest, most imposing man in the room. His air of authority immediately marked him as the trail boss, or even the owner of some big ranch down by the Mexican border. He had wavy brown hair and hazel eyes, and he was still wearing his long canvas duster, even though the weather was warm. She glimpsed the handle of a pistol, strapped low on his left hip.

He turned to her like a compass needle finding north, and a smile twitched at one corner of his mouth, almost imperceptible. There was a trace of mockery in it, as though he suspected she was playing a game, pretending to be someone she wasn't.

He started toward her, his stride long and slow and graceful.

Emmeline, still hovering on the stairs, took an awkward step backward and nearly fell on her bottom.

He gripped the newel post in one leather-gloved hand, watching her. He had removed his hat at the door—that was a rule of Becky's—and she didn't allow guns, either. Not normally, anyway. Whoever he was, this man lived by a code of his own.

"Howdy," he said. It was enough to mark him as a Texan, the way he said that one, honeyed word, caressing it as it rolled over his tongue.

Emmeline concentrated on not swallowing her own.

"Hello," she managed, at last, and felt a hot flush course from her toes to her hairline. She wanted to turn and bolt, but at the same time she was powerless to move.

"You must be new here," he drawled. "I don't remember you from last time."

Emmeline pressed her lips together briefly. "Yes," she agreed awkwardly. "That's right. I'm—I'm new."

He raised one eyebrow slightly. "What's your name?"

She hesitated, glanced in her aunt's direction, and saw that Becky was still blessedly occupied and thus had failed to notice her. "Lola," she said, having read the name in a novel. "Lola McGoneagle."

He smiled again, leaning against the stair rail and watching her. "Well, Miss Lola," he said, "I'm mighty glad to make your acquaintance. It's been a real long trip up from Texas."

Emmeline swallowed so hard that her throat ached. "Oh," she said stupidly.

He grinned. "Buy you a drink?"

Emmeline hesitated, and then decided to live dangerously. She would write about this lovely, dangerous encounter later, in her remembrance book, she thought, and felt a pleasant thrill at the prospect. "Yes," she said. "I would like a drink."

"What's your pleasure?"

This time, Emmeline didn't just swallow, she gulped. Good Lord. He wanted to know what kind of liquor she preferred, and she'd barely tasted the stuff, beyond taking a little brandy in her eggnog last Christmas Eve. "Whatever you're having," she said. When he turned away to approach the elegant table that served as a bar, Emmeline told herself to run. To turn right around and head upstairs and lock herself in the other parlor. Instead, she sat down hard on the step, feeling a little dizzy, and clasped her hands together.

She'd just get her breath, that was all, and *then* she'd flee.

Except that the Texan came back, and seated himself beside her on the step before she worked up enough gumption to stand, let alone make her escape.

"You been in this business long?" the stranger asked, handing her a glass with half an inch of straight whiskey in the bottom, glowing amber.

Emmeline had never even been kissed, let alone done the things she imagined Becky and the others did with men, but she was embarrassed to say so. Another lie leaped readily to her lips, with an ease that both surprised and shamed her. "Oh, yes," she said, flipping through the large repertoire of imagined Emmelines she'd developed over the years. "I came from Chicago, originally. I was on the stage there." It had always been her dream—one of them, anyway—to be an actress, a famous and legendary beauty, in fact, with a fortune at her disposal and countless boon companions. She decided that Lola traveled regularly to Europe, and to all the other places Emmeline had read about as well, enjoying the slavish devotion of kings, princes, and potentates.

He smiled in a way that seemed, well, tolerant to Emmeline, and she was a little stung. "I see," he said. "And now you're—doing this."

She bit her lower lip. No, she said inwardly. "Yes," she said.

He pondered that for a while, very somberly, while sipping his whiskey. Emmeline had yet to imbibe; she held the glass tightly in both hands, willing herself not to spill the stuff on the carpeted stair. "Seems like a hard way to make a living," he observed, after some time.

Emmeline downed the whiskey in a single swig. "Is there an easy way?" she countered, shuddering as the fiery liquid coursed down her throat and burned in her stomach. She was instantly light-headed and gripped a banister post to steady herself.

"I don't guess there is," the man said, and smiled slightly, though his eyes were sad. "More whiskey?"

"Don't mind if I do," Emmeline said. She'd been possessed by some mischievous spirit—that was the only explanation for her present behavior. If Becky caught her at this game, there would be hell to pay.

Still, they talked, Emmeline and the Texan, and drank more whiskey, and the man said his name was Holt, though she couldn't recall, afterward, whether that was his first name or his last. He'd been raised near San Antonio, by an aunt and uncle, and he owned part interest in the herd of cattle Emmeline had seen clogging the street earlier. In time, though how long it was, she couldn't have said, he took her hand, helped her to her feet, and led her up the stairs and into the quiet shadows of the corridor.

There, he kissed her, and though it was pleasant indeed, Emmeline was mildly disappointed. Her reading, and her fantasies, had led her to expect something more, though she couldn't have said precisely what that something was. She sagged against the wall, when it ended, and sighed, causing him to chuckle.

"I thought so," he said wryly.

"Hmm?" she asked, and burped delicately. Her knees seemed a little weak, and she started to slide down the wall, but he caught her, lifted her easily into his arms.

"Your room," he prompted. "Where is it?"

The vague thrill she felt then was neither alarm nor anticipation, but something different, something she didn't recognize. She rubbed one temple, trying to will her thoughts into some semblance of order. "I think you should put me down," she said. "I'm sure this is quite improper."

He chortled at that. "That may be true," he agreed, "but you're in no shape to be wandering around a brothel by yourself."

She sighed again. "I live here," she said.

"So you say," he replied.

Emmeline thought fast, and it wasn't easy, given the fog whirling in her brain. Then she gestured toward the door of a room she knew was empty—only a few days before, Chloe Barker had left Becky's employ, and Kansas City, for good, taking a train west. Emmeline felt a sharp and sudden stab of envy over that, an uncharitable emotion that she'd been able to subvert when she was sober.

"In there," she said. If she could just lie down for a few moments, close her eyes, recover her equilibrium, well, she'd be fine.

The Texan opened the door with a motion of his foot. The ghost scents of lavender water and talcum lingered faintly in the still air, dust motes floating like fragments of stars in the pale gaslight pouring in from the hallway. The bedstead was iron, painted white, and the coverlet was cream-colored sateen, threadbare but still pretty.

Emmeline yawned widely, and the man called Holt laid her down on the mattress, causing the bedsprings to creak. She tried to sit up, remembering that she was still wearing her shoes, aware that there were other, more important matters of concern as well, but he put a hand to her shoulder and she settled deeper into the pillows. She felt a merciful loosening sensation around her ankles as he undid her laces.

That, alas, was the last thing she remembered, for she was caught in a backwash of shadows then, and sent spinning into a place too dark and deep for dreams. When she awakened, the sun was up, and her head ached as though she'd laid it on the railroad track just before the 10:03 came through. The first thing that came to her awareness was that she was alone in the borrowed bed, wearing nothing but her skimpies.

Her eyes went wide as memory returned; bile surged into the back of her throat. Disjointed recollections traipsed one by one through her mind—the red dress, the man from Texas—what was his name?—the whiskey. She stumbled to the washstand next to the window, blinking against the harsh light, bent her head over the porcelain basin, and was violently ill. Then, with frantic motions of her hands, she touched her breasts, her belly, her thighs. She didn't *feel* different. She wasn't sore anywhere, and when she tossed back the bedclothes, holding her breath, there was no blood.

Maybe—*please God*—nothing had happened.

She sat down heavily on the edge of the bed, breathing slowly and deeply, both hands clasped to her stomach, lest it rebel again. And that was when she saw the gold pieces stacked neatly on the bedside table, next to the oil lamp. Emmeline gasped, then fell back on the pillows, yanked the covers up over her head, and wept, for she was surely ruined.

How would she ever explain her foolishness to Becky? Her aunt had spared no effort to make sure Emmeline's life turned out differently from her own. In point of fact, Emmeline would have been sent away to convent school, long ago, if she hadn't begged to stay in Kansas City, and Becky, always tenderhearted, had reluctantly given in. She would regret that decision now.

Just then, the door opened, and Becky stood on the threshold. Her hair was down, brushed to a rich ebony shine, and she wore a silk dressing gown of palest green. "I thought I heard—" she began, and then gasped, her eyes going from Emmeline to the shimmering stack of coins and back again. "Good God, Emmeline," she rasped, *"what have you done?"*

Emmeline bit her lower lip. She was at once too proud and too ashamed to weep before her aunt, and she had no explanation or even an excuse on hand. She merely sat there, wishing she were dead, staring at her aunt's horrified face.

"Who was it?" Becky whispered, white faced and trembling. "I'll shoot the bastard myself—"

Emmeline merely shook her head. Having shifted her gaze to the floor, she found it too heavy to lift again.

Becky hesitated for a few wretched moments, then stormed into the room and slapped Emmeline hard across the face. "You fool, you stupid—ungrateful—little trollop!" she cried, nearly choking on her rage.

Emmeline put a hand to her cheek. Defiance was all that held her together; without it, she would have collapsed, like a building torn from its foundation. "You raised me in a whorehouse," she said. "Did you really think I'd ever be a lady?"

Becky moved as if to strike Emmeline again, then stopped her hand in midair. "Get out of my sight," she whispered. "I can't bear to look at you."

# CHAPTER

## 2

EMMELINE PEERED, through tear-swollen eyes, at the lavish advertisement on the third page of the *Kansas City Star*. She'd been awake all night, weeping and raging by turns, and it could have been said that she wasn't in her right mind that sunny morning.

BRIDES WANTED was the headline, printed in bold type with exclamation points aplenty.

Ladies! Don't wait for that proposal, for it may never come! Start a new and exciting life in the American West! Plenty of opportunity and adventure for everyone! No fee for qualified applicants, all expenses paid! Our fine agency represents men of moral substance and ample means only! Marriages performed by proxy, before departure! Visit Happy Home Matrimonial Service, 67 Fremont Street, Kansas City.

Emmeline sniffled, her imagination stirred, buzzing like a hive full of excited bees. Five minutes later, she pressed a cold rag to her face, donned her best bonnet and her most becoming dress, which was dove gray with black piping around the collar, cuffs, and hem, and marched herself down to the corner, where she stepped aboard the streetcar, paid the one-cent fare, and resolutely took her seat.

She had begun that fateful morning in proud disgrace. When she returned to the boardinghouse, after two hours spent at the Happy Home Matrimonial Service, she was riding in a hansom cab, and she had vouchers for train and stagecoach fare in her drawstring bag, along with a marriage license, signed by a judge and duly recorded at the courthouse.

She was Mrs. Rafe McKettrick, in the eyes of God and man.

She stood stiff-shouldered in the doorway of Becky's office, her trunks hastily packed and waiting on the porch, and announced that she was a married woman now and was leaving to make a new start in the Arizona Territory.

Becky went white at the news. "Good God," she gasped, trying to rise from her desk chair and failing. "You're not serious!"

Emmeline raised her chin a notch. "I have a train to catch," she said.

"This is utter nonsense," Becky said. "You can't just

marry yourself to some stranger and take off for the wilderness!"

"I can," Emmeline told her stiffly, holding up the marriage license. "It's quite legal."

"I'll have it annulled!" Becky pleaded, on her feet now, groping around the edge of the desk to face her niece. "Emmeline, I know I was angry—I struck you and I said things—"

Emmeline shook her head slowly. "None of that matters," she said, somewhat dully. She had a strange, dreamlike feeling, as though she'd fallen into an unseen river and been borne away on the current. There was no going back. "I can't stay here anymore. Not after—" She paused, swallowed hard. "I just can't stay, that's all."

Becky took a desperate, almost bruising hold on her shoulders. "Don't be an idiot, Emmeline! The west is a cruel, uncivilized place, and you can't know what that man is like. Suppose he mistreats you?"

"He won't," Emmeline said. She didn't feel as certain as she sounded, but she probably had Becky fooled. "If he does, I'll leave him."

"And do what? How will you support yourself if this 'husband' of yours turns out to be something less than a prince?" Tears glimmered in Becky's eyes.

"I can teach school," Emmeline replied. "Or maybe dance in a saloon."

Becky's face tightened, filled with grief. "That wasn't funny," she said.

"I didn't mean it to be," Emmeline answered. Then she kissed Becky's cheek, albeit stiffly. "Goodbye," she said. "And thank you for—for everything."

"Emmeline!" Becky called after her.

But Emmeline kept walking.

"Don't think you can ever come back here!" Becky cried. "You leave, and you'd better stay gone for good!"

Tears sprang to Emmeline's eyes, but she didn't reply, didn't look back.

The carriage driver was already loading her trunks into the boot of his cab when she reached the porch, where she stood for a few moments, struggling to recover her composure, watching the shadows of a million leaves dance over the lawn and the stone walkway.

"I'll write," Emmeline said, without turning around, because she knew if she faced her aunt now, she would surely lose her courage and stay. If that happened, she might as well join the business.

Becky didn't speak.

Emmeline descended the porch steps, proceeded down the walk and through the gate. The driver handed her up into the cab, where she arranged her skirts on the cushioned leather seat and kept her eyes straight ahead.

There was a raw spring wind blowing when Emmeline Harding McKettrick finally stepped down off the stagecoach in Indian Rock, Arizona Territory, clutching a satchel in one hand and all her brave, foolish dreams in the other. She pulled her cloak tightly around her shoulders and looked around for a welcoming face amid the rowdy-looking strangers, but it soon became apparent that no one had come to meet her.

Battling the tears she'd been able to hold back throughout more than two weeks of grueling travel, she straightened her spine and glanced up at the crudely carved sign nailed above the door of the stage depot, thinking perhaps she'd alighted at the wrong stop.

Unfortunately, she hadn't.

"Miss?" A young, fair-haired man came across the muddy road, his blue eyes alight with kindness and a sort of good-humored mischief that she sensed was as much a part of his makeup as the beat of his heart and the breath in his lungs. His build was lean, agile, and there was a quiet confidence about him that Emmeline found very reassuring. "Isn't anybody meeting you?"

All the weariness, all the fretting, all the jolting and jostling over countless rough miles very nearly caught up with her when he asked that simple question, despite a staunch effort at shoring up her spirits. She swayed a little, blinked rapidly. "My—my husband," she said. "The agency was supposed to send a telegram—"

The cowboy grasped her elbow quickly. "Here, now," he said. "Have a seat on the edge of this water trough. Get your bearings."

Before Emmeline could protest that she'd been sitting down quite long enough, between the trains, stage-coaches, and even freight wagons she'd ridden to reach this wilderness outpost, and wished to stand instead, raucous shouts of glee erupted from the saloon next door to the depot. The team of dusty horses hitched to the stage-coach nickered and fretted in their harnesses, and the driver, busy unloading Emmeline's trunks, shouted a pro-fane reprimand at the poor creatures and then spat copi-ously for emphasis.

Just then, the swinging doors of the drinking establish-ment parted with a reverberating crash, and a man burst through them, hurtling backward through the air, almost flying, then landing in a graceful roll from shoulder to hip to back. He lay supine for a few moments instead of com-ing directly to his feet, shaking his head once. Then he swore and raised himself onto his elbows.

Emmeline's eyes widened as a truly terrible premoni-tion struck her. "Who is that?" she asked.

"That," said the cowboy, with affectionate resignation, "is my brother, Rafe McKettrick."

Emmeline's knees sagged; she nearly fell into the water trough. "No," she said.

"Yes," said the cowboy, regretfully.

She stood, took one step toward the man lying in the street, then another, until she was standing over him.

"Mr. McKettrick?" she inquired, in profoundest despair.

He looked up at her, squinting against the bright midafternoon sunshine, shook his head again, as though he believed he'd imagined the encounter, then scrambled to his feet and catapulted himself back through the sa-loon doors, where he was greeted by a round of jeers and huzzahs.

"Oh, no," she said.

The fair-haired man, her self-appointed knight in shining armor, came to her side and gently guided her out of the street. "I'm afraid so," he said. "Do you have business with my brother?"

She gave a little cry, pressing one hand to her mouth, and turned to face the beneficent stranger. "Yes," she replied. "He's my husband."

"Well, hell," said the cowboy, flinging his hat to the ground.

Emmeline took a step back, wide-eyed.

"I'm sorry if I startled you," the man said, bending to reclaim his hat and slapping it against one thigh as he straightened. A small muscle pulsed at the edge of his jaw, and he plunked the hat back on his head before putting out a hand. "Welcome to Indian Rock, Mrs. McKettrick," he told her, without smiling. "My name's Jeb and I'm your brother-in-law."

Suddenly the saloon doors sprang open and Rafe came flying through them again. He got up, without so much as a glance in her direction, and rushed back into the fray.

"That sneaking, low-down skunk," Jeb muttered. Then he rallied to his former good cheer, gave a low whistle of exclamation, and turned a wicked grin on Emmeline. "Well, now," he said, smooth as buttered taffy. "It looks like my brother has other things besides his new bride on his mind at the moment. Suppose we load up your things—that's my buckboard right over there—and head for the Triple M. My pa's going to be real pleased to make your acquaintance."

Emmeline had neither the means nor the strength to get back on the stagecoach and travel on in hopes of finding herself in a better situation, which meant that her options were severely limited. Jeb McKettrick seemed polite enough, and he *was* her husband's brother, which made him family, for all practical intents and purposes. She decided to trust him, and hoped her instincts about him were reliable.

"Thank you," she acquiesced, hiding her reluctance as best she could, and ducked her head a little.

Jeb curved a finger under her chin, lifted her face, smiled down at her. She was cheered by the warmth and humor she saw in his eyes. "You're safe with me," he said. "I promise you that." He offered his arm, and she laid a hand on the inside of his elbow. "Are you hungry?" he asked. "There's a dining room inside the hotel if you need something to eat. The food's nothing special, but it'll hold you until we get home." Before she could answer, he went on. "The mercantile down the street carries a few ladies' things. Is there anything you need before we set out?"

Emmeline blushed. "I couldn't eat a thing," she said honestly. "I'd like to—to freshen up a little, though."

He smiled his understanding. Pointing to the alleyway between the saloon and the stage depot, he said, "There's a privy out back. You'll find water and soap for washing up on the bench around the side."

Emmeline's heart sank. She'd tried to prepare herself for the frontier, during the long trip west, giving due consideration to all manner of possibilities, both cheerful and sobering, but not once, in all those flights of fancy, had she reflected upon the probable state of the plumbing.

She hesitated, then collected herself and marched into the alley.

The privy was a true abomination, built of weathered wood and tilting distinctly to one side, but nature would not be denied. Holding her breath against the stench, Emmeline entered beneath a sign that read CLOZ THE DOR, worked the latch, and attended to her business with all possible haste. She came out gasping, and perhaps a little green, minutes later, and hastily washed at the community bucket.

When she gained the main street again, still shuddering a little, she saw that Jeb or the stagecoach driver had loaded her belongings into the bed of a small wagon, drawn by two sturdy black horses. She checked to make sure everything was secure, cast a look of resignation toward the saloon, where her bridegroom evidently preferred to pass his time, and turned to Jeb, who helped her up into the box, rounded the wagon, and climbed deftly up beside her.

*I will not cry,* she promised herself sternly.

Jeb indicated the freight in back with a toss of his head. "Looks like you're pretty well outfitted," he said, probably to make conversation. "That's good, since you'd have to send to San Francisco if you wanted anything fancy."

She smoothed her skirts, patted her hair. Nodded to let him know she was listening. She didn't trust herself to speak just then, for she seemed to be wearing her emotions on her sleeve. She did not wish to make a poor impression on her new family.

"You're sure you don't want something to eat before we leave?" Jeb persisted gently. "It's more than two hours to the ranch, and that's if we don't run into any kind of trouble along the way."

She shook her head, straightened her spine, and fixed her eyes on the road ahead. "I'll be just fine," she said, and tried with all her might to believe it.

The fight over, and his opponent snoozing on the billiard table, Rafe watched as Charlie Biggam, the stagecoach driver, stepped into the saloon and started toward the bar.

"Evenin', Rafe," Charlie said.

Rafe nodded. "Evenin'. "

Charlie glanced toward the billiard table, where Jake Fink was starting to come around, groaning a little. "You and him get to bickering over fencing off the open range again?" he asked.

Rafe set his jaw, swirled his beer around in the mug. "Damn sodbuster," he said. "If Jake had his way, the whole territory would be crisscrossed with barbed wire."

Charlie signaled to the bartender, who brought him

his usual, a double shot of whiskey. "Brought in an inter-
estin' passenger today," he remarked.

Rafe's mind snagged on the woman he'd seen out in
the street, right after Jake had sucker punched him. She
was a pretty little thing, he recalled now, working his jaw
to make sure it wasn't broken. He wondered if she was
taken. "A lady?" he asked.

Charlie nodded, smiling a little. "Nice-lookin'," he said.
"You done real well for yourself, Rafe."

Rafe straightened. An awful feeling settled heavily in
his belly. "What the hell are you getting at?" he demanded.

"Name on the ticket was Mrs. Rafe McKettrick," Charlie told him. "Came all the way from Kansas City. I didn't
know you'd taken yourself a wife."

Rafe muttered, slapped payment for his drink on the
bar, and started for the door.

"No hurry," Charlie called benignly. "Jeb loaded up her
things and the two of them set off for the Triple M half an
hour ago."

Rafe stopped, turned. Jake sat up on the billiard table,
hawked, and spat out a tooth.

"You dirty sum'bitch, McKettrick," the sodbuster
growled, "I ought to carve out your gizzard."

"What did you say?" Rafe rasped, and he wasn't talking
to Jake Fink.

Charlie chuckled. "I reckon old Jake here must have
loosened your eardrums," he said. Charlie considered
himself a wit, and nobody enjoyed his jokes quite as

much as he did. "I said Jeb took your mail-order bride on home, since you was otherwise occupied. Right brotherly of him, I'd say."

Rafe cursed. He'd sent for a wife nearly two months before and forgotten all about her. The least those people at the Happy Home Matrimonial Service could have done was notify him that they'd filled his order.

"Come on back here and fight!" Jake said, swinging both legs over the edge of the table and promptly crumpling to the sawdust floor.

Rafe peeled off a couple of bills and thrust them at Jake's partner, Pootie Callahan. "Get him over to the doc's office," he said, distracted. Then he turned and hurried out of the saloon.

He was halfway to the livery stable when he realized he couldn't ride after his bride looking the way he did. He was filthy, his clothes were torn and bloodied, and he needed barbering. He'd made a hell of a first impression as it was; she was a city girl, most likely, and if he didn't take the time to clean up a little, he'd scare the devil out of her.

No, sir, everything was riding on this, and he had to handle it right.

Charlie Biggam had a mouth on him, and it soon became obvious that most of the town knew about his new wife, who was even now riding toward the ranch with Jeb. No doubt he was pouring on the charm, Jeb was, and the thought made Rafe's collar feel tight. He was legally married to that woman, whatever her name was, but he knew enough about the law to figure out that the deal wouldn't be bolted down until he'd bedded her, and so did Jeb. All she'd have to do, if she changed her mind, was see a lawyer and ask for an annulment.

Rafe wasn't going to let that happen. Though he didn't have Jeb's charm or Kade's talent for spouting pretty words, there were things to recommend him. He'd just have to ponder awhile, that was all, and figure out what they were.

He stormed across the road, and people parted for him, those afoot and those on horseback alike, accurately reading the expression on his face. Anyone who trifled with Rafe McKettrick now did so at his own peril.

Over at the general store, he exhausted his line of credit, buying a new black suit, a white shirt with a celluloid collar, a derby hat, a pair of gold wedding bands, and a frilly white nightgown that would look just fine on his wife.

He ignored the chuckles and whispered speculations as he left the store and headed down the road to the hotel, where he bought himself a bath, a shave, and a room to change clothes in. By the time he'd done all that, and was ready to set out for home, the sun was low in the western sky and a chilly breeze was sweeping down from the high country, up there above the timberline.

Rafe knew that Jeb and the new Mrs. McKettrick would have covered considerable ground by then, nearing the ranch if they hadn't broken an axle or had a horse go lame. He stewed, imagining Jeb's fancy talk. Words came so easily to him, and to Kade, but they generally caught in Rafe's throat like thistles.

He refused to hurry, for all his concern. He was a deliberate man, usually, the sort who took his time, thought things through before he acted. It was just plain bad luck that he'd run into Fink in the saloon that afternoon and they'd gotten on the subject of barbed-wire fences.

He sat up tall in the saddle, raised his coat collar against the wind, and rode on at a steady, even clip. While he traveled, he thought of many things, the first and foremost of which was his brand-new bride. If he had his way, they'd consummate the marriage that very night; that way, they could get on with the business of being married.

He chewed awhile on the possibility that the townspeople were laying bets on which of Angus McKettrick's sons would prevail in this contest—cowboys gossiped, and word of the proclamation would have traveled fast. It galled him to think of anybody betting on Kade or Jeb. As far as he knew, neither one of them had even tried to find himself a decent woman, save a few flurries of effort right after Pa's birthday. In fact, they'd gone right on carousing, his brothers had, right through the winter, acting as if they hadn't a worry in the world.

Now, in retrospect, Rafe realized that he might just have underestimated both Jeb and Kade, just as they'd probably hoped he would do. Hell, they could have brides of their own due to arrive any day now. Why, they might even have answered the same advertisement in the back of the *Cattleman's Journal*.

Just the possibility made him feel downright grim.

He sighed, settled deeper into the warm folds of his coat. He tried to reassure himself; after all, he and what's-her-name were already married, and that was an undeniable advantage. Why, she'd probably be in the family way before morning.

He smiled. Sure she would. Hadn't he bought her a wedding band, and a real pretty nightdress?

Emmeline's spirits rose a little when she saw the long log and timber house, facing the sparkling creek and framed by towering red rock bluffs. Oak trees, still bare of leaves but sprouting green buds, towered along either side of the stream, starkly beautiful. Junipers thrived on the distant hills, melding with tall pines that seemed to climb to the sky.

She drew in her breath as Jeb brought the team to a halt on the far side of the creek. He smiled down at her.

"You like the place?"

She nodded, strangely moved. "It's beautiful," she said.

Jeb released the brake with one foot, slapped down the reins, and drove the team straight into the creek. The whole rig shifted and swayed violently, as if it would surely capsize, spilling Emmeline and all her earthly possessions into the water. She grabbed the edge of the seat with both hands and held on for all she was worth.

Then, to her enormous relief, they were jostling up the

opposite bank, and a tall, white-haired man had appeared in the tall grass in front of the house, leaning on the hitching rail and watching as they approached. She could have measured the width of his shoulders with an ax handle and still fallen short by an inch or two, and he held his head at a proud angle, despite his age.

Jeb's expression turned thoughtful as he brought the team to a stop, set the brake again, jumped down, and rounded the dripping rig to lift Emmeline down by her waist.

"Pa," he said, "this is Emmeline. Emmeline, my father, Angus McKettrick."

Solemnly, his eyes shining, Angus put out a brawny hand. There was a careful tenderness in Mr. McKettrick's grasp, and Emmeline liked him. "How do you do," he said, in a great, Zeus-like voice. "Welcome to the Triple M."

She inclined her head, at a loss for words. She'd done rather a lot of talking on the way out from town, chattering about inconsequential things and revealing little or nothing about her life in Kansas City, using herself up. Now, she felt empty.

Angus regarded his son impatiently, eyes narrowed in that craggy face. "Well," he boomed, "is she your wife, or do I need to send a hand down to the mission to fetch back the padre?"

Jeb studied the distant horizon for a few moments, then heaved a great sigh. "It would seem," he said, "that Emmeline is Rafe's bride. Got here on today's stage."

At last, at last, Angus smiled. In fact, he beamed so that

Emmeline felt almost restored by his regard, and warmed, as if she were standing before a blazing hearth. "Well, now," he said. "Well, well. Why are we all standing out here in the wind? Come on in. We'd best get you settled in."

The invitation apparently didn't include Jeb, who sighed again, adjusted his well-worn hat, and began unloading Emmeline's baggage. Emmeline, meanwhile, allowed his father to squire her into the rustic but spacious house.

"Concepcion!" he shouted, as soon as they were over the threshold, causing her to start. "Come have a look at our girl!"

Emmeline did not mind her father-in-law's gruff way. Angus McKettrick seemed to see her presence as cause for celebration, and that was a nice change from being snubbed or simply going unnoticed in Kansas City.

A tall, slender woman appeared in an inner doorway, her dark eyes bright with speculation and welcome, and Emmeline liked her immediately.

"Concepcion, this is Rafe's bride," Angus said, as proudly as if he'd assembled her himself, from bits and pieces.

Concepcion greeted Emmeline warmly, taking her arm, leading her through the entry and into a long corridor. "Welcome," she said. Then, glancing back at Angus, who was following, she added, "And where, may I ask, *is* Rafe?"

Emmeline's joy, understandably fragile, wobbled a little. Her throat closed up tight, and she found herself unable to answer.

"I reckon he'll be along," Angus said.

"You'll want a nice bath and a long rest," Concepcion said when they reached the kitchen, patting Emmeline on the shoulder in a matronly way. "You just sit down, though, and I'll make you some tea first." Her next remark was clearly directed at Angus. "There'll be time enough for getting acquainted later, won't there?"

Emmeline seated herself, and Angus stood gazing down at her as though she were the eighth wonder. Concepcion gave her the promised tea, along with toasted bread and a thick slice of cheese.

"That Rafe," Concepcion muttered once, glancing toward the window, as if expecting to see him riding in. "What will I do with him?"

"The last time I saw him," Emmeline said, with careful dignity, "he was smashing through the doors of an establishment called the Bloody Basin Saloon."

Concepcion crossed herself; Angus swore under his breath.

"Come," Concepcion said, when Emmeline began to nod over her cup, which had been refilled twice, "you must rest."

Emmeline allowed herself to be escorted upstairs and installed in an airy room with a view of the creek, a glittering golden ribbon shot with crimson and blue in the last fierce light of day. There were lace curtains at the windows, and the crazy quilt on the bed was worn but appealing.

"Is this—?" Emmeline began, and stopped, blushing.

"This," Concepcion said, with gentle understanding, "is the spare room. Rafe sleeps down the hall."

Emmeline was relieved. Her knees sagged, and she left the window to sit gratefully on the thick feather mattress, stroking the pretty quilt with one hand.

Concepcion rummaged through several bureau drawers and produced a flannel nightgown and a damask towel. She laid them on the foot of the bed, then headed for the door. "I'll bring you some hot water. You can wash and then get into bed and sleep."

Emmeline yawned. "Thank you," she said, and she was dozing when Concepcion returned with a steaming basin and a bar of soap.

Rafe led his gelding, Chief, into the barn, slipped the bridle off, and hung it over the stall gate. Then he began brushing the animal down, the way he always did after a long ride. Jeb was there, repairing one of the wagon wheels by the light of a kerosene lantern, and he barely looked up.

"Where the devil have you been?" he asked.

"Where is she?" Rafe asked.

Jeb kept working. "I guess you mean Emmeline," he said. "Your wife."

Emmeline. So that was her name. It had a nice, womanly sound, and he liked it. "Long as you have that straight," he said. "That she's mine, I mean."

"She's a woman, Rafe, not a horse blanket or a pair of boots," Jeb remarked tightly.

"I didn't know you were such a modern thinker," Jeb said. He fetched grain and hay and came to stand facing his brother, his arms folded. "Next thing, you'll be out stumping for Women's Suffrage."

"Could be," Jeb said. He wasn't smiling.

Rafe didn't speak again. He just went back into the stall, picked the small stones and mud from Chief's hooves, then headed for the house, carrying the parcel from town in one arm. His pa was waiting in the back-yard when he got there.

"I ought to take a horsewhip to you," Angus growled, mean as an arthritic bear waking up in a den full of slush. "Leaving your own bride stranded in town! Why, if your brother hadn't been there—"

All the fight had gone out of Rafe, thanks in large part to Jake Fink, who packed a hell of a punch, for a dirt farmer. He sighed and moved around his father, mount-ing the steps and walking into the kitchen.

She was there, by the stove, clad in a modest flannel wrapper, her hair in a long, thick braid, and Rafe stopped cold when he saw her, stunned. He held out the parcel.

"I bought you a nightgown," he said, and felt his face go a dull, throbbing red. He thought he heard Angus groan behind him.

Emmeline hesitated, then raised her chin, ignoring the package. If she'd heard him, she pretended she hadn't.

"I am pleased to make your acquaintance, Mr. McKet-trick," she said, after some time. "At long last."

Rafe might have been sixteen, instead of nearly thirty,

for all the awkwardness he felt now, when she was within touching distance.

His wife.

"Likewise," he said, at some length, and drew the parcel slowly back, setting it aside. Obviously, if there was going to be a baby started, it wouldn't happen tonight.

# CHAPTER

## 3

A LATE SUPPER WAS SERVED at the long trestle table in the kitchen. Kerosene lanterns flickered at both ends of the room, casting soft light through the shadows, and the food, some kind of roasted game, venison, perhaps, or elk, along with boiled carrots, potatoes, and turnips, was plain and wholesome. At Angus's urging, Emmeline was seated first, on the bench nearest the cookstove, where the air shimmered with a welcome warmth, and Concepcion took a chair next to her, at the end. Rafe, still flushed from their earlier encounter, when he'd presented her with the nightgown, sat across from Emmeline.

Jeb wandered in at an unhurried pace, pausing to favor Emmeline with an encouraging smile and a nod. Behind him walked another man, a year or two older, probably, with chestnut hair and green eyes. "Ma'am," the second fellow said, with a nod of his own.

She didn't respond, but simply clasped her hands together in her lap, sat up a little straighter, and tried to quell a rush of homesickness for Becky and the boardinghouse and all the misguided "girls" in their scandalous dressing gowns. Tomorrow she would begin a letter home, chronicling the long and arduous journey, describing Rafe and Indian Rock and the house on the Triple M. Becky, with her formidable pride, might, or might not, reply.

"I guess Miss Emmeline already knows Jeb," Angus remarked, while Jeb and his companion pumped water into the sink and scrubbed their hands with yellow soap, "since he was the one to fetch her home from Indian Rock and all." The old man sent a brief, dark glance in Rafe's direction. "I don't think she's made Kade's acquaintance yet, though."

"Kade McKettrick, ma'am," he said rather gravely, as though the occasion of meeting her was one of lasting personal significance, leaving Jeb at the sink to come and sit beside her on the bench. Kade was good-looking, like the others, and smelled of night air and some costly cologne. "I'm the middle brother." He put out a hand, cold from the pump water, and she took it, bemused. Jeb had not mentioned Kade on the trip out from Indian Rock, and she wondered why.

"I'm happy to meet you," Emmeline said politely, though she didn't spare a smile. Her gaze slid back to Rafe, and she saw that his eyes were narrowed and his jaw was clamped down hard. The realization that he was nettled by the attention she paid his brothers cheered her unaccountably.

"Jeb tells me you hail from Kansas City," Kade began, in an engaging tone. "Do you have a lot of family back there?"

Emmeline's throat tightened right up again, as quickly as that. It was dark, she was in a strange new place, not the bustling city she was used to, but a ranch, with miles of untamed frontier surrounding her, and she was married to a man she'd never laid eyes on before that day. What in the world had she been thinking, leaving home the way she had, burning her bridges behind her? "I have an aunt," she said hesitantly, at some length, and very quietly, hoping that said aunt would still be willing to claim her. "Her name is Becky Harding." She looked down, looked up again. "My parents died when I was an infant, and I don't have any brothers or sisters."

Jeb swung a leg over the bench on the opposite side, sitting next to Rafe, whom he studiously ignored, and reached for the bread plate. His smile, like Kade's, was easy, sympathetic, but without pity, and thereby quite endearing. "That must have been a hard thing, growing up without a family." He let a beat pass, then turned the conversation in another direction. "Do you like to ride horseback? I could cut you a pony out of the herd to-morrow—"

Before Emmeline could reply that she'd never actually ridden a horse, though she'd very much like to try, Rafe interceded, glaring at his brother.

"If *my wife* wants to ride," he said, "I'll be the one to provide the horse."

Emmeline was stung by Rafe's rude, officious manner, and she bristled, but Jeb merely grinned and speared a turnip with his fork. His blue eyes were merry with the knowledge that he'd gotten under his brother's skin so handily. Kade, too, seemed amused, though his expression was carefully bland.

"That might not be a good idea," Angus ventured solemnly, from his end of the table, where he did not merely sit but rather *presided,* like the benevolent ruler of some vast and hardwon kingdom. "Miss Emmeline going riding, I mean. Not if there's likely to be a child coming along soon."

Emmeline, who had been eating with good appetite—she had economized on food during her journey, fearing to run short of funds and find herself facing some unforeseen emergency—flushed now, and set down her fork with a clatter. She felt the pull of Rafe's gaze but couldn't bring herself to look at him. Inevitably, she thought of the Texan who had almost certainly had his way with her the night of her grand folly—why else would he have left gold behind in payment, after all?—and wondered if indeed there *was* a child growing within her. Becky had long since explained the mechanics of such matters, and Emmeline had waited in vain for her monthly ever since. Her cycle had never been regular, a fact that gave her small comfort now.

"Angus McKettrick," Concepcion scolded. "What kind

of talk is that? I swear, you have the manners of a warthog!"

Angus reddened, a sound escaped Jeb—a chortle, perhaps, quickly contained—and Kade feigned a cough.

"Now, Concepcion," Angus said, sounding defensive as well as chagrined, "it's not like nobody around here knows that my sons want children, the sooner the better."

"And we all know why," Concepcion said pointedly, frowning the big man into a semblance of submission. Emmeline might have interjected that she, for one, did *not* know why Angus McKettrick's sons were in a hurry to sire progeny, but it hardly seemed prudent to say so.

She was quietly mortified, wishing she could step back in time somehow, to simply vanish from this table and find herself at home in Missouri, rereading library books and stitching still more samplers, giving nary a thought to anything so foolish as dressing up in her aunt's clothes and pretending to be something she wasn't, even for a single night.

Instead, she was here, in the Wild West, a wife expected to produce an heir in short order, and no amount of woolgathering would alter the reality of her circumstances by one whit.

An awkward silence descended. Emmeline, her splendid appetite gone, ate what she could, trying to prolong the meal, and put off the inevitable night alone with Rafe for as long as possible. Kade and Jeb cleaned their plates, had second helpings of everything, and then excused themselves, with Angus hastening after them. Concepcion squeezed

Emmeline's hand in an effort to reassure her, but then she, too, made an exit, intent on some project upstairs.

"I guess they mean for us to do up the dishes," Rafe said, after a long time.

Emmeline wondered just how long such a simple task could be drawn out. She nodded shyly and got up.

"Emmeline," Rafe said, stopping her midway between the table and the sink. "About today, in town—-"

She didn't turn around. "I was rather concerned when you weren't there to meet me," she said quietly.

He laid a hand on her shoulder, turning her to face him. "What my pa said—about the baby, I mean. I reckon I should explain."

She waited, looking up at him through her lashes. Her cheeks pulsed with heat, and again she thought of the Texan.

Rafe sighed. "We can't talk here," he said. "There's a moon. Maybe you'd go for a walk with me, down by the creek?"

She'd heard about the fierce beasts that roamed the wilderness, bears and panthers and snakes, to name just a few, and she wasn't eager to encounter any of them in the dark. On the other hand, she'd be with Rafe, her husband. Surely she could count on his protection. "All right," she said, but cautiously. If he tried to put his hands on her before she was ready to be touched, she'd make him sorry. Something else she had learned from Becky.

He brought her Concepcion's cloak to wear over the wrapper and the nightgown, slipped a pistol into his holster, and opened the back door for her.

She stepped through ahead of him, surprised to see how brightly the landscape was illuminated, keenly aware of Rafe's close proximity.

Outside, he walked a little apart from her, through the tall, star-silvered grass, and she wished he'd take her hand, like one of the men in her romantic fantasies would have done.

She looked around. Did rattlesnakes come out at night?

The stream made burbling music just ahead, and something skittered through the grass, causing Emmeline to give a small, involuntary cry of alarm. Rafe chuckled, and reached for her hand at last.

"Just a mouse or something," he said.

She raised her chin. "I'm not afraid."

"I don't imagine you would be scared of a whole lot," he replied. "It took some grit, coming all this way by yourself, not knowing what would be waiting for you."

Emmeline was flattered, whether he'd meant the remark to be a compliment or not, and she even reflected that, in time, she might come to like this husband of hers, perhaps even love him.

They reached the creek, and Rafe led her to a fallen log, where they sat, side by side, a foot of space between them. He'd released her hand, and now he gazed at the water.

She took that opportunity to study his profile. He was a handsome man, in a rugged, outlawlike way, and just the thought of sharing his bed made her head whirl and her stomach do flipflops. She wasn't sure what she felt, precisely, but it was part anticipation and part mortal dread.

"What made you sign on with the Happy Home Matrimonial Service?" he asked presently. The breeze ruffled his dark hair, which had been barbered since she'd first encountered him in town, sprawled on the ground in front of the Bloody Basin Saloon. His knuckles were scraped, though the fisticuffs had left his face blessedly unmarked.

She wasn't about to tell him the whole story—that she'd grown up in a brothel, slept with a stranger for money, and fled in a fit of disgrace and wounded pride after the confrontation with Becky—so she related another facet of the tale. "It seemed to me that every day was just like the one before it," she said quietly, watching the moon's reflection splinter upon the water of the creek. "I wanted a change. I wanted something big to happen, and I knew it wouldn't, unless I made it." She paused. "What about you?"

He sighed. "I needed a wife," he said, "and fast. I didn't figure it would take all winter for them to send somebody—they sure didn't hesitate to cash the bank draft, though."

Emmeline swallowed. The bank draft.

For the first time, it occurred to her that she'd sold her soul to Rafe McKettrick, as surely as she had her virtue, back in Kansas City, earning herself a few gold coins and a lifetime of secret recrimination. The terms were a little different now, that was all, but a bargain had been struck, money had changed hands, and she was the goods.

She sat up a little straighter on the log, sick with the full realization of what she'd done.

"They might have sent a picture," Rafe went on, unaware, of course, that she was crumbling beside him, fighting not to double over, not to drop to her knees in the grass, weeping, "or at least told me you were on your way."

Emmeline bit her lower lip, willed some starch into her backbone. What was done, was done. Like many, many women before her, she would have to make the best of things. "Are you disappointed?" she heard herself ask. She'd never had her likeness taken, and therefore she hadn't complied with the marriage broker's request for a daguerreotype, which would, most likely, have been forwarded to Rafe for his approval. "In my appearance, I mean?"

"Nope," he said flatly. "I reckon you'll do."

Emmeline's last hope for romance died a painful death. Everything was utterly unlike what she'd imagined. True, the large house and thriving ranch had come as a pleasant surprise, but she'd expected to be wooed, perhaps even cherished. Instead, it seemed she was to be little more than a brood mare.

She drew in a long breath and released it slowly. "You brought me out here because you wanted to say something to me, Mr. McKettrick. What was it?"

The answer was blunt. "I sent for a wife—sent for

you—because I need to father a child right away. If I don't, I'm going to wind up as little more than a hired hand."

She stiffened, barely hearing the last of what he'd said. "Right away?" she echoed. Wasn't Rafe going to court her at all?

He nodded. "Sooner the better," he affirmed.

Emmeline had never been intimate with a man, at least, not that she *remembered,* and she was unnerved by Mr. McKettrick's size and vitality, to say nothing of his rowdy nature. Still, she was here, wasn't she, with nowhere else to go, and if the Texan had indeed made her pregnant, as she feared, then here was her chance to make her child legitimate, with no one the wiser. The baby would simply arrive a trifle early, that was all.

"I see," she said, and just then she didn't like herself very much.

"Have you ever made love, Emmeline?"

These westerners were so straightforward. She shook her head, but she couldn't make herself look him in the eye.

He took her hand again, interlaced his fingers with hers. "That's good," he said.

She sat in silence for a long time, struggling with her conscience. It wasn't right to deceive Mr. McKettrick, but she didn't dare confide in him, either. "Why didn't you just marry someone from around here?" she asked finally. "Instead of sending all the way to Kansas City for me, I mean."

"Nobody here to marry, save a few whores and Daisy Pert," he said with a shrug, "and none of them would make a fitting wife."

She flinched, but only slightly, and again he didn't seem to notice. "I guess you wouldn't marry a—a fallen woman, even if you loved her?"

"Love?" he scoffed. "Maybe folks have time for that nonsense where you come from, but this is rough country, Emmeline. Out here, marriage is a practical matter, a sort of partnership, and love has damn little to do with it." He paused, regarded her solemnly. "I want a family of my own, like I said, and a man doesn't have children with a prostitute."

Emmeline had a strong urge to bolt to her feet and run fast and far, maybe all the way back across the mountains, plains, and valleys she'd crossed to get here, but she sat still as a stone. "A partnership?" she countered, feeling more than a little testy now that her dream of being someone's beloved wife had been thoroughly shattered. She'd been reading about Suffrage in the newspapers, during the endless train and stagecoach rides, and the things she'd learned in the process nettled her brain and her spirit like briars. Why, she would have painted a sign and marched for the cause if there had been a parade passing by. "I'd hardly call it that. Once a woman is married, she becomes her husband's possession, the same as a dog or a buckboard. If she's got money or property, he can take it away and then turn her out into the snow. He can work her like a mule, run her right into the ground, wear her out having babies. He can beat her, if he likes, put her in an insane asylum, and give away their children like kittens from a litter—"

"Whoa," Rafe said, laughing and shaking his head. "If that's what you think it means to be a man's wife, why did you sign on in the first place?"

It was a good question, but the answer was too embarrassing to share. She hadn't bothered to consider the potential drawbacks of marriage until it was too late. Now, she held her tongue, since her only other option was to beg for mercy.

"I don't mean to do any of those things to you, Miss Emmeline," Rafe said, very reasonably, when she didn't speak. "What I'm suggesting here is a kind of contract, since you obviously don't care for the word *partnership*. Here it is, plain and simple: You make a home with me, and give me children, and I'll see that you never lack for anything for the rest of your life. I'll expect you to cook for me, of course, like any wife, and certainly to share my bed. I won't abide lying, and God help you if you shame me with another man." He smiled, pleased with himself, spreading his hands to indicate that he had finished stating his terms. "Seems like a fair deal to me."

Emmeline was glad she wasn't armed. She wet her lips with the tip of her tongue, tried to be sensible. Now was the time to tell him about Holt, about the baby she might or might not be carrying; if those things came out later, she was certain he would never, ever forgive her. Even knowing that, she couldn't bring herself to say what she knew she must; she didn't have the courage and, besides, she was too furious. "Suppose *you* shamed *me,* by keeping company with another woman?" she challenged.

He looked at her with consternation. "That's not the same," he said.

Emmeline's self-control snapped. She shot to her feet, which were beginning to feel damp, since she was wearing a pair of Concepcion's slippers in place of her own sturdy shoes. "I beg your pardon? Are you telling me, sir, that *you do not intend to honor our wedding vows?*"

His handsome face hardened slightly. "A man has needs—"

Emmeline didn't let him go one word further; she put both hands on his chest and, before he had time to brace himself, shoved him, hard. He tumbled backward, landing on his rear in the moist grass, with the heel of one boot snagged on the log.

Emmeline made no move to assist him. Indeed, she was sorely tempted to spit square into his face. "I do believe I have made a serious mistake," she said.

Rafe rose slowly, and with dignity, brushing himself off. "That you have," he replied in a cold voice. "I have half a mind to turn you across my knee and show you who's the boss in this family."

"You try it," Emmeline responded, drawing on conversations she'd overheard in the corridors of Becky's place, "and I'll whack off your privates with the first sharp knife I can find!"

His mouth dropped open in shock, then he narrowed his eyes. "Madam," he said, "you are no lady."

Those words wounded Emmeline more deeply than anything else he might have said, but she would have died before she let him know that. She whirled on one heel and started for the house at a run. When she looked back, to see if he was giving chase, she stepped in a hole and fell headlong into the grass.

Rafe, reaching her within a moment or two, chuckled at her plight, though he did extend a hand to help her up.

She slapped it away. "Don't touch me, you ruffian!" she cried.

"Why, you little spitfire," he said, annoyed again.

Emmeline scrambled to her feet and backed away.

He moved in, undaunted, and hoisted her over his shoulder as though she were a sack of barley.

"Put me down!"

"I'd love to," he replied. "Right in middle of the creek. I'd do it, too, if I didn't think you'd catch your death and make me a widower before I got my money's worth out of you."

Emmeline saw red, but she kept her voice calm. "I'll scream," she told him.

"Go ahead," he said cheerfully. "Things have been pretty quiet around here lately, and that would surely stir up some excitement. Both my brothers would most likely rush to your rescue, too, and then, of course, I'd have to shoot them."

She didn't believe he would actually shoot Kade and

Jeb, not for a moment, but she definitely wanted to be rescued. She drew in a deep breath, fully intending to emit an ear-splitting shriek, but the air went whooshing out of her when he took another step, causing her middle to bounce hard against his shoulder.

"Put—me—down!" she repeated.

He gave her a hard swat on the bottom. "Hush," he said, quite jovially. "Did anybody ever tell you, Miss Emmeline, that you talk too much?"

She doubled up both fists and pummeled his back with them.

"Little hellcat," he said, and this time he sounded amused, which made her madder still. "I like a woman with some spirit."

They reached the kitchen, where Emmeline hoped for salvation, but there wasn't a soul around. Just her luck.

"Where," she whispered fiercely, "are you taking me?"

"Straight to bed."

Emmeline gasped in horror.

He started up the back stairs.

"Help," she said, but it came out as a whisper, which was quite the opposite of what she'd planned.

Rafe laughed. "You're going to have to do better than that, Mrs. McKettrick. This is a big house, and the walls are chinked logs, more than a foot thick in most places."

They were moving along the corridor now, passing the spare room where she'd napped earlier. At the end of the hallway, Rafe pushed open a door and strode into a darkened room. *His* room, she knew.

She began to kick, but he clamped one steely arm across her legs, effectively stilling them. He shouldered the door shut, then crossed the floor and dropped her, from what seemed a very great height, onto the bed. The pleasantly masculine scent of him wafted from the covers.

Emmeline struggled to sit up, but he placed a hand on each of her shoulders and held her down easily.

She kicked, and he sidestepped the assault without releasing his hold. She lay still, biding her time, but he wasn't fooled. He bent down, so his face was less than an inch from hers.

"Behave yourself, you little wildcat," he said moderately, "or I swear by all that's holy, I'll bare that lovely little bottom of yours and blister it."

"You wouldn't dare," she breathed.

"Try me," he said.

"I will not," she conceded haughtily. "It's obvious that you're nothing more than a ruffian. Perhaps you *would* stoop so low as to strike a defenseless woman."

"Defenseless, hell," he scoffed, still holding her down. His eyes were very blue, almost indigo, she noticed, quite against her will, and his teeth appeared to be perfect. "I'd sooner wrestle a she-bear."

"Then go and find one and leave me alone!"

He laughed.

She jutted out her chin. "Go ahead," she hissed. "Ravish me. I'll tell the world what a scoundrel you are!"

His eyes danced. "The world," he drawled, "will not be at all surprised."

Incredibly, at that worst of all possible moments, he kissed her. Not roughly, as she would have expected, but very gently, and with exquisite thoroughness.

A blaze roared through her blood, and her back arched slightly, of its own accord. A humiliating moan escaped her, and when Rafe drew back, she could only stare up at him with wide eyes, her lips still tingling from the contact. She had been kissed only once before in her life—by the man called Holt—but that experience had left her singularly unmoved. Rafe's kiss, on the other hand, had changed her in some profound and utterly mysterious way.

Rafe tasted her mouth again, at his damnable leisure, then straightened. Emmeline lay completely still, as though stricken by some strange, delectable paralysis.

If he had undressed her then, and made love to her, she wouldn't have, *couldn't* have, made a move to stop him. Knowing that about herself was bad enough; seeing that he knew it as well was mortifying. Or at least it would be, once he released her from whatever spell he'd cast.

He turned away from the bed.

"Where are you going?" she asked very quietly. Only moments before, she'd wanted him to leave. Now, the mere prospect of his going weighed upon her as nothing had ever done before.

He looked back at her over one shoulder. "Town," he said.

She turned her head, so he wouldn't see the tears that came to her eyes. Waited to hear the bedroom door open, then close again. The sound didn't come.

"Emmeline?"

She sniffled. "What?"

The bed gave a little as he sat down. From the sounds, and the shifting of his body, she knew he was kicking off his boots. "I've never forced a woman to make love, and I don't intend to start now." He sighed. "All the same, this is my bed, and you are my wife, and I'm going to sleep right here, so you might as well move over."

She sidled toward the wall, keeping her eyes averted. "Very well," she said stiffly.

He chuckled, moving again, probably shedding his clothes. Then he crawled into bed beside her, settled himself, and sighed contentedly. "Good night, Mrs. McKettrick," he said.

She didn't answer.

# CHAPTER

## 4

EMMELINE HAD NOT PLANNED to sleep, but exhaustion won out. When she awakened, many hours later, the sun was up and she was alone in her marriage bed. She heard voices drifting up through the floorboards, the words indistinguishable, the tones ordinary, companionable.

Recalling the events of the night before, particularly her involuntary responses to Rafe's kisses, Emmeline blushed and covered her face with both hands. Rafe had been right, as they'd sat beside the creek, when he'd touched upon her deepest and most private fear.

She was no lady.

She longed to pull the covers over her head and spend the whole day hiding in bed, but she knew it wouldn't work. Hers was a restless nature and, besides, she needed to use the privy.

She dropped her head over the side of the bed and

peered underneath, but there was no chamber pot. Sighing, she got out of bed.

There was clean, if tepid, water in the pitcher on the bureau top, and she poured some into the matching basin, then washed hastily, ever conscious that Rafe might come striding into the room at any moment and catch her at her ablutions.

She soon discovered that her brush and comb were there, too, and one of her dresses, a practical brown calico, was hanging on a wall peg, neatly pressed. At some point, Concepcion must have slipped in, taking care not to awaken the new bride.

No doubt, she, along with the rest of the household, believed that Rafe and Emmeline had consummated their union the night before. Once again, Emmeline considered hiding out in bed, but not for long. Her bladder felt as though it would explode if she didn't get herself to the outhouse.

She brushed her hair quickly, plaited it into a single braid, and hurried down the back stairs.

The kitchen was warm, filled with sunlight and delicious smells. Emmeline nodded to Angus, who was seated at the table reading a heavy tome, and to Concepcion, who stood beside the big cookstove with a pressing board set up, ironing more of Emmeline's travel-rumpled clothes. She spared each of them a nod and a nervous smile in passing, then dashed out the back door, across the porch, and down the long path to the outdoor toilet.

The barn was not far away, and Emmeline noticed her husband out front, saddling a horse, though she didn't take time to acknowledge him. She was intent on the first order of business, and in no particular hurry to face Rafe McKettrick on any account.

She had just finished when she heard a distinctive rattling sound from the plank floor. In an instant she was standing on the bench, one foot planted on either side of the hole, holding her skirt in both hands and screaming fit to rouse the dead. In the corner, a full-grown snake coiled, hissing.

The door flew open, slamming against the outside wall, and Rafe was there in the chasm, gun drawn. The snake, distracted, struck at him, but, miraculously, Rafe was quicker. He fired, and the creature's head splintered.

Still terrified, Emmeline jumped down off the outhouse bench, forgetting that her drawers were still around her ankles, and stumbled into Rafe with enough force to send them both toppling onto the path outside the door.

Rafe laughed, though she thought she saw something like sympathy in his eyes.

"I hoped you'd come around to my way of thinking," he said, "but this is neither the time nor the place for expressing your affection, Mrs. McKettrick."

Scared, fuming, and wildly confused, Emmeline pushed her way to her feet and wrestled her drawers up, nearly falling again in the process. Rafe remained on the ground, propped on one elbow, grinning up at her. "Thank you!" she shouted, and stormed off toward the house.

Rafe scrambled to his feet and followed, catching up with her long before she reached the porch steps. He took her arm and turned her around to face him.

"I'm sorry," he said, but his mouth kept trying to quirk into a grin, and his eyes were bright with merriment. "Are you all right, Emmeline?"

She drew a deep breath and straightened her spine. Her nerves, flaring like tree limbs tossed in a gale, were beginning to settle down again. Her heart, though still beating rapidly, was no longer struggling to escape her chest, and she was most surprised to hear herself laugh. "I nearly died of fright," she admitted, running a hand over the loose tendrils of hair tickling her forehead. "That *was* a rattler, wasn't it?"

Rafe stepped back into the outhouse, emerging momentarily with the snake's body dangling from one hand. The thing must have been three feet long, even without its head. "Yep," he said, showing her the rattles.

She laid a hand to her stomach, willing herself not to vomit. A cold sweat was drying on her skin, and she shivered.

Rafe tossed the snake aside, into the tall grass. "I was beginning to think you meant to sleep the day away," he said.

She might have bristled, but he'd just saved her life, even if he had laughed at her for getting tangled in her bloomers, so she smoothed her hair again and smiled a little. "I should have thought you would be hard at work by now," she said.

He caught the jibe, and grinned. "I finished my day's

work already," he countered. "You want to go riding? Have a look at the place?"

Emmeline had missed breakfast, and she was starving, but her eagerness to try riding a horse and to see more of the Triple M overruled the emptiness of her stomach.

"Yes," she said. "I'd like that. Provided you promise to be a gentleman."

He leaned in a little and lowered his voice. "I think I've proven that it's safe to be alone with me," he replied, obviously referring to the night just past, during which they had shared a bed without incident. "When I make love to you, Mrs. McKettrick, you'll be more than willing."

She let the remark pass, for the sake of the peace, though her cheeks burned. Something happened inside her, too, something reminiscent of last night's kisses and the secret havoc they'd wreaked, but she would have died before telling him as much.

He caught her chin in his hand and made her meet his eyes. "Everybody in the family thinks you overslept because you were worn out from the wedding night," he said, enjoying her instant, wide-eyed chagrin. "Pa's so happy, he made me foreman of the Triple M first thing this morning and gave me my choice of sites for a house. I'd like to show you the place I have in mind."

Emmeline had never had a real home, at least not the respectable kind where she could entertain company, and the hope of having one at last had been a large factor in her decision to offer herself as a mail-order bride. "I'll be ready in a few minutes," she said, and forgetting all about the snake, she turned and hurried into the house.

Half an hour later, she met Rafe outside the barn. Concepcion had outfitted her with trousers, a shirt, and boots, all outgrown, long ago, by one of the McKettrick sons, then contributed a hat and coat of her own.

Rafe smiled at the sight of her. His gelding waited at the hitching rail, impatient to be away, and he'd saddled a smaller horse for Emmeline, a pinto he introduced as Banjo.

She felt a flutter of fear, looking at that animal, but her love of adventure prevailed. She stepped closer, reached up to grasp the saddle horn, and tried to put her foot in the stirrup, as she'd seen other riders do. Before she could attempt to hoist herself up, however, Rafe closed strong hands around her waist and swung her into the saddle.

His touch stirred a flock of new feelings, rising to swamp her senses like some mystical flash flood, and leaving her spinning and light-headed when they ebbed.

"Ready?" he asked, squinting a little in the bright spring sunshine as he looked up at her.

Emmeline simply stared at him for a long moment, feeling like an idiot and quite incapable of speaking the English language. Then, mercifully, she recovered. She nodded, the breeze setting tendrils of hair dancing around her face, and he untied his horse and mounted.

"She's a lively one," he said, indicating Emmeline's horse as he came alongside. "Good-hearted, though—except when she's in heat."

Emmeline looked away, toward the red mesas looming in the distance, then back to her husband's face. "You wouldn't be trying to shock me, would you?" she asked sweetly, hoping he wouldn't notice that the knuckles of her right hand had gone white where she gripped the saddle horn. Emmeline did a lot of brave things, as a general rule, but that didn't mean she wasn't scared—it meant she was determined not to give in to cowardice.

"No, ma'am," he said, ducking his head in a vain effort to hide a grin. "I wouldn't think of it."

Emmeline rolled her eyes. "Of course not," she said. She sat very stiffly in the saddle, its thinly covered leather seat hard as stone beneath her bottom, and her legs were so far apart that she feared she'd be split up the middle like a wishbone at the slightest jolt. She closed her eyes and silently instructed herself not to be a ninny; she was a rancher's wife now, and ranchers' wives rode horses. Among other things.

"Miss Emmeline?" It was Rafe's voice. Close-by, and quiet. He was right beside her on that big gelding, the man and animal as much a part of each other as if they'd been born together, one creature. Both of them seemed to generate heat and energy, as though they had great, silent machines working away inside them.

"What?" she asked, a mite testily, perhaps. She'd used most of her self-control just getting past the rattlesnake experience, and now she was sitting on a horse's back for the first time in her life. This was a morning worthy of an entry in her remembrance book, and it would make a fine contrast to ones she had written in Kansas City, such as, "Went to the library" and "Saw Mary Alice's father on the streetcar."

She heard Rafe's chuckle. "Take it easy," he counseled. "Anybody who can jump onto an outhouse seat with their britches around their ankles can stay on an old mare with no trouble at all."

Was he praising or mocking her? She couldn't tell. His words made her feel good, though, and a little more confident. She *was* physically agile; she'd loved gymnastics at finishing school and won several awards for juggling Indian clubs. She would be good at riding, too, in time. She was sure of it.

"Shall we go?" she asked very primly, and then couldn't stop herself from laughing a little, for pure joy. The sun was bright, the air was fresh, and the ragged patches of dirty snow were all that remained of winter. There was a faint thrum of exhilaration building inside her, too, just because she was alone with Rafe, though whether or not this was a favorable development was yet to be seen.

He answered by urging the gelding forward with a click of his tongue, and Banjo ambled alongside. Emmeline jostled rigidly as if she had a flagpole on her back, and willed herself not to cling for dear life. They hadn't traveled more than a dozen yards and already her thighs were aching from clenching the horse's sides; after a day of this, she'd be lucky if she could put her knees together.

Rafe smiled. "Let out your breath, Miss Emmeline, and then take in another. Try to loosen your hinges a little.

You'll be mighty stiff and sore by tonight if you ride with your muscles locked up like that."

Emmeline tried, really tried, to comply, seeing the common sense in his words, but her heart was pounding, partly with terror and partly with excitement, and her breath came in quick, shallow gasps. Her many sojourns of fancy, in which she'd ridden elephants over the Alps with Hannibal, raced camels along the road to Damascus, and outrun the wind on the backs of great steeds from the stables of Alexander the Great himself, had done precious little to prepare her for a single overweight mare with the plodding gait of a plow horse.

They traveled on the road for a while, then cut across a meadow, Banjo slogging diligently along behind the gelding, bridle fittings jingling. After a few minutes of rhythmic breathing, Emmeline was able to spare some of the concentration she'd been devoting to immediate survival, and began to take in fragments of the majestic scenery rising all around them.

The horses continued to climb, leaving the meadow behind now, picking their way over trails littered with red rock. The land, which looked so barren from the lower country, was alive with small, skittering animals, vociferous insects, and the occasional snake. Every time Emmeline spotted a slithering reptile, she relived both the horror and the humiliation of the outhouse for a moment.

Inexperienced as she was, Emmeline knew she would love riding from that day forward. Everything was so beautiful—the wind played in the juniper trees and made the newly sprouted oak leaves rustle cheerfully. The sky was an acute blue, just beyond her reach and soft as finely spun silk. Birds twittered in noisy concert, and rabbits raced across the path.

Presently, they came to a high, grassy clearing, surrounded on three sides by timber. Rafe got off his horse and walked back toward Emmeline. Banjo, unconcerned with bit and bridle, bent her head to nibble at a tuft of clover.

Emmeline caught her breath when Rafe lifted her down, stood her on her feet on the lush virgin ground. They stared at each other for a long moment, then he turned her gently, pointing out the vista he'd brought her to see.

The view was indeed splendid, sweeping in all directions. It seemed to Emmeline, in those first drunken instants of discovery, that they had ridden into the sky itself, and staked their claim on a cloud, or even a tattered edge of heaven itself.

To the north, she saw the creek winding along its glittering way, and the big house, small as a party favor in the distance, blue smoke curling from its chimneys. There were the barns, the bunkhouse, the silos, and other outbuildings, all of them tiny enough to close her fingers around and tuck into her pocket. To the west, there was more red-rock country, mesas and buttes and deep ravines, and the ever-present saguaro cacti. In the distance were great stands of timber. Indian Rock was plainly visible to the east. To the south, Emmeline knew from her geography, lay the harsh desert lands, with sage and sand and more cacti, and, farther still, Mexico waited, as mysterious as another world.

She laid a hand to her heart. "Oh, Rafe," she breathed, "it's magnificent." When she chanced to look up at him, she caught him watching her with an expression of quiet pleasure.

"This tract of land is pretty far from everything," he said. He picked his way through the words, as though one of them might prove jagged and do injury of some sort. "No stores for miles. No schools, either. When—when we have children, I reckon you'll have to teach them yourself, like Ma did with Jeb and Kade and me."

Everything seemed so gloriously possible in that time and place, even a family of little McKettricks, seated around a kitchen table with slates and lesson books. They seemed so near in that moment, those dark-haired, blue-eyed children, that she could almost say their names.

Emmeline spread her arms and made one swirling turn. "If this were Europe," she said, "there would surely be a castle standing here, with fine turrets, and flags, and a drawbridge."

Rafe looked both worried and hopeful. "Is that what you want, Emmeline? A castle?"

She laughed, and the sound startled the horses, made them look up, just briefly, from their feast of sweet grass. "Why, Rafe," she said, "if you pitched a tent on this spot, it would do as well. It's the view that makes it so magical, the height—why, it's almost like flying." She whirled again, on impulse, arms out wide. "Like being a bird."

He laughed, too, then, and took a step toward her, and she suspected he wanted to take her into his arms and kiss her, but he was not as bold as he had been the night before, it seemed. Instead, he reached into the pocket of his coat and brought out a small packet of folded paper. His big rancher's fingers fumbled a little as he opened it to show her the contents.

Two gold wedding bands glimmered inside, almost lost in the width and breadth of his leather-gloved palm.

Emmeline looked at the rings, then up at Rafe's face.

He held out his hand a little farther. "Take it," he said. Then, with a slight motion of his arm to prompt her: "The little one's yours."

She smiled at the clarification, and he chuckled, though he'd reddened a little at the base of his jaw, and his expression had an element of shyness about it. She took the ring, held it between her thumb and forefinger, and turned it slightly, enjoying its cool smoothness, its glow. Rafe, meanwhile, made some shifting motions, pulling off his riding gloves and jamming them into his coat pocket. Rather like a carnival magician performing sleight of hand, he managed to end up with his band lying in his palm. He hooked it onto his little finger, then took both her hands in his.

"We've got a lot of things to work through," he said huskily, "but in the meantime, will you wear my ring?"

She felt something tighten in her throat, some sweet and spiky pain, and could only nod her head, even though good sense told her to refuse until she was sure she wanted to stay on the Triple M.

His big hands trembling a little, Rafe slipped her ring onto her finger. Emmeline was as moved as if they'd been standing in a cathedral, clad in the finest wedding garb, instead of on a towering hill, buffeted by an ever-chillier breeze. Without ado, she took Rafe's ring, and his left hand, and pushed the band onto his finger. The two of them just stood there, then, hands still clasped, unable to meet each other's eyes.

"Well," Rafe said finally, in a husky voice, "I reckon I ought to kiss you. Seal the bargain and all."

She couldn't answer, but just stood there huddled inside Concepcion's coat, miserable with hope.

Rafe put a finger under her chin, raised her face so that she had to look right at him. She did so, and her gaze held steady, despite her many misgivings and uncertainties. The forbidden night she'd spent with the man called Holt, back in Kansas City, tugged at the hem of her conscience, and a sense of sorrow settled over her, quieting her joy.

Rafe rested his hands lightly on either side of her waist, while she was thinking those thoughts, and lifted her onto her toes, bending his head to find her mouth with his. Emmeline shivered a little, with anticipation as well as guilt, and Rafe paused, lifted his head, and searched her face for any sign of reluctance. "Emmeline?" he asked.

She knew she should tell him the truth about herself and get it over with, but she was still afraid, and, besides, she didn't know precisely what the truth *was,* where her virtue was concerned. She did recall being soundly kissed, back in Kansas City, in the shadowy upper hallway of the boardinghouse, and wondered if Rafe would be able to tell that she was a woman of experience. The prospect scared her twice as much as the rattlesnake in the outhouse had, but this time, there was nowhere to jump.

"Just kiss me, Rafe McKettrick," she said, flushing.

He sighed, then touched his lips to hers, tentatively at first, softly, and once more Emmeline's passion was immediately awakened.

Rafe responded by deepening the kiss, and when it ended, sometime later, and only because they were both in need of air, they stood close together like that, his hands on her waist, her arms around his neck, just staring at each other in bewildered marvel.

It was Rafe who stepped back. "I thought we could put up the house over here," he said gruffly. "Facing the creek, and Pa's place."

Emmeline was still recovering from the revelation of his kiss. She smoothed her flyaway hair, raised the collar of her coat. "Yes," she managed to agree, and cleared her throat delicately. "That would be nice." Would she even be here when the house was built, or would she be far away, trying to make a new life for herself somewhere else?

Rafe paced off the length of the house, showing her where the windows would be, and the front door. They decided on the locations of various rooms—the kitchen, the parlor, his study, her sewing room, the master bedroom and nursery. It was a sort of game to Emmeline, a grown-up version of playing house.

Having laid their plans, they stood where their bed would be, should they actually get that far, and, stricken to silence once more, looked everywhere but at each other.

Rafe had brought sandwiches along, packed in his saddlebags, and they sat side by side on a flat rock where their kitchen table might stand one day, eating and sharing his canteen of water.

Emmeline stole the occasional surreptitious glance at this contradictory man she'd married, framed in sunlight beside her like a young god, and prayed that she would never love him. It would be unbearable, to care for someone so much and not be cared for in return. Oh, it was all very romantic, the land, the matching rings, the dream of a house, but Emmeline had not forgotten what Rafe had said about love the night before. Marriage was like a business agreement to him; he was scornful of the more tender sentiments.

She thought of the Texan again, and the shadow resting across her heart lengthened. She needed to tell Rafe what had happened, get it off her conscience. "Rafe—"

He turned that indigo gaze on her, solemn and patient, waiting for her to continue.

She stared at him, and something turned over in the most fragile part of her spirit, doing damage, leaving a web of fine cracks behind. She looked away, made herself look back. "Are you sorry you sent for me?"

He touched her cheek with the backs of his fingers, ever so gently. "Are you sorry you came?" he countered.

She considered the matter, then shook her head. "No," she said, "but I don't know if I'm glad, either."

He smiled at that. "Fair enough." He sighed, then reached for the canteen and the saddlebags, preparing to leave.

She touched his arm, and was surprised by her own boldness, though she guessed she shouldn't have been, considering how she'd felt last night, when he'd kissed her, and the way she'd acted back in Kansas City, putting on dance-hall clothes, swilling whiskey, and taking up with a total stranger. "Not so fast, Rafe McKettrick," she heard herself say. "You didn't answer my question."

Rafe stopped, canteen in one hand, saddlebags in the other, and looked down at her. "No," he said forthrightly, "I didn't."

She waited, arms folded.

A sunny grin broke over his face. "I believe you wanted to know if I was sorry I sent for you," he said.

She could have shaken him for drawing things out that way, but she was too stubborn to prompt him with so much as a word. She narrowed her eyes slightly and tapped her fingers against her upper arms.

He chuckled. "No," he said. "I reckon you'll serve the purpose."

Emmeline was at once jubilant and mildly insulted, and her expression must have reflected her quandary, for Rafe laughed loudly, the sound ringing against the sky.

Then he picked her up by the waist, spun her around in a great, dizzying circle, and finally hoisted her into Banjo's saddle. Neck and cheeks pulsing with embarrassed heat, she scrambled to get a grip on the saddle horn, and that delighted him even further.

He stood looking up at her, one hand resting lightly on her thigh, branding its image there. The wind had picked up and, for the first time, Emmeline noticed that the clouds were clustering together, conspiring somehow, gray and heavy at the belly.

"We'd better get back down to the ranch," he said. "There's a storm coming on, and Jeb and Kade and the boys will have their hands full with the herd if it gets noisy."

She felt a swift, fierce frisson of alarm at the prospect of Rafe riding after cattle in a violent storm, even though she told herself he was an able horseman, raised on the frontier. Surely he could look after himself, even in circumstances that would have sent her scurrying for cover.

She didn't give voice to her concerns but merely nodded.

Rafe mounted his horse, and they started down the mountainside, the sky growing darker as they went. By the time they reached the ranch house, more than an hour later, the first warm, fat drops of rain were beginning to pock the dry dirt.

Rafe dismounted, helped her down, then turned Banjo over to a ranch hand to be fed, watered, and groomed.

"Go on inside, Emmeline," he said, "before you get soaked."

"Aren't you coming?" she asked, reluctant.

He glanced up at the thickening clouds, the rain wetting his face and his lightweight coat. "There are cattle to round up," he said. Then he was back in the saddle and riding away.

*"Foreman?"* Kade barked, slapping his thigh with his leather gloves, which he'd just yanked off, finger by finger, using his teeth. "Pa made Rafe foreman? When were they planning to tell us?"

Jeb, who'd stopped and dismounted to inspect his horse's left hind hoof, used the point of his jackknife to remove the offending pebble and then straightened to look up at his brother, who was still in the saddle. They'd ridden separate fence lines all morning, and now, in midafternoon, with the wind picking up and the formerly placid sky turning ugly as a new bruise in the distance, they'd joined forces to round up strays. If there was going to be weather—and it looked like there was—they wanted the herd bunched up close and boxed into Horse Thief Canyon. While there was no way they could gather all the cattle on the Triple M together in one place, even with the help of several dozen hands working on various parts of the ranch that season, they could bring in a good share of them.

"I guess they weren't," Jeb replied belatedly. "Planning on telling us, I mean."

Exasperated, Kade turned his head and spat. "Then how do you know it's true?"

"I overheard Pa and Rafe talking about it this morning, in the kitchen."

Saddle leather creaked as Kade shifted his weight, impatient to ride. "I'll be goddamned," he said.

Jeb grinned. "Probably," he agreed cordially.

Kade shook his head, looking amused and disgusted, in equal measure, the way only he could do. "Hell," he said. "Rafe will be impossible to get along with from now on. You know how power goes to his head."

"We've got to do something," Jeb agreed, swinging up onto his horse's back in a single smooth movement. Like his brothers, Jeb didn't recall a time when he hadn't ridden; Angus had put each of them in the saddle as soon as they could sit up on their own.

"Just what do you suggest?" Kade asked.

The irony in his brother's tone, something Jeb could usually overlook, if he was feeling charitable, made him want to fight today. But then, he reckoned, just about anything would have had that effect, given his mood.

"I don't know what you mean to do," Jeb answered, reining his horse toward the high meadow, where there were always a few strays to be found, knee-deep in the sweet grass, "but I'm going to get myself a wife. Right now, I don't much care who she is, either, as long as it isn't Daisy Pert."

Kade prodded his mount to a gallop, with a light tap of his heels, and rode alongside Jeb's butter-colored gelding.

"How do you figure on finding a woman?" he asked. "It isn't as if we haven't turned the country upside down, trying to scare one up. You had those posters put up all over San Francisco and Denver, and I ran advertisements in four different newspapers back east. Unless you want to marry a whore—"

"New people coming in all the time," Jeb broke in, re-settling his hat and glowering a little. "Why, there are some homesteaders just the other side of our southern boundary line, or so I hear. One of them must have a marriageable daughter."

Kade gave a raspy hoot. "Maybe," he agreed. "The question is, are any of them over twelve?"

"Something's bound to happen," Jeb went on, letting his brother's remark pass. He'd been thinking about this wife situation a lot, at least since Miss Emmeline had arrived the day before, pondering his way through a flock of unspectacular options. "Maybe I'll ride on down to Tucson, or Tombstone, one day soon, and size up the social situation there."

Kade swept off his hat, without slackening his pace, and ran an arm across his forehead. "Bring back a spare," he said.

"By next winter," Jeb vowed, "we'll be married men."

"By next winter," Kade said, "we could be uncles, and taking orders from Rafe on a permanent basis."

"Instead of just temporarily, like now?" Jeb retorted dryly, raising an eyebrow.

Kade shuddered. "I love this ranch," he vowed, "but I

figure I could live another fifty years—hell, look at Pa—and that's a mighty long time to take guff from Rafe."

Jeb sighed. There was no refuting Kade's logic. Yep—he would definitely ride down south a ways and see what he came up with. One thing was for damn sure—Kade could go find his own woman. "I think I'd rather be strung up for an outlaw than have Rafe telling me what to do for the rest of my life. The misery would be over a lot quicker."

Kade nodded, and they rode on, climbing now toward the high country, leaning forward in their saddles as their horses cut through the brush. Sure enough, there were a couple of dozen strays in the meadow, mostly cows and yearling calves, and the two brothers set themselves to the task of rounding up the critters and driving them down a gentler slope, toward the relative shelter of the canyon.

There was a lot of whistling and cursing, and the pair of them were splattered with rain and red mud by the time Rafe finally rode up, looking as cool and unruffled as if he'd just taken high tea in a lady's parlor. The mere sight of him made Jeb want to haul him off that horse and kick his ass, just on general principle.

"Good job," Rafe commended his brothers, tugging at the brim of his hat as he got within speaking distance.

"Nice of you to show up," Kade commended, both hands resting easily on the saddle horn.

Rafe smiled, stood in the stirrups for a moment, stretching his legs, and sat down again with a self-satisfied sigh. "Least I could do," he said, "now that I'm foreman."

"So," Kade said, his jaw tight, his horse sensing his disquiet and spooking a little. "Jeb was right."

Rafe sliced a glance in Jeb's direction, eyes narrowed. "Yup," Rafe said. Hot damn, but he looked cool as a springhouse egg. Seething, Jeb wheeled his horse in a little closer, thinking he might take the new foreman down a peg or two.

Rafe's look invited him to try, and the two brothers sat facing each other in stony silence, their horses restless beneath them. Overhead, thunder rolled across the sky and boomed against the mountains, and the cattle took to bawling and flailing around like a bunch of bugs in the bottom of a tobacco can.

"Let's get these critters into the canyon," Kade said, raising his voice to be heard, "before they take a notion to stampede."

# CHAPTER

## 5

"WHERE IS EVERYBODY?" Rafe asked, looming in the kitchen doorway, his clothes as soaked and muddy as if he'd been rolling about on the ground—and perhaps he had. Cowboying was surely rough-and-tumble work.

Emmeline, seated near the stove, where she'd been mending the hem of her best petticoat, looked up at her husband. The shadows made the room seem especially cozy, even as rain lashed at the windows and struck the roof with a furious rhythm.

"Angus is helping find lost cattle," she answered, "and Concepcion left a note, saying she went to pay a call on a neighbor."

"In this weather?" Rafe asked, evidently unconcerned with his father's whereabouts, or that of his two brothers, for that matter, as he kicked off his boots and set them behind the stove. "She knows better than to do a damn fool thing like that."

Emmeline didn't care for his tone, which was officious, and she passed him a glance meant to convey her thoughts. Granted, the storm showed no signs of relenting—indeed, it seemed to be growing more ferocious by the minute—but Concepcion was an intelligent woman and must have had good reason for making the trip. Emmeline rose from her chair, set her sewing on the seat, and went to peer through the misted window over the sink, as though by looking she could cause her friend to appear.

"Did she ride, or take the buggy?" Rafe wanted to know. He looked—and sounded—as irascible as before.

Emmeline flinched as thunder shook the house and lightning split the sky, outlining trees and outbuildings in an eerie, blue-gold glow. "I'm not sure," she admitted. Her irritation at Rafe's attitude had given way to a quiet but elemental fear. "Do you think she's all right?" A whisper.

"A lot of things can happen in this country, especially in this kind of weather," Rafe said. "I'd better go and find her." He rummaged around on the covered porch for another pair of boots and yanked them on. By then, Emmeline had fetched her cloak from the peg next to the door.

"I'm going with you," she said.

"No, you're not," he replied flatly.

Emmeline put her hands on her hips. "While we're standing around arguing, Mr. McKettrick, Concepcion could be catching her death of pneumonia out there."

"And you figure it makes sense for you to rush right out and catch it too?" he retorted.

"You might need my help."

"I can't imagine ever needing your help," Rafe said.

He might as well have struck her. She opened her mouth, and promptly closed it again, too stricken to speak.

He leaned in, jamming his arms, one by one, into the sleeves of a dry coat. "Just stay here," he snapped.

Emmeline fought back humiliating tears. Was this the same man who had given her a gold wedding band on top of a mountain, after showing her where their house would stand? "No!" she snapped back. "I *am* going, whether you like the idea or not." In fact, maybe she would just point herself toward Indian Rock, once they were sure Concepcion was safe, and keep right *on* going.

"If you want to make yourself useful, start heating up some water. I'm going to want a hot bath when I get back here."

"Heat your own bathwater," Emmeline said, striding across the porch and picking her way down the steps to the yard. "I intend to find my friend!" With that, she dashed across the rain-swept grass toward the barn. The creek was roaring in the near distance, swelling its banks, the sky was ugly as a new bruise, and the rain came in torrents.

Rafe caught her by the arm and goose-stepped her the rest of the way, practically flinging her into the cool dampness of the barn. "Listen to me," he rasped. "I might have been a little gruff back there in the kitchen, but the plain fact is, you're only going to slow me down."

Emmeline's cheeks flared with indignant color, but she

held her tongue. She marched to Banjo's stall, threw a halter over the mare's head, and led her out into the main part of the barn. She didn't bother looking for the saddle; she wouldn't know how to put it on the animal anyway. Surely, she reasoned, she could manage a bridle.

With a gusty sigh, Rafe turned away from her, throwing his hands into the air, and proceeded to saddle a horse for himself. His gelding, Chief, remained in his stall, steam rising off his hide because of the wetness in the air.

Emmeline chose a bridle, wrestled it onto Banjo's head, and led the poor beast to stand alongside a bale of hay, which she used as a mounting block. Rafe and his horse were already approaching the burgeoning creek when she finally persuaded her recalcitrant little mare to leave the shelter of the barn.

Keeping up was impossible; the rain was a smothering, impenetrable curtain between her and Rafe. Emmeline knew she should swallow her pride and go back to the house, but she couldn't make herself do either of those things. If she was ever to amount to anything as a ranch wife, she had to be able to cope with any emergency.

Rafe stayed close when they crossed the creek—Emmeline's feet were already numb with cold—then rode ahead. She persisted, and he wheeled around to ride beside her again. "You're acting like a damn fool!" he yelled over the downpour. "People get struck by lightning storms like this—-they get themselves thrown from their horses and hit their heads on rocks—they drown in flash floods!"

"Exactly why we need to find Concepcion!" she cried in reply, sputtering as the wind buffeted her face, stopping her breath.

"Hell!" Rafe roared. Then, before Emmeline knew what was happening, he leaned over, hooked an arm around her waist, and dragged her off Banjo, settling her behind him on his horse. Deftly, he removed Banjo's bridle, gave the animal a light swat on the flank, and sent her racing back to the barn. "At least *she's* got some sense!" he shouted. "Hold on, damm it!"

With a motion of his heels, he set the gelding in motion again, and Emmeline was forced to cling for dear life. She reached around his middle and took handfuls of his coat, then buried her face in the slight hollow between his shoulder blades. The ride was a rough one, wet and cold and slippery, but when the overturned buggy came in sight, just ahead, Emmeline was glad she'd come along. Concepcion had unhitched the horse, and the two of them, woman and beast, stood shivering beneath an overhang of rocks.

Rafe was down off his horse in an instant, while Emmeline followed more slowly. She was stiff, and the balls of her feet ached mightily when she walked, causing her to limp a little.

"He's lame," Emmeline heard Concepcion tell Rafe, as she stroked the animal's muzzle.

"What about you?" Rafe shouted over the driving rain. "Are you all right?"

Concepcion nodded. "Just feeling a little stupid," she confessed.

Rafe gave her a look designed to convey his opinion of females who didn't have the sense to stay out of the rain, but said nothing. He checked the buggy horse, an ancient dappled gray, and then straightened. "He's sound enough to carry Emmeline," he said to Concepcion. "You can ride back with me."

"What about the buggy?" Concepcion asked. "Are we just going to leave it out here?"

"Yes," Rafe said, giving the rig a cursory inspection. "The axle is broken. I'll come back for it when this lets up."

He hoisted Concepcion onto the gelding's back and, with even less ceremony, flung Emmeline up onto the gray. The muscles in her thighs screamed in protest, but she didn't make a sound. During the brief moment when her gaze locked with Rafe's, the two of them sparked lightning of their own.

Emmeline jutted out her chin.

The return trip was necessarily slower than the ride out had been, due to the dappled gray's injured foot, and once or twice, from beneath the brim of her bonnet, Concepcion looked back at Emmeline, a troubled expression in her eyes.

Reaching the ranch house, Rafe deposited the women near the back door, then rode off to the barn, the gray plodding along behind him.

"What happened?" Emmeline asked, when she and Concepcion were safe, if not yet warm, in the welcoming kitchen. It was obvious that there had been a mishap of some sort, but she wanted details.

Concepcion added wood to the fire in the stove, stoked

the blaze with a poker, then nodded toward the back stairs. "We'd both better change out of these wet clothes before we do any talking," she said.

They retreated to their rooms, returning minutes later, wearing their warmest dresses. Emmeline huddled close to the stove, blotting at her wet hair with a towel, while Concepcion brewed tea.

Concepcion sighed as she measured fragrant leaves into a pot. "You should have stayed here, Emmeline," she said. "It's dangerous out there."

"I could say the same to you," Emmeline pointed out reasonably.

Concepcion smiled. "Indeed, you could," she admitted.

The door banged open, and Rafe stormed in.

"Are you two pleased with yourselves?" he demanded, shedding his coat, shirt, and boots, flinging them back out onto the porch. He was still wearing a button-up undershirt and his trousers and socks, but Emmeline found herself flushing as hotly as if he'd stripped himself naked, right there in the kitchen.

Concepcion squared her shoulders. "Thank you for coming to fetch me, Rafe," she said, very calmly. "I do appreciate it. I will not, however, have you raising your voice to me as though I were some greenhorn."

He subsided, but only slightly and only long enough to turn his ire on Emmeline. "I suppose you have something to say, too?" he challenged.

Emmeline shook her head, holding her chin a notch or two higher than usual.

"Good," he retorted, waggling a finger at her. "Because I've got plenty—"

"Go and change your clothes," Concepcion interceded mildly. "You're dripping all over my clean floor."

For a moment, Rafe looked as if he might bellow like a bull, or turn the kitchen table onto its top, but then he simply crashed his way up the stairs and along the hallway to his room. Both Concepcion and Emmeline flinched at the distant slamming of a door.

"He'll get over this," Concepcion said.

Emmeline realized that her eyes had gone wide, and willed herself to relax. "I was only trying to be a good ranch wife," she confided.

Concepcion chuckled. "I think your idea of being a wife might be a little different from Rafe's," she said. The water in the teakettle began to boil, and she poured it into the crockery pot, raising a cloud of deliciously scented steam. "When Rafe sent away for a bride, he expected someone who would follow his orders, cook his meals, clean his house, and bear his children." She paused. "What did *you* expect, Emmeline?"

She shrugged, feeling dispirited and exceedingly far from home. "I guess I wanted to belong somewhere," she said.

Concepcion patted Emmeline's shoulder, then took two cups from the shelf next to the sink. She inclined her head slightly, urging Emmeline toward the table, and they both sat down, on opposite sides, the teapot between them.

"Rafe wanted me to stay here and heat water for a bath," Emmeline continued.

"Terrible," Concepcion said, and smiled, over the rim of her cup. Her ebony hair was sagging from its pins and still dripping a little. Her dark eyes twinkled.

Emmeline sighed. "I suppose I should have done what he asked, but he was so heavy-handed about it."

Concepcion chuckled, took a sip of tea. "Rafe McKettrick has met his match," she said, and she sounded pleased. She glanced toward the rear stairway, and then the door, probably assuring their privacy. "With the men in this family," she whispered, "you have to choose your battles wisely. They've got skulls as thick as a bull's, all of them, and they'll argue one side of a question until they've convinced God and his angels that they're right, then take up the other side and make just as good a case, for the pure sport of it."

Emmeline's shoulders sagged with discouragement. She might as well catch a stage out of town right now, and let fate have its way with her, for she would never learn to "choose her battles" and, besides, she wasn't cut out to take orders from anyone, especially when she considered those orders unreasonable. She supposed she'd acquired that trait, like so many others, from long association with Becky.

Concepcion poured more tea into Emmeline's cup. "Just give him a little time," she said. Rafe's footsteps echoed from upstairs, and Concepcion leaned closer and whispered, "Marriage requires patience and compromise."

"Yes," Emmeline agreed, rather pettishly, "but only from the wife, it would seem."

Rafe looked damnably attractive, standing at the base of the stairs, his skin ruddy, his dark hair tousled from a vigorous toweling. He wore clean denims, another button-up undershirt, and a pair of gray wool socks, but no boots.

Emmeline sniffed at the sight of him. It was difficult to believe that, only hours before, just prior to the storm, they'd shared a picnic lunch on a lower rung of heaven, slipped gold wedding bands onto each other's fingers, and talked about children.

"Tea?" Concepcion offered, holding up the pot.

Ignoring the invitation, Rafe took a cup from the shelf, approached the stove, and sloshed in a dose of coffee, grimacing when he tasted it. "Where," he asked, very quietly, "did you have to go that was so important?"

Concepcion sighed. "I was at the Pelton homestead," she said. "Phoebe Anne's baby is due any day now, and her husband's laid up with some kind of grippe, and he hasn't been able to work the farm in a long time. I took them a kettle of soup, a few eggs, some canned goods."

"Squatters," Rafe said with distaste. He disappeared into the pantry, returned with a bottle of whiskey, and poured a generous dollop into his coffee.

"They have a valid claim on that land," Concepcion said evenly.

"The hell they do," Rafe countered. "It's five miles this side of our eastern boundary. Soon as I have the time, I'm going to move them off."

Emmeline blinked. "Surely they're not hurting any-one," she said. "The Peltons, I mean."

"They're on Triple M land," Rafe said.

"But he's ailing, and she's about to have a baby—"

Rafe was apparently unmoved. "They'd be better off in town, where the doc could look after them."

"I think I'll go and lie down for a while," Concepcion said, sounding weary. She left the room, by way of the rear stairs, and Emmeline found herself alone with Rafe.

He finished his whiskey-laced coffee, then made a great deal of noise getting pots and kettles from the shelves and pumping water into them at the sink. He set them on the stove top, one by one, and began to build up the fire.

Emmeline watched him, sipping her tea and saying nothing. He was an enigma, this man, kind and generous one moment, almost callous the next. He was willing to ride out into a storm to look for Concepcion, but the plight of the Pelton family seemed not to matter to him at all. She wondered how the other McKettrick brothers felt about the homesteaders, not to mention Angus, and made up her mind to find out at the first opportunity.

And the next time Concepcion visited the Peltons, Emmeline meant to go along.

Meanwhile, Rafe dragged a large copper bathtub in from the back porch and set it beside the stove, out of the way of the door. He brought a folding screen from a nearby room, then fetched towels and a bar of soap. The time had definitely come to leave the room, Emmeline decided. She set the teapot in the sink, along with her cup, and retrieved her sewing from the seat of the rocking chair, where she'd abandoned it earlier to join Rafe in the search for Concepcion. She planned to sit in the rarely used parlor, at the front of the house, and watch the storm as she stitched.

"Emmeline," Rafe said quietly, just as she was about to pass through the doorway.

She stopped, but did not turn around. Her fingers tightened around the already crumpled petticoat.

"This is your bath," he told her.

She faced him, stunned. "Mine? But—"

"You must have taken a chill out there," he said. "Your lips are blue, and you're still shivering a little."

"I'm fine," she said, though in point of fact, he was right. She was still cold, despite her dry clothes, the copious amounts of tea she'd consumed, and the comforting warmth of the kitchen stove.

He gripped the back of his father's chair at the table. Then he took her by surprise by grinning at her. "You're as stubborn as I am," he said. "Makes me wonder what our sons and daughters would be like."

Emmeline's heart skittered over a beat. Just for a moment, she imagined herself as a true wife and mother, the hub of a happy home, high on a mountaintop, and she was desperate with hope. "I couldn't bathe here," she said. "Someone might see."

Rafe smiled. "The screen will solve that problem," he said. "Besides, we've pretty much got the place to ourselves. Kade and Jeb are playing poker in the bunkhouse—they'll be at it awhile, since they're both losing—and Pa's been on the range all day, so he's likely to spend the evening in his study, by the fire. Bad weather always makes him melancholy."

"Why?" she asked. She truly wanted to know, but she was stalling, too. A hot bath would be the purest of luxuries, and she *was* cold, but the prospect of removing her clothes in the kitchen, even with a screen to hide behind, was a daunting one. Back home in Kansas City, there had been a room reserved for the purpose, with hot and cold running water, no windows, and a lock on the door.

"Because of my mother," Rafe said. "A storm came up, like this one, and she rode out to help round up some heifers and calves. It was nothing she hadn't done a hundred times before. This time, though, a clap of thunder scared her horse, and she was thrown into the creek. She came up laughing, and swore she was all right, but she caught a cold, sure enough, and that turned into a fever. She died the next night."

Emmeline laid a hand to her throat. Now she realized why Rafe had not wanted her to join him on the search for Concepcion. He was trying, in a roundabout way, to explain his behavior, if not to apologize. "I'm sorry," she said. "That's terrible."

"Things were different around here, when she was gone," Rafe mused, gazing at the rain-darkened window. Then he met Emmeline's gaze again. "Don't let that water go cold," he said. "And don't worry about being caught naked. I'll stand guard."

He stood at the kitchen sink, looking out the window, his broad back to the room.

Emmeline went behind the screen, removed her clothes, slowly and with stop-and-start motions, keeping an eye out for peepers the whole time, and slipped into the bathwater. It was utter bliss; a benediction from the angels. She sighed aloud.

Rafe chuckled. "There's more hot water on the stove," he said. "Let me know when you need it."

She sank deeper into the tub, covering herself with her arms as best she could. "I won't have you looking," she said.

"You're my wife," he said. She heard him refilling a kettle at the pump.

Emmeline laid a hand to her lower belly. Was there a baby growing there, even now? If so, she was running out of time. Whatever her reservations about a future with Rafe McKettrick, whatever her fears, she needed a husband. A real one.

Rafe rounded the screen, his eyes squinched shut, holding a large kettle by the handles, which were covered with pot holders. He poured the water into the tub, at Emmeline's feet, causing her to suspect that he'd peeked. Steam surged into the chilly air.

"Thank you," she said. The room was shadowy; the kerosene lamps had burned low enough to smoke and flicker, and one of them must have guttered out, for, in the space of a moment, the kitchen was cast into near darkness. "You must be cold, too," she ventured.

He chuckled, and more pots and kettles banged against the sink or the stove top. "I could join you," he teased. "That would definitely warm me up."

Emmeline found the idea more appealing than she would have admitted. "Not," she said, very primly, "in the kitchen."

"Now if I'd known that was the only problem, Mrs. McKettrick," he said, "our being in the kitchen, I mean, I'd have set up that tub in our bedroom."

She blushed, and knew it wasn't because of the deliciously warm water she was soaking in. Her bones, formerly frozen to the marrow, were beginning to thaw, and there was a peculiar ache in the core of her. Instead of answering, she reached for the soap and began to wash, with a lot of splashing.

"I could scrub your back," Rafe volunteered.

Emmeline continued to bathe.

"Emmeline," he prompted.

"All right," she whispered. It wasn't Rafe she'd been resisting, she realized, but herself.

Her response must have taken him by surprise, because several moments passed before he came around the screen, this time with his eyes wide open. His glance, sweeping over her as it did, surely raised the temperature of the water, and Emmeline's breath caught in her throat.

"You're sure?" he asked. He was talking about more than washing her back, and they both knew it.

She nodded.

He knelt beside the tub, lathered the wash cloth with soap. "Lean forward," he said gruffly.

Emmeline obeyed, resting her forehead on her raised knees.

"Scared?" Rafe asked.

She nodded without lifting her head.

"Don't be," he said. He washed her back, rinsed away the soap, then got to his feet, hauling Emmeline with him. He wrapped her in towels, lifted her into his arms, and carried her around the screen, across the kitchen, and up the back stairs.

In his room, Rafe set Emmeline on her feet, wrapped her in a quilt dragged from the bed, and turned away to open the door of the woodstove and get a fire going.

Emmeline perched on the edge of the mattress, noting, as she hadn't the night before, that it was thick and soft, probably stuffed with feathers.

Still huddled inside the blanket, she rested a hand on her lower abdomen. She had hoped to be bleeding by now, but she wasn't, and time was passing. If she waited too long, she would be sent from the Triple M in disgrace, with nowhere to go.

But suppose he knew he wasn't the first? Suppose he rejected her, out of hand?

She decided not to think just then about the choices that would be left to her, should Rafe turn his back on her. She must take things as they came, moment by moment and step by step, or she would surely go mad.

The scent of sun-dried linens, starched and pressed,

teased her nose as she shed the quilt and lay down, pulling the remaining covers over her. She kept carefully to the side she'd occupied the night before, nearest the wall, the blankets drawn up to her chin. She stared upward, into the gloom, her eyes wide, her whole being poised on the edge of a precipice.

And she waited.

Rafe went out, and she dozed, then awakened with a start when the bedroom door creaked open, then closed. When she heard the key turn in the lock, she felt a sweet shiver pass through her. She had no idea how long Rafe had been gone, though the room was quite dark.

"Emmeline?" Rafe asked. He carried a lamp in one hand, and set it on the bureau. He was wearing trousers but nothing else, he smelled of soap, and his dark hair, still damp, lay in ridges left by his fingers.

"Yes," she said. That one word was all she could summon the breath for.

He came and stood beside the bed, looking down at her. She couldn't read his expression, since the lantern was behind him. "I'd like to lie down next to you now," he said, as though he were asking for a dance, "and just hold you in my arms for a while. Would that be all right with you?"

She did not know what she'd expected of him, not brutishness or cruelty, surely, but not tenderness, either. "All—all right," she agreed, and squeezed her eyes shut when she realized that he was unbuttoning his trousers.

The feather mattress dipped as he got in beside her,

bringing a rush of cold air with him, followed immediately by a sense of contained heat. Gently, he stroked the side of her face, the length of her neck.

He drew her against his side, held her loosely in the hard circle of his embrace. She felt his moist hair against her temple, the firm flesh of his shoulder beneath her cheek. The length of his body seemed to shelter her, like a range of mountains shielding a meadow from all but the mildest elements, and he smelled pleasantly of mint and soap, and of the outdoors, the wild, wide countryside that was as much a part of him as his skin and the low timbre of his voice. "Emmeline," he said. Just her name, but with a whole world of meaning.

"What?" she asked unsteadily.

"Let out your breath and loosen up a little. You're stiff as a plank."

She tried to comply, truly she did, but met with small success. She was at a crossroads, and the direction she took was all-important. How could she relax?

He rolled onto his side, still holding her, and brushed his mouth lightly across her temple. "Maybe you need a little help," he said.

Emmeline's heart pounded. If he thought talk like that was going to soothe her, he was sorely mistaken.

His right hand had found its way under her bottom, somehow, and his left came to rest lightly against her hip, bunching the fabric of her nightgown a little as he slid it slowly upward, along her waist and rib cage, to her breast. She gasped when he reached his destination, surprised by pleasure, and he kissed her, deeply and then more deeply still, caressing her all the while.

Emmeline was breathless when he released her mouth, only to nibble at her earlobe and then the length of her neck. The nightgown kept creeping up, at a steady but nearly imperceptible pace, and then suddenly it was off over her head, gone.

The lantern had snuffed itself out, and the storm was still lashing at the house and the land. Rafe was a shadow lover, exploring her with his hands and his lips, and when he took her nipple in his mouth, she was utterly lost. She made a soft sobbing sound and plunged her fingers into his hair, and he moaned as he savored her, cupping her breast in his hand, squeezing gently, tonguing her until the pleasure was nearly past bearing.

Presently, he moved to her other breast, and gave it equal attention. He was an exquisitely thorough man, and Emmeline soon learned that he would not be hurried, no matter how desperate her responses. Indeed, by the time he kissed his way down over her belly, and found her woman-place with his tongue, taking that small nubbin as boldly as he'd taken her nipples, she was perspiring, feverish with need, flailing and tossing on the sheets, instinctively seeking a solace that would be granted only after being denied for a long, long time.

His name was a soft, frantic litany on her lips as he continued his scandalous ministrations, adding to her need by putting a finger inside her, finding the most sensitive place, teasing her there.

She was wild with wanting by that time, beyond thought or reason, and still Rafe asked more and more of her, and still she gave it. She lost the sense of where she, as Emmeline, began and ended; her soul seemed to expand in a dizzying rush, and then she was nothing and everything, pure essence, at one with the lightning searing the night sky, rolling on the crest of the thunder itself.

Satisfaction exploded within her, and, after a long time, her body still spasming, she fell gasping to earth, and to Rafe's bed. Rafe caressed her, spoke soothing words of praise as she settled slowly back into herself. Then, when a blissful eternity had passed, he parted her legs and poised himself over her. She sensed his desire, barely restrained, felt the size and substance of him, about to enter her, and if she'd been in her right mind, she would have been terrified. Instead, she answered the unspoken question, offered by his silence, with a nod of her head and a whispered, "Yes, Rafe. Yes."

He claimed her in a long, deep stroke, and her first response was one of shock. There was pain, too, though it wasn't the tearing sensation she'd expected, even hoped for, on some level of her mind. No, it was Rafe's size that hurt her, in the beginning, and not the breaching of any barrier.

She waited, her heart in her throat, for his scorn, for his furious rejection, but those things never came. Instead of raging at her, he began to move upon her, slowly at first, gracefully, and then with increasing power and speed. He urged her, with his hands and murmured words, to keep pace with him. Once again, her deepest instincts took over, leaving no room for doubts, no room for anything but the delicious friction of their bodies, meeting and parting and meeting again.

When she could endure no more, could climb no further, Emmeline shattered into fragments in Rafe's arms. He groaned, his face buried in her neck, and then his whole body stiffened at the arch of a thrust so powerful that Emmeline's spirit was conquered, as well as her body. She began to weep when it was over, and Rafe held her tightly in his arms, as if he'd never let go.

At some point, she slept, too exhausted even to dream, her fingers still buried in his hair.

Rafe rapped loudly at Jeb's bedroom door as he passed it, early the next morning, and then at Kade's. The storm had moved on, but the aftermath would be wicked. There was a lot of work to be done.

He lingered a moment outside his father's room, heard the old man snoring fit to rouse the dead. Let him sleep; he'd earned it.

Downstairs, in the kitchen, Rafe lighted the stove and put the coffee on to brew. He heard his brothers stirring upstairs and smiled a little. They'd be about as cordial as a couple of old bears prodded out of hibernation, he reckoned, being roused a full hour earlier than usual, but he didn't give a damn what they thought. He took his job as foreman seriously, and Jeb and Kade might as well get used to it, like everybody else on the ranch. He planned to run a tight operation, with no slack in the rigging.

He was whistling under his breath when Kade appeared, unshaved and growly, with his shirttail out. "This had better be an emergency," he said.

Rafe set a skillet on the stove with a resounding clang. Later on, he'd expect Emmeline to get up with him and fix a proper breakfast, but this morning she needed her sleep. He smiled, remembering her response to his love-making. She was one of those women who took to it naturally, and that was a blessing as well as a relief. He had neither the time nor the inclination to coax a reluctant bride. "No emergency," he replied cheerfully. "Just a ranch to run."

Kade narrowed his eyes, but before he could say anything, Jeb came pounding down the stairs, looking even wilder than Kade. "What the hell is going on around here?" he demanded of Rafe. "Do you know what time it is?"

Rafe fetched a chunk of salt pork from a crock in the pantry and tossed it into the skillet, where it started to sizzle right away. "Yeah," he said. "It's time your ass was in the saddle." He paused, sighed magnanimously. "However, because you're my brothers, my own flesh and blood, I'm willing to overlook one slow start."

"Damnation, but you're generous," Kade said, sniffing for coffee. Since it wasn't ready yet, he got a basin off the back porch, filled it with water from the reservoir on the side of the stove, and commenced to wash up.

Jeb glared at Rafe for a long moment, as if he'd like to start a good row, right there in the kitchen, but finally turned and went back upstairs. By the time the coffee was ready and the salt pork had been fried, sliced, and slapped between slices of buttered bread, though, he'd returned, dressed for a long day on the range.

"I guess you think you've got this contest won, hands down," Kade said to Rafe, in a low drawl, as the three brothers left the house together, carrying mugs of coffee with them, their hats pulled low against the early morning chill and the collars of their canvas coats raised.

Rafe merely arched an eyebrow and smiled. He was too much of a gentleman to come right out and say that if there was any rhyme or reason in all creation, he and Emmeline had started a baby the night before. Which wasn't to say he didn't feel like shouting the news from the roof. Some things were private, that's all.

"You missed supper last night," Jeb said, frowning.

"So I did," Rafe agreed blithely.

His brothers exchanged troubled glances.

"You knock on my door before dawn again, Big Brother," Kade warned, "and the house had better be on fire, because if it isn't, I'm going to throw you down the front stairs."

"Anytime you think you can manage that," Rafe said, "you just go ahead and give it a try."

For a moment it looked like there might be a good fight after all, the backyard being more suitable for a skirmish than the kitchen, but the sun was spilling thin light over the hills to the east, and a full day's work awaited. Smoke twisted from the bunkhouse chimney and light glowed from the windows, and some of the hands were already saddling up in front of the barn. Rafe tossed the contents of his coffee into the mud and resettled his hat. Best get the day started.

"Jeb," he said, "you take a dozen men or so and ride south. There are bound to be a hundred head of cattle or more stuck on the far side of the river, and I want them back with the main herd before the rustlers and sodbusters get to them."

Jeb wanted to argue, Rafe could see that, but in the end, he decided against it. He raised his coffee in a mocking toast and headed for the barn without another word.

Kade waited for his orders, watching Rafe, narroweyed, through the steam rising from his mug.

Rafe kept his brother in suspense for another heartbeat or two, and enjoyed doing it. "You go into Indian Rock and bring back some lumber and tar paper, so we can get started on the new roof for the bunkhouse," he said. "One more storm like this last one and the whole thing will sag like a whore's mattress."

Kade weighed the instructions. "Anything else?" he asked tersely, and in his own good time.

Rafe thought about asking his brother to buy something for Emmeline, a pretty comb or a book or even some perfume, but when it came down to it, he didn't want Kade or anybody else choosing presents for his bride. He did wish he'd asked her if she had a letter to post or anything like that, though. Trips to town weren't all that frequent, given the distance involved, and he aimed to be a considerate husband. "Check with Concepcion before you head out," he answered. "She might need some things from the mercantile."

Kade nodded and headed for the barn to hitch up a wagon and choose one of the men to ride shotgun. Rafe considered reminding his brother that the visit to Indian Rock was for business, not pleasure, so he ought not to get himself into a poker game there, or a whore's bed, but he was feeling especially generous that morning, so he held his tongue.

Rafe was still congratulating himself on his leadership abilities when he saddled his horse, appointed ten men to ride with him, and led the way north, in search of more stray cattle. The sky was bluing up nicely, and spring was in the air.

Rafe looked back once, just when the house would disappear from sight, and wished he'd stayed in bed with his pretty wife for just a little while longer.

# CHAPTER

## 6

THE BUCKBOARD, driven by one of the ranch hands, drew up in front of the house. Concepcion drew a deep breath of the rain-washed air, smiled, and started down the front walk. Emmeline walked beside her.

The driver tugged at his hat brim, climbed down to the moist, shimmering ground, and offered a hand up to Concepcion. "You sure you ladies don't want me to go along?" he asked. Concepcion handed him a large covered basket, which he set in the back of the buckboard. "They's been some outlaw trouble around these parts lately."

"Thank you, Red," Concepcion said pleasantly, "but we'll be just fine on our own."

Concepcion settled herself on the seat and took up the reins. Emmeline, meanwhile, rounded the wagon to the other side. Red hurried to assist her, as he had Concepcion. She arranged her skirts and waited.

"They's a rifle under the seat, like usual," Red said, with

good-natured resignation. "Anybody gives you any grief, you just shoot 'em." Plainly, he'd had this conversation with Concepcion before.

"I'll do that," Concepcion said, and released the brake lever. "Good day to you, Red."

The grizzled old man pulled at his hat brim again. "Ma'am," he acknowledged. "If Angus or Rafe should ask where you've gone—"

"Tell them we're visiting the Pelton family," she replied, and gave the reins a flick. The two horses hitched to the buckboard immediately shambled into motion.

Concepcion drove skillfully across the creek and up the opposite bank, toward the cattle track that passed as a road. Emmeline, not nearly as confident as her friend, glanced back over one shoulder. She hadn't told Rafe she intended to visit the Pelton homestead with Concepcion; in the two weeks since the storm, when Rafe had made her his wife in every sense of the word, things had been going remarkably well between them. She didn't like deceiving her husband, but she wasn't eager to go nose-to-nose with him, either. Her monthly still hadn't arrived, for one thing, though she prayed for it every day and often lay awake, in the depths of the night, suffering a crisis of conscience while Rafe slept beside her, exhausted by a long day of hard work and by their love-making.

If she was going to have a child, she wanted that child to be Rafe's. The uncertainty she lived with was taking its toll, chipping away at her spirit day by day and moment by moment. The intimate times with Rafe were ecstasy, transporting Emmeline to heights that literally took her breath away, but he was a different man outside their bed—stubborn, opinionated, and usually distracted.

Now, jostling along in the buckboard, Emmeline glanced at Concepcion, wishing she dared ask her advice, or at least confide in her. She couldn't take the risk, of course. Though she and Concepcion were friends, the other woman's loyalties, in a case like this, would naturally lie with the McKettrick family.

"Have you sent word to your people that you've arrived safely?" Concepcion asked, when they'd been driving awhile.

Emmeline was greatly relieved; here was a question she could answer honestly, and without hesitation. "Jeb mailed a letter to my aunt when he went to town," she said. Although the missive would take a long time to reach Kansas City, she was certain her aunt already knew where she was. She'd left several clues behind—most notably the newspaper, folded open to the advertisement for the Happy Home Matrimonial Service—just in case Becky ever got into a forgiving state of mind.

Knowing that her aunt's pride was even greater than her own, however, Emmeline did not hold out much hope for reconciliation. She sniffled once, and looked away.

The Pelton place was small, just a makeshift cabin with a lean-to barn attached to one end, one old cow for stock, and a patch of garden that had dried up before it really got started.

A tiny woman, enormously pregnant, stepped out onto the porch. She smiled and waved at Concepcion and Emmeline, her other hand resting on her distended belly. Her calico dress, worn to near transparency, was crumpled, but fairly clean, while her dark brown hair had been sheared off at a variety of lengths.

"That's Phoebe Anne," Concepcion confided to Emmeline, smiling at the woman as she secured the wagon. "I thought she'd have her baby by now."

Emmeline felt anxious, having never been acquainted with a pregnant woman, but she, too, smiled.

Phoebe Anne came out to meet them, shading her eyes from the bright morning sun. She touched her butchered tresses self-consciously, and the gesture moved Emmeline, for there was such vulnerability in it.

"Phoebe Anne," Concepcion said, "this is Emmeline McKettrick. She's Rafe's wife."

Phoebe Anne's smile faded a little at the mention of Rafe. No doubt she and her husband had had more than one run-in with him already, over the land; he was determined to send them packing before winter set in again.

"How do you do?" she asked, as Emmeline climbed down off the wagon. Concepcion did the same, after reaching back to claim the basket.

Emmeline gave a polite answer, and smiled.

"How's Seth?" Concepcion asked, putting an arm around Phoebe Anne's waist. "Better, I hope?"

"He's still right sickly," Phoebe Anne said. "He went hunting, though. We don't want to eat any of these chickens if we don't have to—'cause that would stop the eggs comin'." She led them through the tall grass, where a flock of chickens were feeding, and inside the cabin.

The sour smell of sickness struck Emmeline like a slap across the face, and she was glad Phoebe Anne's back was to her, so she didn't see her automatic grimace. Concepcion took note, and nodded slightly.

Emmeline looked around. There was one narrow bed, a stone fireplace, hastily built and already crumbling, a rickety table with a lamp on top, and two crates for sitting. Light slanted between the unchinked log walls, and the floor was hard-packed dirt. The thought of living in a place like that, let alone giving birth there, truly appalled Emmeline, though again she took care not to let her feelings show.

"How about you, Phoebe Anne?" Concepcion went on, setting the basket on the table. "Isn't it past time for that baby to come?"

Phoebe Anne's gaze was fixed on the basket, and Emmeline reckoned the Peltons had been going hungry lately; the knowledge filled her with a combination of sorrow, shame, and indignation. Her own problems were small in comparison to all these poor homesteaders faced, and Rafe might have helped them, instead of adding to their worries.

"I'm not sure everything's right with this baby," Phoebe Anne said. "It don't move like it used to, and it should have been out for a while now."

Concepcion gave the basket a little push in Phoebe Anne's direction and drew back the blue and white checked cloth that covered the contents. "You need to see a doctor," Concepcion said, as Phoebe Anne crept closer and peered into the basket, which contained a good-sized ham and a variety of preserves, among other things.

"There's no money for such as that," Phoebe Anne said. She was openly digging through the basket now, eager as a child at Christmas. There was a whole fried chicken, wrapped in dishtowels, and at the sight of that she gasped with delight. "You hungry?" she asked, looking from Concepcion to Emmeline.

Both women shook their heads, and Phoebe Anne immediately bit into a chicken leg.

"I think Doc would wait for his pay," Concepcion urged gently.

"How would I get there?" Phoebe Anne asked, between bites. "Seth sold our team and wagon off last fall." The realization that Emmeline and Concepcion were standing showed in her face. "Where are my manners?" she said anxiously, indicating the crates. "Mama would shoot me. Please, sit down."

Emmeline and Concepcion sat. Phoebe Anne perched on the edge of the bed, looking far more like a child than a woman grown. Occasionally, she cast a fretful look toward the door, probably expecting her husband.

"I'll drive you to town myself," Concepcion said. Plainly, she was not about to be turned aside from her objective. "And I'll explain the situation to Doc."

Phoebe Anne bit her lip and glanced at the door again. "Seth don't hold much with charity," she confided.

"The devil take Seth Pelton and his fool pride," Concepcion said flatly. "He ought to see the doc himself."

Phoebe Anne's eyes widened; maybe she'd never seen Concepcion take such a hard stance. Emmeline certainly hadn't, and she was fascinated. She also felt a growing admiration for her friend. "He was fit to be tied after you brought us that food two weeks back, when the big storm came in. Said he ought to just shoot himself, since he was good for nothin' anyways. Said I'd have a chance to get myself a real husband, if he was out of the way."

Emmeline felt the bottom drop out of her stomach and, glancing at Concepcion, saw that her friend was unsettled as well.

"You don't think he was serious," Concepcion said.

Phoebe Anne's expression was bleak. She looked at the chicken bone she'd practically denuded, and tossed it onto the cold hearth. "Seth's been real melancholy this last little while. He says he shouldn't have brought us all the way out here, when we could have stayed and helped his folks on the home place, back in Iowa. At least there was always enough to eat, 'cause of the garden and the hogs."

"Now, there's no sense in despairing over what's done with," Concepcion counseled. "Maybe you and Seth could go back to Iowa, back to his folks. Once you've had the baby and everything."

Emmeline closed her eyes. She was no fortune-teller,

but in those moments she was as certain of imminent tragedy as she was of tomorrow's sunrise.

"I wanted to do that," Phoebe Anne said sadly. "I thought we could write Pa and Mam for the train fare and just head on home, but Seth said he couldn't face his folks, failin' like we have here."

"Why don't you just come back to the ranch with us, right now?" Concepcion asked, her tone revealing none of the anxiety Emmeline saw in her eyes and the set of her face, "We'll drive into town in the morning, together. You can see Doc and send a wire to Seth's folks. Just tell them things are real hard out here and you'd like to come home. If they want you, and I'm sure they will, they'll probably wire you right back to say so. You could show their telegram to Seth; knowing there's a place waiting for the both of you in Iowa, he might stop being so stiff-necked." She paused. "As for the fare—I'll lend you that myself. I have plenty saved."

Phoebe Anne blinked back tears. "I been dreamin' of goin' home," she said softly, "and I'll sure go to town with you tomorrow, but I can't leave the place with Seth gone. He'd be real mad. I've got these chickens and old Molly to milk."

Concepcion smiled. "All right," she said, surprising Emmeline with her easy acquiescence. "We'll come by for you in the morning."

"Seth—"

"I'll deal with Seth," Concepcion said firmly.

Phoebe Anne nodded. "Thank you," she said. "Thank

you for bringin' this food, especially. Seth won't like it, but he'll be glad there's something to eat in the house, too."

Emmeline and Concepcion stood. Emmeline's heart was breaking at the prospect of leaving Phoebe Anne alone in this desolate, hopeless place, and she suspected that Concepcion felt the same.

"It was real nice makin' your acquaintance," Phoebe Anne said, shaking Emmeline's hand.

Emmeline smiled. "Likewise," she said. "We'll see you tomorrow."

"Tomorrow," Concepcion reiterated, affectionately stern. "You be ready."

Phoebe Anne nodded, and Concepcion and Emmeline took their leave, both of them silent for most of the drive back.

That night at supper, Angus made a grim announcement.

Several of the Triple M hands had been out looking for strays, he told the small gathering—from which Kade and Jeb were conspicuously absent—and they'd heard a shot, then come across Seth Pelton sprawled in a dry wash, with the top of his head blown off. Evidently, he'd put the barrel of his hunting rifle in his mouth and pulled the trigger.

Emmeline threw down her napkin and jumped to her feet, surprising everyone at the table except Concepcion, who had done the very same thing.

"I knew it," Emmeline cried. "I *knew* something terrible was going to happen!"

"She's all alone over at that place," Concepcion fretted, twisting her apron in both hands. "Poor little thing—-"

"What's all this fuss?" Angus asked, genuinely surprised. He obviously didn't know about Concepcion's friendship with the Peltons. "Jeb and Kade took the body back to the missus. If she needs anything, they'll see to it."

"Why didn't somebody tell me about this?" Rafe asked.

"You're the foreman," Angus retorted. "You're supposed to know what goes on on this ranch." He looked at Concepcion, then at Emmeline. "Now the two of you just set yourselves down. It makes me nervous, all this hen clucking and carrying on."

"A man is dead!" Emmeline burst out.

"Things like this happen all the time," Rafe said quietly. "Sit down, Emmeline, and finish your supper."

"Don't tell me what to do, Rafe McKettrick!" Emmeline cried.

"Now there's no sense in everybody getting all riled up," Angus said.

"Be quiet," Concepcion told him.

"We have to go over there right now," Emmeline said.

Concepcion nodded.

"Hold on," Rafe said, standing. "Nobody's going anyplace. It's stone-dark out there. Kade and Jeb will bury Pelton and see that his wife is looked after."

"Rafe is right," Angus said, rising.

Before either Emmeline or Concepcion could reply, they heard a wagon approaching. They both made for the back door.

Kade was at the reins of the buckboard, with Phoebe Anne sitting rigid and pale on the seat beside him and the Peltons' milk cow tied to the back. Jeb rode alongside, leading Kade's gelding.

"Seth's dead," Phoebe Anne said woodenly. "He kilt himself."

Kade exchanged glances with Concepcion and Emmeline, then set the brake and climbed down. He reached up for Phoebe Anne, setting her gently on her feet.

Concepcion and Emmeline immediately rushed forward to claim the girl, each draping an arm around her, escorting her toward the light and warmth of the house. Rafe and Angus, who had followed them into the yard, parted to let the three women pass.

Becky Harding, who prided herself on courage and fortitude, almost wished she could just stay on the stagecoach, when it rolled into Indian Rock early that summer afternoon, and keep right on heading west until she hit San Francisco or Seattle, somewhere, anywhere, else, but that wasn't to be. She'd tracked Emmeline this far for a purpose, and she meant to see it through, no matter what the difficulties involved.

"Is there a good hotel in this town?" she inquired of the driver, as he was unloading her trunks and valises from the boot at the back of the coach. The weather was dismal, and the roads had been muddy for days. She yearned for a decent cup of tea, first, closely followed by a hot bath, fresh clothes, food, and, ultimately, sleep. Hours and hours of uninterrupted sleep.

The bearded and unwashed driver, who had introduced himself as Eustis Bates at the last stop, favored her with a gap-toothed grin. "Well, now, ma'am," he said, pointing a gnarled forefinger, "there's the Territorial Hotel, right down that there street. I don't know how 'good' it is, but they've got a fair dining room, and they're well away from the saloons, so it's peaceful."

Becky gazed in the direction indicated, shading her eyes with one hand; the sky was a brilliant blue, and the sunlight dazzled. "There?"

"Yes, ma'am," Eustis replied. "Just past the telegraph office. You can see the side of the building from here."

She nodded, raising her parasol over her head and snapping it open. "Thank you," she said, glad for a chance to stretch her cramped legs with a short walk. "I shall send someone for my baggage." Having made this pronouncement, she set out, taking care not to be run down by a wagon or a horse as she crossed the rutted, manure-strewn road, headed for the Territorial Hotel. Once she'd secured her lodging and recovered a bit from the arduous journey, she would make her way to the Triple M Ranch, and Emmeline.

She had a few things to say to that young woman.

The inn, euphemistically called a hotel, was a two-story structure of raw lumber, new enough that it hadn't weathered to the usual gray-brown. There was a wooden sidewalk out front, along with a hitching rail and a horse trough, and flour-sack curtains graced the four visible windows on the upper floor.

Becky swept in, crossed what passed for a lobby to the makeshift registration desk—two barrels with planks stretching between them—and thumped the hand bell with one gloved palm. She closed her parasol and rapped the floor with it once, out of simple impatience.

A curtain covered the doorway behind the desk, and it wriggled a little. Then a scrawny little hatchling of a man in a cheap, ill-fitting suit appeared, beak first, twitching all over.

His small eyes widened behind his spectacles when he saw Becky standing there in her wool travel suit, which was a sensible shade of brown, trimmed in jet-black braiding. She'd taken every care to look the part of a lady, as she did whenever she set foot outside her boarding-house, but it was always possible that she'd be recognized. Maybe this little creature had visited her establishment in Kansas City at one time or another, though she doubted it. He didn't look as though he had the necessary equipment, let alone the courage.

"Yes?" he asked.

She suppressed a sigh. "I should like to take a room," she said. She would have thought her purpose would be obvious, since she had presented herself at the registration desk.

The man looked past her, first on one side, then on the other, as though expecting to see someone else standing there. "You're alone?" he asked, making no effective effort to hide his surprise.

"Yes," Becky said, somewhat tautly.

"I don't know what our policy is in regards to letting rooms to ladies traveling by themselves," he fretted.

Becky, used to giving orders and having them obeyed, was inclined to grab the little man by his cheap celluloid collar and haul him to his tiptoes, but she restrained herself. "Perhaps," she said, in a careful voice, "you had better find out."

He flushed vividly, cleared his throat. "I'll be right back," he said, and dashed out from behind the desk, across the lobby, and out the front door. Becky stared after him in consternation, then marched around behind the desk, examined the registration book, and deduced that rooms 2, 5, and 8 were available. She plucked a pen from the stand, dipped it in the inkwell, and wrote her public name beside the numeral 8 with a grand flourish. Then she collected the key from its peg on the wall and made her way upstairs.

She had chosen wisely, as it turned out. Rooms 2 and 5 faced the street, and would therefore be noisy, while number 8 was at the back of the hotel, and closest to the communal bathroom. She unlocked the door, inspected the sheets for signs of previous use and vermin, ran her fingers over the bureau top. The bedding was clean, and the place was only moderately dusty. In a place like Indian Rock, this was probably the best accommodation one could reasonably hope to find.

She rested her parasol in a corner, removed her gloves, and left the room. She reached the lobby just as the anxious desk clerk was returning with the marshal behind him. The lawman grinned when he saw Becky.

"Howdy, ma'am," he said, tugging at the brim of his hat. He was a disreputable-looking sort, to Becky's mind, but he was unapologetically male, too, and she liked that. "Clive here tells me you're a woman alone," he said.

Becky drew herself up, well aware that she made a picture, standing there at the base of the stairs, one hand resting gracefully on the newel post. Becky had had a lot of practice at striking poses, and she knew how to use appearances—and almost everything else—to her advantage. "Is that a crime?" she asked, with a wry—and admittedly coy—twist just at the corner of her mouth.

"No, ma'am," he said. "It just doesn't happen much out here. Clive needed a frame of reference, I guess, so he came to me."

"Judge Struthers is drunk again," Clive explained, to show that he'd tried to consult the highest possible authority. "And there's no talking to him when he's like that." He scampered back to his post behind the desk, saw the name she had scrawled in the registration book, and twitched at her. "Mrs. Charles Fairmont III?"

"Yes," Becky said.

"You have a husband?" the marshal asked. He didn't seem pleased by the prospect.

"He died," Becky said. "Run over by a freight wagon six years ago, in St. Louis."

"That's too bad," the marshal responded, but he looked like he'd gotten over the revelation handily enough. "What brings you to the Arizona Territory?"

Clive was still blustering. "You can't just rent yourself a

room!" he sputtered, before Becky could answer. "There are procedures, protocols—"

"Oh, for heaven's sake," Becky said, and though she was speaking to Clive, she was still looking at the lawman, "shut up. You wouldn't help me, so I helped myself. Please be so kind as to send someone for my baggage, and mind you have a care with it, too."

The marshal stood patiently, hat in hand, watching her. Waiting for a response to his question.

"I've come to visit a relation of mine," she said, supplying it.

"And who would that be?" the lawman persisted.

If Becky had had a fan, she would have snapped it open and flicked it back and forth in front of her face a few times. "Do you question everyone who comes to your town, Marshal?"

He smiled. "Pretty much," he said, and then waited again. He was, Becky concluded, a damnably patient man.

"Very well." Becky sighed. "I believe my niece is living near here. Her name is Emmeline—Mrs. Rafe McKettrick."

Recognition lighted the marshal's pale blue eyes. "The mail-order bride," he said. "She's out on the Triple M, I reckon. That's about two hours from here."

Two hours. Becky sighed inwardly. As important as the upcoming interview with Emmeline was, it would have to wait until she'd rested. She wanted to be at her best when she saw her niece again.

"You could get a buggy over at the livery stable," the

lawman went on, when he saw that Becky was at a loss. "You know how to drive a rig, ma'am?"

Becky had never had occasion to take up the reins, running her business in Kansas City. She'd ridden in cabs then, or walked. "Yes," she said. After all, how hard could it be?

"Fine, then," said the marshal, and he put out his free hand, still holding his hat in the other. "Name's John Lewis," he said. "Welcome to Indian Rock, Mrs. Fairmont."

Becky hesitated, then responded by putting out her own hand. "Thank you, Mr. Lewis," she said. Then she turned to poor Clive. "Do send someone for my things," she added crisply. "I'll want hot water for a bath, as well, and supper brought to my room at seven. Meatloaf would do nicely—not too spicy, mind."

"We don't serve meatloaf," Clive said in a pettish tone, but John Lewis ran right over his words with a remark of his own.

"I'd be pleased and honored if you'd take your supper with me, Mrs. Fairmont, in the hotel dining room. The cook is a reasonable fellow, likely to make up whatever dish you want, if the price is right."

Becky smiled gaily and nodded once, graciously. She had never been able to resist a man who took charge and got things done—not that there was any earthly reason to resist. "Are you married, Mr. Lewis?" she asked.

The marshal shook his head. "No, ma'am," he said. "Not as I recollect."

Becky was pleased. "Then I should be happy to take my supper in your company."

And so the matter was settled. They met at seven sharp, in the hotel's small dining room, sharing a table next to the window, and the meatloaf was delicious, plentiful, and not too spicy.

Phoebe Anne didn't make it even as far as the back porch before she gasped and doubled over between Emmeline and Concepcion. A rush of water soaked her skirts.

"The baby," Concepcion said grimly.

"I want to die," Phoebe Anne sobbed, "same as Seth did!"

"Nonsense," Concepcion replied. "Emmeline, run ahead and light a lantern in the spare room. We'll need some hot water after that."

Emmeline didn't hesitate. She hurried inside, grabbed a handful of matches from the metal container on the wall next to the cookstove, and rushed upstairs. Rafe soon joined her, carrying a whimpering Phoebe Anne in his arms, Concepcion at his heels, warning him to be careful.

Emmeline, having lighted the lantern, drew back the covers on the spare-room bed, and Rafe gratefully laid down his burden.

"I'll see to the water," he said. "Pa sent Kade on to town, to bring back the doctor."

Concepcion was already unlacing Phoebe Anne's shoes, which were as pitifully worn as her dress. She nodded, without looking at Rafe, and he went out. Concepcion and Emmeline undressed Phoebe Anne, and Emmeline brought her a nightgown to wear, the one Rafe had given her the day she arrived on the Triple M.

"I'm real scared," Phoebe Anne said, her eyes huge with grief and pain, as well as fear. "What are me and this baby gonna do, with no man to look after us?"

"Don't fret about that now," Concepcion said kindly. "You'll go home to Iowa, soon as you're well enough, and Seth's family will take you in."

Emmeline hoped Concepcion was right, but it seemed to her that the other woman was placing a lot of confidence in the elder Peltons. Nobody knew better than she did that families could be very fragile institutions.

"I'm hurtin' somethin' fierce!" Phoebe Anne confided.

"I know," Concepcion said gently. "I know. It'll all be over soon."

Phoebe Anne tensed, then let out a haunting shriek. Blood gushed out of her, soaking the sheets and the delicate nightgown.

"Dear God," Concepcion muttered, barely above a breath.

Phoebe Anne didn't seem to hear her; she was screaming now, flailing blindly with both arms.

Concepcion tore the top sheet off the bed and began tearing the clean parts into strips. A pile of bloody cloth mounted on the floor at her feet.

"Help me," Phoebe Anne pleaded. "Oh, God, help me—"

Bile scalded the back of Emmeline's throat. She wanted to run away, to put this horrible scene out of her mind, but another, stronger part of her wouldn't have it. "What can I do?"

Concepcion shook her head, trying her best to stop the bleeding by packing Phoebe Anne's most private place with cloth. It seemed, after a hair-raising few minutes, to work.

Emmeline thought of Kade, off to fetch the doctor, and wished him Godspeed. Two hours to town, and who knew how long, searching for the physician, then two hours back.

Phoebe Anne began to sob, and her breath came in ragged gasps that were terrifying to hear. "It's comin'!" she cried. "The baby's comin'!"

There was another rush of blood, saturating the bedding and even the mattress. Concepcion had already thrown back the covers, and sure enough, the baby slipped from between Phoebe Anne's legs, slick and bloody and very, very still.

Concepcion looked at Emmeline and, ever so slightly, shook her head.

"Get me some clean sheets," Concepcion said. "Some shears, too. And see what's keeping Rafe with that water."

Emmeline nodded and hastened out of the room. In the hallway, she paused, certain she would swoon, and drew in a deep breath. Then Rafe was there, at the top of the kitchen stairs, a bucket of steaming water in either hand.

"I'll take those," she said, reaching for the buckets. "Concepcion wants clean linens and some scissors."

Rafe nodded, taking in Emmeline's bloodstained dress, and allowed her to take the heavy buckets. By the time he returned with the items she'd requested, she and Concepcion had washed the impossibly small infant boy, wrapped him, and laid him on top of the bureau.

Emmeline cut and tore the sheets and, once again, Concepcion packed them inside Phoebe Anne, who had already lost consciousness. Rafe lingered in the doorway for a moment, then left the room, closing the door behind him.

Emmeline had not expected Phoebe Anne to survive the night, but when Kade returned just before dawn, with the doctor in tow, the young woman was sitting up in bed, holding her stillborn baby and stroking his downy head with slow, gentle motions of her index finger.

"Seth and our baby, both gone," she murmured in an almost singsong tone. "Whatever am I going to do?"

Emmeline slipped out of the room and stood in the corridor, with both hands pressed to her face. She sagged against the wall and sobbed uncontrollably; her spirit had gone dark with sorrow, and she was exhausted.

She hadn't heard Rafe approach, didn't resist when he took her arm.

"It's going to be all right," he said.

She shook her head.

He led her into their room, where the copper bathtub waited in front of the small woodstove, the water steaming. He undressed her, garment by garment, as though she were a weary child, helped her into the tub, and carefully washed away all traces of the horrid night just past.

She wept softly, not only for Phoebe Anne but for herself, and for all women. The realities of childbirth, she'd just discovered, bore no resemblance to the lovely experience of her imaginings.

# CHAPTER

## 7

JEB AND ONE OF THE RANCH HANDS built two pine-board coffins, one large and one small, and Seth Pelton and his baby boy were buried side by side on the homestead. Angus officiated at the funeral, reading solemnly from the Good Book, since the circuit preacher was miles away. Phoebe Anne was well enough to attend, though just barely, and she swooned, toward the last, and had to be taken back to the Triple M ranch house before the service had ended.

Emmeline explored the tumbledown shack of a cabin while Rafe and Kade and two men from the range crew filled in the graves and mounded them over with stones.

It was sobering to think what it must have been like for Phoebe Anne and her husband, living in that cramped little space, with no creature comforts and barely enough to eat, knowing all along that a baby was on the way.

Emmeline's eyes filled with tears as she gathered the

things she knew Phoebe Anne would want most—a battered Bible, a brown dress with frayed cuffs and collar, a mourning brooch fashioned of human hair, and a few letters from the family she and Seth had left behind in Iowa. The Peltons' other belongings, pots, utensils, tools and the like—and these were pitifully few—could be gathered later.

Rafe dusted his hands together as he stepped through the front door of the Pelton cabin to find Emmeline sitting forlornly on the bed, Phoebe Anne's humble treasures in her lap.

"You ready to leave now?" he asked quietly. Things had changed between them in the two days since Phoebe Anne had lost both her husband and her child; Emmeline kept to her own side of the bed at night, and Rafe didn't reach for her.

She nodded. "This is such a wretched place," she said.

Rafe held his round-brimmed hat in one hand and ran the other through his dark hair. "You blame me for this, don't you, Emmeline?"

Her attention had wandered; now she looked directly at her husband. "No," she said. "It's not your fault that the baby died, or that Seth Pelton shot himself."

"Then why, Emmeline? Why are you keeping your distance? Even when you're right beside me, it seems you're a thousand miles away."

She lifted her chin, unable to answer the question for him because she had yet to answer it for herself. "No one from town came to the service, even though Doc Boylen surely spread the word when he went back to town. None of the neighboring ranchers were here, either. Why is that, Rafe?"

"The Peltons were squatters," Rafe said in a calm, matter-of-fact tone.

"Phoebe Anne wasn't, and neither was that poor little baby. They were on this land because Seth brought them here."

Rafe thrust out a heavy sigh. "You do blame me," he said.

"You could have been kinder," Emmeline told him. Their arms brushed as she passed him, carrying Phoebe Anne's things, headed for the surrey waiting outside.

Rafe followed, but he didn't speak. He helped Emmeline into the rig and walked around to climb in beside her and take the reins. The drive back to the ranch was a silent one, for Emmeline was lost in the landscape of her thoughts.

"Don't be a fool," Kade told Rafe, in an earnest undertone, when Emmeline had gone into the house and the two men were out by the barn, unhitching the surrey. "Emmeline's scared, that's all. Hell, any woman would be, after watching somebody go through what Phoebe Anne Pelton just experienced."

Rafe knew well enough what horrors Emmeline had seen; he'd washed the blood off her, carried her to bed, and soothed her until she slept. He'd held her, when she woke sobbing from a nightmare, and in the morning, he'd helped Concepcion scrub down the spare room from top to bottom. He'd burned the mattress and brought another one in from the barn, where he and Kade and Jeb used to sleep on hot summer nights, when they were boys.

He shook his head, but the remembered horrors of Phoebe Anne's ordeal held fast to his mind. "I'm damn near as scared as she is," he admitted, "but like I said, it's more than fear. Emmeline thinks none of this would have happened if I'd welcomed Seth Pelton, told him sure, go ahead, take a piece of our land—"

Kade laid a hand on his brother's shoulder. "She's upset," he said. "Give her some time."

Rafe sighed, then nodded. The brothers finished their work, then headed into the house.

Concepcion was busy at the kitchen stove, getting an early supper ready, and Emmeline was preparing a tray, probably for Pelton's young widow, who was most likely settled again in the spare-room bed upstairs. Emmeline wouldn't look at Rafe when he tried to catch her eye.

Kade hung his hat beside the door and shrugged out of his coat. Then he gave Rafe an almost imperceptible push toward Emmeline.

"Let me take that," Rafe said, reaching for the tray.

She shook her head, still refusing to meet his gaze.

Concepcion added a chunk of wood to the fire in the cookstove. She was still wearing her funeral clothes, as Emmeline was, though they'd both donned aprons. "Emmeline will be all right, Rafe," the older woman said quietly. "Just let her be for a while."

Rafe wanted to take Emmeline aside and tell her that she'd never suffer the kind of horrors Phoebe Anne had, that he'd keep her and all their children safe, no matter what. The only problem was, he couldn't rightly make such a promise—no honest man could. Life was just too damn unpredictable.

He took in what Concepcion said and nodded grimly.

Twenty minutes later, he and Kade and Angus and Concepcion were seated around the table, dining on cornbread and beans, when Emmeline finally descended the stairs.

Kade, who'd been to town most recently, was in the middle of telling them about the new arrival in Indian Rock, a Mrs. Charles Fairmont, from Kansas City, who already had practically everybody in town calling her by her given name, which was Becky.

The color drained out of Emmeline's face. Her hands trembled and, before Rafe could make a move to help her, her tray tilted and a full load of crockery clattered to the floor with a reverberating crash.

Becky Harding—alias Mrs. Charles T. Fairmont III— was indeed registered at the Territorial Hotel, just as Kade had said at the ranch the night before, after the funeral. In fact, when Emmeline entered the lobby, Rafe having gone on to the livery stable to leave off the horses and wagon, Becky was right there, holding court, clad in an exquisite day dress of royal blue, with a fine coat to match. She stood square in the center of the room, a statue of Aphrodite brought to life by means of some wicked magic, looking positively ageless.

Catching sight of Emmeline, she narrowed her eyes and swept toward her, admirers, gentlemen, and ruffians alike falling back in her wake, like a sea divided.

"Well," she said, in that familiar, imperious voice. There was no embrace, as one might have expected—anyone besides Emmeline, that is—after a separation. "Emmeline. I was just on my way to see you at the Triple M. What a stroke of good fortune to find you here."

Emmeline took in the bevy of prospectors, fancy men, cowboys, and farmers assembled to pay homage to her aunt, and whispered, "What are you doing here?"

Becky took her hand in a grip tight enough to fuse her knuckles together. "Why, I came to see you, my dear," she trilled, and proceeded to drag Emmeline toward the stairs. "We will discuss our business in private. I'm sure these gentlemen will understand."

Emmeline wouldn't have dared to object; she had too much to lose if Becky were to explain their affiliation in too much detail. She looked back at the crowd of spectators, all of them staring up at her and Becky, and wondered how much they already knew about Mrs. Rafe McKettrick's scandalous past.

Becky pulled her into a spacious room at the rear of the hotel and slammed the door hard. Emmeline had never seen her aunt cry, not even in the worst of times, but there were tears in her eyes now, furious ones.

"I wouldn't have believed you'd actually leave!" Becky raged, in a whisper. "How could you, after all—" She paused, took a breath. "Emmeline Harding, if you *knew* the things that went through my mind—"

"I wrote you a letter," Emmeline said softly. She regretted the terms she and Becky had parted on, and she was very glad to see her aunt again. Still, she'd come to the Triple M to live with Rafe as his wife, and, hard as it was, she wanted to make the marriage work. If Rafe ever found out what she'd done that night in Chloe's old room, with a complete stranger, and for money, she'd be run out of town on the proverbial rail.

Becky was in a position to ruin everything, and she clearly knew it. She pointed imperiously at a chair. "Sit," she said.

Emmeline sat, but grudgingly, and with a little flounce of her skirts. She folded her hands and held her head high, though a part of her, the little-girl part, wanted very much to fly into Becky's arms and cling to her, to say she was sorry. "If you're planning to ask me to come back to Kansas City," she said instead, "please don't."

Becky had been pacing, arms folded, but at Emmeline's words, she stopped and flushed to her hairline. "That," she snapped, "is just about the *last* thing I'd ever do."

"Then why did you come here? Obviously, you're still angry with me."

"Angry? The word hardly suffices. I'd like to throttle you," Becky said, and then began pacing again, even faster than before. "Have you any idea of the things that could have happened to you between Kansas City and this godforsaken outpost? Women traveling alone have been robbed, kidnapped, and even killed. More than a few wind up in Indian camps, slaves, tattoos covering their entire bodies, or find themselves in the hold of some riverboat, bound for New Orleans and a kind of life you couldn't imagine in your worst nightmares!"

Emmeline swallowed, squirmed a little, waited for the diatribe to cease or at least subside. There would be no reasoning with Becky until some of the steam had escaped.

"Emmeline, I was out of my mind with worry!" Becky cried, coming to a standstill at last. "If you'd only stayed, we could have worked things out—"

Emmeline sighed. "You know what would have happened, and so do I," she said quietly. "And as much as I love you, I don't want to be what you are."

She had not meant the words unkindly, but she saw that their impact was shattering to Becky, even though she shouldn't have been surprised. Becky had always wanted a different life for Emmeline; that was why she'd sent her to school, encouraged her interest in books and music, and kept her strictly separate from the family enterprise.

Until the Texan arrived, that is.

Becky's face took on a grayish cast, and Emmeline felt every bit as guilty as if she'd drawn back her hand and slapped her aunt with all her strength. "And what, exactly, am I, Emmeline?" she asked.

The ensuing silence was shrill.

"You are my aunt," Emmeline said. "You are the only blood relation I have."

"And I am—or have been—a prostitute."

Emmeline's stomach turned over, and though she tried to speak, she couldn't utter a word. She'd tried many times to separate what Becky did for a living from what she was—a strong, vital, intelligent woman and a determined survivor—but it was hard, given society's attitude in general. And Rafe McKettrick's in particular.

"Do you feel superior to me?" Becky asked mildly. Her elegant nostrils had reddened a little, and there was fire in her eyes.

Emmeline shook her head. Whether a woman sold her body once or a thousand, times, she was still a whore. Emmeline had a stack of gold coins to remind her of her own fallible nature; she was in no position to throw stones. "Of course not," she whispered, but she couldn't meet Becky's gaze, even though she felt it burning into her. "I was never ashamed of you. Never. Only of myself."

Becky started to speak, then stopped. She raised both hands, signaling a respite from their discussion, swept over to the door, opened it, and called for someone named Clive. A few moments later, he arrived, and Becky slipped out to speak with the man in the hallway, ordering hot tea, with plenty of milk and sugar, and cookies, if there were any to be had.

"Mr. McKettrick's here, asking about his wife," Clive said, in response.

Emmeline thought she'd exhausted all her sorrows,

but now tears threatened once again. As soon as Rafe heard the complete story, and Becky was in just the mood to tell it, she might have no choice but to follow in her aunt's footsteps.

"I'd like to meet him," Becky said to Clive, but taking care to make sure Emmeline heard. "Do send him up."

The door closed. "Do you love him?" Becky asked. "This husband of yours?"

Emmeline nodded, then shook her head, then blew her nose in the starched handkerchief Becky provided. "I don't know," she said. She knew what she'd always *imagined* love to be, but what she and Rafe were building together was something different, and not so easily named. "I think we could be happy together, given time."

"And you're afraid I'm going to spoil that for you?" Becky had returned to her chair now, and she looked deeply into Emmeline's eyes.

"I hope not," Emmeline said, glancing nervously toward the door.

Becky sighed and settled back, her elegant hands resting gracefully on the arms of her chair. "I would never do such a thing to my own child," she said. "But the truth has a way of coming out, Emmeline. That's the sad fact of the matter."

*My own child.*

Now it was Emmeline's turn to be stunned. She had considered the possibility before, of course, but always dismissed it. It was as if the sky and the earth had just changed places; nothing, whether Rafe ever learned what she'd done or not, would ever be the same. She put one hand to her mouth.

"I didn't plan to tell you this way," Becky said, her usually straight shoulders stooping a little. She met Emmeline's gaze steadily, even proudly, but with a sheen of tears glimmering in her eyes. "Not so bluntly, in any case. But now I've said it, and there's no turning back. You're my child, Emmeline."

Emmeline hardly dared ask. "My father—?"

Becky smiled sadly. "Charles T. Fairmont III," she said. "I get a small measure of satisfaction out of using his name whenever I need an alias, as you know. He was a business associate of your grandfather's. A sophisticated, older man, very charming and handsome. I thought he would marry me when I told him about you." She sighed and, for a moment, an old grief shadowed her eyes. "I was wrong. He had already married someone else, and of course he promptly denied any involvement with me. My father pronounced me a trollop and threw me out of the house for good."

Stricken to silence, Emmeline could only stare at the other woman. Her mother. On one hand, she felt pity for that long-ago girl, frightened and spurned by her family as well as her lover. She had made some terrible choices in order to make a home for herself and for Emmeline. On the other hand, Emmeline resented, bitterly, all the years she'd been led to believe that she was an orphan.

"You kept your secret for so long," Emmeline managed, after some time had passed. "Why?"

A knock sounded at the door, and both women fell silent. Becky rose and admitted Clive, who was carrying a tea tray. "Mr. McKettrick said he'll be along in a while," the anxious little man said. "He's gone to do some business at the Western Union office."

Emmeline closed her eyes, almost dizzy with relief. She would have to face Rafe eventually, but she was grateful for a brief reprieve.

Clive went out, after glancing curiously at each of the women, and Becky made a ceremony of pouring tea. A minute, two minutes, the silence seemed to go on forever.

"Why, Becky?" Emmeline repeated.

"Why didn't I tell you sooner? I guess I was afraid—I thought you'd be ashamed to have a—to have me for a mother."

"There's something more," Emmeline said. She had always been perceptive where her aunt—*her mother*—was concerned, but apparently not perceptive enough.

"Yes," Becky admitted. "A great deal more, but quite enough has been said about the past, for one day. I should like to speak of happier things."

Emmeline was not content to let the matter drop just yet, even temporarily. "What about your—your boardinghouse?" She had never known Becky to take a holiday from her business, no matter what the emergency. Emmeline used to dream that they'd go far away to the shore for a few weeks, or even a whole summer, she and her aunt, where no one knew them, and there, in that magical place, they would be treated as ordinary people.

"I've sold it," Becky said. "Lock, stock, and barrel. A share of the money has been put in trust for you, in my bank in Kansas City."

"What are you going to do without your business?" Emmeline asked, unable to take it all in. She would be assimilating these revelations for some time, she knew, and she did not look forward to the process.

Again, Becky was silent. Just when Emmeline was certain she couldn't bear it for another moment, her mother replied. "Well, it depends whom you ask," she said, with a shaky little smile. "If you ask me, well, I'm going to start all over again, maybe in San Francisco or Denver, somewhere like that. Have myself a respectable life, so far as possible." She paused, and a tiny frown creased the smooth skin between her eyebrows. "If you ask my doctor—"

Emmeline was out of her chair and on her knees at Becky's side within the space of a heartbeat, panicked. "Your doctor? What are you saying?"

Becky patted her shoulder. "Now, now, it's nothing to get so worried about. It's time I slowed down a bit, that's all. Had a change of scene."

Emmeline had taken Becky's hands in her own, their tea forgotten on the small table between their chairs. "It's something serious!" she fretted.

"A few fainting spells, that's all," Becky said wryly, and laid a gentle hand to Emmeline's cheek, wiping away a tear with the pad of her thumb. "Listen to me, Emmeline. I will never betray you. Still, this is a small town and by now it's all over the place that you and I are related. If my past were ever to come out, yours might, too. Can you live with that?"

Emmeline, so shaken by the morning's events that she was dizzy, rose awkwardly to her feet, groped for her chair, and fell into it.

A few more sips of tea revived her to some degree; although she was still in shock, she was no longer teetering on the verge of hysteria. They sat in silence, Becky and Emmeline, and, in time, Rafe arrived.

The dark-haired woman was tall and handsome, elegant in her well-made and probably costly clothes. Rafe had learned, while filling Concepcion's grocery order over at the general store, that the marshal was already sweet on her, and now, meeting her, he could see why. Yes, indeed, she was a looker, if a little past her prime.

"Mr. McKettrick," she said, putting out one hand.

He didn't know whether to kiss that hand or shake it. He made a decision and shook it, glancing uncomfortably at Emmeline, who sat in a chair, teacup in hand. He noticed that it rattled a little against the saucer.

"How do you do, ma'am," he said, and bowed a little.

"My name is Mrs. Fairmont," the woman said, smiling, "but you can call me Becky. Your wife is my niece."

Out of the corner of his eye, he saw Emmeline relax a little.

Emmeline had mentioned having an aunt back in Kansas City, so her appearance was no great shock to

Rafe, but his wife looked shell-shocked, sitting there. Rafe wondered if there was bad blood between the two women.

"I came to Indian Rock to meet her husband," Mrs. Fairmont went on pleasantly. "I do hope you are treating my girl well, Mr. McKettrick. If you do not—well, I cannot be responsible for my actions."

Rafe liked Emmeline's aunt. She was as straightforward as he was, which meant that the two of them would understand each other. "So far," he said, glancing again at his wife and stretching the truth a little, "we seem to be doing just fine."

Emmeline stood and took a step toward him, then stopped, and her hesitation made him wonder again. It made him uncomfortable, too.

"I just rented room 2, downstairs," he said, perhaps a mite too loudly. "I thought Emmeline and I would stay in town tonight. Sort of like a honeymoon." He reddened, realizing, too late, the implications of the word *honeymoon*.

Mrs. Fairmont—Becky—smiled. Emmeline bit down on her lower lip and looked away.

"Will you be staying on in Indian Rock?" Rafe asked, looking for a way to hold up his end of the conversation. He wasn't much of a talker, any way you looked at it, and there was no sense in trying to pretend that he was.

"Probably not," Becky answered. "I've lived in Kansas City most all my life. I expect I'd be happier in a bigger place." She looked around ruefully. "Which is not to say that this hotel isn't suitable, though it *could* use a new owner. It's dismally mismanaged, you know."

Rafe grinned. "My pa will be sorry to hear that," he said. "I believe he owns it."

Becky looked chagrined, but only mildly so. "He ought to pay more attention to the way it's being run," she remarked.

Emmeline had, by this time, made her way to Rafe's side. She took his arm, and he felt a surge of protective pride go through him. She didn't say anything, she just stood there next to him, like a cat ready to race up a tree at the first sign of trouble.

What the devil was going on?

"I imagine the two of you have business to attend to," Becky said. "I won't keep you any longer. Perhaps, though, we could have an early supper together?"

"That would be fine," Rafe said. He liked Becky Fairmont; she was a bit outspoken, but he considered that a positive trait. A man liked to know where he stood and what was what. No mincing words, no pussyfooting around. "You're sure you don't want to help Emmeline pick out the material for a party dress or something? I've got some business at the bank, and down at the feed store."

"Why would I need a party dress?" Emmeline asked, almost suspiciously.

"I figure it's time we threw a shindig," Rafe said, although he hadn't, until that moment, figured anything of the sort. The thought had simply erupted, full blown, in his mind. "To celebrate you and me being married and everything. We could all use some cheering up, it seems to me."

A look passed between the two women and Rafe indulged in a private smile. He was right proud of his quick thinking.

"Suppose we go our separate ways, then," Becky said, "and meet here at the hotel later on. Say around four o'clock?"

Rafe looked questioningly at Emmeline, and she smiled, nodding.

He was at once relieved to be spared the shopping junket and let down at the prospect of being separated from Emmeline, even for a few hours. He knew he didn't love her, they hadn't known each other long enough for that, but he surely enjoyed her company, and missed her sorely when they were apart.

"It's settled, then," he said, somewhat expansively. "I'll walk you ladies to the mercantile and leave you to planning the party."

He deposited them, with a tug at his hat brim, in front of the general store, and walked away whistling.

"I love a party!" Becky confided, quite unnecessarily, as she and Emmeline entered the store. The place was surprisingly well stocked, Emmeline thought, for a country mercantile, with goods everywhere, in barrels, on shelves, burdening long wooden tables. The windows were dirty and fly specked, and the floor was littered with sawdust, but the items for sale were of adequate, if unspectacular, quality.

"Morning, Mrs. McKettrick," said the storekeeper, a skinny woman with gaps between her teeth and an avid expression. "I'm Minnie."

Emmeline put out her hand to Minnie and smiled. "I'm glad to meet you," she said, in all truth. In Kansas City, due to her association with the boardinghouse, she'd been a social pariah. Merchants there had never greeted her in a friendly fashion; instead, they'd watched her closely, as though expecting her to steal something, and were visibly relieved when she made her purchases and left. "This is my—my aunt, Mrs. Fairmont," she added, when Becky nudged her.

The look Minnie gave Becky was more of a sizing up than anything else. "How do you do?" she said.

"Just fine, thank you very much," Becky said. "And how do *you* do?"

Minnie looked disconcerted, as if she didn't know quite what to make of Becky's friendliness. No doubt there had been considerable speculation about this new woman in town, so beautiful, so bold, and so finely dressed. And traveling alone. "Well—I—just fine, I reckon." She turned her attention, with some relief, to Emmeline. "Now, how can I help you ladies?"

Emmeline related what she knew about the forthcoming party, which was precious little. "Of course, you and your husband are invited," she finished.

Minnie beamed. "This town could stand some good

news," she said. "We'd be right proud to join the festivities, Mrs. McKettrick."

Emmeline loved being called "Mrs. McKettrick." She fairly floated over to the bolts of fabric lining a table set well away from the windows. "To start with," she said, running her hand over silks, brocades, velvets, woolens, and cottons of various weights, "I should like material for two gowns, Concepcion's and my own."

Minnie's eyebrows shot up. "Concepcion? Ain't she the Mexican housekeeper?"

Becky made a humming sound, under her breath, and Emmeline knew she was trying to hold her temper. Perhaps because she'd experienced so much prejudice and snobbery herself, Becky tended to be exceedingly tolerant.

"Yes," Emmeline said quickly, anxious to avert even the possibility of social disaster. "Concepcion is the housekeeper and she does hail from Mexico. She is considered a member of the family."

"Hmm," said Minnie. "Well, you just look over them yard goods and let me know if you need help."

"I will," Emmeline said sweetly.

"This green brocade would look wonderful on you," Becky said, fingering a lovely silk and narrowing her eyes. "Puffy sleeves, I think, and a fairly low neckline. Not too low, of course."

Emmeline liked the green brocade, but she wanted to extend the expedition for a while. On the drive into town, Rafe had told her to buy whatever she wanted, and he'd settle up with the storekeeper when she was finished. She'd been too nervous to think about shopping then, with the reunion with Becky still ahead of her; now, she planned to splurge on a book, and perhaps a box of marzipan, in addition to the fabric for her dress and Concepcion's. She would bring back something for Phoebe Anne, too, of course.

She insisted on looking at everything, every fabric, every thread, every button and trim. In the end, though, she bought the green brocade, yards and yards of the stuff, along with thread and small, plain buttons, to be covered with the same cloth. She selected a silvery gray silk for Concepcion, and pretty pearl buttons. The marzipan was next, chosen piece by delectable piece, and she took her time selecting a book, too, knowing she would read it many times. She finally chose a novel about a French noblewoman who became a pirate. For Phoebe Anne, she purchased a simple blue dress, very likely the first ready-made garment the young widow would ever own.

"Shall I just put these things on the ranch account?" Minnie asked. Her cheerful mood indicated that the bill would tally up to a considerable sum.

Emmeline nodded, a little flushed. Although she had never known a hungry day in her life, thanks to Becky, never gone without anything she truly needed, it was a heady thing to buy whatever she wanted, without looking at the price.

"If you wouldn't mind sending everything over to the

Territorial Hotel," Becky put in. "Mrs. McKettrick will be staying in town until tomorrow, you see." She'd made a few selections of her own, Becky had, a scientific volume about butterflies, a packet of tea leaves, and some linen undergarments, and she paid for it all in cash, taken from her drawstring purse with some ceremony.

Minnie warmed up to Becky right away when she saw the money. "Yes, ma'am," she said. "I'll wrap your things up nice, in brown paper and string, and send them right over."

"Thank you," Becky said. Then she took Emmeline's arm and marched her out of the store. On the sidewalk, she straightened her spine and looked in both directions. "I'm famished. Let's have something to eat."

Emmeline was surprised to discover that she was hungry, and even more surprised to realize that she and Becky had spent almost three hours in the mercantile. "All right," she said. She felt a little light-headed from the bright sunlight, after the dimness of the store.

"You should have told me long ago," Emmeline reiterated, perhaps half an hour later, when they were seated in the hotel dining room, having tea and meatloaf left over from the night before. They were the only customers, so they could talk freely, but they still kept their voices down.

Becky took a sip from her cup, made a face, and added coarse brown sugar from the bowl in the center of the table. A fly blundered repeatedly against the glass in the window beside their table. "That you're my daughter, you mean? Well, as I said before, it did occur to me that you might be less than delighted to discover that you had a lady of the evening for a mother."

Emmeline lowered her eyes for a moment, then made herself meet Becky's gaze. "What now?" she asked.

Becky arched one eyebrow. " 'What now'?" she repeated. "It's simple, Emmeline. You go on with your life, and I go on with mine."

"It's not so easy as that," Emmeline whispered. "If Rafe ever finds out—"

"If you're smart," Becky said, salting her meatloaf with a liberal hand, "you won't tell him. Men are such hypocrites when it comes to this sort of thing. They sure don't mind indulging, now and again, but bring a whore into the family, and they'll have a conniption fit."

Emmeline shuddered. She was beginning to feel ill again. She pushed away the meatloaf.

"You're not thinking of telling Rafe about that night in Kansas City?" Becky asked. "That would be a damn fool thing to do."

"No," Emmeline said, wholly miserable on every level of her being. "I've thought about it—I hate living a lie—but I'm afraid."

"Have you and he—consummated your marriage?"

Emmeline reddened. "Yes," she whispered.

"And he didn't comment afterward?"

She shook her head.

"Then what's worrying you? You look as though you're about to leap right out of your skin."

Emmeline lowered her voice still further. Even if somebody was listening at the kitchen door, however, they were much too far away to overhear. "I haven't had my monthly since—since before," she admitted. "Before Kansas City, I mean."

Becky set her fork down with a thunk, the meatloaf forgotten. "Oh, my stars."

Emmeline bit her lip. "I was never very regular anyway," she said lamely.

"But you might be pregnant."

The words struck Emmeline like an arrow in the heart; she couldn't answer. Couldn't even nod.

"Well, now," Becky lamented dryly, "it seems like things are never so bad they can't get worse."

"I know I should tell Rafe the truth about everything, but—"

"There are times, my dear," Becky interrupted, "when the truth is no sort of kindness, and this is one of them. Rafe McKettrick is a good man, but I know his sort. You'll lose him if you tell him you might be carrying another man's baby."

Emmeline bit her lower lip, and a tear slid down her cheek. "He deserves better," she said.

Becky patted her hand. "Now you listen to me," she said in a stern, quiet tone. "Whatever mistakes you might have made, there *is* nobody better than you. You're beautiful, you're smart, and you're genuinely good, and I don't want to hear another word to the contrary."

"Too many secrets," Emmeline murmured, gazing out the dust-clouded window at the street, where a steady stream of buggies, wagons, and horsemen were passing by, along with a good many pedestrians. "How can I live my life with so many secrets?"

"People do it all the time," Becky said.

A moment passed, and then another. "You should know," Emmeline said, thinking once again of all the times she'd longed for a mother, as a child and as a young woman, unaware, all the while, that she had one.

"Have a care how you speak to me, Emmeline." Becky spoke with her usual authority, but there was tenderness in her eyes, and deep understanding. "I know you're angry with me," she said, "and not without some justification. But I did the best I could, with what I knew and what I had to offer. I've always loved you, and you know that."

Emmeline thought of a particular instance: When she was a little girl, eight or so, she came down with scarlet fever and nearly died. Even now, all these years later, she remembered the scent of Becky's perfume in the sickroom, the cool touch of her hand as she sat with her, hour after hour, keeping her vigil. Love, she thought, is not a simple thing.

"Yes," she said. "I know. And I've always loved you as well."

"Then we'll be able to work out everything else," Becky decreed, and went back to her reheated meatloaf with an enthusiasm Emmeline didn't even attempt to match.

Rafe's blue eyes lit up when he saw Emmeline later that afternoon, when they met in the lobby of the Territorial

Hotel, and she felt a pang of sorrow because she was deceiving him. It was no consolation that she did not have a choice.

He kissed her lightly on the forehead. "Where's your aunt?" he asked.

"Becky has a headache," Emmeline said. She wanted to pour out the whole story, right then and there, to tell Rafe about the man in Kansas City, the man whose baby she might be carrying even then, to confide that the woman she'd always known as her aunt was really her mother, and to weep in his arms because Becky was sick, despite all her protestations that it was nothing serious, and maybe even dying. The burden was too great to carry, too complicated to sort out alone, and yet she couldn't make herself share it. She didn't want to lose Rafe, or the hope of home and family he offered.

Rafe, bless his heart, frowned with genuine concern, and Emmeline nearly broke down. Ironically, it was the fruition of Becky's earlier statement, that things were never so bad they couldn't get worse, that prevented her from doing just that. And then she nearly fainted dead away for, at that moment, a familiar frame strode by the hotel's front window.

The Texan, the very man who had ruined her, walked right into the lobby, big as life, and straight up to the desk. Clive was nowhere to be seen.

Impatient, he pounded on the bell, then glanced in her and Rafe's direction, looked away, and looked back. Her fleeting hope that he wouldn't recognize her was gone in an instant, for a slight smile curved his mouth. *Well,* his expression seemed to say, *hello there.*

That was it. Emmeline's knees buckled, the world shrank to a black speck, and she folded to the floor.

When she awakened, she was lying on the lobby sofa with a cold cloth on her forehead, and Rafe was perched beside her, chafing her wrist and saying her name over and over again. She could see the stranger standing a little distance away, his arms folded, watching her thoughtfully.

She blinked, trying to make him disappear, like some vestige of a bad dream, but he was still there when she opened her eyes again.

Rafe was visibly relieved that she'd come around, but there was something more in his expression, too. Delight. She thought she knew what he was thinking—that they'd conceived a child already and he would have the heir he wanted so much. She would have cried, if she'd had any tears left.

"Should I fetch a doctor?" the Texan asked. What was his name again? Holt Something, or Something Holt. The devil take him, what was he doing in Indian Rock, of all places? With the whole country to choose from, he had to end up there?

"No, thanks," Rafe said, still smiling. "A good night's sleep and my wife will be just fine."

"Good," said the Texan. His expression was pensive.

Rafe lifted Emmeline into his arms as though she were an invalid. Then he went behind the registration desk, still carrying her, and managed to take the key to room 2 from its box. He nodded to the stranger, who nodded in return, and headed for the corridor at the back of the lobby.

Emmeline, looking over Rafe's shoulder, met the Texan's laughing gaze. He waggled his fingers in farewell, and Emmeline squeezed her eyes shut and didn't open them again until the door of number 2 closed behind them with a crisp click.

Rafe laid her tenderly on the bed, unlaced her shoes, and pulled them off her feet. Then he spread a coverlet over her. "You just rest," he said quietly. "I'll get you a glass of water."

The kindness he'd shown her made Emmeline's throat constrict, along with her heart, and she could only nod. He left the room, returning a few minutes later with the promised water, which he set on the bedside table. Her purchases at the mercantile had been sent over earlier; she saw the brown-paper bundles resting on the bureau top, neatly tied with string.

She began to cry, dry-eyed and hurting.

"Shhh," Rafe said, stroking her forehead.

She cried harder. "Don't be so nice to me!" she wailed.

"Why not?" he asked, his fine brow knitted into a frown.

"I don't know!" she sobbed, and he only looked more confused.

He patted her hand. "You just rest, now," he said. Then he kicked off his boots, removed his suit coat, and stretched out beside her on the bed, sharing the coverlet, holding her gently in his arms, as though he feared she might break. "Just rest. I'll be right here if you need me."

She closed her eyes and, almost instantly, she slept.

When she awakened, the room was dark and she was alone. She sat bolt upright and felt an immediate flash of pain in her midsection. She knew then that her monthly had come, at last, and with a vengeance. She got up, found some towels, and addressed the situation as best she could.

Rafe returned to find her sitting in the one chair the room boasted, a blanket spread over her lap. Becky, feeling better herself, had stopped by to check on her, found her ailing, and provided a heated brick, wrapped in flannel, and some aspirin powder. She was sitting on the edge of the bed, which she had remade with fresh sheets and blankets, sipping tea and keeping a motherly eye on Emmeline.

"What's the matter?" Rafe asked, clearly alarmed. He had a package under his arm, and he set it aside on the bureau, with the others, before approaching Emmeline and bending to kiss her cheek.

Emmeline would have expected to be glad about her monthly, but she wasn't, entirely. "I'm—" she began, but then her voice just fell away, and she couldn't finish.

"She's having her womanly time," Becky said diplomatically.

Rafe's face registered the meaning of that, and disappointment moved like a shadow in his eyes, but he recovered fairly quickly. "Do you hurt?" he asked.

Emmeline swallowed hard, nodded. "I've spoiled our honeymoon," she lamented.

He shook his head. "No," he said gently. Then he retrieved the square package he'd set on the bureau, laid it in her lap. "Open it," he urged.

Hands trembling a little, Emmeline wrestled with the string and paper, revealing a leather keepsake album embossed with gold letters: OUR FAMILY.

"We've got plenty of time," Rafe said softly.

Emmeline looked at the album, and then at her husband, and then she began to cry again.

Rafe was obviously confounded, but Becky patted his shoulder. "It's all right," she said. "She's just happy, that's all."

# CHAPTER

## 8

"WELL," BECKY SAID, assessing her old friend thoughtfully, as the two of them sat at a table in the dining room of the Territorial Hotel, having tea and coffee, "what brings *you* to Indian Rock?"

Holt Cavanagh grinned, drained his mug, and signaled the waiter—the redoubtable Clive—for a second serving. "I might ask you the same question," he said. "You're about the last person I expected to run into out here." He paused, frowned slightly. "Or, maybe, the second to the last."

Becky smiled sweetly. "I asked you first," she said.

"So you did," he admitted. He waited until Clive had poured his coffee and scuttled away before saying, "I have some family business to take care of."

"Isn't that a coincidence?" Becky replied. "So have I."

Holt chuckled. "You planning on putting down roots around here?"

"I'll probably move on in time," Becky said, picking up the plain crockery teapot and pouring herself more tea. When, and if, things got bad, as her Kansas City doctor had warned they would, she didn't want to be a burden on Emmeline and her new husband. Far better to be off on her own someplace, like an old bear holed up in a cave. "What about you?"

"I probably won't stay put," Holt said. "Never have so far." Until then, Becky had never really noticed how attractive he was, with his broad shoulders, wavy brown hair, and mischievous hazel eyes. She reckoned Holt was probably somewhere in his mid-thirties, and although he talked like a drifter, she knew he'd prospered in the cattle business. The two of them had made several joint investments and done well. He'd been a good customer during his infrequent visits to Kansas City, and a favorite with the girls at the boardinghouse. Becky didn't see clients personally, and hadn't for some years, so she'd never been intimate with him, and she was glad of that now that they were face-to-face in an environment outside her place of business.

"You plan on announcing to everybody in Indian Rock that I ran a brothel back in Missouri?" she asked, after making sure that odious Clive fellow wasn't lurking within hearing distance.

Holt sat back, causing his wooden chair to creak. "Now, why would I do that?" he asked, sounding a bit indignant. There was a wicked light dancing in those eyes of his, though, giving the lie to his expression of affronted innocence.

Becky leveled her gaze at him. "You'll forgive me," she said dryly, "if I have acquired a somewhat suspicious approach to the subject of human nature over the years."

He smiled. "I suppose you have," he said. "As it happens, so have I, so I reckon we understand each other, you and I." He waxed solemn, looking out the window just as Rafe and Emmeline came along, arm in arm, back from one of their promenades. "That young woman—" he began.

"My niece," Becky hastened to say. "She and Mr. McKettrick are newly married. I think they make a lovely couple." She paused, measuring him, and his apparent interest in Emmeline. Becky hadn't run a thriving brothel all these years for nothing; she knew when a man was interested in a woman, and when he was *interested*. "Don't you?"

Holt didn't answer, but when Emmeline and Rafe came into the dining room, he rose from his chair. Despite his odd fascination of moments before, he seemed more interested in Rafe now than in Emmeline, studying him the way he did, with both intentness and solemnity.

Emmeline went pale at the sight of Holt; Becky noticed that right away, although Rafe seemed blithely unaware of his wife's discomfort. *Typical,* Becky thought. Men worried about all the wrong things, and all the wrong people, and then were blindsided by a situation or a foe that should have been obvious to them from the beginning.

Holt put out a hand to Rafe. "Hello," he said, a little too

heartily, in Becky's opinion. "Name's Holt Cavanagh." He nodded to Emmeline as he and Rafe shook hands. "I hope you're feeling better today, ma'am."

Emmeline dropped gratefully into the chair Rafe drew back for her. "Yes," she said weakly, fooling no one. "I am much recovered, thank you."

"Rafe McKettrick," Rafe said.

"Good to make your acquaintance," Holt replied.

Becky took Emmeline's hand, squeezed it reassuringly, as Rafe, too, sat down. Emmeline was plainly uncomfortable in Holt's presence, and Becky wondered why. She hadn't mentioned that she and Holt had known each other in Kansas City, of course, and she was grateful that Holt had the good sense not to do so, either. So what was it?

The possibility, when it struck her, had the impact of a speeding freight train.

Dear God, she thought. Oh, dearest God.

"You two seem to know each other," Rafe said easily, his gaze moving from Holt to Becky, after Clive had brought coffee for him and tea for Emmeline.

"Actually," Holt replied, without missing a beat, "we just got acquainted this afternoon. I was sitting alone, and Mrs. Fairmont very kindly invited me to join her."

Emmeline's eyes, while still huge, looked slightly less feverish. Her hand shook a little, though, as she reached for her teacup and raised it to her lips.

"We've just about finished our business in town," Rafe said, blissfully unaware of all the complex nuances at play in their midst, "so I reckon we'll head out for home." He smiled at Becky. "You'll join us, won't you? Pa will want to meet you."

Becky nodded and acted pleasantly surprised by the invitation, though in point of fact she'd intended to pay a call at the Triple M in any event. She wanted to see for herself what kind of home her precious girl was settling into, and she had some advice for Angus McKettrick concerning the management of his hotel. From what she'd seen of that establishment, she expected him to be a bit of a dullard. "Of course I'll join you. If I won't be imposing."

Emmeline tossed her a frantic look, and Becky didn't know for sure whether the girl wanted her to come to the ranch or stay away. Instead of saying anything one way or the other, Emmeline just lowered her head and took another sip of tea.

Becky wanted to shake her. Emmeline had not been raised to act like a mouse, after all, but a strong woman. Why else had Becky tolerated the girl's insane penchant for adventure, if not to assure that she would learn to take care of herself?

"Pa will be real happy to meet Emmeline's aunt," Rafe went on, oblivious. "It's worried him some, and me, too, that she was so far from any people of her own."

Holt cleared his throat, managed something like a smile. "Your pa would be Angus McKettrick, then?" he asked Rafe, in the tone of someone who was confirming a suspicion. What *was* he up to? Becky wondered. Emmeline had a part in it, surely, but there was more—she was sure of that.

"That's right," Rafe said. Becky figured he must have taken a few thumps in the head somewhere along the way, though he seemed pretty intelligent and well spoken, too. He plainly had no idea that all was not what it seemed. Goodness, the very air itself was charged; Becky wouldn't have been surprised to see St. Elmo's fire dance across the tabletops. "We're always looking for hands if you need work."

"I might take a job at that," Holt said easily. "I could use the wages."

Becky narrowed her eyes slightly, pondering. Holt Cavanagh might have been a lot of things, but broke wasn't one of them. She had an unerring instinct where men and money were concerned, and Holt wasn't the kind who let himself run short.

"Then it's settled," Rafe said. "I'm the Triple M foreman, so I've got the authority to hire you. If you can ride and punch cattle, you're hired. You get thirty dollars a month, all the grub you can eat, and a bed in the bunkhouse."

"Sounds good," Holt replied, and it seemed to Becky that there was something a little ironic about his smile. "I'll ride out with the rest of you, if that's all right."

Emmeline clung to the edge of the wagon seat with both hands as she and Rafe and Becky jostled over the countryside between Indian Rock and the Triple M on that hot summer afternoon. She was over the terrible cramps that had heralded her monthly, and Rafe had been very understanding, considering that their honeymoon had been spoiled, but her troubles were far from over.

Now that Holt Cavanagh had arrived, she feared they were just beginning.

The sun was low in the western sky when they reached the ranch house, after a couple of hours of hard travel, and Emmeline was so glad to see the place that she almost forgot what a mess she'd gotten herself into. Almost, but not quite.

Mr. Cavanagh, who rode a fine sorrel gelding, expensively saddled, turned off toward the bunkhouse, as a hired hand might be expected to do. There was a lot of commotion going on over there; some of the cowboys were playing horseshoes.

Emmeline watched him ride away, and might have kept right on staring after him, if Becky hadn't pinched the back of her arm, hard, to get her attention.

Angus came out onto the porch, as he had when Emmeline herself first arrived, with Concepcion at his side. He waved a welcome, and looked pleased to see that they had an unexpected guest. Concepcion, Emmeline noticed, seemed less enthusiastic, though she was very polite.

Rafe pressed the brake lever hard with one foot before winding the reins around it and climbing down. He lifted Emmeline after him, then assisted Becky.

"Mrs. Fairmont," he said, "this is my pa, Angus McKet-trick."

Angus put out a big, work-worn paw. "Howdy," he said.

"Hello," Becky replied.

"Mrs. Fairmont is Emmeline's aunt," Rafe said.

Concepcion drew near, standing just half a step behind Angus, her brown eyes missing nothing.

"This is Concepcion," Emmeline hastened to say, pulling her friend forward a little way, to meet Becky. "She's been ever so kind to me."

Becky, having shaken Angus's hand, shook Concepcion's as well. A look passed between the two women as they greeted each other. "I will always be in your debt," Becky said. "My niece is precious to me."

Concepcion relaxed visibly. "Come in," she said. "It is just like these McKettrick men to keep a guest talking in the dooryard, when there's hot water for tea on the stove, and fresh molasses cookies to go with it."

Rafe and Angus set about bringing in the bags and parcels stuffed into every spare inch of the wagon bed, while Concepcion led the way into the house, through the entryway and the dining room, and into the warm, welcoming kitchen. There, she took Becky's lightweight wrap, and then Emmeline's, and shooed them to the table.

"I have missed you," Concepcion told Emmeline, as she bustled about, gathering the best china pot, a tin of tea leaves, cups and saucers. "These men!" Having set everything down, she threw her hands in the air for emphasis. "They are sorry company, indeed. Not five words said between them, the whole time you were gone!"

Emmeline smiled, glad to have been missed. "How is Phoebe Anne?"

"She's mending," Concepcion said. "Taking a walk by the creek at the moment. Was there any word waiting in town, from her folks?"

"Rafe brought an envelop from the telegraph office," Emmeline said.

"What did it say?"

Emmeline shook her head. "I don't know. The message was addressed to Phoebe Anne, so he didn't open it." She looked at Becky, then back at Concepcion. "Did you know there's going to be a party? I brought lovely fabrics for our gowns."

"A party?" Concepcion beamed, still busy at the stove. "Even after what happened to the Peltons, I'd say we have plenty of reason to celebrate. You and Rafe are married, and now your aunt has come all this way to visit."

Emmeline glanced at Becky, and thought she looked a bit tired. Her joy at the prospect of a celebration waned a little, and she was filled with concern. "Maybe you'd like to lie down, after tea," she began, but Becky cut her off before she could go on.

"Nonsense," she said. "I feel fine. If anybody's fragile around here, Miss Emmeline, it's you, not I."

Emmeline subsided slightly, feeling almost as though

she'd been reprimanded. "I'm perfectly all right!" she protested, after a brief pause spent rallying.

Concepcion served the tea and sat down in her usual place at the table for a chat. "Emmeline didn't tell us you were planning to come and see her," she said, watching Becky over the rim of her cup.

"It was meant to be a surprise," Becky said, somewhat airily. "And I'll be moving on quite soon."

Concepcion absorbed this news with equanimity. "Not too soon, I hope," she said. "We are very fond of Emmeline here, but I'm sure she's been homesick, and longed to see a familiar face."

Becky refrained from comment.

"When is this party to be held?" Concepcion asked, after an interval of comfortable silence.

"No date's been set," Emmeline answered. "We wanted to speak to you—and to Angus—first."

"Knowing Angus," Concepcion mused cheerfully, "it won't be long. He's been itching for an occasion to kick up his heels and let the other ranchers know he's finally got a daughter-in-law."

Becky chuckled. "I take it that Mr. McKettrick is pleased about the marriage?"

"Oh, he's pleased, all right," Concepcion said. "And he ought to be, considering that he practically forced it."

There was an awkward pause.

"Forced it?" Emmeline echoed quietly, at some length.

Concepcion squirmed a little, and took a rather noisy sip of her tea.

"Concepcion," Emmeline insisted, forgetting all her private doubts and worries for the moment, "what did you mean just now, when you said Angus 'practically forced' the marriage?"

"Oh, dear," Concepcion said.

Emmeline waited, and so did Becky.

Concepcion looked as though she wished she could disappear through a crack in the floorboards. "It's nothing, really."

"Then you won't mind explaining," Emmeline said.

Concepcion bit her lower lip, let out an enormous sigh. "Madre de Dios," she murmured, and crossed herself. Her lips continued to move, but silently, for a few moments, and then, reluctantly, she went on. "It is just that Mr. McKettrick—Angus—wants grandchildren, very much. He has been feeling his age, worrying that he would die without ever seeing his sons married, with families of their own. So he—he sort of helped things along."

"How?" Emmeline asked, very quietly. Becky, though listening intently, said nothing.

"It was his birthday," Concepcion said, looking harried. "He was melancholy. He told Rafe and Kade and Jeb that he would give control of the ranch to whichever of them married first *and* gave him a grandchild."

Emmeline had known all along, of course, that her marriage to Rafe was not a love match, and he'd made it perfectly clear that he wanted a child right away, but it wounded her, just the same, to realize he hadn't made the decision to take a wife on his own volition. She was a means to an end to him, a convenience, and probably little more. He would have married *anybody*, because he needed a wife and a child to get control of the Triple M.

"I see," she said, to no one in particular.

"No," Concepcion argued, under her breath, "I do not think you see at all. Rafe cares for you. In time—"

"In time," Emmeline echoed, standing up.

"She's just tired," Becky said hastily, rising, too. "Perhaps a short rest—"

Emmeline shook her off. "Please let me be," she said, very softly. "Both of you."

Becky and Concepcion exchanged concerned glances, but they subsided, let her climb the back stairs without tagging after her.

She moved briskly along the upstairs corridor, saw through the open doorway that Becky's things had been brought to the spare room, where she'd slept that first night after her arrival. A cot had already been set up for Phoebe Anne.

She went on to Rafe's room, opened the door, stepped inside. It was empty, but his scent was there, and so were the sweet memories of their lovemaking. She sighed, then turned the key in the lock, crossed the room to the writing table, and opened her remembrance book.

She sat down, opened the ink bottle, reached for her pen, dipped it, and began to write. At her elbow was the album Rafe had given her in Indian Rock, with its taunting gold lettering. *Our Family.*

She paused in her writing, and a shiver moved along

her spine. If Holt betrayed her to Rafe, there would *be* no family for her.

"I do not intend," Becky told Angus McKettrick that evening, after supper, when the two of them were alone in his study, each with a snifter of brandy at hand, "to over-stay my welcome. I will be returning to Indian Rock in a few days, where I have taken a hotel room."

Angus had graciously asked her permission before lighting the cigar he was so obviously enjoying, seated be-hind that grand, if rustic, desk of his. His sons, and Em-meline, were elsewhere in the house, as was Concepcion, but Becky had no doubts whatever that all of them were wondering what kind of discussion was transpiring be-hind the study doors. "No need to be hasty about leav-ing," he said. "This is a big house."

*Not big enough,* Becky thought wryly, remembering the tension she'd seen in Concepcion's face and bearing upon her arrival that afternoon. Angus probably didn't have the first idea, she reflected, that Concepcion loved him, and had for years. It was even less likely that he knew he felt the same way about her. These McKettrick men, she decided, had thicker skulls than most.

"I am used to looking after myself," she said. She had taken the chair across from his desk, next to the crackling fire. She smiled a little, gazing at the flames. "I have been in business for some years, though I am now retired."

Angus didn't ask what sort of business; maybe he knew. After all, how many women drank brandy and talked about profit and loss, the way they'd been doing? More likely, though, he assumed she'd run a millinery shop or something like that. "You'd be a welcome addition to Indian Rock, that's for sure," he said, in that pleasantly gruff way of his. "Why, you could rope yourself a good husband in two twitches of a mule's tail, if you wanted."

Becky's smile widened a bit, before she brought it under control. "That's very kind of you to say, but I'm not really looking to marry. I have a little money set aside, and I'm an independent sort." Understatements, both. She couldn't imagine taking orders from some man, just because he'd put a ring on her finger, and she had considerably more than "a little" money spinning gold in her bank account. Why, when Emmeline saw what her share alone added up to, she'd probably faint.

"Of course," she went on, when Angus didn't say anything, "if I came across the right business arrangement, I might choose to settle down. Have you ever thought of selling the Territorial Hotel, Mr. McKettrick?" Was that her talking? She didn't want that crude place, with its shared bathrooms, rough plank floors, and flour-sack curtains.

Did she?

Angus savored his cigar for a while. "Are you fixing to make me an offer, Mrs. Fairmont?"

Becky smiled, recognizing a kindred soul, another sharp trader. It almost seemed that Angus had known what she intended before she did. "I might be," she said.

"You understand, that hotel is in a sorry state of affairs. It would take a lot of hard work and money to bring it up to my standards."

"Would it, now?" Angus asked. He was enjoying the encounter as much as Becky was, that was clear.

"Still," Becky mused aloud, playing her part, "I think it has possibilities. A town of any size at all needs a decent hotel."

"I agree," Angus said generously. "I'll admit I've neglected the place. I never was much interested in the hostelry business. Bought it for taxes when the first owner went bust, two or three years ago."

"Then you ought to be able to give me a good price," Becky said. It was a game to her, this genteel haggling. She loved it for its own sake, though all the while she was wondering what in the world had possessed her to start the conversation in the first place. Just about the last thing she needed was a hotel in a backwater place like Indian Rock, way off in the Arizona Territory. Why, in five years, given a financial calamity or two, the whole kit and caboodle could be nothing but a ghost town, full of empty buildings, sagebrush, and jackrabbits.

"I was thinking I'd offer you a share of the profits," she said. "Whatever you paid in taxes, up front, and a third of what I make for the first five years. After that, it's all mine."

Angus leaned back in his chair, smoking and cogitating. He took his time, but Becky wasn't ruffled. If he accepted, she'd have a project to occupy her mind while she kept an eye on Emmeline, made sure she was safe and settled. If he refused, well, she wouldn't be saddled with a miserable excuse for a hotel.

"You are quite a horse trader, Mrs. Fairmont," he said presently.

"Becky," she corrected, "and yes. I am."

Angus chuckled, stubbed out his cigar in the ashtray on his desk. "You have yourself a deal, Mrs.—Becky."

Becky rose, as did Angus, and they shook hands over the top of his desk, two people who understood each other.

Emmeline's manner was very stiff that night at the supper table, but Rafe didn't set much store by that. He figured she was still feeling delicate, with that female thing and all. For his part, he was glad to be home again, eager to push up his sleeves and get back to work.

He remembered the telegram, midway through the meal, and handed it to Phoebe Anne, who looked a mite perkier, all gussied up in the blue dress Emmeline had brought her from town.

All eyes turned to Phoebe Anne. Her hands shook as she opened the envelope and unfolded the sheet inside. Gradually, as she groped her way through the words written there, a light bloomed in her thin face.

"They want me to come home!" she cried, jubilant. "Pa and Mam Pelton want me to come home, soon as I can get there!"

Cheers erupted at the table, and Emmeline unfroze

herself long enough to go over and hug Phoebe Anne tightly. All the women got teary.

Good, Rafe thought. Now I can burn that claptrap cabin to the ground, and there'll be an end to this homestead business.

He'd build a fence around the two graves first, of course.

He finished his supper and excused himself from the table when Angus did, leaving the womenfolk to their chatter. His pa went to the study, while Rafe headed outside.

He found Kade and Jeb in the bunkhouse, enjoying a game of poker with half a dozen of the men, while that many more looked on. The new man, Cavanagh, sat over by the stove, watching.

Red, the cook, if you could call him that, laid down three aces and a pair of tens.

"Son of a bitch," Jeb said, throwing in his cards.

Kade shook his head. "I'm out," he said.

The other players offered good-natured laments of their own, but they were eyeing Rafe speculatively at the same time.

"Maybe you'd like to join us in a game," Red said to him.

Rafe thought of his bride, up there at the big house. She'd be all right without him for a little while, he supposed, visiting with her aunt and the like. By now, he reckoned, they'd have gone over Phoebe Anne's impending trip home and moved on to planning the shindig.

"Don't mind if I do," he said, feeling confident, and drew back a chair.

"Got room for another player?" the new man asked.

"You can have my chair," Kade told Cavanagh. "I can't afford to let Red pick my pockets again."

Jeb wasn't going to play again, either, but he always took an unabashed interest in other people's folly, so he pulled his chair out of the way, turned it around, and straddled it, his arms resting across the back. A matchstick jutted from the corner of his mouth. "I'm too broke to do anything but watch," he said. He slid a glance in Rafe's direction. "Big Brother's pretty flush, though, now that he's foreman and all."

Rafe let the remark pass. Petty jealousy, that's all it was.

Cavanagh took Kade's seat, and Kade leaned against the wall, his arms folded.

"Where you from, cowboy?" Red asked the new man, as he shuffled.

Rafe noticed that Cavanagh never took his eyes off the cards, not for so much as a second. "Texas," he answered.

Another man, Dusty, gave a hoarse guffaw. He gathered up his cards as they were dealt, as did the others at the table. "Hell," he said, "half the wranglers I ever met up with claimed to be from Texas. Ain't nobody from Kansas? Or Iowa?"

"Where you from, Dusty?" Denver Jack wanted to know. He was at the stove, brewing up some of his infamously bad coffee. The other men claimed he washed his socks in the stuff before he poured it.

Dusty ducked his head, grinned, showing front teeth that overlapped a little. He probably hadn't seen his seventeenth birthday yet, Rafe thought, and wondered if the kid had people someplace, watching the road for him. "Ohio," he said.

"Ohio?" chorused four or five of the men, nudging one another.

"We got us a sodbuster here," Red remarked, assessing his cards with all the concentration of a surgeon deciding where to cut. "Don't know as we ought to put up with it."

There was more good-natured joshing, but the game was under way, and it was in earnest. One by one, the players dropped away, over the course of the evening, until only Rafe and the Texan remained. The pile of chips in the center of the table was a significant one, and Rafe was sweating a little under the collar. He had two months' salary in the pot, money he didn't actually have at the moment, despite his promotion to foreman. If he lost, he'd have to borrow from Angus, or even Concepcion, to make good on the debt.

He resisted an urge to wet his lips with the tip of his tongue and waited.

Cavanagh drew the moment out as long as he could, then laid down his cards. "Two pair," he said, showing eights, jacks, and a lone ace.

Rafe let out his breath, literally and figuratively. "Three of a kind," he said. There they were, the other three aces, a deuce of hearts, and a five of clubs. He raked in the chips while the others pounded his back and hooted in congratulations.

"Must be a bridegroom's luck," Red observed jovially. He still had money, having pulled out of the game early on, and he'd probably taken a pull or two on the whiskey jug, too.

"Must be," Rafe agreed. "And speaking of that, I'd better be getting back to my wife."

Jeb and Kade glanced at each other in some unspoken exchange. Kade pushed away from the wall, and Jeb got up from his chair with an exaggerated groan of weariness.

"Think I'll turn in myself," Jeb said. "Unfortunately, I'll be alone."

Kade slapped his younger brother on the back. "Poor, lonely soul," he said, with a fair amount of drama. "We can't all be as lucky as our big brother, Rafe. Why do you suppose that is?"

"Somebody get a harmonica," Red said. "We need us a sad song played here."

Enjoying his brothers' good humor, perhaps because he knew it would be short-lived, Rafe laughed, and happened to glance at Cavanagh, saw him watching with a solemn look in his eyes. He was not a man to inspire pity, this fellow from Texas, but he looked kind of lonesome, sitting there, like he'd been shut out of something.

"I expect those fences around the Pelton place to be mended tomorrow," Rafe said, "bright and early."

Jeb saluted, Kade shook his head, and the new man grinned a little, then looked away.

\*     \*     \*

The green silk brocade glowed like liquid emerald, lying in folds on the freshly scrubbed kitchen table. It was full dark outside, and the room was lit only by lanterns. The stove seemed to shimmer with warmth. Phoebe Anne sat in a rocking chair, smiling and reading her telegram over and over.

"Oh," Concepcion breathed, admiring the fabric Emmeline had just unveiled, "it is *lovely*."

"Here is yours," Emmeline said excitedly, pushing a large parcel toward the other woman. "Open it!"

Concepcion did so, eagerly. She gasped when she saw the silver-gray silk, and laid a hand to the base of her throat, murmuring in Spanish.

"Isn't it beautiful?" Emmeline asked. Only then did it occur to her that Concepcion might not like the cloth as much as she did. Maybe she would have preferred red, or the green Emmeline had chosen for herself. "Concepcion?"

"Oh, yes, " Concepcion whispered, and her eyes were shining with joy when she looked up at Emmeline. "I have never had anything so fine. Not even my wedding dress—"

Emmeline went around the end of the table and embraced the other woman, who sniffled as she returned the hug.

Rafe came through the back way just as they were carefully folding the lengths of cloth and wrapping them in the brown paper again. In the morning, they would cut their patterns from newspaper, using the carefully chosen designs in *Godey's Ladies' Book* as a guide, and then the sewing process would begin. Emmeline had never stitched anything more ambitious than a simple shirt-waist, but Concepcion was an accomplished seamstress. Together, with Becky to supervise, they would have the gowns ready in no time at all.

Concepcion cleared her throat, when she saw Rafe, and hastily excused herself. Becky was still shut away in the study with Angus, and Kade and Jeb, who came in just behind their elder brother, tipped their hats and made themselves scarce.

Rafe stood gazing at Emmeline, handsome as Apollo in the lantern light.

"Good evening, Mr. McKettrick," Emmeline said formally.

"Evenin'," he said, still frozen in place, hat in hand. "You look right pretty," he added, when the silence had lengthened significantly.

"Thank you," Emmeline responded, and kept her distance.

"Your aunt settled in and all?"

She nodded.

"Is something wrong?"

Emmeline spread her hands. "What could be wrong?"

"You're acting kind of strange, that's all. You have been, all evening."

She pretended to be busy wiping down the already spotless table. "Tell me, Mr. McKettrick," she said, "would you have sent away for a wife if the Triple M hadn't been at stake?"

He was quiet for a long time, and she couldn't bring himself to look at him. "Probably not," he said, finally.

"You would have gone on carousing and drinking and fighting and chasing saloon women forever, I suppose," she said.

"Not forever," he said miserably. "For a while longer, though, I reckon."

At least he was honest, Emmeline thought. That was more than she could say for herself. She'd have to get down off her high horse, difficult as that would be, and make the best of things. She was married, she had a real home, and in time there would surely be children. It was everything she wanted, everything she'd hoped for, save one.

Perhaps it would be asking too much to expect love as well. At that point, she wasn't sure the true article even existed, outside of fairy tales and her silly dreams.

"I want to thank you, Rafe," she said quietly.

He looked startled. "Thank me?"

"Yes," she replied. "You've been kind to me, and patient."

"Are you—well—over that other thing?"

She smiled at his embarrassment. "Not for a few days yet," she said.

"I reckon you must be about worn out. Maybe you'd better turn in. I want to have a word with Pa, and then I'll be up."

She nodded, went to him, stood on tiptoe to kiss his cheek. Then, without another word, she climbed the back stairs and made her way along the corridor to their room.

He gave her plenty of time to change into a nightdress, brush her teeth, and get into bed before tapping lightly at the door and waiting for her answer. He stood shyly on the threshold for a few moments, then came into the room, closing the door behind him.

"I brought you this," he said shyly, and handed her a brick wrapped in felt.

# CHAPTER

## 9

"You bought the Territorial Hotel?" Emmeline asked, looking up from her sewing. Several days had passed since her aunt's arrival at the Triple M, hectic days in which they'd done a lot of cooking, cleaning, and furniture moving, and spent hours, with Concepcion and a subdued Phoebe Anne, planning the party. Concepcion had given up her bedroom to Becky after the first night and moved in with Phoebe Anne in the spare room.

Emmeline had not had a chance to sew during that time, but she had finally managed to cut out the pieces of her party gown after breakfast that morning, the lush green brocade flowing like a river over the kitchen table, and now she was preparing to gather the top of one sleeve. She and Becky were alone in the seldom-used parlor, with the windows open to the warm summer day.

Becky watched her shrewdly for a few moments before

nodding. "You heard right," she said. Never much for needlework, she'd been reading one of Angus's books, *The Life of Copernicus*, purloined from the study earlier. She closed the volume carefully, let it rest in her lap.

Emmeline was delighted by the news, on one hand, because it meant Becky would be staying in Indian Rock, and she would see her often. On the other, well, her aunt's chosen career wasn't exactly one to inspire family pride; in a small community like that one, it would spell certain ruin. "You've been here almost a week," she said very carefully, "and this is the first I've heard of it. When did you strike this bargain?"

Becky's eyes twinkled. She pursed her lips, then gave in to impulse and laughed. "The first night," she said. "Angus and I came to terms pretty quickly." She tilted her head to one side, studying her daughter. "What's the matter, Emmeline? You don't truly think I'd start another—boardinghouse—do you?"

"I think," Emmeline said sweetly, dizzy with relief, "that you would do whatever struck your fancy, and devil take anyone who objected."

That brought a saucy smile. "You have been paying attention, then," Becky said. She seemed to sparkle all over at that moment, like a prism refracting the late June sunshine. It was difficult, no, impossible, to believe that she might be seriously ill. "Never fear, darling. I shall be the very touchstone of staid respectability, from now on. The Territorial Hotel will be just that—a hotel. Of course, the place needs lots of work."

"You might begin," Emmeline said, wielding her needle again, "by changing the name. Not to mention the curtains."

"My dear," Becky assured her, "you will hardly recognize that establishment once I'm through with it."

"Won't it cost a great deal?"

"There will be some expense involved," Becky allowed. "Since I have rather a lot of money at my disposal, however, that won't be a problem." She leaned forward in her chair and whispered mischievously, "Emmeline, I'm rich."

Emmeline's eyes widened. "Really?"

"Well," Becky said, "not as rich as your father-in-law, it's true. But I've got enough that I'll never want for anything, and neither will you."

"I wouldn't think of accepting a cent," Emmeline said.

"Because the money is tainted?" Becky asked, and for the first time, Emmeline realized Becky's greatest vulnerability. Always independent, always thumbing her nose at the scornful matrons of Kansas City's upper crust, Becky wanted, perhaps even needed, Emmeline's respect and approval.

"Money," Emmeline said, stitching even more busily than before, "is money. You've obviously saved, and invested wisely over the years. I'm refusing to accept any of it because I'm a grown woman now, and married. I should be an asset to you, not a liability."

Pride glittered in Becky's eyes. "My girl, you have never been a liability to me, not ever. You were, and are, the great joy of my life, and my money means nothing at all, if I can't share it with you."

Emmeline was moved, unable, for the moment, to speak *or* sew. She knew, then, the full extent of Becky's sacrifice—she'd prostituted herself, and established one of the best-known brothels in Kansas City, *for her.* The knowledge left Emmeline breathless.

Rafe chose that moment, bless his soul, to loom up in the parlor doorway, wearing dirty work clothes, his battered hat in one hand. Emmeline felt a peculiar squeeze in the deepest regions of her heart, just to look at him. Lord, but he was a fine sight to see, even clad in dungarees, muddy boots, and a chambray shirt, with his dark hair rumpled.

"Am I interrupting something?" he asked.

Both women sniffled, then turned bright smiles on him. "No," they said in chorus. Becky laughed and rose from her chair. "As a matter of fact," she said, "it's time I started packing to go back to town. I've got a lot of hard work ahead of me, and I'd better get started."

"I'll have one of the hands drive you in, in the buggy," Rafe said, crossing the room to stand beside Emmeline's chair. "It's not safe for a woman to travel that distance alone."

"Thank you," Becky replied, favoring Rafe with a look of genuine fondness, and swept out of the room in grand style. Emmeline happened to know that she'd done all her packing before breakfast; she just wanted to give the McKettricks some time alone.

Rafe leaned down and kissed Emmeline on the top of her head. "How's your party getup coming along?" he asked, noticing the large sleeve piece in her lap.

"Do you have time to take a ride with me, up the mountain? There's something I want you to see."

An outing sounded like just the thing, especially on such a pretty day. It might keep her from waxing melancholy over Becky's departure, too. Even though she would be only two hours away, in Indian Rock, Emmeline would miss Becky sorely, once she'd left the Triple M. "I'd like that," she said.

Rafe's smile was a little shy, and a flush burgeoned along his jaw line. Emmeline marveled that a man so forceful, so decisive, could be so incomprehensibly shy when it came to a simple conversation with a woman. She wondered if he'd been such a retiring type before their marriage, then remembered her first sight of him, hurtling out through the swinging doors of the Bloody Basin Saloon, and almost laughed out loud. She knew a little, mostly from Kade and Jeb's accounts, about his scandalous past. No, she decided, distinctly pleased, Rafe was bashful only around her.

"I'll hitch up a buckboard," he said. "Maybe you could throw together a few sandwiches and the like, for a picnic?"

She nodded, stood to face him. He kissed her, but gently, as if he thought she might shatter into pieces if he didn't take care. He'd been a most understanding husband during the past few days, kissing her chastely at night, and keeping to his side of the bed. She appreciated these considerations but missed being held in his arms, missed, too, the feverish intensity of their lovemaking and the way it transported her.

When she went into the kitchen, Rafe having headed for the barn, Concepcion had set a basket out on the table and was busy frying chicken. There was a loaf of fresh bread, wrapped in a checkered table napkin, along with a bottle of wine, glasses, plates, and utensils.

"Here," the older woman said, beckoning Emmeline to the stove and handing her a large meat fork. "This is just about ready to turn."

While Emmeline oversaw the sizzling, deliciously fragrant chicken, Concepcion hurried into the pantry, returning with several jars of preserves. There were cinnamon pears, Emmeline could see, and jewel-bright strawberry jam. Crimson beets, probably pickled, completed the menu.

"Good heavens," Emmeline said, having noted a dozen eggs in a saucepan boiling at the back of the stove, "we're only going for an afternoon drive, not setting up camp."

Concepcion looked cheerfully flustered. "Rafe is a big man," she said, setting the jars one by one in the basket, with more checkered napkins stuffed in between them, to prevent breakage. "He has a big appetite."

Emmeline turned the chicken pieces, one by one, careful not to burn herself with splashing grease. A roaring sound rose from the skillet, along with the familiar, savory aroma. She began to feel hungry, even though she'd eaten a hearty breakfast only a couple of hours earlier.

"I can't imagine why he wants to go up there, he's been so busy with the cattle and the new fence lines and everything. The place can't have changed that much since we were there a few days ago."

"Perhaps he simply wants to be alone with you for a while," Concepcion suggested, with a sly little smile. "You must admit, it's a mite crowded around here these days, what with Mrs. Fairmont visiting, and poor little Phoebe Anne."

Emmeline felt a little thrill of anticipation at the prospect of a few hours alone with Rafe. "Perhaps," she said, and blushed a little.

"You'd better dress warmly," Concepcion counseled, edging her aside and taking over the meat fork and the skillet again. "It's cooler up the mountain, and besides, you never know when a storm might blow up out here. Take some blankets, too, and some woolen socks. If you broke an axle on the wagon, or one of the horses went lame, you might not get back before nightfall."

Emmeline privately thought her friend was being somewhat overcautious, but she did as she was told, taking bedding from a large cedar-lined trunk in the upstairs hallway, packing a spare set of clothes for herself and Rafe. When he brought the buckboard up to the back of the house and came inside to collect Emmeline and the picnic basket, he saw the stack of blankets and the satchel and smiled a little.

Though naïve in many ways, Emmeline knew precisely what he was thinking. She happened to be thinking along the same lines.

Becky came downstairs to say goodbye, taking Emmeline's hands and kissing her on both cheeks. "If you need me," she said, "you know where to look."

Emmeline laughed. "The Territorial Hotel," she recited dutifully. "Indian Rock, Arizona Territory."

Becky rolled her eyes. "It sounds so rustic," she said.

"Denver Jack will be waiting for you out front, ma'am, when you're ready to leave," Rafe told Becky. "He's got the buggy all rigged out for the trip to town."

"Thank you," Becky said, and surprised Rafe with a light kiss on the cheek. Then she assumed an expression of mock sternness, narrowing her eyes and raising one finger, as if to shake it under his nose. "Now you look after my darling girl, Rafe McKettrick. There will be a severe accounting if you don't."

"I will," he said, very softly, and Emmeline felt a pang, because it was almost like a wedding vow, the way he framed those two simple words. She wished they'd had a real ceremony, instead of being married by proxy. She would have liked a dress to save for their own daughter to be married in one day, and a daguerreotype of her and Rafe as bride and groom, to paste in the album he'd given her.

"And you bring your bride to town to visit me soon, do you hear?"

Rafe smiled. "Yes, ma'am," he said. "I'll do that."

Emmeline and Becky said goodbye again and went their separate ways.

Emmeline was reflective as Rafe helped her up into the seat of the buckboard. He set the basket in the back, along with the blankets and the valise containing their extra clothes. Holt stood in the doorway of the barn, watching them, and Emmeline suppressed a chill.

"You must be expecting to stay up there a while," he commented, climbing up beside Emmeline, taking the reins in hand, and releasing the brake lever. The two mules pulling the buckboard responded immediately to his one-word command, and they were moving.

Emmeline did not look back at the house, suspecting that she would see Becky watching from the back porch or one of the windows if she did. It was hard to leave her, after just finding her again, even for a short time.

"What is it you want to show me?" Emmeline asked, a mile or so along the road, before they turned off to climb the rutted track leading to their home site. Rafe had been grinning, all along, like he was holding in some vast secret.

"You'll see when you get there," he said.

Emmeline sighed, knowing she'd get no more out of him, no matter how she tried. She might as well sit back and enjoy the drive, which, while rugged, was breathtakingly beautiful. The sky was a pure and fragile blue, fit to break her heart, it was so pretty, and the oak trees along the winding creek were cloaked in new, wind-rustled leaves. Yellow wildflowers peppered the grass, raising their faces to the sun.

Every now and then, as the trail got steeper, the mules balked, and Rafe urged them on with a light snap of the reins. The wheels of the buckboard jostled over rocks and sank into ruts, and still they traveled. The air grew thinner as they climbed, and Emmeline yawned once or twice, unaccountably sleepy.

Rafe smiled down at her. "Almost there," he said.

She rested her cheek against the curve of his shoulder, just for a moment. "It's so beautiful up here," she said.

"Yes," he agreed, in a low voice, but he wasn't looking at the countryside, he was looking at her. It would have been a perfect moment if an image of Holt Cavanagh watching them go hadn't come into her mind just then, a persistent reminder that she was on very shaky ground. Granted, her worries about an unwanted pregnancy were over, but one word from Mr. Cavanagh and the whole dream of husband, home, and family would come crashing down like a house with no nails to hold it together.

Rafe must have seen her expression change, for he touched her mouth with one gloved finger. "Why so sad?" he asked.

She smiled. "I'm not sad," she said, and that was true enough. She couldn't be, not on this sunny day, with Rafe at her side and a picnic basket tucked away in the back of the wagon. If anything, she treasured every hour of every day all the more, because she knew just how fleeting happiness could be. "I guess I was just wondering if all this can possibly last."

"All what?" he asked, very quietly. "Are you telling me you're happy here, Emmeline? On the Triple M, I mean, with me?"

She flushed, lowered her eyes, nodded. And suddenly she was desperate to know. "What about you, Rafe? Are *you* happy?"

He bent his head, tasted her mouth in a teasing way that sent sweet shivers through her. "Yes," he said, putting a lusty emphasis on the word.

They drove on, Emmeline painfully conscious of all the wicked forces Rafe had so easily aroused in her, Rafe smiling and keeping his thoughts to himself.

Just ahead, the track converged with another, newer trail snaking up the mountainside from the direction of Indian Rock.

When they finally reached the site where their home would be built, Emmeline felt a rush of excitement. Stacks of massive, cleanly planed logs had been brought in, some of them notched at the ends, so they could be fitted together into sturdy walls, strong enough to keep out the worst weather.

"Oh, Rafe," Emmeline whispered, clasping her hands together. "You've begun building!"

He looked pleased, and uncharacteristically modest. "Not exactly. All we've done so far is have the logs brought in. They were cut and milled up around Flagstaff." He drew the team to a halt, set the brake lever and secured the reins, then took a moment to assess the construction project with obvious pride. "Pa said he came into some unexpected money the other day. The logs are his wedding gift to us, along with the land itself, of course."

Emmeline's spirits soared. She stood up in the wagon box in order to see farther, and drew in a deep breath, spreading her arms wide. It was easy to imagine the finished house, sturdy and strong, a frontier castle with smoke coming from its chimneys and light glowing in its windows.

"I wish we could stay," she said. "Not even go back, but just stay right here, you and me, in our own house, under our own roof."

Rafe laughed. He'd come around to her side of the wagon and now stood looking up at her, ready to help her down. "I reckon you'd get restless soon enough," he said, raising his arms for her.

He closed his hands around her waist, held her suspended above him for a few moments, during which her heartbeat raced and her breath turned rapid and shallow, then lowered her slowly toward the ground, but stopping just short, letting her slide along the hard length of him as she descended. Then he kissed her, and the hussy in her came out for a fact. She returned his kiss with fervor.

"Oh, Lord," he groaned, coming up for air. "Are you *trying* to drive me insane, or does it just come naturally to you?"

She smiled mischievously. "Both," she answered.

"Well," he told her, his eyes dancing, "you've bitten off more than you can chew this time, little lady. Suppose I just lay you down in the sweet grass right now and have my way with you?"

She gave him a temptress's kiss, or what she imagined as one, sultry and slow, before replying. "Suppose you do," she challenged.

He eased them both to the ground without another word, and they kissed for a long time, there in the cool, damp grass, never bothering to fetch a blanket from the wagon.

Usually, their lovemaking was a lengthy process, but that day they were too eager for each other to wait long, or even to fully undress. Rafe opened the bodice of Emmeline's dress, baring her breasts, reveling in them, and she unbuttoned his shirt, splaying her fingers over his chest, savoring his warmth and his strength.

He raised her skirts and petticoat, bunching them in one hand, and she felt the soft ground through her pantaloons. They were soon gone, too, down around one ankle, and Rafe was unfastening his trousers. He teased her for several long, excruciating minutes, and she finally pleaded with him. He was inside her in one deep, powerful stroke, and her need, pent up for so many days, unwound like a watch spring freed from its casing. She was crying out, and hurling herself against him in the first throes of release, from the very beginning.

Now that he was inside her, though, Rafe took his time, guiding her through one climax, and then another. She was all but exhausted when he finally lost control himself, and delved deep. He threw back his head and shouted in triumphant surrender, and his body buckled on hers once, twice, a third time. She felt his warmth inside her, and hoped—*prayed*—they'd conceived a child.

They lay entangled for a while, and Emmeline wondered dreamily if they would ever be really separate again, after such a joining. It seemed to her that, this time, their very souls had fused into one, just as their bodies had. She wound a finger 'round and 'round a lock of his hair, just below his collar.

He raised himself, trembling, to look down into her face. "That," he said slowly, still out of breath, "was worth waiting for. I've got to admit, though, there were times in the last week when I thought I'd go out of my mind, wanting you."

She merely smiled, feeling as voluptuous as Cleopatra on her barge, and stretched, making a little crooning sound of sensual contentment, way down in her throat. Rafe moaned and instantly began to grow hard inside her.

Her eyes widened. "Rafe," she said, "I can't . . . Not yet."

He nibbled at her lower lip. He was harder still, now, and bigger.

It was her turn to moan.

He began to move on her, inside her, slowly. Very slowly.

"Oh," she groaned, drawing out the word, like someone falling over a cliff.

He slipped his hands under her bare bottom, raised

her a little, plunged to the core of her, and found fire there.

Her hands were wild under his shirt; she grasped his back, pulling, trying to draw him into her very soul. Within moments, she was climaxing again, with a violent abandon so wild and so primitive that she barely recognized herself. All the while she was shouting his name to the skies, all the time she was meeting him thrust for thrust and coming apart in his arms, she wondered what force had taken her over.

Rafe's release was as fierce as her own, and when at last it ended, he fell beside her, fighting for every breath, his eyes tightly closed. It was as if he had depleted all his senses in loving Emmeline, and must wait for their recovery.

He didn't stir until much later, when a chilly breeze began to blow. Only then did he carefully, but awkwardly, button her bodice, covering the breasts he loved so well, and lower her skirts. He held up her pantaloons, like a flag, and smiled when a blush rose in her cheeks.

"You won't be needing these quite yet," he said, and sent them sailing up into the back of the wagon. He ran a hand through his hair, dark as ebony, and mussed by Emmeline's eager fingers. "What do you say we have that picnic now? Build up our strength a little, before the next round?"

She blushed harder still. "You are incorrigible, Rafe McKettrick."

"And insatiable," he added.

She laughed. "Such fancy words. You must have been a very good student."

"Better at some things than others," he admitted, kissing the backs of her fingers. Then he stood, deftly pulling her right along with him. He turned his back to her, to fasten his trousers and then button his shirt. He was still in a state of appealing dishabille when he faced her again, took her in his arms, and kissed her soundly.

If we never had any more than this, Emmeline thought, it would be so much more than I ever dreamed of.

"Let's get a fire going," he said when the kiss ended, and for a moment, Emmeline didn't realize that he was talking about gathering sticks and lighting matches. "It's getting cold out here."

Emmeline found firewood, branches and twigs, mostly, fallen and dried, and Rafe made a circle of stones to contain the blaze. Once the campfire was going strong, he unhitched the mules and staked them nearby, where there was plenty of grass and a small spring.

Emmeline, meanwhile, spread one of the blankets on the ground, well within the radius of warmth cast by the fire, and laid out the picnic. She was ravenously hungry, and so was Rafe; little wonder, the way they'd exerted themselves earlier. She reddened a little, just to recall her unbridled responses.

Rafe, standing at the edge of the blanket now, bent to take the wine—elderberry, made by Concepcion herself—from the basket, along with two empty jelly jars. He uncorked the wine easily, then poured for Emmeline and himself.

"A toast," he said, holding up his glass.

Emmeline knew her eyes were shining as she held hers up in response.

"To us, Emmeline. To you, and me, and our children, and our children's children. To this house, and this land."

She touched her glass to his, and they drank, and to Emmeline there was something sacred about the exchange.

The wine was heady stuff, and she had more with her dinner, and more still afterward. When Rafe laid her down amid the remains of their feast and took her again, this time slowly, she was transported, rising and falling on the tides of a sweet, quiet passion that had no beginning, it seemed, and no end.

They slept afterward, huddled together under the other two blankets they'd brought along, and woke to find twilight descending. The wind was raw, and the fire was nearly out.

"We'd better head back," Rafe said, without particular enthusiasm.

Emmeline nodded, wishing again that the house were finished, and they could stay where they were, on their own ground, just the two of them, for just a while longer. She opened the valise she'd brought, found a pair of pantaloons inside, and put them on behind the wagon, out of Rafe's view.

It seemed a silly pretence of modesty, given that he'd

removed the first pair with so little resistance from her, but there it was. She felt taut as the strings of a fiddle inside, tuned and resonant, all her senses humming. Indeed, she suspected that if Rafe so much as touched her in the most remotely intimate way, she would shatter like a clay pigeon at a skeet shoot.

She didn't look at him while they were gathering the blankets and the remains of their picnic, and when he'd hitched up the mules and hoisted her into the wagon box, she took great care to keep to her side of the seat.

He chuckled, wrapping one of the blankets around her, pulling her close to his side. She hesitated, then settled against him with a sigh.

It was dark by the time they crossed the creek, a few hundred yards downstream from the ranch house, with its glowing windows, and rambled up the other bank, mules and wagon wheels dripping water.

Rafe stopped the rig behind the house, near the steps leading to the enclosed back porch, and helped Emmeline down from the wagon box first thing. She was stiff from the long, rugged ride down the mountain, but she felt a deep, secret contentment, too. That, she knew, was the legacy of Rafe's lovemaking.

He carried the picnic basket and blankets as far as the porch, then went back out to put away the team and wagon. Emmeline was hoping to find the kitchen empty, for she knew there was a silly, dreamy look about her, one she couldn't quite hide. She might have been treading on air, several inches off the floor, so light was her step.

And then she saw him.

Emmeline stopped cold, staring at Holt.

He smiled and hoisted his coffee mug in an impertinent salute. "Hello, Mrs. McKettrick," he said.

She couldn't speak.

Holt sighed and shook his head, affably bewildered. "Have you forgotten what we were to each other?" he asked. He chuckled when she didn't answer, set his mug in the sink, and went out.

Emmeline collapsed into the rocking chair near the stove, her knees having turned to water.

Jeb reached into the back of the wagon, just as Rafe was leading the mules into the barn to be brushed down and fed, and came up with Emmeline's discarded pantaloons. "What's this?" he teased. "A flag of surrender?"

Rafe left the mules standing and went back to snatch the knickers out of his brother's hand. Once he had them, he didn't know what to do with them, and he made several false starts before stuffing them inside his shirt. His face felt hot as a stove lid with a January fire burning beneath it.

"One more word," he warned, waggling a finger at Jeb and frowning so hard, it hurt. "Just one more word, Little Brother, that's all it's going to take."

Jeb was trying hard not to laugh, and he held up both hands, palms out, in a gesture of peace. His cheeks kept puffing out, though, and he was making a wheezing sound. Under any other circumstances, Rafe would have whacked him hard on the back, thinking he was choking.

Instead, he turned his back on his brother, commending himself on his forbearance, and stalked over to take up the mules' halter ropes again. Damn, but he'd be glad when he and his wife had their own place.

Jeb followed him into the barn. Typically, he didn't help put the mules away, he just leaned against the stall gate, watching Rafe work and grinning like a cat with feathers in its whiskers.

Rafe finally snapped. "What?" he barked, tossing the brush he'd been using into an old bucket full of similar items, and forcing Jeb to step back by opening the stall gate.

"I reckon we'll be starting on that house of yours soon," Jeb said.

Rafe glared at him, suspicious. "You're up to something," he said. "What is it?"

Jeb tried to look injured. "Me?" he asked, thumping his chest with both hands. "If anything, Brother, I'm stricken with admiration. Who'd have thought you had such a way with women?"

"What way is that?" Rafe asked in a very low voice, glowering. He was taller than Jeb, so he made a point of looming a little.

Jeb reached out, patted the lump on Rafe's chest where the bloomers were stashed. Unbelievably, he'd forgotten all about them. "That must have been some picnic," he said.

Rafe lunged for him, but Jeb was quick as a rabbit, and he got out of the way. He gave a hoot of laughter and Rafe went over the edge, chasing the little bugger clear out of the barn and around the horse trough. When he got his hands on Jeb, he meant to drown him.

The ruckus drew a crowd from the bunkhouse, including Kade and the new man, Cavanagh.

"What's that in your shirt, Rafe?" Denver Jack wanted to know. "You fetch home a pup or something?"

Jeb found the inquiry uproariously funny and let out another guffaw. Rafe saw red. He knew Jeb was just ribbing him, and normally he wouldn't have let him get under his hide, but he was mighty sensitive where Emmeline was concerned, and he didn't want the whole bunkhouse speculating on how she'd come to be separated from her knickers.

Jeb took to dancing around, dukes raised like a prizefighter. He'd always been a show-off, and he loved an audience. "Come on, Rafe," he urged good-naturedly. "You know you want to throw a punch. Let's see your best."

Rafe made a roaring sound low in his throat, like a bull, and he knew his eyes were bulging a little. He made another lunge for Jeb, and this time he connected, landing a solid punch in his middle. Jeb flailed backward and Rafe, propelled by his own momentum, got sucked into the undertow. Both of them landed in the horse trough with a resounding splash.

Jeb came up sputtering and laughing at the same time. Rafe scrambled to his feet, his temper considerably cooled, and found himself flying backward onto the hard ground when Jeb's foot struck his middle.

And so they fought, these brothers, like a pair of young bulls, soaking wet, cheered on by the bunkhouse crew, and laughing fit to be tied, until they finally gave up in exhaustion and headed for the house, each with an arm around the other's shoulder.

# CHAPTER

## 10

SMOKE ROILED DARK and greasy against the sky, and Emmeline hurried anxiously to meet Rafe as he rode in, the morning after their trip to the mountaintop. "Rafe," she gasped, "what—?"

His face hardened slightly—or had she imagined it? "Don't worry," he said. "It's just the Pelton place."

Emmeline stared at him. "What do you mean, 'just' the Pelton place? Are you telling me that fire was deliberately set?"

Rafe swung down from his horse in front of the barn and gave the reins to a ranch hand. "I set it myself," he said. "There are men watching it, keeping it under control, if that's what's worrying you."

"How could you?" she whispered, horrified.

"I told you before," Rafe said, plainly losing patience. "That's McKettrick land. The last thing I want is another bunch of squatters moving into that cabin."

Emmeline clenched her hands at her sides, glanced back toward the ranch house, where preparations for the party were going on. The party celebrating their marriage. And Phoebe Anne was in there, too, resting up for the long trip home to Iowa; Phoebe Anne, who had buried her dreams just a few hundred yards from that cabin. "You had no right!" she said.

"I had *every* right!" he retorted.

The extent of his insensitivity was breathtaking. "The least you could have done was wait until Phoebe Anne left for Iowa!"

Rafe glowered down at her, eyes narrowed. "You've got a lot to learn about living out here. We don't set a whole lot of store by *waiting* to do anything that needs doing. Furthermore, if I let every hard-luck farmer who took a fancy to this place slap up a cabin and hoe himself out a vegetable patch, there'd be no room left to graze cattle!"

Emmeline stood on tiptoe, her face as close to Rafe's as she could manage. "Rafe McKettrick," she said, "that poor woman lost her husband and her baby, in the same day. Now you've burned her home to the ground. Have you no trace of human kindness or understanding in you?"

He pulled back, ever so slightly, as if she'd slapped him. "First of all," he said evenly, "the place *isn't* her home and it never was. And second, she doesn't mean to live there anyhow!"

"Seth and the baby are buried on that land! Did you just let the flames rush across their graves?"

Rafe threw his hat to the ground. "Hellfire and damnation," he bit out. "What kind of man do you think I am?"

"I believe I have made that clear," Emmeline replied. Then she turned and stormed back to the house.

Angus, who had business with a neighboring rancher, was taken aback to find his eldest son standing in the barnyard with one foot planted in the middle of his own hat. He reckoned he shouldn't have been surprised, though, since he'd just passed Emmeline on his way out of the house. She'd been in such a steaming rage that she hadn't even said howdy.

"What's the trouble, Son?" he asked, slapping Rafe on the back. He felt charitable. Today, he meant to buy the Chandler place, just north of the Triple M, and double the size of his holdings. Now that *one* of his boys had taken hold and landed himself a wife, Angus had hope for the future.

Rafe looked exasperated, and a little embarrassed, too, as he stooped to recover his ruined hat and slapped it distractedly against one thigh. "We're burning the Pelton cabin," Rafe said. "Emmeline isn't taking it too well. I explained that it was on Triple M land in the first place, but—" He spread his hands, then let them fall to his sides. Enough said.

Angus sighed. "Women don't usually put so much stock in deeds and titles and the like as we do," he said, and shook his head. He'd always found the female of the species purely confounding, and never pretended otherwise. "They seem to reckon that if somebody comes along in a broken-down wagon, hangs up some curtains and builds a chicken coop, that's claim enough."

Rafe thrust a hand through his hair. "There's no reasoning with that woman," he muttered, staring at the house intently as if he hoped to see through the walls.

Angus laughed. "Don't even try," he said. "You'll save yourself years of suffering."

Right then, the new cowhand rode in, mounted on a big sorrel gelding, one of the finest pieces of horseflesh Angus had ever seen, which was saying something, since he'd been around horses all his life. He'd heard about this Cavanagh fella, but this was the first time he'd actually laid eyes on the man, and something in his bearing gave Angus a jolt. Without thinking about it, he laid a hand to his heart, half expecting it to give out on him, right there in the barnyard.

"You must be Cavanagh," he heard himself say. He felt odd, as though he were sleepwalking, but with his eyes open.

"Yes, sir," came the reply, as the wrangler swung down from the saddle. His gear was good, like his horse—better than a man making thirty dollars a month and three squares a day ought to be able to afford. That saddle was Mexican, if Angus wasn't mistaken—and he seldom was, when it came to good tack or anything else that had to do with ranching. Silver conchas gleamed in the richly tooled leather on the canticle, and the bridle fittings and breast strap were just as fancy.

Angus put out a gloved hand. "Angus McKettrick," he said, frowning.

There was something cocky about the man's grin, and a little familiar, too. That was the most disturbing thing of all—the sense that he ought to know this fellow. "Yes, sir," drawled the newcomer. "I figured that's who you were."

Angus ruminated on that. "I knew some Cavanaghs once," he said. "They were neighbors to my first wife's people, down in Texas."

"That so?" the younger man allowed. "Truth is, I just took on the name because I didn't care for the one I was born with." He turned his attention to Rafe. "We found some dead steers up there in the ravine, the one overlooking the springs. Looked like wolves got them."

Rafe swore. "How many?" he asked.

Angus could barely keep his mind on the conversation. There was an odd thrumming inside him, like a far-off drumbeat rising from an enemy camp. He hoped he wasn't about to keel over in some kind of codger fit and make a damn fool of himself. "You put me in mind of somebody," he said, thinking out loud.

"That so?" said Cavanagh, real breezy-like. He didn't ask whom he reminded Angus of, and that was fine, because Angus couldn't have answered with any certainty anyhow.

"You planning on staying around awhile, or are you just passing through?"

By then, Rafe was studying Angus as though he feared he'd lost his mind, and little wonder. Any other time, those dead cattle would have been the only subject he cared to talk about. He'd have gone out looking for the thieving scavengers himself, with a loaded rifle and plenty of spare bullets.

Cavanagh looked at Angus for a long moment. "I'm not sure," he said. "Sometimes I get the yen to put down roots someplace." He paused and grinned. "Other times, I just want to see what's on the other side of the next rise."

Angus nodded. He'd been like that, too, when he was younger. He'd thought he'd be in Texas forever, when he got married the first time. Raise a whole flock of children there, build a ranch. But then his young wife had passed on, trying to give him a son, and he'd been wild with sorrow for a long time after that, unable to light anywhere, always moving. He followed the herds for a long while, before settling in the Arizona Territory, sending a bank draft for the boy's keep whenever he could scrape the money together.

It saddened him to think of that child, for he'd missed him sorely, more so after the other boys came along, rather than less, like he might have expected. He still did, sometimes.

"What do you want to do about those dead cattle?" Cavanagh asked, turning to Rafe, when the silence lengthened.

"We'd better bury them," Rafe said, with an exasperated sigh. "Let's hitch up a wagon and load some picks and shovels. After that, I mean to see if I can track that wolf pack."

Cavanagh nodded and led his horse to the barn.

Angus watched him, still shaken.

Becky almost collided with Marshal John Lewis on her way out of Indian Rock's one and only bank that fine sunny morning. She had already visited the telegraph office and sent the necessary wires to Kansas City, and her mind was busy with staffing decisions. She meant to keep the cook, but that Clive fellow would have to go; he was about as cordial as a rattlesnake sealed up in a lard can, and it took diplomacy to work in a hotel. She had to hire at least one maid and one waiter, as soon as possible, though she could handle the registration desk and the ledger books herself.

"Mornin', ma'am," said the marshal, tipping his hat. His hair was thinning, and his face was long, and a little gaunt. For all that, Becky thought, he was an attractive man, if you liked the rough and rugged type.

She smiled winningly. "Why, good mornin' to you, Marshal," she said. She wasn't flirting, she told herself silently. If she was going to conduct business in this town, she had to be on cordial terms with the locals, that was all.

Lewis smiled. "I hear you've bought the Territorial Hotel from Angus McKettrick," he said, falling into step beside her as she proceeded along the uneven wooden sidewalk, a ruffled parasol shading her delicate skin from the sun.

"That's true," she said. His eyes were watchful and a little shrewd, even though he kept on smiling, and for one terrible moment, Becky wondered if he knew who she really was, and how she'd earned her living in Kansas City. "I mean to change the name, and spruce the place up a bit."

The lawman grinned. "Angus never took much of an interest in the hotel business, far as I could tell," he said. "Picked up the whole shootin' match for a song when it went for taxes a few years back. I don't believe that man's ever passed up a bargain if he could help it."

Becky decided she was being fanciful, worrying that somebody would recognize her. Kansas City was a long way from Indian Rock, and even if the marshal *had* been there, it didn't mean he'd ever frequented the boarding-house. She brightened her smile and twirled her parasol once, for effect. "He must be an astute businessman," she allowed. "From what I've seen, Mr. McKettrick has done very well for himself."

"That he has," Lewis allowed, unruffled. His expression turned serious. "You want to be careful, ma'am. You being a woman alone and all. Indian Rock is a real nice town, and all, but we get our share of drifters and gunslingers."

"I assure you, Marshal," Becky said, "I can take care of myself."

"Be that as it may," said the lawman, undaunted, his strides lengthening a bit as Becky picked up her pace. "You'll want to have a care." She didn't mind his company, but she had a great deal of work to do if she was going to make a success of the hotel, and she wanted to get started. "You have any trouble, don't hesitate to send Clive for me. Any hour of the day or night."

She stopped, there on the sidewalk, and looked up into his craggy face, squinting a little in the band of sunlight that found its way under the fringe of her parasol. "I promise you that I will not hesitate to summon you if the need arises, Marshal," she said. "I intend to discharge Clive, however. He has a poor disposition for working with the public."

Lewis grinned. "I wouldn't be too hasty, ma'am," he advised, taking her arm. Just like that, they were strolling again. "About showing Clive the road, I mean. He's a mite testy sometimes, it's true, but that's only because nobody's ever taught him how to deal with folks. He's a bright kid, real good with numbers, and he and his mama depend on what he earns."

"I will reconsider, then," Becky said, after weighing the marshal's words for a few moments. They had reached the front door of the hotel, and stood there looking at each other.

Lewis tugged at his hat brim again. His gaze was steady, his eyes clear. He needed a shave, but on him, a scruffy countenance was oddly attractive. "I'd like to buy your supper tonight, Mrs. Fairmont," he said. He grinned a slanted, outlaw's grin. "Course, your dining room is the only place I could take you."

She was charmed, and that troubled her not a little. For a long time, she'd seen men as hardly more than vary-

ing combinations of suits, cigars, and fancy hats, oppo-
nents to be outwitted and, whenever possible, relieved of
excess funds. Now, after all this time, here was Marshal
John Lewis, wanting to take her out to supper.

He chuckled, evidently amused that she'd been struck
speechless. "If you're inclined to refuse," he said, "that's
fine. No hard feelings. But you look surprised, ma'am, if
you don't mind my saying so, and that puzzles me some.
A beautiful woman like you must get a lot of social
invites."

Becky opened her mouth, closed it again. Narrowed
her eyes. "Have you ever been to Kansas City?" she asked.

He shook his head. "No, ma'am. Got as far as Independence one time, though. Why?"

She took out her fan, popped it open, and waved it
under her chin. "No reason," she said. "I was just wondering."

He waited, cleared his throat. Smiled. "About supper?"

"What about supper?" Becky snapped, wondering
when she'd turned so short-tempered.

He leaned in a little, lowered his voice. "Are we taking
supper together tonight, or not?" he asked.

"Yes," she said, knowing all the while that she should
have said no. Turning, she marched into the Territorial
Hotel. Clive was behind the desk, fussing and fretting.

"Whatever is the matter with you?" Becky asked, her
tone admittedly peevish.

"The stage will be in any minute now," Clive said.
"Sometimes, there are people on it."

"Yes," Becky said, with an effort at patience. "That is the point of running a passenger service, I believe."

"I don't like talking to people. They give me nerves."

Becky gazed heavenward for a few moments—as if she could expect any special dispensation from *that* quarter. "If you are going to work in a hotel, it stands to reason that you must expect to deal with the general public."

"I get hives," Clive said, and indeed, he did appear to be breaking out in a rash along the length of his throat. "See?" he cried, tugging at his collar to indicate his infirmity.

A great racket arose on the main road, which was less than a block away. The stage was coming in. "Get a hold of yourself," Becky ordered, but not unkindly, going over a mental checklist even as she spoke. All the beds were clean, she'd taken care of that task herself, and she'd given her cook a suggested menu and a list of items to buy on account at the mercantile. They were ready for guests. "These are ordinary travelers, not marauding outlaws. Just take their money and give them keys and try not to insult them."

Clive looked miserable. He brought a dime novel out from under the counter and showed it to Becky, turning to a page showing a rather sensational drawing of a dangerous desperado shooting down a bartender in cold blood. "Just look at what can happen," he said.

Becky made a clucking sound as she inspected the illustration and the first few lines of the story. Trash, that was all it was, yellow journalism calculated to fill people's heads with nonsense. "I would imagine," she mused, at some length, "that the poor man asked for meatloaf, and was told, in rather rude tones, that it wasn't available."

Clive's eyes widened, and he went pale behind his hives. Becky shook her head, swatting at him over the counter with the soft-covered book.

"I will be right here," she said. "I promise, if anyone tries to shoot you, I'll stop them immediately." Unless, of course, she thought wryly, that "anyone" is me. "Do leave off pulling at your collar that way. You'll only make the eruptions worse."

Poor Clive looked as though he might break down and weep with agitation, and he stayed close to Becky when the first customers straggled in, dusty and tired from their long trip on the stagecoach. There wouldn't be a departing coach until the next afternoon.

Two spinster sisters started the rush, bony, angular women with long, thin necks, sparse brown hair, and beaklike noses. They signed in as Hester and Esther Milldown, and said they meant to settle near Crippled Cow Springs, on a ranch that had belonged to their dear, departed brother. Becky welcomed them, trying, as she did so, to demonstrate to Clive how customers should be greeted, and showed them to the most spacious room, apart from number 8, of course, which she'd kept for herself.

She'd just returned from room 5, having helped the Milldown sisters with their bags, when the nun came in. She wore a black habit much the worse for wear, and her face seemed very small inside her wimple. The poor thing must have been sweltering under all that heavy material.

It was her eyes that really caught Becky's attention, though: they were enormous, the color of aquamarine, and full of fear. She'd seen *that* look often enough, back in Kansas City. This child, nun or not, was running from something, and she was terrified.

"I don't have much money," she said in a very small voice, addressing herself to Becky. "Perhaps I could work for my keep? I wouldn't need much—just a cot someplace—and I can get by on one meal a day."

The kid was sincere, at least where wanting work was concerned; Becky would have spotted a con game right off. "You plan on staying around Indian Rock for a while, I presume?" she asked quietly. "I have need of a maid."

The quick eagerness in that worried little face touched Becky, and that was no mean accomplishment. She'd seen just about everything in her time, and she was not easily swayed by sentiment. The girl nodded. "I can do any work that needs doing," she said. "You'll never regret it if you take me on."

Clive's skin condition was subsiding, since no gunman had showed up wanting meatloaf, and now he came up with the courage to speak. "Don't you have to live in some convent or something?" he asked. It was a reasonable question, Becky thought, if a little roundabout.

The newcomer smiled shyly and ducked her head a little. "I'll be teaching at a mission school, outside of Tucson," she said. "But it might be some time before Father Meyers can spare anyone to come for me. I—I had money to travel the rest of the way but we—we were robbed a few days ago by road agents, and I lost all but what I had hidden in my—what I had hidden."

"Well, you poor thing," Becky said, rounding the desk and putting her arm around the waif. "You're among friends now, and you're welcome here at the hotel for as long as you need to stay. We'll telegraph Father Meyers, to let him know you're safe."

"Oh," the girl said, just a shade too quickly, "please don't trouble yourself. I'll send a letter myself."

Becky smiled warmly. She knew a secret when she met one; she'd kept a few herself. "I'm Mrs. Fairmont, and this is Clive," she said. "What shall we call you?"

"Mandy," said the nun, and flushed a little. "Sister Mandy, I mean."

"Sister Mandy," Becky repeated. "Well, well, well. Are you required to wear that habit all the time, Sister? I have a couple of spare dresses we could take in. They'd be more comfortable, I'm sure, when the hot weather comes."

The longing in that girl's face was something to see, but in the end, she shook her head. "I'd best wear my nun clothes," she said. "That's what they told me to do."

Becky was fairly certain that the "they" in question wasn't the Holy Roman Catholic Church; she could tell a nun from a scared kid playing dress-up. "Let's get you settled in," she said. "There's a nice little room just back of the kitchen. All we have to do is move a few boxes and bring in a bed."

The wolves were elusive. After three days spent hunting them, Rafe called the search to a halt and set his mind on getting the house built. Emmeline was still fractious over the burning of the Pelton place, and they weren't talking much. He hoped this would appease her a little.

Coming back to the hilltop without her had a lonely feel to it, Rafe thought, even though he'd been there by himself a thousand times before she'd come to the Triple M. He glanced at the circle of stones where their fire had burned, and at the place in the grass where they'd made love, ducking his head a little so that his hat brim hid his face. If he let anything show, he'd be in for another round of joshing from Kade and Jeb, and he just wasn't up to that.

He swung down from the saddle to stretch his legs, as did his father and the other riders. The supply wagon, necessarily slower than their horses, was still laboring up the track with the crosscut saws, various tools, kegs of nails, and an assortment of other things they'd need to start building. Rafe felt a rush of excitement at the prospect of coming home to this place after a day's work, or, more specifically, of coming home to Emmeline. Eventually, he hoped, there would be a passel of kids hurrying out to greet him.

Kade elbowed him. "What are you grinning about, Big Brother?" he asked, but it was plain that he'd already guessed. There was a look of friendly amusement in his eyes. "You're a lucky son of a gun, you know that?" he added.

"Yeah," Rafe said, a bit hoarsely. "I know."

There was a pause. Then Kade rubbed his hands together. "Let's get to work," he said, for Rafe's benefit and that of the other men. "You got the rooms marked off?"

The lines of the house weren't staked, except in Rafe's head. In his mind, he could have gone through the place blindfolded, pointing out every nook and cranny.

Eager to get started, he paced off the outside walls while they waited for the wagon, and he and Kade set rocks at all the corners. In the meantime, Jeb and Cavanagh and a few of the others set up a camp, of sorts, building a fire to keep the coffee flowing, while others tended to the horses. The animals were relieved of their saddles and bridles and left to graze in the knee-deep grass.

Angus seemed bent on helping out, though he was obviously a little distracted, as if he were gnawing on something way at the back of his mind. Rafe had seen that look in his pa's eyes often enough to know that it didn't necessarily bode well, and he hoped the old man wasn't fixing to say the house ought to face in the other direction or something. There was likely to be an argument if he did.

The wagon arrived, finally, and the sun was up, making the dew sparkle in the grass and the leaves of the oak trees shimmer. Angus kept glancing at that Cavanagh fellow, like he thought he ought to know him from someplace, but he didn't commence telling everybody what to do, and for Rafe that was enough.

By midmorning, the first logs were set into the ground and chinked with mortar, top and bottom, and by noon, the structure was waist high, with the openings for the doors and windows cut away. The men drove themselves hard, shirtless and sweating, working the crosscut saw, using the wagon mules and lengths of heavy chain to hoist each log into place.

While they ate the grub Red had packed at the bunkhouse, and drank some of the worst coffee Rafe had ever tasted, Angus stood beside him, admiring the beginnings of the house.

"That's going to be a fine home," Angus said. "Makes me feel old, seeing one of my boys take a wife and put up walls and a roof of his own."

Angus was rarely sentimental, and his present mood worried Rafe a little. He slapped his father on the back. "You'll be up here visiting all the time, Pa," he said, "bouncing those grandchildren on your knee."

A light of anticipation gleamed in the old man's eyes. "Reckon I will at that," he said. About that time, there was a shout, followed by a thundering roar, and Angus and Rafe turned to look just as one of the largest piles of logs gave way, shaking the very ground itself as they rolled.

"Sweet Jesus," Angus rasped.

Rafe, for his part, was struck dumb, momentarily at least. The whole thing was over in a few seconds, but it was like watching an avalanche, or a dam breaking. He shook off his paralysis and ran toward the site. "Anybody hurt?"

"That Cavanagh fella's pinned!" one of the men yelled.

Sure enough, there was the Texan, his face as white as bleached linen, his right leg wedged under a log as big around as a man's middle. There probably weren't enough men on the whole ranch to move that thing off him—not without doing a lot more damage to Cavanagh's leg in the process. Worse, if they weren't careful, and lucky as all hell, they'd set it rolling again, and it would crush the man to death before they could get him clear.

"Bring the mules," Angus said, crouching beside the fallen man. "You're going to be all right," he added. "You need a swallow of whiskey?"

Cavanagh was sweating with pain, and fear, too, if he had any sense, but he turned down the whiskey with a shake of his head. "I could do with some water," he said, "and a prayer or two."

Rafe and another man brought the mules, then fastened the chains around the ends of the log, making sure they were secure. Cavanagh took a few sips from Angus's canteen and raised himself onto his elbows. Kade and Jeb were behind him, ready to take him by the shoulders and drag him out when the time came.

Rafe crouched next to the log and peered beneath it. "You feel any rocks or anything like that under your leg?" he asked Cavanagh.

The Texan shook his head. His hair was wet with perspiration, and his jaw was clenched tight. A lot of good men would have been screaming by then, if they hadn't passed out, but he hadn't so much as groaned. "I don't feel anything but pain," he said. "There's a good bit of that."

Rafe exchanged glances with Angus. Then he waved his arm, and the men driving the mules shouted and slapped down the reins for all they were worth. The chains rattled, clanked, sprang taut. The log didn't budge at first, then it gave a creaking lurch, and Cavanagh bit clean through his lower lip at the pain, drawing blood. Kade and Jeb yanked him free and dragged him to safety a second before one of the chains snapped like a length of frayed string, sending one end of the log into a long, lethal sweep, leaving a deep gash in the earth to mark its passing. Fortunately, men and beasts were clear of its path, and it finally ground to a stop.

Angus got down on one knee beside Cavanagh and cut away the leg of his pants to reveal the twisted, bloody flesh beneath. The bone was sticking right out, and for a moment Rafe felt light-headed.

"I need a tourniquet," Angus said, all business. "And a flask." He looked down at Cavanagh's contorted face. "This time, you don't get a choice. You're going to need whiskey, and plenty of it, to get down that mountain without dying from the pain."

Rafe squatted down beside his father. "I'll send a man for the doc," he said to Angus. Then he turned to Cavanagh and spoke with frankness, which was all he knew to do. "You'll never stand the ride into Indian Rock—just getting back to the house is going to be rough enough."

Cavanagh nodded. Damned if he didn't try to smile, too, and him with his leg in such bad shape that it might have to be sawed off. "Where's that whiskey?" he asked.

They put a blanket under him, a man at each corner, and lifted him carefully into the back of the supply wagon. The mules were harnessed and hitched up. While Kade rode for town, Jeb took the reins of the rig, with Denver Jack riding in back, to hold Cavanagh's leg steady, and loosen or tighten the tourniquet as need be. Angus rode alongside, keeping a close watch.

Rafe stood watching the rescue party move away, hoping to God Kade would find Doc sober, hoping, indeed, that he'd find him at all. Boylen was a skilled physician—as he'd proven, caring for Mrs. Pelton—unless he'd been overtaken by a melancholy state of mind, which was most of the time. When he was cheerful, he could handle just about anything. When he commenced to sorrowing, though, he drank, and when he drank, he was just plain worthless. It was probably a mercy to the general population of Indian Rock and the surrounding countryside that he tended to hide out at those times.

After a few moments, Rafe turned to face the remaining men, all of them quiet, all of them watching him, waiting for him to tell them whether to keep on working or head back to the ranch. He'd been champing at the bit to run the Triple M for years, but now that he was actually in charge, he was beginning to see the gray cloud behind that silver lining. He had a new respect, and a new sympathy, for his pa, and all the decisions he'd had to make over the years. It all boiled down to one thing, it seemed to Rafe—whatever else might be happening, he had to get on with the task at hand.

"We've still got a few hours of daylight," he said, "and there's a house to put up. Let's get back to work."

Kade found Doc Boylen in the Bloody Basin Saloon, stone sober and winning at faro. Boylen was a small man, with wild red hair and a beak the size of a potato. He always smelled faintly of carbolic acid, and he had the personality of a porcupine with its quills bristled.

"That poor Pelton woman having trouble again?" he asked when Kade approached the faro table.

"A man's been hurt," Kade said quietly. "Got himself pinned under a log, up at Rafe's new place. Jeb and Pa took him to the ranch."

"How bad?" Doc Boylen barked, throwing in his cards.

"Real bad," Kade said. "His right leg was crushed."

Doc swore. "Reckon I'll need my surgical kit then, and some ether. Laudanum, too. I'll stop by my office, and meet you at the livery stable. If they haven't got a fast horse for hire, I'd better take yours."

Kade nodded and turned to go.

As it happened, the livery stable didn't have any horses on hand at all, except for an old swayback that would never make it as far as the Triple M, let alone get there fast. Kade surrendered his chestnut gelding, Raindance, with resigned reluctance. He'd pass the night at the Territorial Hotel, if there was a room available, and wait for someone from the ranch to bring back his horse. Doc might be out there for several days.

He saw Boylen off in front of the livery stable, then returned to the Bloody Basin for a few drinks and a round or two of faro. Doc had been enjoying good luck when he broke up the last game; maybe it was still floating around there somewhere, waiting for somebody else to smile on.

It was early evening, and his pockets were considerably lighter, when Kade headed for the hotel. Apparently, Doc had taken his run of luck right along with him; Kade hoped it would rub off on Cavanagh, the poor bastard. Just thinking about the shape that fella's leg was in made Kade want to turn around and go back for another drink.

He thought he was seeing things when he stepped into the lobby of the Territorial Hotel, and blinked a couple of times. That didn't clear his head; the nun was still standing behind the registration desk, big as life. She smiled at him.

"I need a room," he said, feeling downright befuddled. What was in that whiskey?

She handed him the hefty registration book. "Sign here," she said. "It's a dollar a night, if you want supper included. Chicken and dumplings."

He scrawled his name, leaving a few blotches of ink on the page in the process, and noted the signatures of Hester and Esther Milldown, entered above his own. He'd known a no-account claim jumper by that same name, a couple of years back. The rascal had up and disappeared one day, and not a soul went looking for him, either, even though he owed money to half the men in the territory.

Kade took out his wallet, extracted a silver dollar, and laid it on the counter. He definitely wanted supper; the pickled eggs he'd eaten at the Bloody Basin while playing cards were already wearing off. He narrowed his eyes, gazing at the nun, and pushed his hat to the back of his head in consternation. He was pretty sure that under all that heavy black cloth, there was a good-looking woman. "Are you—?"

"Yes," said the girl, raising her chin. "I'm a nun."

Damn the luck, Kade thought, and scooped up the key to room 4.

# CHAPTER

## 11

"I DON'T LIKE THE LOOKS OF THIS," Concepcion said as she and Emmeline stood in the side yard, watching the team and wagon toil across the creek. Angus rode alongside, his horse up to its knees in the rushing water. Even from a distance, the grim expression on his face was plain to see.

Emmeline felt a chill of fear. Rafe, she thought, forgetting all their differences, and started toward the wagon, her heart pulsing in her throat. Where was Rafe?

Concepcion caught hold of her arm and stopped her flight. "We'll know what's happened soon enough," she said quietly. "There's no sense rushing out to meet bad news—it will always find its own way."

"Rafe," Emmeline whispered, in anguish.

"Hush, now," Concepcion scolded kindly, giving Emmeline a hasty squeeze. "If it is Rafe, you can't afford to fall apart. He'll need you to be strong."

Emmeline stood watching through tears of terror and frustration as the wagon lurched and rumbled toward them. Angus rode ahead, and swung down off his horse, leaving the reins to dangle.

"That new man, Cavanagh, got himself rolled on by a log," he said, addressing his words to Concepcion and finding some strength, it seemed to Emmeline, in just looking at her. "He's hurt real bad."

Emmeline was wildly grateful that it wasn't Rafe who'd been injured.

"Bring him inside," Concepcion ordered, as the wagon drew up alongside the house. "He can stay in the spare room, and we'll move Phoebe Anne in with me."

It struck Emmeline then, what it might mean, having Holt Cavanagh in such close proximity, and she was ashamed to catch herself wishing they'd taken him somewhere else. Suppose he said something, either intentionally or in delirium, about the night they'd spent together?

She couldn't think about that now. She turned and hurried into the house.

Phoebe Anne sat by the stove, rocking and reading over the old letters Emmeline had brought from the cabin, the day of Seth and the baby's funeral. "What's happened?" she asked, her eyes going wide. By then, Phoebe Anne knew the cabin had been burned, and she'd taken the news with a strange calmness. It was encouraging to see her register any emotion, even alarm.

"It's the new hand—Mr. Cavanagh," Emmeline said hastily. "He's been injured in an accident." There were voices at the back door; no time to explain further. She hurried upstairs to the spare room to put fresh linens on the bed.

Cavanagh was unconscious when they brought him in, using an old door to support his weight, and he was so covered in blood and dirt that he was barely recognizable. Emmeline wished she'd waited to change the sheets, and then was stricken with guilt because she'd entertained such a petty thought.

"He's going to need a lot of tending," Angus said quietly, standing next to the bed. He was a strong man, Angus was, but he looked brittle to Emmeline in that moment, and somehow fragile. "He might not make it, anyhow. He's lost a lot of blood."

Emmeline stepped back, hands clasped together so hard that her knuckles hurt, and watched as Concepcion moved to the side of the bed to examine the broken man lying so still on the mattress.

If Emmeline could have been granted a single wish, by some passing fairy godmother, even an hour before, she probably would have asked for Holt Cavanagh to disappear as suddenly as he'd arrived, never to be seen or heard from again. That way, her secret would be safe. Now, though, seeing him mangled and broken, perilously near death, she felt nothing but compassion.

Concepcion rolled up her sleeves. "Jeb, Emmeline," she said crisply, without looking back, "I'll need hot water and all the clean rags you can find. Angus, if you aren't going to help, kindly get out of the way."

Emmeline rushed to obey, racing down the stairs to the kitchen, snatching up a basin, ladling steaming water from the stove reservoir to fill it. Jeb started pumping water into kettles and setting them on the stove to heat, and even in her agitation, Emmeline noticed that he kept glancing up at the ceiling, a look of solemn reflection on his face.

Phoebe Anne fetched the rag bag in from the back porch without being asked, and started sorting, setting the larger scraps aside to be used in cleaning Holt's wounds.

Emmeline, meanwhile, scalded her thumbs, carrying that first basin up the stairs.

Concepcion had already commandeered all the clean handkerchiefs to be had, and when Emmeline arrived with the water, she soaked one and began cleaning Cavanagh's wounds, in an attempt to assess the damage. The water in the basin soon turned crimson, and Emmeline went back to the kitchen to replace it with a fresh supply. Jeb accompanied her when she returned, having filled a couple of tin buckets from the stove reservoir.

"Is Mr. Cavanagh going to die?" Emmeline asked her brother-in-law, when they paused in the hallway outside the spare room.

Jeb's face, boyishly handsome and usually full of mischief, was grave. "He left a trail of blood down the mountainside," he said, shaking his head at the memory. "We tried to control it, but by the time we got to the creek, the stuff was seeping through the floorboards of the wagon." He sighed. "I don't reckon his chances are all that good."

Emmeline lifted her chin. "Was anyone else hurt?"

Jeb knew she was asking about Rafe, and he smiled a little, though his azure-blue eyes were still sad. "No," he said. "Nobody. Kade went for the doc, and Rafe and the rest of them are still up there, working on the house."

They descended to the kitchen again, and Jeb worked at refilling the reservoir and heating more kettles while Emmeline built up the fire. Phoebe Anne had delivered the rags Concepcion wanted and was busy scouting out more. Angus remained upstairs, helping Concepcion clean Mr. Cavanagh's shattered limb. The bleeding had stopped by then, or at least slowed to a trickle, but the poor man was deathly pale, and still unconscious, which was a mercy, Emmeline supposed. He would suffer dreadfully when, and if, he awakened.

"We need blankets, Emmeline!" Concepcion called from upstairs, and that command was just the tonic she needed. Jeb had taken over the hot water detail, and he was handling it so efficiently that any efforts on her part would be more hindrance than help.

She and Phoebe Anne raided the blanket chest, at the far end of the upstairs corridor, and carried armloads into the spare room. Concepcion and Angus wrapped Mr. Cavanagh as best they could, while leaving his injured leg bare.

After that, for Emmeline time seemed to run together and blur, like a palette of watercolors left behind in a hard rain. The sunlight at the windows changed, first glaring, then fading its way through a series of colors, before disappearing entirely, and Emmeline fetched lanterns from the shelf on the back porch, filled them with oil at the kitchen table, trimmed the wicks, and scrubbed the glass chimneys. Soon, the spare room glowed softly.

There was no sign of Rafe.

Working steadily, Concepcion had loosely bandaged Mr. Cavanagh's leg, and she sat beside him, holding a cold cloth to his forehead, whispering soothing words, now in Spanish, now in English. Angus, even more pensive than usual, had dragged in a couple of chairs.

Emmeline remembered that Concepcion's husband had died violently, and felt certain that her friend must be reliving that experience as she tended Mr. Cavanagh. Maybe she'd looked after her Manuel in the same quiet, desperately efficient way, only to lose him in the end.

She went to Concepcion's side, took her arm gently. "You need to rest," she said softly, but in a firm tone. She glanced at Angus. "You, too. I'll look after Mr. Cavanagh for a while."

Just then, there was a commotion downstairs. Emmeline strained to hear Rafe's voice, and heard the doctor's instead. Jeb must have pointed him toward the stairs. "Up there, in the spare room," she heard him say.

"Tarnation," fretted the doc, as he made his entrance moments later, "it seems like I spend half my time on the Triple M these days."

Concepcion and Angus moved aside so he could approach the bed, and he stood looking down at the patient, shaking his head.

"Sweet heaven," he muttered, "what happened to this man?"

"He got in the way of some runaway logs," Angus said. "Hello, Boylen."

The doctor didn't even spare him a look. His attention was all for Mr. Cavanagh and his mangled limb. He made a harrumph sound and barked, "I need to wash up before I do anything. And somebody might want to put Kade's horse away for the night—he worked up quite a lather getting out here."

"The kitchen is this way," Emmeline said. "You can wash there."

"I'll see to the horse," Jeb said from the doorway. "I take it you and Kade didn't ride double on the way out, so he must have stayed in town."

"He'll be there until I get back, I reckon," said the physician. "My guess is, he'll find plenty of ways to amuse himself in the meantime."

Jeb looked thoughtful at that, but he left the house to put Kade's gelding up for the night.

In the kitchen, Emmeline provided the doctor with a bar of yellow soap, a towel, and a basin of hot water, and watched as he scrubbed his hands. Phoebe Anne had started a supper of fried ham, potatoes, and onions; she greeted the new arrival with quiet friendliness, then set another place at the table.

"I won't have time to eat for a while," Boylen said, watching her with a paternal interest as she moved about the kitchen. "You been feeling all right, Mrs. Pelton? When I saw you last, you were in pretty bad shape."

Phoebe Anne smiled slightly. "I'm gettin' stronger by the day," she said. "The McKettricks have been real good to me."

Except for burning your home to the ground, Emmeline thought, and felt a fresh spurt of irritation at Rafe, even though she was wishing he'd ride in, so she'd know he was safe.

"Well," said the doctor, "you just get your rest, and take in all the fresh air and good food you can. You still look a mite bony to me."

Phoebe Anne nodded a little. "I'll keep a plate warm for you, Doc." She turned her steady if somewhat haunted gaze toward Emmeline. "What about you, Emmeline?" she asked. "You'd best have something."

"In a little while," Emmeline agreed. She didn't have the slightest appetite, but she knew she had to keep up her strength, if only to be ready for the next crisis. It seemed to her that life on the Triple M was one calamity after another.

Up in the spare bedroom, a few minutes later, Doc Boylen began unpacking equipment from his bag. He brought out a bottle of ether, a mask of some sort, and a variety of surgical instruments.

Emmeline swayed, just looking at them.

"Buck up," ordered the doctor; apparently, he'd seen her reaction out of the corner of his eye. "I'll need your help. Concepcion is ready to collapse, and Angus oughtn't to be under this kind of strain." He paused to peer at both of them over the rims of his glasses. "Contrary to what he'd have the rest of us believe, Angus McKettrick is not made of steel."

Emmeline swallowed a throatful of protests that she couldn't possibly assist in an operation, and stiffened her spine. Whether she liked it or not, this was the lot that had fallen to her. Concepcion and Angus had been watching over Mr. Cavanagh for several hours; indeed, they might well have kept him alive thus far, but for the time being they'd given all they could. It was her turn.

Reluctantly, they left the room, and Emmeline heard their quiet voices as they went downstairs.

"Just tell me what you want me to do," she said.

The doctor looked up from the bandages he'd been peeling away.

"Go and scrub your hands. We're going to put this leg back together."

Knees trembling, Emmeline nodded and went to the kitchen, where she began washing up. Angus and Concepcion were there, drinking coffee Phoebe Anne had made for them, watching numbly as she set the table to serve a light supper.

"You don't have to do this, Emmeline," Angus said.

She turned from the sink, drying her hands on a clean towel. They looked as if they'd been through a war, the two of them, Concepcion dazed, her dress bloodied, Angus wan and pale.

"I'll be fine," she said, but she couldn't help glancing toward the darkened windows when she heard horses passing by, moving in the direction of the barn and the bunkhouse. Rafe was back, then. How she yearned to see him, if only for a moment. A look, a word, would give her the strength she needed so badly to meet this new challenge.

"Emmeline!" Dr. Boylen called, from upstairs. "What's keeping you? We need to get started in here!"

Emmeline drew a deep breath, squared her shoulders, and marched up the steps.

Frank Boylen placed the masklike contraption over Mr. Cavanagh's face. The patient happened to be semiconscious at the moment, and he was looking up at Emmeline with an unreadable expression in his eyes. Unreadable, that is, except for simple recognition. Holt Cavanagh definitely remembered her from Kansas City, and for whatever reason, he wanted her to know it.

"This bottle contains ether," the doctor went on, shoving it into Emmeline's hand. "Drip it slowly onto the mask. *Slowly.* Give him too much, and it could be fatal."

Emmeline's ears began to ring, and she had to stiffen her knees just to keep them from buckling, but she nodded. She did as Dr. Boylen showed her and, after a few minutes, Mr. Cavanagh closed his eyes.

Dr. Boylen listened to the patient's heart with his stethoscope, nodded to himself, and reached for his instruments, wiping each one with a cloth soaked in carbolic acid. Then he began to cut, mend, and stitch. He pressed the bones back into place with his bare hands, and there was plenty of blood.

Emmeline felt woozy several times during the long ordeal, but she concentrated on administering the ether. Drip, drip, drip.

The doctor's counsel echoed in her head: *Slowly, slowly.*

Mr. Cavanagh must have been very tough indeed, because he lived through that operation. When it was over, Dr. Boylen had worked for more than four hours over the patient, pausing only to wipe sweat from his brow with a bunched table napkin, reassembling bone and sinew like the parts of a puzzle, disinfecting the wound, closing it with sutures, disinfecting it again. Toward the end, he'd shouted for someone to come and run an errand, and Rafe had stepped in, glancing at Emmeline, telling her with his eyes that he'd have taken her away from that awful scene if only he could.

Frank Boylen sent him to cut the ends off a pair of shovel handles, and when he returned with them, the doctor cleansed them with carbolic acid, just as he had the scalpel and other instruments. He used the lengths of hardwood as splints, setting the leg, then binding them in place with long strips of cotton sheeting, the same material Concepcion had used to create bandages earlier.

Emmeline was sitting in the kitchen, bloodstained and exhausted, when Rafe came to her, crouching beside her chair. She'd drawn it up close to the stove, cold to the marrow of her bones, sure that she would never feel warm again.

Rafe took her hand, kissed it, even though it probably smelled of ether. "You did a fine job, Emmeline," he said quietly. "Doc Boylen said so himself."

Emmeline turned her head, looked at her husband. She felt strangely dissociated from everything, as though she were wandering in a dream, unable to find her way out. "I was afraid it was you they were bringing back," she said, almost whispering the words. "When I saw that wagon, I knew someone had been badly hurt, or even killed, and I was so afraid it was you."

He squeezed her hand.

"When—when I saw him—I was glad," she blurted, and clapped her hand to her mouth in a vain attempt to stifle a sob. "I was *glad*—"

Rafe gathered her in his arms, buried his face in her hair. "Shhh," he said. "You're plumb worn out. Let's get you upstairs to bed."

He stood then, and scooped her up in his arms like a child. He carried her to their room, where he helped her undress and get into her nightgown. Then he tucked her in and kissed her gently on the forehead. She was already drifting off to sleep when he put out the lamp and left the room, closing the door quietly behind him.

Angus stood looking down at Cavanagh, asleep in the spare-room bed, his face awash in moonlight, and he knew what it was that had been nipping at the back of his brain ever since he'd first encountered the man, early that morning, out by the barn.

"Holt," he said, and dropped into the chair nearest to the bed, too overcome, for the moment, to stand. He buried his face in his hands for a long moment, remembering the little boy he'd left behind in Texas, his firstborn son. It had torn his heart out at the time, and he'd never gone so much as a day since without wishing there'd been another solution.

Holt opened his eyes. "You," he said. His voice was like a hasp striking rusty metal.

Angus chuckled, even though he felt tears gathering in the back of his throat and behind his eyes, and had to squeeze the bridge of his nose hard, between thumb and forefinger, to keep them back. "Yup," he said, when he could trust his voice. "You hurting?"

"Everywhere," Holt admitted. Then, in the grip of some sudden terror, he tried to sit up, groping wildly with one hand.

Angus put his hands on the younger man's shoulders and pressed him back onto the pillows. "Settle down, Son," he said. "You've still got both your legs."

Holt let out a long breath. "For a moment there, I thought—"

"You'll have to take it easy for quite a while," Angus told him. "In time, the doc figures you'll be able to walk and ride, same as always. Might be a little hitch in your get-along, course." He reached for the bottle Frank Boylen had given him, uncorked it, and poured a generous dose of the brown liquid inside into a serving spoon from Concepcion's kitchen. "Here," he said gruffly. "This'll take the edge off, anyway."

Holt raised his head to take the laudanum and then lay still again, cursing under his breath.

"What brings you to Arizona Territory?" Angus asked, when a long time had passed, and he figured the dope was starting to work. Holt's breathing had evened out a little; it seemed deeper, and less rapid.

Holt turned his head to look at him. "I wanted to get a good look at you," he said, straight out. But then, Angus would have figured any other answer for a bold-faced lie. "My old man. See if you were the polecat I always reckoned you to be."

Angus's shoulders moved, and he laughed, but no sound came out. "Well," he said, after quite a while, "what did you decide?"

"I'm still considering the matter," Holt said. His speech had slowed to a drawl, but he was making sense, anyway.

Angus emitted a raw chuckle, close kin to a sob. He rested his elbows on his knees and steepled his fingers, waiting for Holt to go on, knowing what was coming, and dreading it, too, all of a piece.

"I guess calling myself Cavanagh got to be a habit," he said. He was drifting as the drug took hold, hardly able to keep his eyes open. Angus wished he had something to dull what *he* was feeling, but he reckoned it was his just deserts, this raw and ceaseless ache in the very center of his soul. "I left home when I was twenty-one," he said, stumbling over a word or two in the process. "There was some trouble."

Angus gave him a sip of water from the glass on the bedside table. "Directly after you sent back that money I tried to give you, I reckon," he said.

"I didn't want your damn money then," Holt told him, "and I don't want it now."

"Took you a long time to head this way," Angus said gently. "What kept you?"

"You left when I was a baby," Holt reminded him, as if he needed reminding, his words thick and muddled. He struggled visibly to keep his eyes open and said his piece with slow and painful deliberation. "You ever look back, even once?"

Angus's voice was gruff. "Of course I did," he said. "I was young, and when I lost your mother, I lost my mind, too. For a long time, I was just plain crazy."

"You've got three other sons," Holt said. "You must have married again."

Angus nodded. He had a lot to apologize for where Holt was concerned, but he would *not* apologize for Georgia. Marrying her was the smartest thing he'd ever done. "She was a fine woman," he said.

Holt was rambling now, sort of groping his way from word to word. Angus figured listening was the least he could do, however painful it might turn out to be, so he leaned forward, resting his arms on his thighs, and took it all in.

"I used to tell myself that one day, I'd find you, and cut

your gizzard out. Time passed, though, and I had some luck. Wound up with land and a herd of my own. I decided to let you live."

Angus smiled a little, nodded. "Glad to hear it," he said. "There's been a time or two in my life when I would have welcomed being killed, though. Did they look after you, your mother's people?"

"They did the best they could," Holt said, after a long time. "I learned to ride and shoot and work. God, yes, I learned to work."

Angus closed his eyes for a moment, overcome by sadness, by the loss of those years with his eldest son, years that could never be replaced or redeemed.

It was the drug that made the boy say what he did next; Angus knew he'd deny it, once the stuff wore off. "I used to wonder what it would be like to have brothers," he said. "To be part of a real family."

"I'm sorry," Angus said. It was all he had to offer, under the circumstances.

Holt didn't answer, and for a few seconds, Angus was afraid he'd gone and died. He didn't think he could have borne that. Then the young man mumbled something, and Angus knew he'd merely fallen asleep. Best thing for him.

He sat back in the chair and kept his vigil, his hands folded in his lap, flipping through old memories grown musty in his mind, like daguerreotypes in a forgotten album. Georgia, delighting in their children, teaching them to walk and talk, read and write and figure. Sweet

God, the two of them, he and Georgia, would have been glad to fetch Holt back home and raise him with his brothers; they'd talked about it a thousand times. There'd always been some reason to put off the trip—a hard winter, sick cattle, money running short.

Angus sighed, thinking of his other three sons. He'd never gotten around to telling them about Holt when they were young, partly because he was ashamed of how he'd handled the whole matter and partly because he'd never wanted them to think he was going to ride out one day and leave them behind, too. It was enough that they'd lost their mother.

Of course they were men now, and he could have told them, but somehow he'd never found the words. So he'd kept the secret, even though it nettled him like a burr. All this time, he'd kept it.

He let out a long, despairing sigh, and started a little when he felt Concepcion's hands come to rest on his shoulders. He hadn't heard her come into the room.

"You must sleep, Angus," she said softly. "You're exhausted."

"I reckon I'm afraid to close my eyes," he replied. He glanced back at her, saw that she was wearing a nightgown and wrapper. Her lustrous black hair was plaited into a heavy, gleaming braid, resting over her shoulder and reaching nearly to her waist. Her eyes gleamed in the moonlight. "I'm afraid I'll die if I do," he said, "and go straight to hell for all my sins."

She squeezed his shoulder. "Nonsense," she said, and

though she was smiling, he could see tears in her eyes. "The devil wouldn't have you. You're too much trouble and far too cantankerous."

He chuckled, patted her hand. "I hope you're right," he said.

"Come," she said, urging him to stand. "I will sit with you until you sleep, and chase the devil away if he dares come near you." There wasn't much to Concepcion, she was such a little thing, but she could herd him around right well when she had a mind to, and that night was no exception. She led him out of the spare room and straight down the hall to his own.

"What about the Doc? Did you find him a bed somewhere?" he asked.

"He's sleeping on the parlor sofa," she replied.

Fortunately, Jeb had turned in long ago, and so had Rafe and Emmeline. Angus didn't want any scandals in his life at this late date, and it would have aroused comment, for sure, if anybody saw Concepcion go into his bedroom in the middle of the night. They were always careful when she came to his bed.

She lit a lamp, after closing the door, and Angus sat on the edge of the mattress to yank off his boots. He felt as if he'd been dragged down the mountainside by those mules of his, and then stomped on for good measure.

"Who is he, Angus? This Holt Cavanagh?" Concepcion asked, settling into the chair at his writing table. "There have been a lot of men hurt on this ranch, but you never sat with them half the night."

Angus tossed back the covers on his bed, stripped off his shirt, and shed his trousers. He never stood on ceremony with Concepcion—not when they were alone, anyway. They'd known each other too damn long for that.

"I knew there was something familiar about that boy the moment I met him," he said, stretching out. The older he got, the more his joints ached when he lay down at night; it was as if his damn bones spent the whole day rusting up, just to give him grief. "It was peculiar—I felt like I'd seen him someplace, but I couldn't figure where. Just came to me a little while ago, while I was sitting there, watching over him."

A lot of women might have started in to prattling when he left off talking, but not Concepcion. She had the patience of a bird on a nest when it came to things that really mattered, and she waited.

"I told you I was married once, and widowed, before I met Georgia," he went on. "What I didn't say was, we had a child together. A boy I called Holt, after her mother's folks. I was young when my wife died, and sometimes the grief was so bad that I'd ride out into the countryside and just holler 'til I was too hoarse to keep it up. I commenced to drinkin' more than I should have, too, and I was itching to leave that place behind me. I guess I thought I could outrun the pain someway.

"The boy's aunt finally convinced me that I ought to leave the boy with her and her husband until I got myself straightened out. It didn't have to be permanent, she told me. Just until I could give Holt a proper home and all."

Concepcion came to sit on the side of the bed when he stopped to recover for a moment. She took his big hand in her two small ones and kissed the knuckles. "But it was permanent," she said softly.

He nodded. "I was a long time getting myself headed in the right direction," he said. "Holt's aunt and uncle asked me to let them adopt him, and I agreed. It seemed like the best thing to do at the time, but I always regretted it. Georgia would have been glad to take my son in, and raise him like her own."

"Yes," Concepcion said, smiling. "She would have. She was a wonderful woman, your Georgia."

"By the time we were married, and had the ranch turning a steady profit, it was too late. Holt was somebody else's son by then." He swallowed hard, searched Concepcion's face for any trace of the condemnation he felt for himself, and saw only tenderness there, only warmth and compassion. "I don't know much about what his life was like, but I believe it was a hard one."

"Oh, Angus," Concepcion said softly, touching his face.

"I should have gone back there, Concepcion. I should have made sure Holt was all right. Dammit, he's my own flesh and blood."

She kissed his forehead, touched an index finger to his mouth. "You had every reason to believe he was safe," she said, "and you were more than a thousand miles away, building a ranch, starting a new family. You couldn't have traveled to Texas then without causing a lot of hardship for Mrs. McKettrick and the boys, as well as yourself."

He closed his eyes, sighed. She was balm to his spirit, this woman, simple and practical and sweet, and he began to let go, muscle by muscle, thought by thought, breath by breath, of all his burdens.

In time, he slept, and dreamed that Concepcion was chasing the devil around the front yard with a fireplace poker, railing at him in Spanish.

# CHAPTER

## 12

EMMELINE AROSE WHEN RAFE DID, the next morning, and dressed hurriedly in practical calico while he went downstairs to build up the fire in the cookstove. Although it was now the third week of June, there was a distinct nip in the air, and according to Concepcion and Phoebe Anne, it wasn't unheard of for a freak snowstorm to strike in summer. She glanced out the bedroom and was relieved to see that the ground was bare.

When Emmeline descended the back stairs, she found Dr. Boylen hunched at the kitchen table, talking quietly with Rafe and probably waiting for the coffee to brew. He'd spent the night on the parlor sofa, and had already been up to the spare room to look in on Mr. Cavanagh more than once; Emmeline had heard him passing in the hallway several times.

Despite the fact that he presented a somewhat debauched appearance, Emmeline liked the doctor. She knew he was highly skilled at his profession, and wondered what demons drove him to the occasional and apparently unfortunate excesses in other areas of his life, which she had also heard about from Concepcion.

"Good morning, Emmeline," he said, and smiled. He looked grayish and gaunt, in the first struggling light of day, as if he were caught in the throes of some private and fathomless pain, with no hope of freeing himself.

She nodded. "Good morning, Doctor," she replied, and glanced at Rafe before meeting that too-wise gaze again. "I trust you've been to see our patient this morning. How is he?"

Boylen nodded. "I've seen him. He's hurting pretty bad, but that's to be expected. I gave him a dose of morphine—much as I dared, anyhow. He's got some rough days ahead of him, I'm afraid, but my gut feeling says he'll be all right in time, if he doesn't try to get back in the saddle too soon." He paused, sighed appreciatively when Rafe handed him a cup of the coffee he'd surely put on to brew first thing. He dosed the stuff liberally with sugar and cream, and a dollop of something from a flask drawn from his inside coat pocket, and took a deep draft before going on. "Fact is, Cavanagh ought to be in a hospital. Too bad there isn't one handy."

Emmeline was getting pretty good at making breakfast for her hardworking husband. She brought in the egg basket from the porch—one of the ranch hands gathered them from the hen house each morning—and fetched bread and salt pork from the pantry. While Rafe and the doctor were eating, both of them showing good appetite, despite the events of the day before, she packed her husband a lunch of cold meat sandwiches, fruit preserves, cheese, and, finally, sweet cream sealed in jar. Red, the bunkhouse cook, would feed the rest of the crew, up at the work site.

Angus joined them a few minutes later, fully dressed and noticeably subdued, and Emmeline filled a plate for him, which he accepted gratefully. Apparently, she was the only one who couldn't have forced down a bite of food if it meant her very life. Even Concepcion, when she appeared, ate two pieces of bread, toasted in the oven and well buttered, and she'd been in the thick of the carnage.

"Kade's horse still here?" Dr. Boylen asked presently, chewing. "I'll ride him back to town if you haven't already sent somebody."

Emmeline, standing with her back to the stove, her hands behind her, couldn't hide her misgivings. "You're leaving?" she asked.

Boylen nodded, took a noisy slurp from his coffee mug, swallowed with a gulping sound. Emmeline smiled slightly.

"I've got you and Concepcion here to look after my patient," he explained, as an apparent afterthought. "Two of the best nurses I've ever run across. Cool-headed, both of you."

"But—" Emmeline began.

"All you need to do is watch over him," the doctor went on. "If you see any signs of infection, send somebody to fetch me. Otherwise, just keep him warm and clean, and try to get him to take some broth. He won't have the stomach for much else, not for a while, anyway."

Concepcion gave Emmeline a reassuring smile, along with a slight nod, but said nothing.

"What do we owe you, Doc?" Angus asked, in his booming voice, raising one hip off his chair so he could pry his wallet from a back pocket.

The doctor named a hefty fee, and Angus paid it without equivocation, putting his wallet back and then reaching for the egg platter, intent on a second helping. "You did a mighty fine job, Frank," he said. "I'm beholden to you."

"Not now, you aren't," Frank replied, looking at the payment with open satisfaction before folding the bills and tucking them into his inside coat pocket. "I ought to ply my trade more consistently," he mused, half to himself. "It can be quite lucrative."

Rafe, who had taken the seat at the opposite end of the table from his father, pushed back his chair and stood up. He kissed Emmeline on the forehead, right in front of everybody, and chuckled when her cheeks took fire.

"That was a fine breakfast," he said. He reached for the tin lard pail containing his lunch. "See you around suppertime."

She nodded, and walked him as far as the back door. "You be careful today, Rafe McKettrick," she whispered. "Mr. Cavanagh will testify that it's dangerous work you're doing up there on the mountain." She blushed again, thinking that Mr. Cavanagh could tell Rafe a good deal more than that, if he chose.

Rafe kissed her again, lingeringly, since they were on the back porch, and therefore out of sight of the others, who were still in the kitchen. "It's nice to know there'll be a pretty woman down here, worrying about me," he teased.

Emmeline gave him a little shove, in playful exasperation, just as Angus came out, putting on his hat. He smiled briefly but offered no comment.

"Thought you might stay home today," Rafe said to him, his tone pensive.

"Well, you thought wrong," Angus answered. "Let's get rolling. We're not paying those men to stand around in front of the barn, smoking tobacco and swapping lies. There's a house to be built." Saying that, he winked at Emmeline. "Don't worry," he said. "I'll look out for your bridegroom."

"Thank you," Emmeline said, and hurried back into the kitchen.

Concepcion put wash water on to heat, then gathered the bloody sheets and garments from the day before into a pile on the back porch. She and Phoebe Anne would spend the day washing, so it fell to Emmeline to look after Mr. Cavanagh. After the doctor had examined him one more time before leaving for Indian Rock on Raindance, Kade's horse, she bravely mounted the back stairs, proceeded along the hallway, and rapped at his door.

"Come in," he growled.

Emmeline turned the knob, stepped over the threshold, hoisted her chin up a notch. So far, not one word about the unfortunate incident in Kansas City had passed between them, but she knew it was inevitable. She could have held her peace on the subject forever, but she was not naïve enough to expect the same courtesy from Mr. Cavanagh.

"Good morning," she said, holding out the mug of venison broth she'd heated for his breakfast. "I brought you some soup."

"I don't want any damn soup," he said. He was scowling at the ceiling as he spoke, his features in profile, but Emmeline could tell by the strain in his voice and the pallor of his skin that he was suffering.

She drew a deep breath, released it slowly, and summoned up a smile. "Be that as it may," she said, "you must take as much nourishment as you can. Your—your body needs food to mend properly."

He turned his head to glare at her—maybe it was the word *body*—and his eyes, sunken and shadowed, devoured and then dismissed her, all in the space of a second. "Go away," he said. "I have no need of your singular services. Not at the moment, at least."

Emmeline's face throbbed with indignation; her blood stung like venom in her veins. So, she thought, in miserable fury, he not only recalled their first meeting, he meant to torment her with oblique references to it. Perhaps he would even resort to blackmail.

"I will be glad to go away," she replied tautly, lifting her chin, "as soon as you take some of this soup."

He narrowed his eyes. "What are you doing here?" he demanded, in a low rasp, just when Emmeline felt sure she'd swoon from the tension. She was pretty sure he wasn't asking how she happened to be in his sickroom. He'd probably been as surprised by their encounter in town as she had.

She set the mug on the bedside table, dragged a chair away from the wall, and sat down close to the bed, summarily ignoring his question. "Can you raise your head on your own," she began, "or shall I assist you?"

He kept glowering at her, holding his tongue, stubbornly waiting for an answer to his own. Which, after all, had been put first.

"I'm married to Rafe," she reminded him.

"Ah, yes, Rafe," he said. "Mr. McKettrick's 'firstborn.' " He paused to ruminate for a few moments, then brightened, though his expression was anything but friendly. "Well, *Lola*, my congratulations. You've certainly come up in the world since I saw you last."

It took her a few flustered moments to remember that she'd introduced herself by that name the night they'd met at Becky's boardinghouse. She swallowed painfully, and her face got hot again. Her tongue seemed to be tied in a knot.

Holt actually smiled. In his present state, however, it

was hardly reassuring. Indeed, it was more like the grin of a demon. "Don't tell me you *lied*," he drawled in mocking tones, and if he hadn't already been so badly injured, she probably would have fetched him up alongside the head with the first blunt object she could lay her hands on. "Not *you*."

She fought back a rush of tears, knowing he would interpret them as a bid for sympathy, and never believe any explanation she might offer, no matter how eloquently it was made. "My name is Emmeline," she said.

"I know," he replied. "Becky told me, and Rafe mentions your name in every other sentence." He glared at her. "Give me that damn soup. I think I might be hungry after all."

At any other time, she would have taken serious issue with his tone of voice, let alone his demanding manner, but that morning, she did not have the luxury. She picked up the mug in one hand, and supported Mr. Cavanagh's head with the other, while he took several sips of the broth.

"Enough," he said, choking a little.

She lowered his head to the pillow, then set the mug aside, frowning as he coughed. "Are you all right?"

"As a matter of fact, Mrs. McKettrick, I am not all right," he answered, after a brief and alarming struggle to regain his breath. His tone was scathing. "You see, yesterday, through no fault of my own, a log fell on me, and damn near took off my right leg."

"You needn't swear," Emmeline pointed out stiffly.

He chuckled, but there was no humor in the sound. "Oh, yes, Lola," he said, "I *do* need to swear. It's the only thing, besides a shot of morphine delivered through a horse needle, that gives me any relief at all."

She sighed. "I can see you are set on being difficult," she said.

"A brilliant conclusion, Lola."

"Don't call me that again!" she said, glancing once toward the open door. The last thing she wanted was for someone to overhear his ranting, and start asking questions. Mr. Cavanagh might just be despicable enough to answer them.

"You'll forgive me, but 'Mrs. McKettrick' is just too formal," he said, "after all we've shared, I mean."

"We haven't shared anything," she hissed, getting up to peer into the hallway, which was blessedly empty, and then shut the door. She sat down in the chair again, hard.

He leered a little. "Haven't we?"

"If you say we have, I'll deny it!"

He made another effort at smiling, every bit as unconvincing as the ones before it. "Do you think they'll believe you?" He paused. "Or me?"

"Why should they take your word over mine?" she scoffed, but she was worried, and he obviously knew it.

"Maybe they won't," he allowed, "even though I'm a blood relative. On the other hand—"

Intent on ending their conversation, Emmeline recalled the brief instructions Dr. Boylen had left with her and Concepcion, before heading back to town, and took refuge in the distraction duty offered. All business, she uncovered his leg, peeled back the bandages, and inspected the wound for infection, even though the doctor had surely already done that during his morning visit.

"Emmeline," Mr. Cavanagh said, to get her attention.

"What?" she asked, wincing inwardly at his bruised and inflamed flesh, and the jagged stitches that would leave a map of long, jagged scars from his ankle to his upper thigh.

"I need to use the bedpan," he said forthrightly, "and I'm not about to do that with you here."

"I'll just step out for a while, then," she replied, and nearly tripped over her hem getting to the door.

Mr. Cavanagh's low, gruff chuckle followed her into the hallway, and she stood for a long time, leaning against the closed door and struggling to regain her composure. She had to speak with Becky as soon as possible; her aunt was the only person in the world who would understand, and offer advice.

It was only as she was descending the back stairs that certain of Cavanagh's words hit home. *Even though I'm a blood relative. . . .*

She immediately turned around, against her will, and went straight back upstairs. She rapped at the spare-room door, praying that Mr. Cavanagh had finished answering the call of nature, and stepped over the threshold. He was lying quite still, the pitcher-turned-urinal standing on the floor beside his bed.

When Emmeline closed the door behind her, he smiled, as though he'd been expecting her.

"What do you mean," she demanded, in a frantic whisper, "by 'blood relative'?"

She saw the same mischievous light in his eyes that she'd seen in Jeb's, on several occasions since her arrival in Indian Rock. She waited.

"Suppose I told you that your husband is my half-brother?" he said.

She was sure she'd faint, just slide right down the door into a heap on the floor. "You can't be!"

"I am, though. I'm Angus McKettrick's eldest son. Left behind in Texas, right after I was born." He paused, watching the color drain from her face, his own features void of any emotion at all. "I wouldn't say anything right away if I were you, though," he added. "I believe Angus wants to speak with my half-brothers himself. It seems they don't know about me, either."

Emmeline put a hand to her throat. It was bad enough that she'd been—indiscreet—with this man, worse still that he'd turned up on the Triple M, but the fact that he and Rafe were brothers was downright calamitous. Even if he managed to overlook what she'd done, and decided not to expose her for a harlot, her husband would be reminded of her mistake every time he looked at Holt Cavanagh, and that was bound to poison whatever portion of love and trust fate might allot them.

"Emmeline?"

She straightened, patted her hair with one hand, waited miserably for him to go on. She would need every ounce of dignity she possessed in the days to come, and whatever she could feign, as well. "Yes?" she asked, very crisply.

"I wonder if you'd read to me awhile," he said, surprising her. "I could use something to take my mind off this leg."

She hesitated; then, knowing she couldn't refuse, and not really wanting to, odd as that seemed, she nodded. "I'll find something in Angus's study," she said, groping behind her back for the doorknob.

"Thank you, Lola," Holt said. "I'm obliged."

Sleep soon overtook Holt, or maybe it was the British history text that numbed him senseless. In any case, he was grateful for any respite, however brief and fitful, from the dozens of teeth gnawing at his right leg. All too soon, however, the creatures of his dreams drove him back to the surface again, and he came up gasping.

Emmeline, his reluctant nurse, had slipped away, leaving the book behind.

If he had rested a little, so had the pain, and it came back with breathtaking force. Gasping, he groped for the bottle of distilled opium the doctor had left behind and, not bothering with the spoon, took a great, bitter gulp. He might have been sorely tempted to swallow the rest, had he been anyone other than who he was, and give up the struggle, but he was a hardheaded Texan, half again too cussed to die in bed like some old woman.

He set the vessel down again, with a thump, and lay stiff in the sweat-soaked sheets, waiting, enduring. Finally, the laudanum began to take effect, and he was at least a little more comfortable than he had been before.

He occupied himself by thinking about Emmeline, also known as Lola, and a smile touched his mouth. The temptation to tease her had simply been too great to resist, especially since it had allowed him intermittent moments of forgetfulness—presently, those were at a premium.

A tap sounded at the door, different from Emmeline's, less tentative, and the housekeeper stepped into the room. He remembered seeing her face looming over him a time or two, before the doctor had started cutting on him, and though he'd heard her name, he couldn't grasp it.

She seemed to know that he was searching his memory, for she smiled a little and inclined her head. "I am Concepcion," she said. Bless her soul, she carried a syringe in her right hand, no doubt filled with morphine, left behind by that burnt-out old sawbones, Boylen. "Your father's housekeeper."

So she knew. She and the old man must be close, if he'd confided in her before he had a chance to tell Rafe, Kade, and Jeb about their long-lost big brother. He knew Angus hadn't, since none of them had been in to size him up. They were at a disadvantage in that way, because he'd been taking their measure, separately and as a group, from the beginning.

"Holt," he said, by way of introduction.

"Give me your arm," she replied.

He obeyed gladly, and she stuck him. He felt the morphine and the laudanum doing a merry dance in his bloodstream. After the war, a lot of men had gotten addicted to one or both of those substances, and he could certainly see why—it was the devil's own bliss, far better than whiskey.

She set aside the syringe and threw back the blankets to tug at his bandages. He was glad he'd dosed himself with liquid poppy seeds; the injection hadn't gotten that far yet, for all its frolicking, and it felt as though she were tearing off chunks of his hide.

He drew in a sharp, hissing breath, but that was all he was willing to give up.

"You are a very strong man," she said, without admiration. It was merely a remark, but at least she'd stopped tugging at the bandages.

"Thank you," he replied, "but inside, I'm screaming like the town drunk's third wife."

She smiled again, moved Emmeline's book, and sat down. "We'll wait a few minutes, that will be better."

"I hope you're not telling me, in a roundabout way, that you plan on changing my bandages?"

Concepcion looked rueful, and about as strong willed as old Santa Anna himself. "Doctor's orders," she said. "A new dressing every day. It's very important to keep such wounds clean."

He swore, but under his breath. Concepcion was, after all, a lady. "Have you known my father long?" he asked.

"Yes," she said in a quiet voice. "I came to work in this house when my husband was murdered. The boys were small then, and Mrs. McKettrick was still living."

Holt was glad he hadn't known about Angus's second family when he was young. He'd been a hotheaded kid, in trouble more often than not, and, most likely, he'd have been eaten alive by his own jealousy. As it was, he had trouble warming up to Rafe, Kade, and Jeb.

"I'm sorry about your husband," he said, after some time. A delicious numbness was just beginning to creep through his system.

"So am I," Concepcion replied. "Manuel was a good man." She stood up and started pulling at his bandages again. It hurt like hell—that part hadn't changed—but thanks to the laudanum and the morphine, he didn't give a damn.

She removed the dressings, set them aside, and left the room, returning a few minutes later with a bottle, clean rags, and more bandages, already torn into long strips.

The stuff in the bottle felt like horse liniment on his ravaged flesh, and he damn near bit through his lower lip again, like he'd done up on the mountain, right after the accident.

"Sweet God," he muttered.

She paused to cross herself, but she was smiling a little. "You are very like your father," she said, and she sounded almost fond.

Under other circumstances, he might have taken issue with that statement, scorning any comparison between himself and the man he'd trained himself to despise, but he just plain didn't have the strength at the moment. "How's that?" he ground out.

"You are bone stubborn. For you, that quality is both a blessing and a curse. You will succeed at anything you attempt, because you don't know how to give up, even when it would be best for all concerned. But you will also suffer more than you need to, because you cannot ask another person for help."

Holt waited for her to finish her work. Only when she'd stopped cleaning his wound and started replacing the bandages she'd removed, working carefully around the improvised splints, did he realize that he'd been holding his breath most of that time. He drew in great gulps of air.

"Do you think you could eat something?" she asked, as she went to the window and raised the sash a little way, letting in a soft, clean breeze that swept over him like a blessing.

He'd had nothing since the soup Emmeline had brought, but he didn't feel hungry. "I don't want anything," he said.

Concepcion came back to his bedside. "I didn't ask what you wanted," she said reasonably. "I asked if you could take food. You can't expect to get well if you don't eat."

He sighed. "All right," he said. He definitely wanted to get well, and the sooner the better. Now that he'd had a look at the old man, and found out he didn't have horns and hooves and a pointy tail, he was ready to make some new plans. Maybe he'd hit the trail again.

"I'll bring you some of the pudding Emmeline made for supper," Concepcion said.

And maybe not.


"I want a word with the three of you," Angus said that evening, when the day's work was done and he and Rafe were in the barn, both of them stone weary, putting away their horses for the night. "Find your brothers and be in my study in twenty minutes."

Rafe wanted to see Emmeline, not his brothers, but he knew by the grim set of his father's face that refusal wasn't an option. In point of fact, the old man had been testy and preoccupied all day long, though he'd worked as hard as anybody else in the outfit. "Sure," he said. Jeb was just rolling in, since he was driving the supply wagon, and Kade was probably back from Indian Rock. Generally, when he had time on his hands, Kade liked to hole up someplace with a book. He'd be easy enough to locate.

He left the horse to its feed and his father to his thoughts, whatever they were, and went outside to meet the supply wagon.

"Have Charlie there put up the team and rig," Rafe told Jeb. "Pa's holding some kind of powwow in the study. You've got fifteen minutes."

Jeb simply nodded, turned the wagon and mules over to Charlie, who'd ridden down the mountain with him, and ambled off toward the house.

Passing through the kitchen, Rafe hoped to catch a glimpse of Emmeline, and he was disappointed when there was no sign of her. He mounted the rear stairs and strode along the hall, rapping at Kade's bedroom door.

The reply was an annoyed grunt.

Rafe pushed open the door. Kade was stretched out on his bed and, just as he'd expected, there was a book propped on his chest.

"What?" Kade asked, none too friendly-like, marking his place with one finger.

"Pa's got something on his mind," Rafe answered. "He wants to see us all in the study. Ten minutes."

Kade swore, but he set the book aside, sat up, and reached for his boots. "What's it about this time?"

Rafe shrugged. "Damned if I know," he said. "Whatever it is, it's been chewing on him awhile. Let's just say, this is no time to give him any guff." He paused on the threshold, in the act of turning away. "How's that Texan fella doing, anyhow?"

"Concepcion says he's holding his own," Kade said, standing, making sure his shirttails were tucked in right. "She and Emmeline and Phoebe Anne took turns looking after him all day."

Rafe felt a stab of displeasure at this news, and no amount of cool reasoning would have assuaged it. He didn't know why, but he purely disliked the idea of Emmeline spending time alone with Cavanagh. "You seen her?"

"Emmeline?" Kade asked, as they headed down the hallway to the front staircase. "She was helping hang out laundry when I got back from Indian Rock. Why?"

Rafe didn't answer.

The three brothers converged in the study well before Angus arrived. Jeb stood at the window, with his back to the room, looking out toward the creek and keeping his thoughts to himself, if he had any. Kade took a post beside the fireplace, where a nice blaze was crackling, and Rafe drew up a chair. He realized, with a mild sense of amusement, that they'd always taken those same spots when Angus handed down one of his summonses. They'd marked out their positions as boys.

Angus had changed into a clean shirt and creased trousers before he finally put in his appearance, a full ten minutes past the time he'd decreed that his sons be present.

Rafe, Kade, and Jeb looked at one another, and then at their father.

Angus closed the door carefully and faced his sons with both resolve and reluctance. "I've got something to tell you boys," he said, "and it isn't going to be easy to say. I should have done this long before now."

Rafe felt a tightening in his gut. If Angus was fixing to go back on his word about his being foreman and all, he intended to raise hell about it. He was doing a good job running the ranch, he'd gotten himself a wife, and he was working on siring a child.

Dammit, a deal was a deal.

Angus held up a hand, palm out. He was pretty good at reading Rafe. "Don't go jumping to conclusions," he said. "This isn't about the ranch."

Rafe relaxed for a moment, then waxed fretful again.

"You're not sick or anything, are you, Pa?" Jeb asked, from his place by the window. He was facing their father as he spoke, and his arms were folded.

"No," Angus said. He sat on the edge of his desk, looked long and hard at each of his sons in turn, as if trying to see right through bone and flesh to the very core of the man. "That fella Cavanagh," he began, and stopped to clear his throat. "He—well, he's not exactly a stranger to me. I was married to his mother, a long time ago, down in Texas."

At that point, the room went so silent that Rafe figured he could have heard a feather hit the floor.

Angus folded his arms, still powerful, even at seventy-five, and studied the floor for a good long while. When he looked up, his eyes were full of old sorrows. Rafe, who had always thought he knew everything there was to know about the old man, was taken aback by the suspicion that, in fact, he'd known almost nothing.

"My first wife and I had a son," Angus went on when

he was ready. "She died the day he was born, and I named him Holt, for her side of the family." Simultaneously, Jeb and Kade sat down, Jeb in the chair by the window, Kade on the raised hearth of the fireplace. Nobody said anything, though, so Angus huffed out a despairing sigh and commenced talking again. "The long and short of it is, I left Holt behind, with his aunt and uncle, and later on I signed papers so they could adopt him."

"You're saying," Rafe marveled, grasping the arms of his chair and leaning forward, "that that fella upstairs is our half-brother?" He was certain he must have misunderstood.

Angus took his time answering, looking long and hard at Rafe, then Kade, then Jeb. "Yes," he finally said. "That's what I'm saying."

Jeb looked flushed, and his eyes were hot with anger. "And you're just getting around to telling us about him *now?*"

To his credit, Angus held his youngest son's gaze, though Rafe could tell he wanted to look away. Hell, the old man looked as if he might fold right up. "Yes," he said.

Kade was looking at the floor. "Did Ma know?" he asked.

Angus nodded. "She did," he confirmed. "She wanted me to tell the three of you, right along, but I guess I was ashamed of leaving my own flesh and blood behind for somebody else to raise. Then, when your mother died, well, you were still just boys, and I didn't want any of you thinking I was about to abandon you, the way I did your brother."

"I reckon this changes things," Rafe said. He wasn't sure what he felt concerning Angus's long-standing lie by omission, but one fact troubled him greatly.

He was no longer the firstborn son.

# Chapter

## ❧ 13 ❧

EMMELINE WAS OUT IN BACK of the house, arms raised, taking down the last of the day's laundry, when Rafe found her. She looked like a sprite of some sort, gilded in the light of the failing moon, and she whirled, startled, when he said her name, nearly dropping a ghostly white sheet into the grass at her feet.

She smiled then and caught her breath, and though he knew she was genuinely glad to see him, it was obvious that she was anxious about something, too. Maybe she'd already learned the truth about Holt Cavanagh, but, it seemed unlikely that she'd be bothered about that. To her, it would be an unimportant rustling in the branches of the family tree. To him, it was much more: He felt as if he'd lost his way in a strange country, where he neither knew the customs nor spoke the language. All his life, he'd been Angus McKettrick's eldest son. Now, that had turned out to be a lie, and he wasn't sure *who* the hell he was.

"Rafe," she said. Her chin wobbled a little, and her eyes were soft, and yet it didn't waver or wane, that different *something*. "I'm so glad you're back."

A wound-up placed inside him unbent at her greeting, despite his uneasiness, and he wanted to lose himself in her, or perhaps, find himself there. Trouble was, he wanted almost as badly to ride in to the saloon in town, play some cards, fight a little, and get so drunk he couldn't tell his left hand from his right.

Completely confused, he put out his arms, and she sprang into them, hugging his neck.

He kissed her, but just lightly, mindful that they were in the backyard, with the light of the moon and the kitchen window spilling over them, making them visible to anyone who took the trouble to look.

"It's a little late in the day to be doing wash, isn't it?" he asked, the scent of clean, sun-dried linen rising all around, better than any perfume. His voice came gruffly from his throat, but it was tender, too.

She smiled up at him, but that cautious look lingered in her eyes, and he couldn't help wondering, again, *still*, what it meant. Right then, he didn't know as he could stand any more surprises, good or bad. Maybe that was why he didn't question her.

"Conception and Phoebe Anne did the washing earlier," she said. "There was a lot to do inside, with Mr. Cavanagh feeling so poorly, though, and we both forgot about this last batch of sheets until a few minutes ago."

He helped her unpin the remaining bedclothes and

other items from the line, and together they started for the house. He felt a strange desire to take Emmeline away, far away, right then. Just to hitch up a wagon and head for the home site, on top of the mountain. The two of them would live within the unfinished walls of their house, with the earth for a floor and the starry sky for a roof, keeping to themselves, and it wouldn't matter a whit what went on in the outside world.

Before Rafe could find words to frame what he was thinking, Jeb came slamming out the back door, headed for the barn, his strides long and angry. He was carrying a bedroll and wearing his canvas duster, and he didn't so much as glance in their direction.

Emmeline touched Rafe's arm. "What—?"

Rafe sighed, watching as his brother vanished through the barn doorway. He suspected it would be a while before any of them laid eyes on Jeb again, and even though the kid got under his skin on a regular basis, the thought made him feel sad. Jeb had always had the quickest temper of them all, and his feelings had always been outside his skin. If there was one thing Jeb couldn't abide, it was being lied to, directly or indirectly. Rafe couldn't blame him for that, since he felt the same way.

"Turns out Pa's been keeping a hell of a big secret," he said.

She waited. They'd stopped, the two of them, their arms full of clean laundry, the deep grass rippling around their feet in the evening breeze.

Rafe tilted his head back, searched the sky, and finally

met Emmeline's gaze. "It seems that stranger sleeping up in the spare room isn't a stranger after all," he told her, at some length. "Holt Cavanagh was born Holt McKettrick. He's a half-brother to the rest of us."

Emmeline looked stricken, but not precisely surprised, though Rafe didn't take special notice of that, right then. "That's why Jeb is so angry?"

Rafe nodded.

"You can't let him go," she said. "What if something happens? What if he never comes back?"

He heaved a sigh. "I can't stop him from leaving, Emmeline. The fact is, right this minute, I'd probably ride out myself, if it weren't for you."

"You would? You'd just leave?"

He thrust a hand through his hair. "Sometimes, that's the only way a man can sort things through."

Just then, Jeb led his horse out of the barn. Rafe handed his armload of sheets to Emmeline and strode over to his brother. He put a hand on Jeb's arm, something he would have known better than to do if he hadn't been so distracted by Emmeline's presence, and Jeb whirled around and landed a haymaker right in the middle of Rafe's belly.

The wind was knocked out of him, but he didn't go down.

"What the hell was that for?" he gasped, when he could talk. He sensed Emmeline hovering somewhere close-by, and he didn't like knowing that she'd seen somebody get the better of him like that.

Jeb looked like a wild man. He tossed his hat aside, then the Colt .45 he wore whenever he left the house, then his lightweight jacket. His fists were knotted tight, and his teeth were bared. "That," he growled, "was for twenty years of being 'Little Brother'!"

"Well, I'll be goddammed," Rafe said, stung to fury. An old-fashioned donnybrook would feel good, he decided, and there was no getting around it. "You want to fight? Is that what this is about—Little Brother?"

Jeb lowered his head and rushed at Rafe, catching him in the stomach again, this time dropping him to his knees.

Emmeline fluttered at the blood-red periphery of Rafe's vision, flapping her arms like some demented butterfly. "Stop!" she kept saying. "Stop!"

"Emmeline," Rafe said, never looking away from Jeb, "go in the house and stay there." He got to his feet and went after Jeb, landing a good uppercut in the process. Jeb went wheeling backward, and just when Rafe was about to tan his hide in earnest, Emmeline struck from behind, jumping onto his back and flinging both arms around his neck.

Jeb, bleeding from one corner of his mouth, laughed out loud.

Rafe seethed. He shrugged Emmeline off, took her by the shoulders, and brought her around to face him. "*Go inside* now!" he commanded.

She blinked at him. At least two dozen cowboys had gathered, out of nowhere, to watch the fracas.

"Now!" he bellowed, lowering his brows when she hesitated.

She backed slowly away, her eyes wide. "You cannot talk to me like that, Rafe McKettrick," she sputtered.

"I just did," he pointed out.

The cowboys whooped and applauded.

"Fine!" Emmeline spat. "You and Jeb can just kill each other. See if I care!" She whirled and stomped into the house.

Rafe took a couple of deep breaths, and his ribs felt as though he'd just been kicked by a mule. He hoped they weren't cracked, since the night was still young.

He felt a tap on his shoulder—Jeb—but he had a fist ready when he turned around, and he sent his brother rolling across the barnyard. Jeb came up hard against the horse trough, and was back on his feet in a heartbeat.

They went at each other like two bulls—his little brother, Rafe thought ruefully, had grown up while he wasn't looking, and acquired himself a mean punch—and finally had to call the thing a draw. The two of them were evenly matched.

"Buy you a drink?" Jeb asked, breathing hard and bleeding, as he put an arm around Rafe's shoulders.

"Don't mind if you do," Rafe replied.

The cowboys cheered that, too, the fickle bastards. Then one of them brought Rafe's horse out, saddled and ready to ride. He found it harder than usual to swing up onto Chief's back, but since Jeb was having the same problem with his mount, his pride didn't suffer.

Kade appeared, riding Raindance, as unruffled and smoothly turned out as if he'd just been to church.

"Where the hell were you when the fight was going on?" Jeb wanted to know.

Kade grinned. "Watching," he said. "Rafe, that woman of yours is going to skin you if you go to town. You know that, don't you?"

Red handed up Rafe's hat, and he settled it on his head at a go-to-hell angle. "If I stay," he said, "Emmeline and I are bound to have harsh words. It wouldn't be gentlemanly of me to take a chance."

Jeb laughed. "Last one past the Indian graveyard buys the whiskey," he said.

And the race was on.


Emmeline gathered the discarded sheets from the grass, grabbing them up haphazardly, bunching them in her arms. Her eyes burned with furious tears but she would not cry. By God, *she would not cry.*

When the last of the bed linens had been collected, she marched into the house with them, the laughter of the cowboys, long since silenced, ringing in her ears. She had never in her life been so humiliated as when Rafe had sent her away like a child, then ridden off to town with his brothers.

There was no telling what they'd do when they got there.

She sniffled and raised her chin when she found Concepcion there in the kitchen, waiting for her. She'd already brewed a pot of tea and set out two cups.

Emmeline deposited the sheets, which would probably have to be laundered again, since she'd hurled them onto the ground in her rush to stop the fight between Rafe and Jeb.

"They nearly killed each other," she said, when she trusted herself to speak without losing her dignity completely. "And then they rode into town together!"

Concepcion smiled calmly. "I heard," she said, pouring the tea.

"I'll bet they'll be gone all night," Emmeline fretted.

"Probably," Concepcion agreed.

"There is certain to be more fighting."

Concepcion spoke mildly. "Is that what you're really worried about?"

Emmeline sat down hard on the bench. "No," she admitted.

"I thought not. Don't fret so, Emmeline. Rafe married you, even it was by proxy, and that means something to him. He's building a house for you. He'll come straggling in sometime tomorrow, probably, beat-up, hungover, and otherwise pure as the driven snow."

A sweet, fierce hope rose in Emmeline's heart. "Well," she said, "he needn't think he can get away with treating me the way he did."

Concepcion patted her hand. "Drink your tea," she said sweetly.

\*     \*     \*

Holt sat upright in bed, eating the scrambled eggs Concepcion had made for his breakfast. She stood just inside the door now, while Angus drew up a chair.

"I told them," Angus said. The old man looked gaunt.

Holt didn't trouble himself to hide the bitter satisfaction he felt. "I gathered that," he said, "when I heard that row in the yard last night. Tell me, did the three of them kill each other, leaving me an only child?"

Concepcion let out her breath, muttered something in Spanish.

Holt made no attempt to translate; her tone communicated all he needed to know.

"They took the news moderately well at first," Angus said, with a long sigh. "I should have known all hell would break loose once they had time to think it over."

Truth to tell, Holt wasn't really all that concerned about his half-brothers' hurt feelings, not at the moment, anyway. His leg felt like it had been beaten to a mash with a sledgehammer and then set on fire, and the walls of that bedroom were closing in on him, inch by inch. The one bright spot was sweet little Emmeline. Damned if she wasn't married to the son and heir.

He smiled a private smile. "You'll forgive me, Mr. McKettrick," he said, "if I don't wax sentimental over my brothers' sad plight." After all, Rafe, Kade, and Jeb had enjoyed the luxuries of a fine home, a birthright, and a family.

If they had to do some fancy thinking now, well, so be it.

"There are bound to be some hard feelings," Angus said. He cleared his throat, glanced at Concepcion, probably seeking courage, and went on. "It'll take time for everybody to come to terms with the situation. Still, you're bone of my bone and flesh of my flesh, and there's a place for you, Holt, right here on the Triple M."

Holt had already weighed the meaning of the ranch's name in his mind, having little else to do besides stare at the ceiling and grit his teeth against the pain. He was planning on passing the morning ahead by counting leaves on the oak tree outside his window. "The Triple M," he reflected aloud. "I reckon that's a reference to your three sons." He put just the slightest emphasis on the word *three*.

"Yes," Angus said, leaning forward in his chair. "That's what it means. But a name is just that—a name. Do you mean to stay on when your leg heals up, or not?"

The bottle of laudanum rested on the bedside table. Holt reached for it, yanked out the cork, and drank. He'd asked for morphine a few minutes earlier, and Concepcion had refused, saying he couldn't have another shot for a couple of hours yet. Now, he could see her out of the corner of one eye, looking as though she'd like to snatch the medicine from his hand and put it somewhere out of his reach. He set it back on the bedside table.

"I haven't exactly decided," he replied at last, watching Angus's face.

His father was a tough old geezer, Holt had to give him that much. "That's your choice," he said, rising from his chair. "If you just came here to make trouble, well, rest assured, you've accomplished your purpose."

Holt raised an eyebrow, poked at the remains of his eggs, now cold, with the tines of his fork. "That Chandler fellow," he said carefully. "You manage to buy him out, like you were planning?"

*That* perked the old man right up. "How did you know about that?" he demanded, in a rasp.

Holt smiled. "There was some talk in the bunkhouse."

"*You.*" Angus almost growled the word. "You were the outsider who bought that place out from under me. Chandler wouldn't give me a name."

"Yup," he said. "I might be willing to sell, though."

Angus narrowed his eyes. God, Holt was enjoying this. "How much?" he said, proving what Holt had suspected all along. Angus wanted the Chandler place and wanted it bad. Maybe it was because of the springs that fed the creek flowing past the McKettrick place; why, if a man were to dam that up somehow, and set the water flowing in another direction, the Triple M would be hurting in no time.

The figure Holt named was twice what he'd paid, which was considerable.

Concepcion drew in her breath.

"That's robbery," Angus snapped.

"Water's valuable," Holt said, with a shrug. "Good as gold out here."

"When I get my hands on Buck Chandler," Angus rumbled, "I'm going to squeeze the greedy little sum'bitch out of his hide like a sausage out of its skin. He *knew* I had first claim on that land. We made the agreement months ago."

Holt sighed philosophically. "Folks can be capricious," he allowed. "Especially when there's money involved."

Angus didn't answer. He just closed a fist around the laudanum bottle and set it on top of the dresser, over on the far side of the room. Concepcion stepped aside, without a word, to let the big man pass into the corridor, but then she lingered. Her dark eyes blazed as she looked at Holt.

"What are you trying to do to him?" she demanded, in a fierce whisper.

Holt set the plate of eggs on the table, where the laudanum had been. He wondered if he could hobble over to the chest of drawers without breaking his other leg, and maybe his neck, in the process. He didn't answer her question directly. "Business is business," he said.

She waggled a forefinger at him. "You've set fire to a wasps' nest," she warned, "and you're bound to get stung, Holt McKettrick!"

Holt felt as if one of those theoretical wasps had just stung him on the ass, but of course he didn't admit to it. And he sure didn't have any inclination to explore the fact that he liked hearing himself called by the name he'd been born with, the name he'd coveted in vain for so many years. "I came here because I wanted a look at the man who sired me," he said evenly. "That was the only reason."

"Nonsense," Concepcion replied. "You must have

known he would recognize you. You look exactly as he did, when he was younger."

On the contrary, Holt had known nothing of the kind. He'd been too young, when Angus left, to remember him, and if his aunt had had any tintypes of the man, she'd never shown them to Holt. Maybe, though, on some level, his real aim in coming to the Triple M *had* been to find out if Angus McKettrick would look at him, and see in him some reflection of himself.

"You are angry, and I suppose I can understand that," the woman went on, her voice quieter now, but just as angry, and picking up more and more of a Spanish inflection as the words tumbled faster and faster from her lips. "But as God is my witness, if any harm comes to that good man because of you, I'll see that you rue the day you set foot on this land!"

"Do my half-brothers know you're sleeping with dear old Daddy?" he asked.

She stomped over and slapped him, hard, and with no apparent regard for his injuries. "There are things I will not tolerate," she said evenly, "and talk like that is one of them."

He simply looked at her.

Her voice dropped to a furious whisper. No apology was forthcoming, it seemed. "What do you think will happen when you turn your back on him, and on this place he's spent his life's blood and his sweat to build? When you cause your brothers to turn theirs as well? You will break his heart!"

"Rafe, Kade, and Jeb aren't going anywhere," he said. "They're too smart for that. As for Pa, well, he was able to put me clean out of his mind for better than thirty years. He shouldn't have any trouble doing it again."

She looked at him with a strange combination of compassion and contempt. "You are so sure you understand Angus, and what he did. Well, you have *no idea* what he's gone through, what he's sacrificed, and you're too busy feeling sorry for yourself to think about his side of the story!"

"I can name one thing he's sacrificed," Holt replied. "Me." He yawned. "Is it time for my medicine yet?"

Kade and Rafe watched blearily as Jeb collected his horse from the livery stable in Indian Rock, hauled himself painfully up into the saddle, and reined toward the south, never even raising his hand to wave farewell. He seemed downright ungrateful, after all the drinks they'd bought him last night, on account of his winning the horse race by passing the graveyard before anybody else.

"Think we ought to go after him?" Rafe asked. His head throbbed, and he was nauseated, and his troubles wouldn't even *begin* 'til he got home and had to face Emmeline.

Kade pulled his hat brim down low, probably to shield his eyes from the bright sunlight, and shook his head. "I'd sooner rope a mountain lion, tie some string around his balls, and try to teach him tricks," he said. "That would be easier, and a whole lot less dangerous."

"You know," Rafe observed, studying his brother, "unlike Jeb and me, you came out of this without a scratch or bruise. How'd that happen?"

"I was always the smart one," Kade said, with a slight smirk, and spurred his horse in the direction of home.

Rafe caught up to him. He was beginning to feel fractious again, even though he was painfully sober. "You know, I get the sense that you're up to something, Brother, and that troubles me greatly."

Kade didn't so much as glance at Rafe. His eyes were fixed on the road ahead. "You'd better get that baby started," he warned. "There just might be some other new developments in this contest, besides our brother Holt."

Rafe frowned. "Like what?" he growled, feeling a touch less brotherly than he had moments before.

Kade grinned. "Jeb's not just going off half-cocked, Big Brother," he said. "He's got a plan. Or maybe I should say, *we've* got a plan."

"*What plan?*" Rafe asked.

Kade still didn't spare him a glance, but Rafe would have sworn his brother was humming the wedding march under his breath.

Emmeline, newly in charge of egg gathering, pretended not to see Rafe and Kade riding across the creek toward the house and walked on to the chicken coop, her back straight, her basket swinging in one hand. If that reprehensible man thought he was going to be welcomed back with open arms after the scene he'd made, he was deluded.

Sure enough, she heard his voice outside the coop, even over the squawking of the hens. He was talking to his horse.

Good thing, she reflected loftily. The horse was far more likely to answer him than she was.

She reached under a hen, collected two large brown eggs, and set them carefully in her basket. When she'd first undertaken the task, she'd been afraid of the chickens but now, after just a few days, she approached the roost confidently.

"Emmeline?"

Rafe's shadow fell across the floor of the hen house, and the layers began to cackle and fret. Red feathers filled the air.

Emmeline turned around slowly, saw her husband looming in the small, uneven doorway. He had the nerve to smile at her, too, just as if nothing had happened between them.

She took one of the eggs out of the basket and lobbed it at him, taking great pleasure in the way it splattered on the middle of his chest, and in the shocked expression on his face. A slimy double yolk ran down his front, and she was emboldened, by her good aim, to throw another.

Rafe let out a furious whoop. "*Damn* it, Emmeline," he said.

She hit him in the forehead with the next one.

He wiped his face, took a step toward her. "Why, you little—"

"You stay back, Rafe McKettrick," she warned. She was

out of ammunition, but he didn't have to know that. "I swear I'll let you have it again if you take another step."

For a moment, he looked as though he'd call her bluff. Then, to her great relief, he turned and strode away, covered in raw egg, leaving her alone with a flock of highly disgruntled hens.

"Why, bless your heart," Angus said, in response to Phoebe Anne's shy inquiry that night at supper, "of course there's still going to be a party."

Emmeline, who was still studiously ignoring her errant husband, smiled at Phoebe Anne. "You'll wear the blue dress, won't you? The one Becky and I picked out in town?"

Phoebe Anne shifted a little on the bench next to Kade, looking uncomfortable. "Concepcion was kind enough to lend me the money I need to get back home. I was thinking maybe I ought to leave right away."

"Is that what you want?" Concepcion asked gently. "The party will be a memorable one."

Phoebe Anne lowered her eyes. "I don't know that it would be proper for me to act in a frivolous way, after what happened." She looked around the table, from one face to another. "I don't want to seem ungrateful, but—"

An awkward silence descended.

In the end, Kade was the one to break it. He laid a hand on Phoebe Anne's forearm. "One way or the other," he said quietly, "we'll understand. If you're ready to leave for home, I'll drive you to town and put you on the stage myself."

Emmeline, stealing a glance at Rafe from under her lashes, saw him narrow his eyes as he watched the exchange between Phoebe Anne and his brother.

Tears sprang to Phoebe Anne's eyes. "I don't have much to pack up. I could be ready tomorrow—Pa and Mam are going to need my help on the farm, so the sooner I can get there, the better."

"Fine," Kade said. "Tomorrow it is."

Angus was determined to steer matters onto cheerier ground. Since Holt's injury, and the subsequent revelations, he'd been subdued, so it was nice to know he was looking forward to a social event. "We'll set some men to working on building that dance floor first thing in the morning," he said.

Rafe tried to catch Emmeline's eye, but she dodged his glance.

Kade swung a leg over the bench and stood, carrying his plate and utensils to the sink. "Folks will come from miles around," he said, "if only to find out if the rumors are true: Rafe's married, and Angus McKettrick really has himself another son."

Angus's jaw tightened, and a frightening flush surged up his neck. His jovial mood was gone. "You got anything else to say, Son?" he demanded. "If you do, let's hear it, right now." A vein bulged in his temple. "By God, at least you have the guts to stand your ground. That's more than I can say for Jeb."

Rafe's eyes flashed at this, but he said nothing. Kade, on the other hand, spoke right up. "Jeb always thought every word that came out of your mouth was gospel," he told their father evenly. He stood beside Angus's chair now, leaning down, his voice pitched low. "When he found out different, well, I guess it set him back a ways."

Angus sighed. "You think you have to defend your brother to me? I'm his father, dammit. Nobody on the face of this earth cares more about him than I do!"

"You've got a strange way of showing your devotion, Pa," Kade replied, leaning against the sink, his arms folded. He nodded toward the ceiling. "I reckon Holt would agree."

By then, Angus looked as though he might burst a blood vessel, and it was probably for that reason exactly that Concepcion shot to her feet.

"Enough!" she cried. "That is *enough!* Kade McKettrick, your mother would have had your hide for talking to your father that way, when he's worked every day of his life to make sure there was something to pass on to you and your brothers when the time came!" She stopped to catch her breath, and proud, furious tears gleamed in her eyes. "All of you, you act as if it means nothing to have a family, when it means everything. *Everything!*"

Having said her piece, Concepcion turned and swept out of the kitchen. Emmeline watched her departure with open admiration.

"She's right, you know," she heard herself say. Then she stood, and began clearing the table, getting ready to wash dishes. Supper was over, whether the McKettrick men thought so or not.

Rafe didn't linger while the kitchen chores were done, as he sometimes did, but went upstairs without any comment. Kade glared at his father for a while, and Angus glared back. Then Kade went outside, slamming the back door behind him, and Angus retreated to his study. Poor Phoebe Anne was simply gone, probably hiding out somewhere.

Emmeline was hanging up the dish towel to dry when Concepcion returned to the kitchen, looking slightly more composed than before, but not in the least apologetic.

"You were magnificent!" Emmeline told her, pausing to kiss the other woman's cheek.

"*Madre de Dios*," Concepcion fussed, fanning herself with one hand. "I don't like to lose my temper like that. It's just that these McKettrick men are so exasperating—"

Emmeline laughed. "Yes," she agreed. "They certainly are."

Concepcion prepared Holt's injection. "I'll sit with our patient for a while," she said wearily. "You go upstairs, to your husband. It's time the two of you talked."

Emmeline nodded, resigned. Only hours before, she'd pelted Rafe with eggs, so she wasn't counting on a pleasant reception, but she wouldn't be able to avoid him forever. "Holt has had his supper," she said, as an aside. "I took him a plate before we sat down to eat."

Concepcion started up the stairs. "He's mending, I think."

Emmeline had hoped Holt would get well soon, and leave the Triple M forever, but she'd overheard Angus and Concepcion talking about the Chandler ranch, which Angus had long planned to buy. Evidently, Holt had made a better offer on the place, just before he was hurt, and the land was his, which meant he would be staying.

Emmeline's stomach knotted. When she reached the bedroom, Rafe was already there, seated at the table he used as a desk, a book open in front of him. She stopped in the doorway, taken aback, for she had hoped to have a few minutes to prepare for a private confrontation.

"Come in," he said gravely. Then a smile tilted one corner of his mouth. "Unless, of course, you're planning to start throwing things again."

Emmeline crossed the room to stand behind him, leaning slightly to one side to peer at the title of the volume he'd been reading. *Modern Astronomy*.

He grinned when he saw her eyes widen. "Surprised?"

She shook her head. If the gesture was a bit misleading, well, she had other concerns on her mind. "You spent the night in town," she said.

"So I did," he agreed.

"Do you intend to apologize?"

He chuckled, without humor. "I do not," he said. "Do you?"

She folded her arms. "Of course not," she said.

He frowned, though his eyes were shining. "Well, then, I guess we have ourselves a standoff," he said. He got up from the chair, crossed the room, and closed the bedroom door with a distinct finality.

"I guess we do," Emmeline agreed, glancing toward the bed, then looking quickly away. She'd cried herself to sleep on those very pillows the night before, but if she lived to be a hundred, she would never tell Rafe McKettrick. "Kindly keep to your own side," she said.

He bowed. "Don't worry," he said.

# CHAPTER

## 14

"It was just a little flutter, that's all," Becky told Doc Boylen as he straightened, having bent over her bed to listen to her heart through his stethoscope. She was ensconced in room 8 of her hotel, fully clothed, a spill of summer sunlight washing over her. Through the open window she heard the sounds of a busy community, and they brought her an ordinary but tender comfort. "I'm perfectly all right."

"I don't like what I hear in there," he said, having completed his examination. "Fact is, your time might be running out."

She sighed. "*Everybody's* time is running out," she replied. "You ought to know that better than anyone, Doctor."

He chuckled as if against his will, and his eyes remained grave. He was not an attractive man, and what little she knew of his reputation was entirely unsavory, but Becky liked him anyway. She'd lived in glass houses far too much of her life to go about throwing stones.

"You're right about that," he admitted. "We're all on a slippery flume to the hereafter. I once opened up a feller for an autopsy, after his third wife—I believe Flossie was twenty-two at the time—was accused of poisoning him with prussic acid. He was seventy-nine, and he'd never taken in any poison, far as I could tell, but his ticker was so worn out, it wouldn't have pumped enough blood to keep a chicken alive. He should have kicked the bucket *years* before he did—there was no earthly reason for him to be breathing past the age of thirty."

Becky eyed Doc wryly. "Don't keep me in suspense," she said. "Did the poor young widow go to prison, or live happily ever after?"

He smiled. "She was hitched to the banker's nephew within three months. The scandal turned that town on its ear, but of course they got over it, when somebody else stepped off the straight and narrow and started a whole new round of gossip."

Becky shook her head, having pondered the case and come up with a verdict. "Guilty," she said, with certainty. "She poisoned him, all right. She used something other than prussic acid, that's all. Maybe foxglove."

John Lewis, just entering the room, had evidently overheard enough to pick up the thread of Becky and Doc's conversation, because he grinned as he went around to the other side of the bed. "You've got a real suspicious mind, Rebecca," he said, meeting Doc's gaze. "How is she?"

"I'll thank you, Marshal Lewis, to speak to me directly, if there's something you want to know," Becky said. "I am neither deaf nor dumb, and I'll answer for myself."

Doc pretended not to hear and busied himself putting away his stethoscope, but he was smiling a little.

"Well, then?" John asked, spreading his hands in cheerful concession as he looked down at her. "What's the diagnosis?"

"I'll be fine," she told him. "Just fine." She glanced at the doctor. "What do I owe you, Frank?"

"A steak dinner in that fine dining room of yours," Doc answered, taking up his battered bag. He fixed his gaze on the marshal, taking his measure as if he were a newcomer to Indian Rock instead of a longtime acquaintance. He smiled again. "See that she rests, John," he said. "I mean that."

John nodded, taking Becky's hand and holding it between his own. "I'll make sure of it," he said, and he sounded like he was swearing an oath. "You come on by later, and I'll fry up that steak for you myself."

Doc nodded, then went out, closing the door softly behind him, and John sat down on the edge of Becky's bed, still grasping her hand. "What happened?" he asked quietly. "Clive told me his version, but he was practically hysterical by the time he found me, and I could barely make heads or tails of it."

"It was nothing," Becky said, with a little sigh and a thoughtful sidelong glance at her friend. For all her figuring on the matter, she still hadn't worked out what made

John Lewis tick. She knew he wanted her, in the elemental way that men want women, but he'd never so much as tried to kiss her, even though they'd taken to each other right away, and had spent most of their free time together from the beginning. She wondered, yet again, if he'd found out about her past somehow. "I was standing on a chair, taking down one of those infernal flour-sack curtains, and I had a little dizzy spell. That's all, just a dizzy spell—I didn't even faint. Mandy brought me here—you know, *Sister* Mandy—and Clive went for Doc Boylen."

"Are you telling me the truth, Rebecca?" he asked, with a wry and watchful smile in his eyes. Like Becky, he had his doubts about the young nun she'd taken on as a temporary housemaid—he'd expressed them right off—but he was inclined toward tolerance, at least where women were concerned.

"About this, yes," she said, after a moment's pause.

"But not about everything?"

"Not about everything," she confirmed. Now it would happen. She would tell him about Charles Harding, and Emmeline, and the boardinghouse in Kansas City, and she would lose him as a result. She could trust him not to spread what he learned, she knew that; he wouldn't do anything to hurt Emmeline. He'd be polite about it, tip his hat, and walk away for good.

The regrets Becky would have to live with after that would be bitter ones indeed. She had never dreamed she could care about a man the way she cared about John Lewis, but there it was. She'd been ambushed by fate.

He released her hand, went around to the other side of the bed, and lay down next to her. "If you feel like talking, I'm ready to listen," he said, with a settling-in kind of sigh. "If you don't, well, that's all right, too."

She couldn't help smiling. At the same time, she felt the sting of tears in her eyes, and she was glad they weren't looking at each other. "Who knows? Maybe it will do me good to bare my soul."

"Maybe," he agreed. "I'm listening, Becky."

"I ran a brothel in Kansas City," she heard herself say, and then she was horrified, because the words were right out there, and could not be unsaid. John would simply get up now, walk right out of that room, and never come near her again.

"Did you, now?" he asked. There wasn't a hint of shock in his voice, and Becky turned to stare at him.

"Is that all you've got to say?"

He grinned at her. "Becky," he said, "when folks get to our place in life, they've usually built themselves up a past, if they've done any livin' at all. I didn't figure you'd been spinning straw into gold in some tower all this while, and there was no sign of a husband."

Her eyes burned, and her vision went blurry. Her heartbeat was doing strange things that bore no discernible relation to her medical condition. "John Lewis," she said, "did you *hear* what I said?"

He put his arms around her, snuggled her close against his chest. She loved the scent of his skin, the steady rhythm of his breath, the sound of his strong, honorable heart. "Yes," he said, "I heard you. You ran a brothel in Kansas City. Now, would you like to hear my horrible secret? It's only fair that we swap."

"Not if you're going to say you're married," she said. "I don't want to hear that."

He laughed. "I'm an eligible bachelor," he assured her. "But I did five years in prison, back in Ohio, when I was a lot younger—and a lot stupider—than I am now."

She felt sympathy, rather than alarm or contempt. "What did you do?"

"I took part in a bank robbery," he said. "A man was shot to death."

She lay perfectly still, absorbing this. "Was it you who killed him?"

"No," he said, and she knew he was telling the truth. She'd heard every size, shape, and color of lie, and she could have recognized one anyplace. "I didn't pull the trigger. But I was there, and I was breaking the law all right, so it was partly my fault that that fellow died. I was caught three days later with my share of the money we took—the others got away, as far as I know."

Becky laid a hand on his chest, her fingers splayed. "Oh, John."

"I paid for what I did," he said quietly. "All of that's behind me, for good. Has been for a long, long time. All I care about these days is right now. Right now, and you, Becky."

She started to cry.

"Don't now," he whispered, and kissed her tears away.

"We've both had enough of regrets and sorrow. It's time we were happy, don't you think?"

She settled against him, with a sniffle and a little nod, and began telling him things she'd never told another living soul, but even with John, she knew there were some secrets she must never tell.

Emmeline picked up the bottle of laudanum, poured a dose into a tablespoon, and, holding it out in front of her by at least a foot, approached Holt's bed with a series of short, rapid steps.

He swallowed the stuff, and looked as if he might laugh when she leaped back, but his eyes were full of bad temper. "Thanks," he growled.

"You have no call to be so peevish," Emmeline said, still keeping her distance, her hands resting on her hips, elbows jutting out. "It's not my fault you got yourself pinned under a tree trunk!"

"I have *every* reason!" Holt snarled. "If I don't get out of this bed soon, I'm going to turn loco!"

"Oh, stop your fussing," she told him. She and Concepcion and Phoebe Anne had been running up and down stairs for the better part of ten days, by that time, looking after him, and he never had a polite word for any of them. Certainly he'd never said "please" or "thank you," except in a sarcastic way. "You're behaving like a spoiled child."

"Well, thank you for that, Mrs. McKettrick," he snarled. "Tell me, where is the sweet-tempered Phoebe Anne? I believe I prefer her to you."

"She's gone to Iowa," Emmeline said with snappish dignity. She missed the other woman's company, and any mention of her friend put her in mind of the sad visit the two of them had made to the homestead site, just the day before, so that Phoebe Anne could say her goodbyes at the gravesides of her husband and child. "This is a hard land, Emmeline," she'd said. "It just takes and takes until a body has nothing left to give, and then it takes some more."

Emmeline shivered a little. Would she end up the same way as Phoebe Anne?

Holt assessed her, seeing, she thought, much more than she wanted him to see. "Somebody just step on your grave?" he asked, very quietly. There was a look of speculation in his eyes. "Maybe you wish you'd gone with her, or, better yet, never come to Arizona Territory at all. Don't you like it here on the Triple M, sweet Emmeline?"

She closed her eyes. She was, in fact, quite unhappy. She and Rafe had been tiptoeing around each other ever since the night he'd gone to town with Jeb and Kade and not come back until the next day. They slept in the same bed, and spoke politely when there was a need for it, but there was no tenderness between them, and certainly no passion.

"I like it fine," she said.

"Liar," he replied easily.

She considered pouring the contents of his water carafe over his head, but that would only mean more work for her and Concepcion, in the end, so she refrained. "What do you want from me?" she asked, in a desperate whisper.

"Dangerous question," he said.

She reddened. "If you mean to tell Rafe about us," she asked hoarsely, "then why don't you just go ahead and do it?"

"Ah," he said, "but that's my trump card. What would I do for entertainment, once I'd played it?" He paused, sighed.

Just then, the door swung open, fairly stopping Emmeline's heart in midbeat, and Rafe strolled in. His expression was so fierce that, for one terrible moment, she thought he'd found out, somehow, about her and Holt.

Rafe went to stand at the foot of the bed, his arms folded. "Pa tells me you bought the Chandler place," he said.

Emmeline laid a hand to her chest and tried to breathe. She stared at Holt, a plea in her eyes. He merely smiled a little and shifted his gaze to Rafe.

"That's right," Holt told Rafe. "I'd sell it for the right price, though. You interested?"

"Just what the hell are you trying to do? " Rafe countered. "Put us out of business? Start a range war?"

Emmeline's blood ran cold at the mere mention of a range war; she'd read about such conflicts in the newspapers back home, and, by all accounts, they were brutal affairs, serving no one in the end.

Holt was the absolute vision of innocence. "Now why would I want to do that?" he asked, spreading his hands.

"Pure spite, maybe," Rafe said.

"My buying the Chandler place could put you out of

business?" he reflected, sounding intrigued. "I hadn't thought of it that way."

"Hell no," Rafe growled, albeit a bit too late.

"But you just said—"

Rafe shoved a hand through his hair. "Look," he said, "you leave the springs alone, and keep your cattle off our grass, and there doesn't have to be any trouble."

"I thought you believed in open range," Holt said. "Isn't that why you burned the Pelton cabin and took back the land?"

"It wasn't like that," Rafe snapped.

"Wasn't it?" Holt asked.

Rafe gripped the foot rail of the bed so tightly that his knuckles turned white. "When did you say you'd be well enough to move on?"

Emmeline stood in the side yard watching, the morning breeze ruffling her hair, as Kade and some of the other men laid out the planks for the dance floor. The day of the party, the Fourth of July, was almost upon them.

Kade smiled and approached her, dusting his hands together. "What do you think, Mrs. McKettrick?" he asked good-naturedly. "Will that do for reels and waltzes?"

Emmeline returned his smile, though she felt like something of a fraud. The party was being held to celebrate her union to Rafe, even as the marriage was beginning to fall apart.

She turned her thoughts in a more optimistic direction. She liked Kade; he had a quick mind and a gracious manner, like the gentlemen she'd sometimes seen coming and going by the side door at Becky's boardinghouse, back in Kansas City. She'd have bet, though, that Kade McKettrick never used any door save the front one, anywhere he went. "It will do very well," she said.

"You're going to get your feet run off, you know," he said. A twinkle lit his eyes as he took off his hat. "There're men around here who've never danced with a real lady in their lives. Pa sent Denver Jack and another fella to town to put up notices saying everybody's invited, so half the territory's likely to show up."

Emmeline laughed, enjoying the fresh air and the light conversation. Angus had fashioned a crutch for Holt, and he was learning to get around on his own, for the most part, so she and Concepcion were not required to spend so much time cooped up in the house. As always, though, the thought of her eldest brother-in-law took some of the starch out of her, and her delight turned hollow all of the sudden.

Kade, watching her closely, tilted his head to one side. He was entirely too perceptive at times—maybe it was all that poetry he read. "What is it, Emmeline?" he asked. "What's troubling you?"

She tossed her head, as if to shake off the feeling of dread that was always nipping at her heels, sometimes vague, sometimes so real that she could barely catch her breath for the fear it roused in her. "Nothing," she said. "Really."

Kade sighed, still watching her. "Emmeline," he said

quietly, "there was and is a kind of contest going on between my brothers and me—I suppose you know that already. It's got to do with taking a wife and being the first
to present Pa with a grandchild, and the stakes are pretty
high. Rafe figures he has it won, but Jeb and I are a long
way from giving up." He paused, sighed. "Who knows
how Holt is going to figure in to all this. All that aside,
though, I want you to know that you're as good as a sister
to me now, and you can count on me for help if you ever
need it."

Emmeline looked away, blinked a couple of times, then
looked back. "Thank you, Kade," she said. "I'll remember
that."

"Good," he answered. He glanced back at the crew of
men, busily constructing the framework that would serve
to support the dance floor. Poles were being erected, too,
and wire was to be strung between them, to hang colorful
Chinese lanterns special-ordered from San Francisco. "I
guess I'd better get back to work," he said, putting on his
hat again.

She stopped him from turning to walk away with a shy,
"Kade?"

"Yes, ma'am?" he replied.

"Has there been any word about Jeb? Do you think he's
all right?"

Kade sighed, resettled his hat. "I've heard a few things,"
he admitted. "There's a rumor that he went to Mexico, to
mine for gold. Somebody else claims they saw him just
south of the Triple M, mending fences for a widow

woman, and there's still another yarn making the rounds, too. The storekeeper's wife, Minnie, swears he told her himself that he was headed for Seattle, meaning to board a ship bound for the Orient."

Emmeline was alarmed; Angus hadn't said much about Jeb's absence, but she knew he watched and listened for his return, day and night. If Jeb had indeed gone to Mexico, or secured passage to the Far East, he and his father might never see each other again. "What do *you* think?" she asked.

"I'd bet on the widow woman," Kade said without inflection. Then he tugged at the brim of his hat, turned, and walked away.

Emmeline watched the workmen for a while, then went back into the house. Concepcion had promised to teach her to bake bread, and she hoped to surprise Rafe with her first batch when he came down from the mountain that evening. It might serve as a sort of olive branch.

She was kneading busily, with Concepcion looking on in a supervisory capacity, when Holt came slowly down the back stairs, fully dressed, with one leg of his trousers slit to accommodate his splints and bandages, his crutch thumping the floor.

"I need a bath," he announced cheerfully. Getting around *had* improved his disposition, though Emmeline still preferred to avoid him as much as possible. It was safer that way, and there were whole stretches of time when she could pretend he didn't exist.

Now, involuntarily, she blushed, for a bath was a very intimate ritual, not usually mentioned in mixed company. If her hands hadn't been covered with bread dough, she might have pressed one to her mouth.

"You certainly do," Concepcion confirmed with laughter in her eyes, and something else, too—affection, Emmeline decided. "When Angus and Rafe get back, and supper's over, they can help you. You don't want to get that leg wet."

"Good," Holt said, and there was a glint of mischief in his eyes as he watched Emmeline trying to will away the color that was still pulsing in her cheeks. He lingered for a moment, deliberately making her uncomfortable, she was sure, and then headed for the back door.

Neither Concepcion nor Emmeline attempted to call him back, or to follow. Concepcion fetched some potatoes from the bin in the pantry and began paring them at the sink, to boil up for supper, while Emmeline pummeled the bread dough with new vigor. When something caused her to glance in Concepcion's direction, she caught the other woman smiling.

Emmeline started to ask what was so amusing, thought better of the idea, and held her tongue.

Presently, Holt came back from his wanderings, and it was plain that he'd been up from his bed too long. His flesh had taken on a gray hue, and the light in his eyes had dimmed measurably.

Concepcion hurried to take his arm, and Emmeline automatically went to his other side, ready to help support him.

"Sit down," Concepcion urged, steering Holt toward Angus's chair at the table.

"I guess I overdid it a little," he said, barely able to get the words out because his jaws were so tightly clenched, as he eased into the chair. Emmeline knew he'd made a major concession, for a McKettrick man, just by confessing to a human weakness.

She went to the pump, filled a china pitcher with water, and set it on the table, near his elbow, with a glass. He poured some, and drank it down in a few mouthfuls.

"Thank you," he said, at last.

Emmeline nodded. It was the first time he'd ever said those words, and he sounded as if he actually meant them.

"I will get your brother," Concepcion told him. "Kade and I will help you back up the stairs to your bed."

He sighed. "I'd like to sit here for a while," he said, "if it's all the same to you. It's mighty lonesome up there, all by myself."

Concepcion considered the matter for a moment, then nodded. "We will move your bed to the parlor," she decided, in her businesslike way. "Then you will not be isolated, and you will not have to manage the stairs. Yes. I should have thought of this before."

Within the hour, Kade and several members of the dance-floor crew had been summoned to dismantle the spare-room bed and reassemble it in the parlor, next to a window. The bathtub was brought into that same room, and Emmeline and Concepcion started the lengthy process of heating water while they continued with their supper preparations.

Emmeline was greatly relieved when Holt declared himself in need of a rest and went to lie down. It was as if she'd been wearing a tight corset and finally gotten the chance to loosen the stays.

Her bread had risen beautifully, and was ready to go into the oven, when Rafe returned, at the reins of the supply wagon, his work on the mountain finished for the day.

"I'll make sure the bread doesn't burn," Concepcion said, seeing Emmeline's eager smile. "Go and welcome your husband home."

Emmeline untied her apronstrings, checked her hair in the mirror beside the door, brushed a splotch of flour from her cheek, and dashed outside. It was not yet five o'clock, early for Rafe, and the sun was still fiercely bright on the western horizon, as though, for once, it would refuse to set, and the moon would have to share the sky.

Rafe's McKettrick-blue eyes shone as she approached him. His dark, longish hair was attractively rumpled when he took off his hat. Her impulse was to fling herself into his arms, but she remembered the other men, and the chasm between the two of them, just in time, and came to a stop a few feet short of where he stood, ducking her head. When she looked up, she thought she saw disappointment in his face.

"Hello, Emmeline," he said quietly.

She searched her thoughts for something to say. "Hello, Rafe," she replied when nothing better came to her.

He smiled, pulled off his gloves, and touched her nose with one index finger. "Flour," he said. "You been baking something?"

She nodded, relieved that he'd gotten the conversation rolling. Who would have thought, she wondered, that a woman could do the most wanton things with a man and turn shy as a schoolgirl when facing him in the broad light of day? "Bread," she said. "For supper." She was desperate to keep the exchange going—she missed their old intimacy so much—knowing that he would turn away at any moment and head off to the barn to help put away the team and wagon. "Holt is sleeping in the parlor now," she told him. "Kade and some of the others moved his bed downstairs, so he could get around more easily."

He was silent for a few moments, his jawline tight. As he watched her, his face relaxed, and it seemed to her that he wasn't thinking about his brother, or even about the bread she'd baked for his supper, but of things that had the power to make her blush whenever she was reminded of them. "I thought you might like to ride up with us to-morrow and have another look at the house. We've made a lot of progress on the place."

Sure enough, their picnic came to mind, and she felt her cheeks heat up. "I'd like that," she said.

"We won't be alone this time," he said, his eyes smiling at her. It sure seemed, sometimes, that he could read her mind. "But I reckon we'll get plenty of other chances." He caught her chin gently between his thumb and forefinger, and his sensual mouth curved, as though he might laugh at the high color throbbing in her face. "Tonight, for instance?"

"Rafe McKettrick!" she whispered, trying to sound stern, and failing miserably.

He chuckled, then leaned down and kissed her, right in front of God and everybody. "Tonight," he repeated, and then he turned and walked away, toward the barn, pausing to talk with Kade and admire the raw boards of the dance floor.

After supper, with Angus and Rafe's help, Holt got his bath.

It was a marvel, Concepcion confided to Emmeline, that they didn't drown him.

"Wake up!" Rafe whispered the next morning, shaking Emmeline's shoulder lightly. "It's almost dawn. You're going up to the new house with me, remember?"

They'd been awake late the night before, making love, and Emmeline still felt as though all her bones had melted, like so much warm wax. She yawned, stretched. "Can't I sleep just a little longer? Please?" She raised her head, looked at the window, and plopped her face into her pillow. "It's still dark outside."

He laughed, turned her over easily, and bent his head to nip lightly at her breast through the thin fabric of the nightgown she hadn't even bothered to put on until a few hours before. "Sure," he said. "You can have ten minutes, the time it takes me to get the fire going downstairs and the coffee brewing. If you're not up by the time I get back, well, let's just say we'll both be late getting up to the mountain."

She stretched again, deliberately taunting him, but the truth was, if they made love again, she wouldn't have the strength to get up and get dressed, let alone make the long drive up the mountain.

He kissed her, a long, thorough, hungry kiss, promising a great deal, and then hoisted himself to his feet, with a groan. He stumbled around the room a little, pulling on his boots, and made her laugh. He pretended indignation, pulling his suspender straps out from his chest with curved thumbs and letting them snap back, then left the room.

He was gone longer than the stated ten minutes, though not by much, according to the small clock on the bureau, and when he returned, Emmeline had washed, dressed, and brushed and plaited her hair. She was winding it into a neat coronet at the back of her head when Rafe burst through the door, leering like the villain in a blood-and-thunder melodrama. He expressed comical disappointment at finding her up and around. "I was hoping you were still in bed," he confessed, without shame. "I've missed holding you, Emmeline. Missed touching you."

She slanted a shy look at him but made no comment. Instead, she began making up the bed, and he took the other side, helping to smooth the covers. In those moments, with laughter between them, sharing a mundane task, she was purely, exquisitely happy. As happy, in fact, as she was when he'd taken her into his embrace the night before, in that same bed, and driven her quite mad with a few nips, nibbles, and caresses.

She blushed, yet again, just to think of the effect his attentions had on her, and the way she'd carried on, and he laughed. That time, he was definitely reading her mind.

"It amazes me," he confided, plumping his pillow and putting it in place next to the headboard, "that you can be so bashful in the daylight, and such a little temptress at night." His mouth quirked up at one side, in a mischievous grin. "You're a paradox, Mrs. McKettrick," he drawled. "Don't ever change."

She swatted at him with her pillow, laughing, and he reached across, caught her by the wrist, and threw her down onto her back, making the mattress bounce beneath her. He'd just put one knee on the side of the bed, as if to throw himself on her, when someone cleared his throat a few yards away. Emmeline, realizing that the door was open, shot to her feet, straightening her skirts and staring fixedly at the floor, as mortified as she'd ever been in her life.

"Good morning," Angus said, his deep voice brimming with amusement.

Rafe turned, grinning. "Morning," he said, with a telling degree of exuberance.

Emmeline wished the floorboards would open up so she could fall between them. Raising her eyes to meet her father-in-law's gaze was one of the most difficult things she had ever attempted. She managed a slight nod.

"Concepcion sent me to tell you she's got breakfast started," Angus said. Although he was not smiling with his mouth, his blue eyes were bright with merriment. "She's busy packing a basket so you won't have to eat Red's cooking up there in camp."

"Thank you," Emmeline said.

With that, Angus turned and walked away. Emmeline heard him chuckling to himself as he made his way down the hall.

She waggled her index finger at Rafe. "Next time," she whispered, "close the door!"

He laughed. "Yes, ma'am," he said.

Half an hour later, filled with Concepcion's hearty oatmeal laced with molasses, with a jug of coffee to share on the ride and a lunch tucked away in the back of the wagon, Emmeline and Rafe crossed the creek, its waters shining pink and gold as the sun rose, following a dozen mounted men headed toward the mountain.

The trip was long, and the wagon seat was hard, but Emmeline was glad she'd agreed to come along. She did not know if she loved Rafe McKettrick, the man, but she loved being with him, and she loved the breathtaking scenery surrounding them on all sides. She loved the quick little jackrabbits, watching them pass, loved the sky, breaking open like a jewel as the sun finally mounted the eastern horizon, shining in earnest.

Her first sight of the new house, more than an hour later, its log walls nearly tall enough for the roof to be set upon its beams, literally took her breath away. It was a long, one-story structure, and all the windows and doors had been framed. Through the doorway, in fact, she could see the skeletons of the interior walls, and the stone fireplace at one end was already taking shape, made of colorful rocks hauled up from the creek bed down by the main house.

"Oh, Rafe," she said, purely enthralled. At last, at last, she would have a real home of her own. "*Rafe.*"

He beamed at her, setting the brake, securing the reins, jumping down, reaching up to take her by the waist when she slid to his side of the wagon seat. He lifted her down, setting her gently on her feet, as if she were made of fragile, precious stuff. "What do you think?" he asked, his voice hoarse, and pitched so she and she alone could hear.

"It's a mansion," she said. "A palace!" Then she put her arms around his neck, devil take the watching crew of men, stood on her tiptoes, and kissed him soundly, right on the mouth. The onlookers cheered, as they had once before, but this time she paid them no mind, didn't even blush, or look away from Rafe's face. "Let's move in right now, today. We don't need floors, or a roof, or windows."

He laughed and, taking her hand, led her toward the front door. "That is a tempting suggestion," he allowed. "Come on, Mrs. McKettrick—I'll give you a tour."

They walked slowly through the rooms, Emmeline imagining how each one would look when it was finished, and there was furniture, and rugs on the floor, and pictures on the walls. Here, in the kitchen, she would teach her daughters to bake bread. There, by the fireplace, she would trim her sons' hair, and sweep the clippings into the hearth.

They stepped into the room that would be their own, and Emmeline spotted a bunch of bluebells and buttercups growing where they meant to set up the bed. Rafe followed her gaze, and bent to pick the flowers for her, offering them as hopefully as if he were a lad, barely out of school, come a-courting for the first time. She accepted the fragile blossoms with something akin to reverence, and was careful to wrap them in a moist table napkin so they wouldn't wither.

That night, when they returned to the main house, the long day behind them, the joyous night still ahead, she pressed them between the pages of a huge tome, borrowed from Angus's library. When they were properly dried, she would put them in the album Rafe had given her, the one that said OUR FAMILY on the front, and keep them forever and ever.

# Chapter

## 15

On Independence Day, the official start of the party, which was expected to last three days and nights, wagons and buggies began arriving just after noon, burgeoning with excited passengers. Men came riding mules, as well as horses, and many made the trek on foot. Angus personally greeted everyone, including those Concepcion pointed out to Emmeline as his biggest rivals, when it came to ranching and grandfathering, with an exuberant handshake and a resonant, "Welcome!" Even Mr. Chandler, who had fallen into disfavor by selling his sizable ranch to Holt when he'd promised it to Angus, was received cordially.

The two women, looking on from the spare room, which was now equipped with several hastily constructed cots to accommodate the more delicate guests, smiled at Angus's obvious delight in the occasion.

"He is so proud," Concepcion said, with affection.

Folks had already begun erecting tents in the field east of the house, while others clearly planned to sleep in or underneath their rigs. This gathering was undeniably the biggest social event of the year for many miles around. Horses and mules were unhitched and unsaddled, then turned out to pasture in the high grass down by the creek. Women in calico and Sunday bonnets greeted one another with laughter and embraces, and children ran in the tall grass, stretching their legs after the long ride.

"It looks almost like a gypsy camp," Emmeline remarked, filled with excitement. She imagined dancers in colorful skirts, cavorting wildly around the campfire in the night, and old women with warts, telling fortunes from cards so timeworn that the images barely showed.

Concepcion smiled. "Yes," she said. "See that family over there, with the Conestoga wagon and the flock of red-haired children? They're the O'Learys—their homestead is closer to Tucson than Indian Rock, so they've probably been on the road for several days."

"My goodness," Emmeline said, impressed. She marveled at the distance the O'Learys had traveled, in a wagon drawn by oxen; she had journeyed many more miles, it was true, coming out from Kansas City, but she'd had only herself to look after, not a whole family, and trains and stagecoaches, as uncomfortable as they could be, made considerably better time than a dilapidated old Conestoga.

"They'll have persuaded a neighbor to tend their stock while they're gone," Concepcion said, her gaze fond as she watched the O'Learys greeting Angus and some of the other guests. "It isn't often that there's a party like this. Folks won't want to miss a minute of it, no matter how far they have to come to get here."

"It will be wonderful," Emmeline said, with confidence. She and Concepcion and even Red, from the bunkhouse, had been cooking and setting food by in the pantry and out in the springhouse for days. There was a whole beef roasting underground, in a special pit lined with stone, raising a luscious aroma, and the carcasses of two pigs, bought from a farmer on the other side of Indian Rock, were hanging in the storage shed, to be cooked when the beef ran out.

The dance floor had been sanded, and the Chinese lanterns, which Emmeline and Concepcion had hung themselves, swayed red and blue and orange and green in the sultry breeze of that summer afternoon. The cowboy band, recruited from the bunkhouse and calling themselves the Triple M Three, had been practicing their limited but lively repertoire every night for a week. Emmeline and Rafe had danced together in the moon-washed grass just outside the back door whenever there was music, practicing for the night of the party, the anticipation building with every moment that passed.

Now, at long last, the waiting was over.

When Becky arrived, in a wagon driven by Marshal John Lewis, with Clive and an older woman, who was probably his mother, and, of all things, a nun, all perched in the back, Emmeline could contain herself no longer. She jumped to her feet and ran out of the spare room, fairly leaping down the steps. Such was her haste that she reached Becky's side of the wagon before the other woman could even alight.

Emmeline's heart climbed into her throat when she got a close look at Becky; she'd lost weight since she'd seen her last, and there were dark circles under her eyes. Her smile, however, was as brave and as confident, even impudent, as ever. When the marshal had helped her down from the wagon, she opened her arms to Emmeline.

Emmeline embraced Becky, squeezing hard, but taking care not to crush her, too. She looked as though her very bones would crumble if Emmeline held her too tightly. "I'm so glad to see you," she said.

Becky kissed her cheek. "You are a sight for sore and weary eyes, Emmeline," she said. Then she began making introductions, while the lawman stood quietly at her side, and the other passengers assembled behind her. "My niece, Mrs. Emmeline McKettrick," she said grandly, smiling at Emmeline. "You know Marshal Lewis, I believe," she went on. "And Clive, too. This is his mother, Mrs. Hallowell, and here—" she paused, gripped the nun's sleeve, and pulled her gently to the fore, "here is Sister Mandy."

Sister Mandy? Emmeline set the name aside to puzzle over later, and concentrated on shaking each person's hand, even Clive's clammy one, and welcoming them all, in turn, as she had seen Angus doing from the upstairs window. Mrs. Hallowell, mother of the redoubtable Clive, was a likable soul, small as a child, with lively brown eyes and a sweet smile. The nun was so covered up in black serge that only her face was visible. She had beautiful blue-green eyes, the lashes long and dark, high cheekbones, a bow-shaped mouth, and clear skin. Her hair was completely covered by the wimple, and might have been any color. She smiled slightly at Emmeline and murmured, "Hello," but would not meet her gaze.

Emmeline glanced at Becky, in silent inquiry, but Becky merely raised her eyebrows as if to say, Don't ask me.

"Let's get you three ladies settled in the spare room," Emmeline said brightly, taking Becky's arm. "Marshal, I'm sure you and Clive will want to say hello to Angus. He's over there, by the barbecue pit."

Mr. Lewis smiled and tipped his hat, and when his glance lit on Becky, it was solicitous as well as respectful. "We'll go over and present ourselves properlike right now," he said. "Come on, Clive."

He and Becky looked at each other for a long moment, then the marshal strode away, with Clive following rather reluctantly behind him.

"My Clive is kind of retiring, when it comes to being around a lot of folks," Mrs. Hallowell said, reaching into the wagon for a small, battered carpetbag. "I wish he'd find himself a wife—that might help him get over being so shy."

"He'll be just fine," Becky said kindly.

By then, she and Emmeline had linked arms. Emmeline was eager to ask Becky about the state of her health, but she knew she would get a smart set-down if she brought up the subject in front of other people.

Becky sat down in the kitchen to take tea with Concepcion, who greeted her warmly. Mrs. Hallowell joined them, while Emmeline and Sister Mandy trooped up the rear stairs with the bags.

"Aren't you roasting to death in that habit?" Emmeline asked forthrightly, when she and the young nun had reached the spare room. The cots, with their rope springs and straw-stuffed mattresses, had been made up with crisp sheets, plump pillows, and blankets. "I could lend you a calico dress."

The girl tried to smile, and almost made it. There was something so forlorn about her—she was barely more than a child, for one thing—that Emmeline found herself wanting to take her under her wing. She had no doubt that Becky felt a similar sympathy, which was why "Sister Mandy" was a part of her entourage. "I'm supposed to wear this," she said, indicating the habit with a graceful motion of her hands. "I reckon God expects that."

Emmeline frowned, finding the remark odd, to say the least. She didn't want to commit a mortal sin by persuading a nun to break some sacred rule, but neither could she see the harm in the young woman setting aside those grim and heavy garments for just one night. "Perhaps God would understand," she replied quietly, "if you dressed modestly, and honored your vows."

Sister Mandy lowered her eyes, shook her head. "No," she said. "But thanks."

Emmeline suppressed a sigh. "Well, then, now that you

know where you're to sleep, let's go downstairs and have some tea."

Mandy hesitated, then set her small bundle of possessions on one of the beds, the one farthest from the window and wedged into a corner. "All right," she said, and followed meekly when Emmeline led the way.

The night sky gleamed, studded with stars, and the great bonfire, built well away from any structures or trees, blazed gloriously. People milled everywhere, enjoying roasted beef, baked potatoes, and beans cooked up with molasses and brown sugar, in great crockery pots, all of it served up on plates they'd brought themselves, in wagons and buggies, saddlebags and reticules. The cowboy band was tuning up, having just finished several helpings of supper. Emmeline, standing at the study window in her new green party dress, her hair upswept, an extra pair of Becky's earbobs brushing her cheeks, looked out on the scene in wonder.

"You look very nice," a voice said from behind her. She stiffened, because she knew that voice, and because it wasn't Rafe's.

She turned, very slowly, to face Holt. He was still using a crutch, of course, but with some help from Kade and Rafe, he'd gotten himself spruced up for the celebration, and he looked handsome in his suit, one pant leg altered to cover his splints without binding, a string tie at his throat.

"Thank you," she said politely but without warmth.

"I hope you'll save me a dance," he replied. His face

was in shadow, the study being lit by just one lamp, and she couldn't make out his expression. He spoke quietly, and his tone revealed nothing.

She simply nodded, for there was no graceful way she could refuse, and it would not have been kind to point out that dancing would be awkward, if not impossible, for him.

He offered her his arm, and she took it, and so it was that Mrs. Rafe McKettrick was escorted to her husband, already at the bonfire, talking with neighboring ranchers, by the very man with whom she had compromised herself.

She was barely able to meet Rafe's eyes when they reached him.

He grinned at her. "You are something to behold, Emmeline," he said, taking her hand, nodding coolly to Holt, who stood a little distance away now, looking on in silence. She could feel him watching her and Rafe, and she wondered when, or if, he would betray her. To lose Rafe, and her place in this community, would be devastating, and to look at the other McKettricks, or Concepcion, and see censure in their eyes would be nearly as bad.

She curtseyed slightly. "Thank you, Rafe," she said very softly.

The music had begun, and Rafe led his bride toward the dance floor, into the spill of colored light from the Chinese lanterns, and they swept around and around in each other's arms, with the dance floor all to themselves.

The guests clapped and cheered when the waltz ended, and Rafe gave his wife a brief, tender kiss.

She wanted to take his hand then, as he had taken hers, to lead him away, somewhere quiet, and tell him everything, reveal every secret, regardless of the consequences. He would probably scorn her, once he knew that she'd spent the night with a man, his own brother no less, in return for a stack of coins, but there was also a chance, remote though it was, that he might understand, and find it within himself to overlook her mistake. After all, for all their strife, they had found much happiness together, she and Rafe. They had plans, and a beautiful house nearly finished. When they made love, they knew a wild, strange, soaring joy, far too intense to be ordinary. Perhaps he would not be so quick to throw all of that away.

Alas, she could not bring herself to speak of the matter on that night of nights, with all the music, the laughter, and the dancing to serve as a backdrop for what she had to say. She decided to wait until they could be truly alone, which probably wouldn't be for several days yet. In the meantime, she would enjoy the gathering to the utmost, knowing that it might well mark the high point of her life, with everything going downhill after that.

She danced. Oh, how she danced.

With Rafe first, of course, but then with Angus, and then Kade, and then, calling upon all her inner resources, with Holt, who moved with surprising grace, if not speed or agility, holding her loosely in one arm and keeping time with the music. She thought she saw bewilderment in his eyes, once or twice, but she dared not look too closely, nor would she risk asking.

For all intents and purposes, this man was her mortal enemy. If indeed he intended to blackmail her in some way, well, he'd soon find his plans thwarted. Neither he nor anyone else would ever be able to hold the past over her head again, once she'd told Rafe the whole truth.

After Holt, Emmeline danced with Rafe again, and that calmed her nerves. Her smile, shaky while she was in Holt's arms, came naturally in Rafe's.

He took her aside for a glass of sweet punch, and she enjoyed a few minutes of badly needed rest.

"Are you enjoying the party, Emmeline?" he asked, as they sat together on a bale of hay covered with a horse blanket. He sounded as though her answer truly mattered to him.

She was flushed, and little breathless, and the stars overhead were so bright, she was sure she could reach up and snatch one for a keepsake and tuck it into her evening bag. "Yes," she said. "What about you?"

Out on the dance floor, the Milldown sisters, newcomers to the community, were dancing happily with one man after another. They might have been considered plain, wherever they came from, but in and around Indian Rock, Arizona Territory, they were sought-after beauties. Rafe watched them for a moment, a smile lifting one corner of his mouth, then turned to look at Emmeline.

"I reckon that right now, in this moment, I'm about as

happy as a man has a right to be, this side of the great beyond," he said, with sweet solemnity.

Emmeline's heart did a little flip, and tears burned behind her eyes. "Oh, Rafe," she said. She almost told him everything then, despite her earlier decision to wait, because she wanted to tear down the last barrier between them, for better or for worse, once and for all, so that she never had to be afraid again.

He straightened her lace shawl, draped loosely over her shoulders, and leaned over to kiss her just beneath one ear. She shivered, closed her eyes tightly, and he chuckled at her response.

"I do like it when you say 'Oh, Rafe,' " he teased in a gruff whisper. "Do you suppose anyone would notice if we sneaked into the house, you and I? I'd like to take off your clothes, Mrs. McKettrick, one garment at a time, until all you're wearing are those earbobs of yours. And I'd like to—"

She was falling under his spell, and that simply would not do. No lady left her own party to make love with a man, even if that man *was* her husband. "Rafe McKettrick," she scolded, her cheeks hot, her backbone stiff, and all her senses rioting for more of the very thing she was refusing with such spirit. "Stop that, this instant!"

He laughed. "All right," he said, "but when I get you alone—"

She scooted over a little way on the hay bale, in order to put some space between them, and when she saw Becky and the marshal coming toward her and Rafe, she was so relieved that she bolted right to her feet and almost stumbled over the hem of her dress, hurrying to meet them.

It wasn't until she got closer that she noticed the strain in the marshal's face, and the alarming pallor in Becky's. She was leaning on John a little, a very un-Becky-like stance.

"Is Doc Boylen around anywhere?" the marshal asked, holding Becky with a firm gentleness. She looked as though she might swoon.

Rafe, bless his heart, was close behind Emmeline, and he immediately took charge. "You take Mrs. Fairmont on up to the spare room, John," he said. "Emmeline, you go along, too, and see that she's comfortable. I'll find the doc."

John lifted Becky easily into his arms, against her muttered protests, and the concerned crowd parted, whispering, as the three of them made their way into the house.

Angus claimed the last waltz of the evening with Concepcion, who, like the other women present, fat and skinny, plain and beautiful, wives and spinsters, had barely gotten a chance to take a breath, for dancing with cowboys and prospectors, farmers and ranchers. Only the little nun had sat idle, but he'd seen her toes tapping under the hem of the church getup she wore.

Concepcion was breathless, and flushed, and very beautiful. So beautiful that it fairly made Angus's old heart turn right over in his chest. He tightened his embrace a little, missing more than one step as the dance progressed, and stared down at her as if he'd never seen her before.

She smiled up at him. "What is it, Angus?" she asked.

"Have you always been beautiful?" he countered, frowning.

She laughed. "You old fool," she said, "you've had too much dancing and too much whiskey. I have *never* been beautiful."

The words sounded garbled to Angus, as if he'd stuck his head in the horse trough and come up with water in his ears. Good Lord, how could he have failed to notice Concepcion's grace and humor and, yes, her beauty? He was stupefied by the scope of his oversight.

Concepcion tilted her head to one side. Her lush dark hair, wound into an elegant chignon at her nape, glittered in the starlight and the flickering crimson glow of the bonfire. Her eyes caught the reflections of the colored Chinese lanterns and held them in their dark depths, like fragments of a gaudy rainbow.

"Angus?" she prompted, sounding a little worried now. "Are you all right?"

He felt like five kinds of an idiot. "Of course I'm all right," he grumbled. Maybe it was the moonlight getting to him. Folks said it could drive a sane man mad, if the circumstances were right.

She lowered her eyes, then raised them again, meeting his gaze. "It is a fine party," she said. "You can be proud of yourself, Angus, and of your sons, and your lovely daughter-in-law."

"Of course I'm proud of them," he said, barking out the words without meaning to, feeling like some young whippersnapper, still wet behind the ears, he was so nervous. "I don't see much point in being proud of myself, though—all I did was pay for this shindig. It was you, you and Emmeline and that little Pelton gal, who did most of the real work."

She looked pleased. "So you noticed," she said.

"Yes," he said, still dancing, and feeling as if he'd grown a third foot.

Concepcion arched one perfect eyebrow. "And did you notice my dress?" she asked, with a mischievous note in her voice.

She could have been wearing a burlap feed sack, for all Angus knew. When he looked at Concepcion, he realized that, whether on this magical evening or on an ordinary day, he didn't see her clothes, or even her body, for that matter. He saw her fine, strong spirit, her endless competence, her generosity and readiness to laugh even when crying would have made more sense. He saw the woman who came to his bed some nights, and held him, asking nothing more than to be held in return.

"Yes," he lied. "Of course I noticed your dress."

She placed her hand under his chin, quick as a jackrabbit, so he couldn't look down. "What color is it, then?" she challenged.

He couldn't even guess, and she laughed when she saw the dilemma reflected in his face. "Just as I thought," she said, but she sounded triumphant, not angry.

He all but fell into her eyes, headfirst, rolling end over end like a cowboy flung from a bronco's back. It seemed as if he'd never land. "I believe I love you," he said, amazed by the revelation, since he hadn't known it himself until a minute or so back.

She smiled up at him. "Has that just occurred to you, Angus McKettrick? I've known it for a long time."

Angus managed to break his metaphorical fall, and glowered down at her, stopping in his tracks, right out there in the middle of the dance floor, with his friends, neighbors, and favorite enemies whirling all around them in a colorful blur. "You have?" he asked.

"Of course," she said, sounding smug.

"Well, I guess we'd better get ourselves hitched, then."

She smiled again. "In time," she said. "There is no hurry."

He frowned harder. He couldn't follow her reasoning; he was seventy-five, and might turn up his toes any day now. If that wasn't reason to make haste, he didn't know what was. "Do you love me, Concepcion?" he heard himself ask, and his face flamed, because he hadn't put a question like that to a woman since he'd proposed to Georgia, better than thirty years back.

"Yes," she said. "I do."

"Then why not tell the world?"

"This time belongs to the young people, Angus. To Rafe and Emmeline, to Holt and Kade and to Jeb, wherever he is." She paused to cross herself at the mention of his youngest son, and he loved her even more for that. "You and me, we can go to the mission and get married, if that's what you truly want, but let's keep it to ourselves for a while, if we do."

"How can we do that?" Angus boomed, and was shushed for his trouble. "How can we do that?" he asked again, more quietly. "We've got a houseful, in case you haven't noticed, and I'll be damned if I'll take myself a wife and then sleep apart from her."

Concepcion's eyes flashed, not with anger but with the quiet passion of a woman secure in her charms. "I did not suggest sleeping apart," she said, softly but with no lack of meaning. "There are things happening around us, Angus, in *la familia*. Very important things, written in the stars long, long ago. We might upset the balance, and ruin everything, if we are not careful."

Angus didn't understand, and he didn't pretend to, but he was willing to concede the point, whatever it was, because it seemed so important to Concepcion. "There must be a preacher somewhere in this bunch," he said. Now that he saw a way out, he realized how tired he was of being alone. He'd been a widower for so long; now, as far as he was concerned, it was time to let this bronc out of the chute and watch it buck.

She raised her eyebrows. "Is that your proposal, Mr. McKettrick? Because if it was, well, it's God's own wonder that you ever managed to land one wife, let alone two."

He led her off the dance floor, through the crowd, into the moonlit darkness, well away from the bonfire and the other guests. Then, knowing he might not be able to get up again without help, Angus McKettrick got down on one knee and took both Concepcion's hands in one of his.

"Maybe it's the moonlight," he said. "Maybe it's the whiskey Denver Jack poured in the punch. Whatever it is, Concepcion, I love you, and I want you to be my wife. Will you marry me?"

She smiled down at him. "Yes," she said. "Yes, Angus, I will marry you."

"Good," he said. "Now, help me up, and I'll go round up a preacher."

They became man and wife in secret, half an hour later, in the hay-and-horse-scented privacy of the barn, with Denver Jack and one of the Milldown sisters for witnesses, both of them sworn to secrecy.

Emmeline sat beside Becky's cot, holding her mother's hand tightly, her eyes bright with tears of concern. Doc Boylen had finished his examination, advised quiet and rest, along with a shot of whiskey at regular intervals, and returned to the party. John Lewis and Rafe lingered, both of them as worried as Emmeline, and trying hard to hide the fact.

"You scared me half to death," said Emmeline, who felt no compunction to hide anything at the moment.

Becky patted her wrist. "Well, now, you can just calm down. You heard the doctor. I had just a little too much dancing, that's all." Her gaze strayed to the marshal. "John, maybe Rafe wouldn't mind showing you where the whiskey is. I do believe a drink would do me some good right about now."

The marshal nodded, and he and Rafe left the room together. Becky waited until she heard them on the stairs before speaking again.

"I don't mean to die before I have a grandchild," Becky said in a near whisper, clinging hard to Emmeline's hand. "That would make up for a lot, holding your baby in my arms. So don't you be fretting, thinking I'll be hopping aboard the glory train anytime soon, because I won't be."

Emmeline took a few moments to compose herself. She glanced back over her shoulder, at the closed door, and then turned to Becky again. Her mother. The only person in the world she dared confide in, without fear.

She'd deceived Rafe, and the burden was getting harder and harder to bear with every passing moment. The reason for that was simple, much more than a matter of conscience: She'd fallen in love with him. Somewhere along the line, between her arrival in Indian Rock, when he'd rolled out of the saloon and landed at her feet, and this splendid night, she'd given him her heart, and she knew it was for good, too. Even if Rafe washed his hands of her, cast her out like a painted Jezebel, she would never care for another man the way she cared for him.

"What on earth is the matter?" Becky whispered, her face pinched with concern.

Just about the last thing Emmeline wanted to do was get Becky upset, particularly in her present condition. Why, if she'd had the remotest suspicion that Becky was ill, she never would have hooked up with that marriage brokerage and traveled all the way to Arizona Territory to marry Rafe in the first place. She'd have stayed right there in Kansas City, to look after Becky. So many things would never have happened at all, if she'd done that. . . .

"Emmeline," Becky persisted.

Emmeline glanced at the door again. "That night—in Kansas City—before I ran away—"

Becky stroked Emmeline's hand, her touch gentle and reassuring. "Oh, baby," she said. "You haven't told him about that, have you? You haven't gone and told Rafe?"

Emmeline shook her head. "No," she said, and dashed at a tear with the heel of one palm, "but it's eating me alive, keeping a secret like that." She didn't, *couldn't*, bring herself to say that the man she'd spent the night with was none other than Holt McKettrick, though she suspected Becky might have guessed.

"Now, you listen to me," Becky said fiercely. "It's none of Rafe's concern what you did before you came here. Did he tell you about every woman he's ever bedded? I think not." The sound of male footsteps could be heard mounting the front stairway. Rafe and John Lewis were coming back with the medicinal whiskey.

Emmeline considered taking a shot of the stuff herself.

"You keep what happened that night to yourself, do you hear me?" Becky hissed, practically crushing Emmeline's fingers with the strength of her grip. "No good can come of Rafe's knowing. None at all!"

Emmeline bit her lower lip. If only it were that simple,

she thought, but Holt knew. Dear God in heaven, Holt knew, and he was holding the secret over her head, too. Any day now, he might make some improper demand on her, and what would she do then? Refuse? She didn't dare. Comply? She couldn't do that, either. She'd made more than her share of mistakes, but she still had a conscience. And she loved Rafe McKettrick, as hopeless as that made her feel sometimes.

The door opened then, and John came into the room, carrying a crystal glass with a double shot of whiskey in the bottom. Rafe loomed in the doorway, handsome in his good clothes.

Emmeline stood, so that John could take her place in the chair and help Becky sit up, and hold the glass to her lips. She took small, steady sips.

Rafe held out his hand to Emmeline, without speaking, and she went to him. She wanted to lie naked in his arms, to murmur his name over and over again, to soar past the farthest star on the joyous swell of his lovemaking. She wanted to forget that anyone, or anything, existed in all the natural world, besides Rafe McKettrick and herself.

There were two kerosene lanterns lighting the room, and she could see in his eyes that he understood her need for solace, even if he couldn't possibly know the reasons behind it. She lifted his hand, kissed the backs of his fingers.

She looked back, saw Becky watching her.

"You'll send for me, if you need anything?" Emmeline

asked her. "You'll tell Mrs. Hallowell or Mandy to come knock on our door?"

"Yes," Becky said, "but I'll be just fine. This whiskey will help me sleep, and John will sit with me until I nod off, won't you, John?"

He nodded. "I'll be right here," he said, never looking away from Becky's face.

Rafe said good night to Becky and the marshal; then, still holding Emmeline's hand, he drew her out into the darkened corridor, walking slowly toward their room.

"Shouldn't we say good night to our guests?" Emmeline asked.

"No," Rafe said flatly, opening their door, pulling her inside, closing the door and turning the key in the lock. He stood her in the shaft of shadow-partitioned moonlight pouring in through the windows, and drew in a sharp breath. "Lord, Emmeline, but you are a fine-looking woman. I must be the luckiest man who ever drew breath, sending away to some outfit in Kansas City and getting *you* back."

Her heart ached in her throat, and her chin wobbled. She couldn't have said a word for anything, right then.

He came to her, drew her shawl off her shoulders and set it aside. Then he unfastened her earbobs and laid them carefully on the bureau top. Emmeline knew what was coming, of course, and she trembled with the wanting of it.

Rafe turned her so she was facing away from him, but still bathed in moonlight, and began unfastening the buttons at the back of her dress, one at a time. That done, and it took a very long time, he smoothed the whispery fabric away from her shoulders, down her arms. The dress caught at her hips, and he sent it gliding to the floor in a pool of emerald. Her petticoats followed, with all their ruffles and ribbons, and he took away her camisole, baring her breasts, leaving her wearing only her pantaloons, the garters and silk stockings beneath, and her dancing shoes. He knelt, like Prince Charming in a fairy tale, but unlike the prince, he wasn't trying to put a slipper on her foot, he was taking one off. His hands were strong, yet gentle, stroking one calf, then the other.

He reached up to caress her breasts with his hands, giving a low groan as he stroked the nipples. She tilted her head back with a sigh of surrender, and her hair tumbled, of its own accord, down over her spine and shoulders to tickle the soft backs of her thighs.

Rafe supported her—she would have fallen if he hadn't—and slowly drew down her pantaloons. Only the garters were left now, and the stockings. He kissed the soft swell of her thighs, above the tops of the stockings, nuzzled the center of her femininity, now bared to him.

She groaned, entwining her fingers in his hair. "Oh, Rafe," she whispered.

He parted her, nibbled. Outside, the band played a lively tune, and the dancers stomped and clapped, making more than enough noise to cover the involuntary cry Emmeline uttered.

Still enjoying her, Rafe unfastened one stocking and

rolled it slowly down the length of her leg. He did the same with the other.

"*Rafe,*" she pleaded.

Somehow, he maneuvered her to the edge of the bed, laid her down gently, and draped her legs over his shoulders.

"Rafe!" she cried again, more loudly this time.

He murmured some response, never taking his mouth from her, and she clutched at the covers of their bed, certain that she would go hurtling through the roof and far beyond the borders of the night sky itself if she didn't hold on tightly. And sure enough, a few glorious minutes later, she was spinning, somewhere beyond the moon, all her fears and worries left far behind in the world of ordinary mortals.

# CHAPTER

## 16

THE PARTY LASTED for three days, and by the time the last of the guests had straggled off for home, Becky was well rested. Color bloomed in her cheeks, and, since Concepcion and Emmeline had been feeding her at every opportunity, she had even filled out a little. John Lewis, along with Mrs. Hallowell, Clive, and the mysterious Sister Mandy, had gone back to Indian Rock early, for they all had jobs to do.

Emmeline, watching in thoughtful silence as the other woman rocked contentedly on the front porch of the ranch house, might have thought that nothing was wrong, indeed, that nothing had *ever* been wrong, to look at her aunt now, so marked was the change.

Becky, fanning herself with a copy of *Godey's*, gave Emmeline a sidelong glance and smiled. "What are you thinking?" she asked.

"That you'll surely live to be a hundred and ten," Emmeline answered, without any hesitation at all.

Becky laughed. "A hundred and ten? God forbid! Can you imagine what I'd *look* like? All shriveled and wrinkly and toothless, like one of those dried-apple dolls, with tiny black seeds for eyes, that's what." She fanned herself more vigorously. "No, thank you!"

Emmeline, leaning against the rough-hewn railing of the porch, smiled at the picture Becky had painted in her mind. "Are you in love with John Lewis?" she asked. The question had been lurking in the back of her mind since Becky's near collapse, the first night of the party, but she'd managed to hold it in check until now.

Becky sighed, gazing not at Emmeline but at the creek, sparkling in the near distance. The acres beyond that stream seemed especially beautiful to Emmeline, a land of milk and honey, gently sloping down toward the water, every inch thick with verdant grass. She knew, from Rafe's brief accounts, that his mother had planned on homesteading there, all on her own, before Angus McKettrick came along and swept her off her feet. She must have been a spirited woman, Angus's Georgia, and Emmeline wished she could have known her.

"I'm not sure what I feel for John," Becky answered, after due consideration. "He's a fine man, and strong. I like him very much. The fact is, it scares me a little, finding out that I'm inclined to lean on another person. I've made a point of getting by on my own for a long time, you know."

"Yes," Emmeline agreed softly, thinking of the years Becky had run her business, answering to no one but herself. She had made a great deal of money, but it had surely been a lonely struggle in many ways. "I know."

"And it's not as if I'm any kind of great prize," Becky went on, and only then did she look at Emmeline again, her gaze direct and unflinching. "Oh, I don't mean because of what I did for a living all these years; he knows about that, and he understands. Has a few things posted in the liability column himself, John does. No, I'm talking about this temperamental old heart of mine."

Emmeline was silent, sorting through the things Becky had said one by one, and putting them in their proper places. Finally, and carefully, she said, "You just told me you were going to live for a long while yet, didn't you?"

Becky sighed. "I reckon I will, but that's no cause to think a good man like John ought to be tied down to a wife whose going to be swooning like some silly debutante at a cotillion every five minutes, now does it?"

"Swooning aside, I guess that should be *his* choice," Emmeline reasoned, smiling a little. "Whether or not he chooses to be married, and take the good with the bad, I mean."

Becky laughed, waving the magazine at her. "Emmeline McKettrick," she said, "I declare you could have been a lawyer, you argue so well."

They were quiet for a while, comfortably so, enjoying the summer weather, with its soft, fragrant breezes and pale blue sky.

"You told John about the boardinghouse," Emmeline

ventured presently, now that she'd had time to digest the implications, "and he wasn't angry or upset?"

Becky shook her head. "I was so scared, but I did it. Thought he'd walk right out and never spare me so much as a nod again, but he didn't, bless his soul. He listened, and he held me in his arms, and he told me some things he'd done that he wasn't proud of. Nothing really changed between us, except that we got closer."

Emmeline looked down at her feet. She was wearing her everyday black lace-ups, and she missed her dancing slippers a little. "Maybe it would be like that with Rafe and me, too. If I told him what happened."

Becky's glance was sharp. "It's different for the two of you," she said, lowering her voice, even though they both knew Rafe was miles away, with a crew of men, working on the new house. "You're young, and Rafe's young, and that changes things, Emmeline."

Emmeline wet her lips with the tip of her tongue, still looking down at her feet, but said nothing in response.

"Why are you so set on telling Rafe about that night?" Becky demanded in a hoarse whisper. "Do you *want* to ruin everything, Emmeline?"

"Of course not," Emmeline said, blinking and glancing away. "I love Rafe. I don't want any secrets between us, that's all."

"Don't be a fool. Everyone has secrets."

Just then, the sound of an approaching rig reached them, and both women looked up to see John Lewis approaching, at the reins of a hired horse and buggy. They watched as the team, rig, and driver splashed through a shallow place in the creek, the spindly wheels sending up plumes of sun-shimmered water.

"Don't be a fool," Becky repeated in a stern whisper, but her attention was all for John by then. She rose from her chair, smiling, and waved. Her knight-in-shining-armor pulled off his hat and waved it exuberantly, his grin visible even though they were still separated by several hundred yards.

Before an hour was out, Becky had told Concepcion and Angus farewell and much obliged, and set out for Indian Rock with John. Just before the marshal helped her into the buggy, having secured her things in the small space in back, she hugged Emmeline, kissed her on the cheek, and whispered, "Mind what I said, now, and hold your tongue."

With that, she was gone, and Emmeline watched her out of sight, torn between Becky's sensible advice and her own sense of right and wrong. She knew, even then, that her conscience would win out, if only because it plagued her night and day.

Rafe arrived home just as the sun was setting that evening, and he looked so tired, and so full of pride in the work he was doing, that, despite her earlier resignation, Emmeline nearly put aside the decision that had been troubling her so much.

There had to be an end to the deception; she couldn't bear it any longer. Before her new and fragile feelings for her husband deepened, before she and Rafe conceived a child together, complicating matters even more, or moved up the mountain to that fine, new house, she had to tell him about Kansas City, and about Holt. She was anxious all the time, and felt sure she couldn't live another day with the very strong possibility that Holt, or someone who'd gotten the story secondhand, would tell Rafe the sordid truth before she did. She knew he would find her silence almost as hard to forgive as the incident itself, and if he was going to hear it from anyone, it had to be from her.

She couldn't eat a bite at supper, for the painful grinding in the pit of her stomach, and while Angus, Concepcion, and Kade seemed to notice her reticence, Rafe himself was blissfully unaware. He beamed, telling them all he'd accomplished that day at the building site, and declaring that his place and Emmeline's would be the finest home in the Arizona Territory when he was through with it—save the ranch house, of course.

"Let's take a walk, Rafe," Emmeline said quietly, laying her hands on his shoulders when the dishes were done. Rafe was still seated at the table with his brother and father, the three of them studying a hand-drawn map, trying to figure out where a hundred-odd stray cattle might have gone. According to Kade, they were missing at least that many from the main herd.

Kade and Angus had been stealing intermittent glances at Emmeline all during the conference, perhaps seeing something in her face or hearing something in her tone of voice that troubled them, and Concepcion, putting away silverware, gave her a penetrating look when she spoke of leaving the house, but Rafe was oblivious to every nuance.

"Sure," he said. "It's a nice night. Lots of stars out."

"Yes," Emmeline replied, and hoped she wouldn't break down crying before she got everything said.

They left by the back door, walked around the house, arm in arm, and made their way to the creek bank. Emmeline's throat was tight, and her eyes burned so badly that she was tempted to kneel and splash them with water from the stream. She straightened her shoulders, instead, and fixed her gaze on the expansive meadow across the creek. She pictured a rustic house, a dream castle, standing there, and saw it fade away into nothingness.

"I wonder why none of you have built a house on the far side of the creek," she said. "It's so pretty, especially in the sunlight, and there's water handy, too."

Rafe followed her gaze. "I don't know," he replied. "Ma would have liked that, knowing one of her sons had built a home on the land she staked out for herself, way back when."

"She must have been an amazing woman," Emmeline said, and she meant it. For a woman alone even to attempt homesteading, in the present day as well as in those early pioneering times, was an Olympian accomplishment.

"She was," Rafe said, with a remembering kind of smile. "Independent as all get-out. After her folks died— her family lost just about everything in the War Between the States—she gathered up what little was left and struck out on her own. Got all the way here from Louisiana, stopping along the way every now and again to teach awhile, and replenish her grubstake. Pa never did have the heart to tell her that he already owned that half section she'd pegged out for herself. There'd been some kind of mistake at the land office in Tombstone, he reckoned."

So, Emmeline thought, what Becky had said was true: Most everybody had secrets. Still, Angus's had been a harmless one; her own was like a stick of dynamite, rolling around at their feet, with the fuse lit.

"Do you think she'd have been upset, your mother, I mean, if she'd ever found out the truth about her homestead?"

Rafe didn't hesitate. "She'd have been madder than a hen dunked in pancake batter," he said, grinning. "Pa admitted he was mighty relieved that she never found out."

Emmeline tried to smile, but she couldn't. Her heart was beating outside her body, trapped there, exposed, with no way to retreat to safety. She looked up at the stars for a long time, saw them blur into one blazing silver light, and finally met Rafe's gaze. Only now, when he'd seen her tears, did he turn thoughtful.

"What is it?" he asked.

"If there was something about me—something I'd never told you—would you want to know? Even though knowing might be the end of everything?"

He stared at her, then sat her down on a large rock next to the whispering stream before taking his place beside her. "Put like that," he said gravely, "I don't reckon you've left me with much of a choice." She wished he'd take her hand, but he didn't, and she thought she could already feel a distance growing between them, wider with every heartbeat. "What is it, Emmeline?" he reiterated.

She couldn't look at him, so she looked at the water instead, splashed with starlight. Under the surface were rainbow trout, surely, living out their whole lives without ever having to keep or share secrets. She envied them, in that moment, and wished she too were a slippery, shiny fish, going about her business, ignorant of the concerns of men and women. In telling her story, she would be revealing not only her own past but, by necessity, Becky's, too. She hoped that Becky would forgive her, even if Rafe didn't.

"I told you that Becky was my aunt, and that she ran a boardinghouse in Kansas City," she began miserably, still unable to look at him, her hands clenched so tightly in her lap that the joints ached. "Turns out, she's my mother—I was illegitimate, actually—and the boardinghouse was really a—a brothel."

Rafe was silent, listening so closely that he was rigid. He'd gone cold, too. Emmeline felt the changes in him, even though they weren't touching.

"I was sheltered, and I never got near the business," she said. She paused, shuddering with emotion. "Anyway, Becky sent me to a good school, did everything she could to raise me as a lady. But I had no friends, because of the stigma. I was foolish and bored, and probably spoiled, as well, and one night—" she paused, bit her lip so hard she tasted blood, "one night I decided to dress up in fancy clothes and pretend to be a—a lady of the evening. Just as a diversion." She waited again, but Rafe remained stone silent. "I went and sat on the stairs, just watching, planning to slip away if anyone noticed I was there, and all of a sudden this man was walking toward me."

She glanced at Rafe, sidelong, and saw that he'd closed his eyes. His jaw was set, as if he was bracing himself for a blow.

"He—he sat by me, on the stairs, and gave me whiskey," she went on, for there was no going back now. "We talked, and he made me laugh, and it all seemed so harmless. I felt special and, well, *chosen,* somehow. Nobody had ever noticed me like that before. I had more and more whiskey, and then I was sure Becky or one of the others would find me out, and I'd be in more trouble than I'd ever thought possible—" She stopped, laughed bitterly at the naïveté of that concern. "I wanted to slip away. The man came with me, into the hallway, and it was dark there. He kissed me a couple of times, and—and I started to feel really dizzy. He asked me where my room was, and I lied to him. One of the girls had just left, and hers was vacant, so I claimed it was mine, and—"

Rafe stood up suddenly, turned his back to her. His

broad shoulders looked stiff, outlined by the diffused starlight reflecting off the creek, but he still didn't speak.

"I remember that he carried me into that room, and untied my shoes." She swallowed, thinking frantically that Becky had been right, and she should have kept the confession to herself, but it was too late now. It was far, far too late to stop. "I woke up the next morning, alone in the bed, and there was money on the bedside stand."

Silence.

"Rafe," she whispered. "Rafe, you have to say something—please."

He turned, very slowly, and looked down at her. His hands were clenched into fists at his sides, and, although she knew he wouldn't harm her physically, his rage and his pain were palpable. "You were—" His voice was raspy, hurtful to hear. Emmeline wanted to put her hands over her ears. "You were a *whore?*"

She began to cry then, miserably, hopelessly, like a wounded child. "No," she said. "No! It was one time, a mistake—I don't even remember if—"

"One time or a thousand," Rafe ground out, "you slept with a man for money."

As horrible as this was, it wasn't over. "There's one thing more," she said, ready to curl in on herself, return, somehow, to the safety of the womb.

"Good God," Rafe whispered rawly. "What?"

"The man—the man I was with was Holt," she said.

The silence was terrible; shouts and accusations would have been easier to endure, but there was just that awful, pounding silence.

"Rafe," she said. "I'm sorry."

He walked away from her then, just as she'd feared he would, his strides long, carrying him not in the direction of the house, where Angus or Kade or Concepcion might have been able to calm and comfort him a little, but toward the barn. Like Jeb, he was going away, maybe for good. Unlike Jeb, he wasn't leaving the land, or his father and brothers. Rafe was leaving *her*.

She stood, for in spite of it all, her instinct was to go after him, but all the while she knew that would do no good. Besides, her knees were shaking so badly that she had to sit down again, right away, lest she tumble into a heap.

Minutes passed, then Rafe rode out through the barn doors at a lope, and by the time they reached the creek, his gelding, Chief, was running full out. They seemed to set the waters churning, man and animal, as they crossed that stream, and Emmeline was sure they'd both founder and drown in the torrent they created, but within moments they were climbing, dripping wet, up the other bank.

"Rafe," Emmeline whispered, knowing, for the first time in her life, the true meaning of a broken heart. "Oh, Rafe."

She cried, and waited to be strong enough to go into the house and start packing her things. Before she could manage that, however, Holt came limping across the expanse of the yard and down the creek bank to stand over her.

"Are you all right, Emmeline?" he asked. "The way Rafe rode out of here just now—"

She looked up at him, her nemesis, and wondered if he'd come to gloat. "I told him," she said simply. "About Kansas City. About us."

"Us?" He stared down at her. "Sweet God, Emmeline, you don't mean—"

"Yes," she answered, too broken to feel anything now besides despair. "I told him the truth about what happened that night."

"Good Lord," Holt said, with such gravity that Emmeline was confounded. Maybe, she thought, he was irritated because he wouldn't be able to blackmail her, now that her great sin was out in the open. "What possessed you to do a thing like that?"

She stood, at last, buoyed by a rush of angry frustration. "What possessed me?" she snapped. "I wanted to tell him before you did."

"Before I told him what?" he demanded, looking a lot like Rafe in that light, or the lack of it. "Dammit, Emmeline, there was nothing to tell. You put on somebody else's clothes and got drunk. I didn't want to tell Becky what you were up to, and I didn't want to leave you for one of the other men to take advantage of, so I put you to bed and left. That was the end of it!"

Emmeline's mouth dropped open. "But those coins—"

"I thought maybe you needed money, that you were in some kind of trouble, and desperate."

Emmeline sat down again. She felt as though she might throw up, or even faint.

"Emmeline?"

"I thought we—that you and I—"

"Jesus," he murmured. Then he turned and started away from her, stumping determinedly toward the barn.

"Where are you going?" Emmeline cried, at last finding the strength to break her strange inertia and move her feet.

"None of your damn business!" he called back.

She hurried after him, tried to take hold of his arm. "You can't," she said quickly. "Holt, you can't. You're hurt—if you ride—"

"Stay out of this," Holt said tersely, shaking her off. "You've done enough damage as it is." They were almost to the barn.

"Don't go after Rafe," she pleaded. "He'll kill you, or you'll kill him, but nothing good will come of it!"

His eyes were hot. "Go in the house, Emmeline."

She stood speechless, one hand clasped over her mouth, staring after him as he stormed into the barn.

He managed to saddle a horse, put the bridle in place, and even mount, all without help. Emmeline was still standing where he'd left her when he came riding out into the moonlight; on the ground, he was a cripple, in the saddle, he was his old self.

"At least let me go with you!" she cried.

He paused beside her, reining in the prancing gelding, and got in one last volley. "Oh, you'd be a lot of help," he scoffed furiously. "You've already made enough trouble to keep us all busy for the next hundred years, picking up the pieces!"

With that, he rode away.

The log house loomed, in long lines and shadows, against the spectacular sky.

Rafe, breathless from the hard ride up the mountain, the legs of his trousers still wet with creek water, jumped down from Chief's back and left him to graze, reins dangling. The saddle looked to be slipping a little, because the cinch had come loose.

Too bad it hadn't given way on one of those steep, narrow trails he'd just ridden over, Rafe thought, having consumed three-quarters of a flask of whiskey during the journey. His head was spinning, and he'd turned his heart out, like some wild beast, and drove it away from him, unable to bear the pain of Emmeline's words, and of the images she'd drawn in his mind. It was hard enough to think of her selling herself to another man. Knowing that other man was Holt, his enemy, his brother, made a hell of his very soul.

He gave a great scream of anguish, roaring at the sky. He walked around the house, once, twice—he couldn't stand to go inside—and then, his movements calm and methodical, for all their admitted madness, he began piling dry brush and wood chips in the main doorway.

He'd expected to carry his bride across that threshold in just a few more weeks, when the roof was finished and the floors and windows had been put in. Now, he never wanted to set foot in the place again.

He doused the chips and twigs and small limbs with the remains of his whiskey, then struck a match and tossed it down.

A blaze flared up immediately, and he stared at it blankly for a moment, quelling an instinctive urge to stomp out the fire before it caught the walls. Instead, he thought of Emmeline, doing with Holt the things she'd done with him, and he bellowed again, like a creature snared in jagged teeth of a trap, and started rushing around, gathering up every piece of fuel he could find, hurling twigs and grass and scrap wood into the flames.

Rafe stood back, but not so far that he couldn't feel the smothering heat, watching as the fire leaped from here to there, from window ledge to rafter. Within a few minutes, the whole place was burning, spitting sparks, a fire big enough to see from heaven.

"Jesus, Rafe," a male voice shouted beside him, "get back!" He didn't move willingly, indeed, he was dragged away from the blaze by the other man, the two of them stumbling. When they were a good distance from the house, and he saw that it was Holt who'd come riding out of the night, he took a swing at him, not giving a damn that he was a cripple. He wanted to kill him.

Holt dodged him easily, for even though he had a

game leg, Rafe was drunk, and out of his mind with sorrow. "Listen to me," he said.

"You go to hell!" Rafe responded. "Damn you, Holt—and damn her—"

Holt's face tightened, and he nearly lost his balance, using both hands to shove Rafe backward, onto his ass. Remarkably, he caught his crutch before it fell, and jammed it back under his arm, breathing hard as he leaned on it, and gazed down at Rafe. "There's a real good chance that I'll go to hell someday," Holt said, breathing hard and fast, "but it won't be because of anything I did with Emmeline!"

Rafe tried to stand, but he was winded, and he wanted to come up swinging. He wiped his mouth with the back of one hand. "She told me what happened," he said.

"Get up, you damn fool. She told you what she *thought* happened."

Rafe rose, dusting himself off, still trying to decide whether or not he'd be justified in sucker punching his half-brother. "She said she spent the night with you and you gave her money for it," he said. It made him sick, the picture that came to his mind, and he felt the heat and heard the roar of the fire behind him, consuming his dreams.

"She was drunk that night," Holt said, his eyes flashing with the reflected light of the fire, and with fury. "I didn't touch her, except to take off her shoes and that stupid outfit she had on. And I paid her, yes, because I figured she must be pretty hard up for money to pull a stupid stunt like that."

Rafe swayed on his feet, his fists still knotted at his sides. He couldn't, and wouldn't, hit Emmeline, but he sure as hell wanted to hit somebody, and Holt would do just fine. Trouble was, his brother kept shifting in and out of range, even though Rafe would have sworn he was standing still. He splayed the fingers of one hand and thrust them through his hair, realizing only then that he'd lost his hat somewhere along the way. It had been his favorite, too; he'd paid three dollars for it in Denver.

"You're just trying to cover your tracks," Rafe said.

Holt sighed. "Emmeline told me you'd think that," he replied. "Dammit, Rafe, don't be an idiot. Put aside your bloody pride. Go back to the house and *talk to your wife*, before you lose everything." His gaze flicked toward the blazing structure behind Rafe. "You can build another house," he said, lower. "Hell, you can build a hundred houses. But there's only one Emmeline."

Rafe wheeled away from Holt, overcome by everything he was feeling. He'd been through tough times before, but nothing since his mother's death had hit him as hard as Emmeline's confession. He ran a hand over his face and struggled with his emotions, wanting to believe Holt, wanting that more than he'd ever wanted to believe in anything, and that was precisely why he was afraid to trust his own judgment at that moment.

Holt laid a hand on his shoulder. "Let's go back," he said quietly.

Rafe shook his head, keeping his back to his brother. They stood in silence for a little while, then Holt withdrew his hand and walked away. Rafe heard him whistle for his horse.

When he turned, Holt was in the saddle, with that one splinted leg sticking out toward the horse's head. "If I had two good legs," he said, looking down at Rafe, "I swear I'd bring you back to the ranch, one way or the other, and you wouldn't have any say in the matter. As it stands, I reckon there's nothing I can do to keep you from making a fool of yourself, so maybe I'll just stand back and enjoy the show."

Rafe felt something cold settle over his spirit, in spite of the great heat, turning all his innards to icy stone. He'd been hornswoggled once already. He wasn't going to let it happen again.

He nodded toward Holt's broken leg. "See that you don't catch that on a tree," he said. Then he turned and walked away, and when he had occasion to look back, sometime later, his brother was gone.

"It's gone?" Emmeline asked Holt, in a hollow voice, blinking in the morning sunlight. "The whole house?" Bile surged into the back of her throat, and she gripped the side of the buckboard for support.

She'd packed her few belongings the night before, after an emotional conversation with Angus and Concepcion, and Kade was reluctantly hitching up a team to drive her to town. She intended to stay with Becky until she figured out what to do with the rest of her life.

Holt nodded. "I'm sorry, Emmeline."

She swallowed, shook her head. "I should have told him right away."

Angus came out of the house, with one of Concepcion's food baskets in his hand. His voice was grave as he neared them, and when he stood at Emmeline's side, looking down at her with a fatherly expression in his eyes, she nearly broke down.

"Concepcion won't say goodbye," he explained gruffly. "She says you oughtn't to leave, Emmeline. And that's what I think, too. It was just a mistake, what you did, and Rafe will come to understand that, once he calms down."

Emmeline bit her lower lip as she gazed up at his fine, craggy face, so full of kindness and strength and character. One day, after he'd done more living, Rafe would probably look much as his father did now. Her heart squeezed, because she'd wanted so much to grow old along with him, surrounded by their children and their children's children.

"I have to get away," she said, standing on tiptoe to kiss his beard-stubbled cheek. "While I've still got enough pride to hold my head up. You understand, don't you?"

Angus's eyes said he didn't, but he nodded. He put the food basket under the seat, and handed Emmeline a sealed envelope. "You need anything," he said, "anything at all, you go over to the bank and show Big Mike Jenkins this letter of credit."

"I couldn't," Emmeline said.

He pressed the envelope into her hand. "You're the closest thing I've ever had to a daughter," he told her, nearly strangling on the words. "No matter what happens, you'll always be my girl. So you take this paper, missy, and I don't want to hear another word about it."

She sniffled, wiped her eye with the side of one thumb, and took the envelope, shoving it into the pocket of her cloak. No one else seemed to be cold, that July day, but Emmeline was chilled to the marrow. "Thank you," she said.

Angus only nodded, that time, looking as though he didn't trust himself to speak. He kissed her forehead and helped her up into the wagon seat, and Kade scrambled up on the other side, taking the reins in gloved hands. His gaze was fixed straight ahead. He hadn't said one word to Emmeline since that morning, at breakfast, when she'd announced that she was leaving.

Now, it was real. Emmeline was seated in that wagon, riding away from the Triple M, toward Indian Rock. She did not allow herself to look back.

They passed the burned-out homestead, where the Peltons had lived, and Emmeline remembered Phoebe Anne's words: *This is a hard land. . . .*

"What happened, Emmeline?" Kade asked, when they were well away from the house. He hadn't been present when she confided in Concepcion and Angus, and Rafe was still gone. Holt, too, had packed up, early that morning, saying it was time he moved onto his own ranch.

She lowered her head. "I made a terrible mistake," she said. "I'd like to leave it at that."

Kade gave her a sidelong glance, then patted her hand in a brotherly fashion, as if to say everything would be all right. That only went to show what *he* knew.

Nothing was ever going to be all right again.

# CHAPTER

## ❧ 17 ❧

"EMMELINE HARDING MCKETTRICK," Becky said furiously that afternoon, in the relative privacy of her tiny office behind the registration desk, when the unexpected guest presented herself, and the rudimentary details of her separation from Rafe had been explained. "I have never suffered fools gladly, and I do not intend to begin with you!"

Emmeline's control over her emotions was growing more tenuous by the moment. Her back ached, after the long ride from the Triple M to Indian Rock, jolting and jostling over a rough track, perched on the hard seat of a wagon. She and Kade had said very little during the trip, because she didn't want to explain why she was leaving, and he was keeping his thoughts to himself. Her heart was in pieces, and scattered all about, like pearls from a necklace, spilling off a broken string. Her worst fears had come to fruition: Rafe had put her aside for good, like some biblical harlot, and now she must face Becky's angry recriminations as well. She opened her mouth, and when no words came, she closed it again.

Becky shook a finger at her. "I warned you," she reminded Emmeline. "I told you that Rafe wouldn't understand!"

Emmeline lowered her head, but only for a moment, then she was looking directly into Becky's eyes again. "I had no other choice," she said.

"Oh, indeed," Becky ranted in an outraged whisper, well aware, as Emmeline was, that Clive was probably just outside the room, with one ear to the keyhole. "Well, my dear, you haven't just finished your own reputation in this town, you've put an end to *mine*, as well. Lacking your penchant for spoiling a good thing, I had planned on making a new start." She sighed, her expression thoughtful now. "Once word gets around, that may be quite a difficult thing to do."

"I do regret that part of it, truly," Emmeline said with feeling. "It's just that I couldn't think of a way to clear the air with Rafe without revealing how I came to be in such a situation in the first place. Therefore, I had to tell him that I grew up in a brothel, and naturally, that meant—"

Becky rolled her eyes. "Saints preserve us," she murmured. It was the closest Emmeline had ever heard her come to offering a prayer, though the tone of it was more like swearing. "Well, my girl," she said after an interminable, steaming silence, "what do you intend to do now?"

"I have no idea," Emmeline admitted. "I was hoping to

stay here with you, until I come to some decision. I can certainly help with the work."

It seemed, for one dreadful moment, that Becky would turn away from her, just like Rafe had done. In the end, though, Becky simply walked over to the wall safe, opened it with a few deft spins, this way and that, and reached inside to pull something out. She handed Emmeline a thick packet. "This is the documentation concerning the funds I put aside for you after I liquidated most of my interests in Kansas City. You can have the money transferred to the bank here in Indian Rock, but I wouldn't recommend it—John tells me the place has been robbed four times since it opened."

Emmeline stared at the packet. "Are you sending me away?"

"Dolt," Becky snapped, and gave an annoyed little sigh. "Of course I'm not. You and I are family. I'm your *mother*, for heaven's sake! Remember—I told you there was money when I first visited you at the Triple M."

Emmeline found a chair, sat down hard. "I'd forgotten," she said. "Is it a great deal?"

"Yes," Becky said, nodding briskly at the envelope, which rested in Emmeline's lap. "See for yourself."

Hands shaking, Emmeline opened the packet, drew out the papers, unfolded them. It took a few seconds for her to find the line marked, "Balance on Deposit," and when she did, she gasped aloud. It was a small fortune.

Becky's smile was a welcome sight, even if was a bit

ironic. "You are a wealthy woman in your own right, Emmeline," she said. "Does that surprise you?"

"Yes!" Emmeline burst out. "I had no idea—I can't possibly accept—"

"Stuff and nonsense," Becky said, cutting her off. "You will inherit three times that much when I pass away, and this hotel into the bargain, such as it is."

Emmeline pressed one hand to her mouth, shook her head. Even in her wildest flights of fancy, she'd never imagined having so much money. With such wealth, she could do anything she wanted to do, travel to any part of the world, wear the finest clothes and bedeck herself in the kind of jewelry she'd always coveted, and still have a fat balance in her bank account.

The strange thing was that she would have given all of that up, and gladly, every penny of the money, every luxury such riches afforded, if only she could be with Rafe, back in that tenuous golden time before she'd shattered his image of her. She lowered her head, a great sob rising into her throat, and Becky took her into her arms.

"There, now," she said. "We'll work this out somehow."

"I was trying to do the right thing," Emmeline wept.

"I know," Becky commiserated. "I know."

Emmeline had been at the hotel a week, cleaning rooms with Mandy, helping the cook in the kitchen, and working at the front desk whenever a stagecoach came in, and there were customers to be dealt with, when Holt came into the dining room one afternoon.

He took off his hat. "Hello, Emmeline," he said.

Emmeline, who had been setting the tables for the supper trade, went absolutely still. "How is Rafe?" she heard herself ask. It was as though she had two voices, her normal one, and this other, speaking up when she least expected it, quite independent of her brain.

Holt stood leaning on his crutch, watching her. "I couldn't rightly say, since I've been on my own place, and haven't seen much of him. He came by once to make sure I hadn't dammed up the springs." He paused to consider. "I'd guess from the looks of him, though, that he's miserable as a rattlesnake circling the bottom of a rain barrel."

Although she tried not to show it, Emmeline was relieved that Rafe hadn't left the territory; the ranch was an integral part of him, the physical counterpart of his soul. She was also illicitly pleased that he was miserable. "He is a stubborn man," she said, thinking aloud, and was immediately sad. "Sit down, Holt. I'll bring you some coffee." A customer, after all, was a customer.

He nodded his thanks and took a seat at the nearest table, propping his crutch against the wall. Emmeline went into the kitchen, poured a cup of coffee from the big pot on the stove, and carried it back to the dining room. The cook, a small Chinese man who went by the unlikely name of Stockard, was out in back, chopping wood for the huge cast-iron stove, Becky was in her room, taking a rest, and Mandy and Clive had gone out to run various errands.

Holt stood, very awkwardly, and waited until Emmeline was seated across from him before sinking into his chair again. He grimaced a little, and she knew he was still in considerable pain, but he was a hardheaded McKettrick, whatever name he went by, and, as such, it would take more than a badly broken leg to prevent him from riding all over the countryside just as if he were in the peak of health.

He added sugar and cream to the coffee she'd brought him, stirring with a clatter of the spoon, while Emmeline waited for him to state his business, being well aware that he hadn't stopped in to pay a social call.

"I was wondering," he said finally, after taking a careful sip from his cup, "if you've got any woman friends back east."

She looked at him quizzically. "Why? Are you looking to get married?"

He chuckled. "No," he said. "I need a housekeeper."

Immediately she thought of Mandy, and said so.

"The nun?" Holt asked, plainly surprised.

Emmeline sighed. "She *isn't* a nun," she confided. "She's just pretending."

"Why would anybody pretend to be a nun?"

She glanced around, to make sure no one was listening. "I think she's hiding from somebody," she said. "Maybe she's in trouble."

"Now, there's a great recommendation," Holt said. "I'm looking for somebody to cook and clean and sew, not rob me blind, or get me shot by a jealous husband."

"That's not very chivalrous," she said.

"I am not a chivalrous man," he replied. "Emmeline, why don't you go back to the Triple M?"

She turned her head toward the window beside their table, fixing her gaze on a mule drinking at a moss-covered horse trough on the other side of the street. "I can't," she answered quietly. "Seeing that look in Rafe's eyes again— *ever* again—well, it would be worse than dying. I just couldn't bear it."

He waited, taking another taste of his coffee.

"Why didn't you tell me before that nothing really happened that night we were together?" she demanded suddenly. The question had been gathering speed inside her, like a runaway locomotive, ever since the night of her confrontation with Rafe. Now, it came out of her mouth all on its own.

Holt leaned forward slightly, his eyebrows raised. "I figured you knew, Emmeline. It isn't as if there aren't— well—indications."

Of course there *were* indications; she knew that now. Still, she blushed, wildly embarrassed, incapable, for the moment, of answering. An experienced woman would have been aware, of course, but Emmeline had not been any-thing of the sort. Indeed, she was *still* woefully ignorant about a great many things, despite those unconventional chats with Becky, during her girlhood. Nothing Becky had ever said had prepared her for the glorious, soaring joy, the melding of souls, she'd known in Rafe's bed.

"You truly didn't know," Holt marveled, his voice quiet.

She shook her head.

"Damnation," he muttered, sounding exasperated, and after that he seemed to be at a loss for words.

Emmeline's eyes felt as though they'd been pricked with needles at the inside corners. She'd gone to Rafe's bed as a virgin, and now he'd spurned her for a whore. It was all her fault, and no one else's, however much she would have liked to share the blame with somebody.

"What are you going to do now, Emmeline?"

She shook her head. "I don't know. I have some money. Maybe I'll move on to Denver or San Francisco or somewhere, and start over."

"Bide your time," Holt counseled with a solemn shake of his head. "I told Rafe that I never touched you, except to put you to bed for the night. He *wanted* to believe me, I could see that."

"Don't you see that it doesn't make any difference to him, that we didn't—didn't do anything? As far as Rafe's concerned, I was *willing* to sell myself for money, and that's the same thing as whoring."

"Maybe," he admitted ruefully.

"What would you do, in his place?"

Holt sighed. "I don't know," he said, and Emmeline knew immediately that he was lying. He would have put her aside, just as Rafe had done.

"Do you think you'll ever make peace with your father and brothers?" she asked, after a long silence.

"Hard telling," he said, just as Becky entered the dining room from the lobby, looking refreshed after her nap.

Whatever else Holt might have added to his brief response was lost as he stood to greet Becky.

Her eyes shone with affection as she took his hands in her own. "Holt Cavanagh," she said. "How good to see that you're recovering from your injuries. Tell me, do you bring us happy news? We'll settle for just about anything."

He glanced at Emmeline before meeting Becky's sparkling gaze again. "Things are pretty much the same all around, I reckon" he said. "I was in town on some personal business, so I decided to stop in and pay my respects."

"We would never have forgiven you if you'd passed us by," Becky said. Her eyes fell on the coffee cup on the table, now empty. Emmeline stood to clear it away, suddenly needing something to occupy her hands. "All you had was coffee?" she asked. "It's true that dinner's well over, and supper won't be served for a couple of hours yet, but we could surely serve you something more nourishing. Is there any of Stockard's wonderful beef stew left over from last night, Emmeline?"

Emmeline didn't get a chance to answer; Holt spoke too quickly.

"I had a big meal at my place," he said. "And I've got to be headed back to the ranch now anyway." He rose, nodded to both women, and left the dining room.

"You and Holt are good friends," she mused, watching Becky watch his departure. "I don't think I realized that before."

"Yes," Becky said, meeting Emmeline's gaze and hold-

ing it without flinching. "We go way back, Holt and I do.
We've even shared in a few business deals."

"He's looking for a housekeeper," Emmeline said.

"He doesn't need a housekeeper," Becky said briskly.
"He needs a wife." With that, she dispensed with the
subject.

Emmeline let out her breath. She'd expected to get
over missing Rafe so much, but it was worse than ever.
The malady seemed to grow keener and more painful
with every passing day, rather than better, as it should, by
rights, have done.

"Any word of Rafe?" Becky asked gently, laying a comforting hand on Emmeline's forearm.

"I asked after him," Emmeline admitted. "Holt said he
was 'miserable'—and just as stubborn as ever. I believe he
thinks that if I go back to the Triple M to live, Rafe might
get over his anger sooner."

Becky took her by the shoulders and gave her a slight
shake. "You love the man, don't you?"

"Yes," Emmeline said wretchedly.

"Then go to him. Tell him so." The look in Becky's eyes
was urgent. "Oh, Emmeline, life is so short—if there's a
chance in all the world of making Rafe see—"

Emmeline shook her head again, looking not at Becky's
face now, but through the dining-room window to the
street. John Lewis was passing by on the sidewalk, a bunch
of wildflowers in his gun hand; a few moments later, both
women heard the bell ring at the registration desk.

"Go to him," Emmeline said, kissing Becky's cool, carefully powdered cheek. "As you said, life is so very short, and you mustn't waste a minute."

Becky hesitated, then straightened her spine and put on her most brilliant smile. "Well," she said, "I'd be a hypocrite if I didn't take my own advice, now wouldn't I?" With that, she strolled out into the lobby to greet her suitor warmly, while Emmeline stayed rooted to the spot for a long time, her eyes full of tears, smiling at her mother's hard-earned happiness.

Rafe kept himself away from the former Territorial Hotel, now called the Arizona and already looking considerably spiffier than it had under his pa's ownership, with lace curtains at the windows and flowerpots on the sills. There was talk over at the Bloody Basin that Becky planned to build on to the place; Hyde Wilkerson, the saloon owner, who sold lumber from trees harvested up around Flagstaff as one of several sidelines, said she'd already ordered the supplies.

Biding his time on the corner by the telegraph office, dressed up in his best clothes, Rafe kept an eye on the hotel, hoping for a glimpse of Emmeline, but so far he hadn't seen hide nor hair of her. He'd sure enough seen Holt, though, walking right into the Arizona Hotel, like he had every call to go in there. And he'd still been fuming over that when Marshal Lewis had come up behind him and caught him unawares.

"Howdy, Rafe," he'd said, grinning. He had a handful of pink and yellow flowers, probably gathered in the vacant lot behind the livery stable, where such things flourished because of the manure pile. He took in Rafe's good suit of clothes. "You got business in town, or do I have to arrest you for loitering?"

Rafe had eyed the flowers and resettled his hat. "Just waiting for my horse to be shod," he said.

"Thought you did all your blacksmithing right on the ranch," Lewis replied, with an eloquent glance toward the hotel. Once old John got a man on the hook, he didn't like to let him off easy. "Why don't you go over there and say hello to that bride of yours? Fetch her home, like you ought to have done a week ago?"

Rafe's neck felt hot, and it seemed to swell, too, making him want to unbutton his collar and shove it into his coat pocket—or toss it into the first alley he passed. "What goes on between Emmeline and me is our business and nobody else's," he said.

John's easy shrug made Rafe see red. "Well, then, have the decency to divorce her, will you? This town is chockfull of men looking to take a wife, and Miss Emmeline is prime pickings. Folks are already speculating on when she'll be back on the market."

Rafe's right hand clenched into a fist of its own accord, but he consciously opened his fingers. Much as he'd like to knock John Lewis into the nearest horse trough, he figured he couldn't afford the indulgence. Punching an officer of the law was bound to be a crime, and he'd most likely end up behind bars for a good long while.

Besides, fighting didn't have the same appeal it once had.

John smiled and nodded, as if he'd followed Rafe's thought processes. "I'd best be going," he said, indicating the flowers, which were already starting to wilt, clutched in his big hand the way they were. "I've got a good woman waiting for me."

The marshal was referring to Becky Fairmont, of course, and even though Rafe could have told the man a few things about his "good woman," he would never have done so. A confidence of any sort was safe in Rafe's keeping, gall him though it might, whether telling it served his purposes or not. Anyway, he liked Becky, even admired her.

He pulled at the brim of his hat in unspoken farewell. "I'd just as soon you didn't mention me when you get there," he said, turning to leave. He'd head himself in the direction of the livery stable, like he was going there to pick up his freshly shod horse. Maybe jaw awhile with Old Billy, who ran the business. When it was time to head for home, he'd fetch Chief from the fenced pasture in back of the mercantile, where he'd been grazing all the while, and saddle up.

Rafe made his way to the stable, watching Old Billy run the forge, and marveling. The man was eighty if he was a day, but he still had a full head of black hair, a chest like a bull's, and upper arms the size of a ham hock. His face and clothes, especially his leather apron, were covered with soot, and his hammer rang as he laid a red-hot horseshoe on the anvil and pounded it into shape. There was a sizzling sound, and a rise of steam, when he thrust his pinchers and the shoe into a trough at his feet.

He blinked, evidently having forgotten that Rafe was there. "What do you want?" he demanded, even though they'd been talking about the coming of the railroad just five minutes back. It would seem that Old Billy's mind hadn't held up to the passing of time as well as his body had.

Rafe chuckled, but before he could answer, Billy's gaze drifted past him, and a silly smile cracked his blackened face.

"Howdy, ma'am," he said, with genuine admiration. He even made a little bow.

Rafe turned and saw Emmeline standing a few feet away. She'd just rounded the corner of the building, it appeared, and stopped in her tracks when she saw him. She flushed, and raised her chin in that stubborn way she had, but she didn't say a word. Rafe was pretty well tongue-tied himself; he'd been hoping for a look at Emmeline, all right, but at a distance, so he could keep his feelings to himself.

He nodded, pretty sure he was growing roots that would keep him pinned to that spot for the rest of his natural life, like a tree.

She found her voice first. "What are you doing here?" she asked, like he needed her permission to set foot in Indian Rock.

He pushed his hat to the back of his head, stuck for an answer. "What are *you* doing here?" he countered, stalling.

Her eyes flashed. He loved her eyes. They were blue sometimes, gray at others, like a changing sky. Today, there was a storm brewing, with plenty of thunder and lightning. "I've been bamboozled," she said, sounding purely disgusted.

He wanted to laugh—he loved her temper as much as her expressive eyes—but he couldn't quite summon up the wherewithal because, at the same time, he felt as if something vital had been yanked right out of his middle. Sweet God, what had come over him?

"Dammit," the smithy put in, at Rafe's side all of the sudden, nudging him with a filthy elbow. Irascible old goat. "Say something!"

"Wait until I get my hands on those two!" Emmeline ranted, her cheeks pink. She tossed her head for emphasis, and her hair started coming loose from its pins. He loved her hair, longed to let it down and run his fingers through it. "I should have known they were up to something."

Old Billy was fixing to elbow Rafe again, so he stepped out of range, dusting off his coat where the old man had marked him with soot the time before.

Rafe didn't need to ask what Emmeline was talking about; he knew well enough. John Lewis had been on his way to the hotel when he and Rafe met, and it didn't take a great mind to figure out that he and Becky had had themselves a powwow and then cooked up some excuse to send Emmeline to the livery stable, hoping the two of them would meet up.

"Say something!" Old Billy ordered, moving in for another jab.

Rafe sidestepped the smithy and made himself approach Emmeline. He took off his hat and looked down at her face and wondered how the devil he'd be able to stay mad at her for the rest of his life. It would take some doing, he decided, but he'd manage.

All he had to do was think of her selling herself to Holt.

"I'll walk you back to the hotel," he said, as if they were cordial strangers.

She stiffened her spine. "Don't trouble yourself," she replied, with a lift of her chin. "I'm perfectly capable of walking two blocks in broad daylight."

"Young people today," complained Old Billy, shaking his head. "They just don't know how to spark." His great shoulders were bent as he went back to his forge.

Emmeline closed her mouth on what might have been a smile, or even a laugh, and turned to march away.

Rafe fell in beside her; he hadn't intended to, after she'd put him in his place like that, but there he was, doing it, still holding his hat in one hand. Why, a part of him wished he had those flowers of John's to give to her. Wished he'd read some poetry books along the way, too, like Kade had, so he'd have something fancy to say. He tended to read about practical subjects, like water tables and animal husbandry and timber management—not much romance in those things.

"You all right?" he asked.

"Oh, I'm just fine," she snapped, picking up her pace a little.

He lengthened his stride. Damned if she was going to leave him behind. *He'd* do all the leaving behind that was going to be done. "Well, then," he said, "I guess there's nothing more to say."

She hesitated only a beat, but it was long enough for Rafe to figure out that she wasn't as dead set against him as she'd like him to believe. "I guess not," she agreed tersely.

He caught hold of her arm, stopped her, right there on the sidewalk, with half the town of Indian Rock probably looking on, like it was any of their darned business what happened between him and Emmeline, anyhow. He said her name, ragged-like, and then didn't know how to go on from there.

She pulled her arm free. "You owe me an apology, Rafe McKettrick!" she said in a furious whisper.

Getting mad was something he knew how to do. He was almost grateful to her for shaking him out of his fuddled state. "*I* owe *you* an apology? How do you figure that?"

She narrowed her eyes. "You know what I'm talking about!" she seethed.

His nose was an inch from hers, he'd leaned in so close. "The hell I do!" he shot back. "You're the one who—" He stopped, unsure how to phrase the rest of that sentence in a socially acceptable way. They were, after all, in public.

"You *know* exactly what I'm talking about, Mr. McKettrick!"

"Do we have to discuss this on the sidewalk?" Without waiting for an answer, he took Emmeline by the wrist again, making sure not to hurt her, and pulled her down the street and straight into the lobby of the Arizona Hotel.

Clive, the nun, and a peddler, just signing for a room, turned to stare as they entered. Becky and John Lewis were probably keeping themselves out of sight, until things settled down a bit, which only showed they were brighter than Rafe would have given them credit for.

He dragged Emmeline to the back of the lobby, behind a potted palm tree with yellowing fronds, and glared at her. She glared right back.

"You know, Rafe," she insisted. "Holt told you nothing happened that night." She paused. "You're just being hardheaded!" Her color was still high, and her eyes were flashing. He could see her pulse thrumming at one temple, and at the base of her throat. And he wanted, more than anything, to kiss her so she stayed kissed.

"What I know," he rasped, "is that you told me you were a whore!"

She turned crimson, and the palm fronds rustled where she pushed them aside to peek into the lobby, in case anyone was listening. Clive and the nun were gone, but that didn't account for the traveling salesman.

"Well, I was mistaken," she said.

He was astounded. "It's true? You didn't—?"

"That seems to be what she's saying," observed the peddler, from the upper landing. He was bending over the banister and peering down at them.

Rafe nearly pulled his pistol on the fellow, though he wouldn't actually have shot him, of course. Just made him dance a little. "I'll thank you to stay out of this discussion, mister," he growled.

Wisely, the man made himself scarce. Almost immediately, they heard the sound of a key grinding in a stubborn lock, followed by the closing of a door.

"Go away, Rafe," Emmeline said. "Go home to the Triple M and don't come back until you're ready to say you're sorry for treating me the way you did."

He stared at her, furiously confounded. "You want me to say *I'm* sorry? I didn't start all this!"

"You've treated me abominably," she said. "You burned down our house, and you were ready to believe the worst about me, even after all we'd been to each other."

By then, Rafe was struck dumb, and his collar was cutting off his air. He tore it off and sent it sailing, and it landed in the upper part of the palm tree, dangling there like a half moon made of celluloid. He couldn't have uttered a sensible word for anything just then.

"Out!" Emmeline said, pointing dramatically in the direction of the door. "Just get out!"

Rafe had been thrown out of saloons before, and even a bathhouse once, in Denver, but never a respectable hotel. He stood his ground, folded his arms, and wished to God he knew what to say.

He was saved by Becky's appearance. She swept down the stairway, next to them, in a cloud of perfume and gracious goodwill.

"Why, Rafe," she said, extending a hand and smiling for all the world as if they'd met at some fancy party, "how wonderful to see you!" She hooked her arm through his and steered him away from Emmeline and across the lobby, toward the dining room. "How are Angus and Concepcion? Has there been any word from your youngest brother?"

With Emmeline, Rafe had felt as though he had a whole apple stuck in his throat, but with Becky, he found he could talk. Maybe it was just that he'd taken off that damnable collar.

"Your daughter, or niece, or whatever she is," he sputtered, letting her polite questions go hang, "is one infuriating female!"

Becky laughed. "Yes," she agreed. "Isn't she wonderful?"

The stage driver ambled in then, covered with trail dust and carrying a battered envelope in one hand. He touched his hat to Becky, but addressed Rafe.

"Just the man I wanted to see," he said, smirking a little. "I got a letter for you. You got another bride on the way, Rafe?"

Frowning, Rafe stepped forward. He took the missive, read the return address, and was struck by a terrible premonition. *The Happy Home Matrimonial Service.*

He tore open the envelope, unfolded the page with a shake of his wrist.

"Dear Mr. McKettrick," it began. "We at the Happy Home Matrimonial Service regret to inform you . . ."

He found a chair and fell into it. Read the letter again, and then once more, just to be sure.

Becky laid a hand on his shoulder. She seemed worried, and rightly so, if he looked the way he felt right then.

"Rafe?" she asked quietly. "What is it?"

He looked up at her. "There was a legal problem—something about the proxy—" he managed.

Becky frowned, waiting.

Rafe didn't know whether to shout for joy or break down and cry like an old woman. "Emmeline and I," he said, and paused to swallow hard, "we aren't married after all."

# CHAPTER

## 18

EMMELINE BLINKED. The plank floor of the hotel lobby went soft under her feet. "What?" she gasped, thinking of the times she'd given herself to Rafe McKettrick, like a shameless hussy, without a trace of modesty or reserve.

"We're not married," Rafe said. Clive and Sister Mandy looked up from the registration book at the desk, where they'd been conferring over something, and Becky hovered nearby, as if she might be called upon to catch Emmeline in a grand swoon.

Emmeline slapped a hand over her mouth, then reached out and snatched the letter from Rafe's hand. She read the damning words over several times before she was really able to take them in.

"Emmeline," Rafe said gruffly, "I'm willing to make an honest woman of you. We can go find the preacher right away and—"

"*Make an honest woman out of me?*" Emmeline raged, shoving the letter, now crumpled in her fist, at Rafe. "Of all the arrogant, insensitive, *wretched* things to say—"

Rafe flushed, and straightened his spine. "Well," he said, in a way that obviously seemed reasonable to him, "it isn't as if you're *pure* or anything—"

Emmeline lost control of herself in that moment and did something she'd never even imagined doing before— she struck Rafe McKettrick across the face so hard that he rocked back on the heels of his boots. "Get out!" she screamed, while another Emmeline stood apart, astounded and appalled. "Get out of this hotel and don't ever come back!" She saw Becky at the edge of her vision, closing her eyes and shaking her head.

"That," Rafe yelled back, "is exactly what I mean to do!" He turned and stormed across the room to the doors, which were open to the sunshine and relatively fresh air, and even before he hit the sidewalk, Emmeline wanted to call him back.

Her pride wouldn't allow it. She looked at Becky in a fever of desperation.

"Oh, Emmeline," Becky said, very softly, "this is no time to be pigheaded. Go after the man."

But Emmeline was unable to move. She watched through dry, burning eyes as Rafe strode past the front window, never so much as glancing her way.

"If he wants me," she said, raising her chin, "he'll have to come courting." With that, she turned, climbed the stairs with all the dignity of a reigning queen, and promenaded along the second-floor corridor to the room she shared with Becky. There, she opened the door with decorum, stepped over the threshold, grabbed the pitcher from the washstand, and flung it hard against the nearest wall. It shattered with a satisfying, almost musical clatter.

The basin soon followed, splintering into a hundred tinkling shards.

Emmeline slammed the door behind her, marched herself over to the bed, and flung herself onto it, face-down, stricken by an unendurable grief.

She was now officially a fallen woman, used merchandise. And Rafe *pitied* her.

She began to sob, letting go of years of secret mourning, weeping not just for the loss of her marriage but for the little-girl parties she'd never been invited to as a child, for the times on the street, when she'd been running some errand or other, and women had swept their skirts aside as she passed, for all the dances she'd never danced, and all the flowers she'd never been given. For all the times she'd been brave, and raised her chin, and said it didn't matter.

Here, at last, was something that *did* matter, unequivocally, undeniably: the link between her heart and Rafe's. And now that was gone, too, just another flight of fancy.

Presently, Emmeline sat up, wiping her face with the heels of her palms.

It was time she put away childish things, once and for

all. She was a woman, and there would be no more pretending.

Rafe was pacing off measurements and driving stakes into the ground when Kade rode across the creek, no doubt having spotted him from the barn, and sat there, leaning on the canticle of his saddle, watching him.

"What the hell are you doing?" he finally asked, when Rafe volunteered nothing. By that time, word was probably all over the territory that his marriage to Emmeline was nothing but a farce, and she probably had half a dozen suitors by now. Kade had to know, and now he was just looking for a chance to rub it in.

Rafe picked up a hammer and drove in a stake with one blow. "Fixing to build myself another house," he said, with appropriate irony. After all, it would have been obvious to a blind man, what he was doing.

Kade narrowed his eyes, resettled his hat. Got down off the horse. "Why, so you can burn it down in a fit of temper, the way you did the last one?"

Rafe favored his brother with a scathing glance. "I mean to take another wife," he said. "Start over from scratch. This time, I'll have a house ready. Do things right."

Kade stared at him. It wasn't often that he was at a loss for words, but this time, he appeared to be choking on his own tongue. "What about Emmeline?" he demanded. "Or are you taking up bigamy now?"

"They made a mistake, at the Happy Home Matrimonial Service," he confessed, and he felt some of the starch going out of him, just by saying the words. "Turns out Emmeline and I were never legally married."

Kade let out a long whistle of exclamation, and Rafe, watching his brother through narrowed eyes, couldn't rightly tell if he was sympathetic or not. "Son of a gun," he said.

"I figure this is my chance to take up with somebody more suited to life on a ranch," Rafe said.

"Like who?" Kade demanded, wrenching off his hat. He looked like he might take a bite right out of the brim. "Just exactly who do you figure on marrying? That little nun at the hotel? Or maybe you mean to chase after Phoebe Anne's train and drag her back?"

"I'll find somebody," he said, pounding hard at one of the stakes in the ground.

Kade sighed and wheeled his arms once, for emphasis, Rafe guessed. "I knew you had your head stuck up your ass," he said, "but I never reckoned how far!" He took a step toward Rafe, like he wanted to punch him, and then stopped, which was a wise choice on his part. If he wanted a fight, Rafe would oblige, and this time it would be no good-natured, brotherly scuffle, like the one before Jeb left. "Are you crazy, or what?" Kade persisted. "Emmeline is beautiful. She's sweet, and smart, too—the kind of woman any man would be proud to have for a wife, and the mother of his children."

"You want to marry her?" Rafe drawled. And then he frowned. It hadn't occurred to him that one of his own brothers might step in and offer himself as Emmeline's next husband. Now, he knew it was a real possibility—he could picture either Kade or Jeb riding to the rescue, and Emmeline might go along with such a plan out of sheer spite.

"I might just do that," Kade said, and he looked like he meant it. "I'd sure as hell treat her better than you have. Not that that would take much doing, Big Brother."

Rafe looked at the sharpened stake in his hand, looked up at his brother. *Nah*, he thought. Violence never really solved anything, and, besides, Pa would be sure to spot the body right away, since this was one of his favorite places to walk when he was brooding over something.

"Stay away from Emmeline," Rafe said. He couldn't help reflecting on what it would be like if she took up with another McKettrick. He'd have no choice but to pack up and leave the Triple M for good.

Kade put his hat on, took it clear off again and slapped one thigh with it before slapping it back on his head. His horse, grazing a few yards away, got fretful, and did some fancy sidestepping before calming down. "Have you even tried to talk to her about this?"

Rafe felt the sting of Emmeline's rejection all over again. He'd offered to do right by her, despite all she'd put him through, and she'd thrown his suggestion right back in his face. "The time for talking is past," he said. He paused, swept a hand through his hair. His voice was lower when he spoke again, and sort of ragged. "Word around town is, Emmeline's come into some money. She's the independent kind, anyhow. Like as not, she'll move on."

Kade looked patently unconvinced. "Did she *say* she was going to do that?"

Rafe shook his head. "No," he said. "But I figure when she hears I've ordered up a new bride, she'll pack up and go." At least, that was what he hoped she would do. A contrary woman like Emmeline could be downright unpredictable, though.

"You sent away for another bride, after what just happened? Are you out of your mind?"

Kade looked as though he'd like to deck him, right then and there, but, wisely, he showed some restraint. Something flickered in his face—the same look he got when he drew a good poker hand—and then he asked the question that struck Rafe's solar plexus like a fist. "What if she's pregnant, Rafe? You ever think of that?"

He hadn't, what with all that had been going on, and now he felt as though his knees might give way.

"You didn't, did you?" Kade challenged, when Rafe failed to answer.

Rafe dropped the stake, dropped the mallet. Grabbed Kade by the front of his shirt. "You know something I don't?" he demanded, in a whisper sharp enough to saw at the inside of his throat.

Kade knocked Rafe's hands away, adjusted his shirt indignantly. "Big Brother," he said, "I know *plenty* of things you don't."

"Right now," Rafe said, flexing his fingers, "I'm only interested in one of those things." He wanted to grab Kade again, but he resisted the temptation. There'd be a fight for sure if he did, and he needed to keep his head. "Tell me about Emmeline."

"There are a few rumors going around town, that's all," Kade said. He looked almost contrite now, though there was a glint in his eyes that Rafe didn't care for at all.

The thought of folks gossiping about Emmeline, for any reason, made Rafe spitting mad. They had no damn right, poking and prodding, making judgments, prying into other people's private business. "Like what?" he asked, his voice low.

"She and Becky mean to build on to the hotel," Kade answered. "That's general knowledge. She's supposed to be heading for San Francisco one day soon—Emmeline, I mean—on some kind of buying trip. Might be gone for some time, according to Minnie, over at the mercantile. Folks are saying Emmeline's in the family way, and planning to have the baby there on the coast, where nobody knows her."

"Since when," Rafe rasped, shoving his hands into his pockets to keep them from going for Kade's throat, "are *you* privy to that kind of woman-talk?"

Kade smiled. "Since I've been looking for a wife," he answered. "I make it a point to talk to everybody who might have an unattached female relative. You see, I still haven't given up on turning the tables on you, Big Brother. Fact is, I've been getting letters from half a dozen marriageable women back east." He paused. Smiled. "How would you like to take orders from me?"

Rafe spat in answer to that, then turned, half blinded

by fractiousness and despair, and stomped off toward his horse. Chief, always a dependable critter before, whinnied and tossed his head, keeping himself and his dangling reins just out of Rafe's reach. No doubt, he'd picked right up on Rafe's mood, and wanted no part of his plans.

Behind him, Kade laughed. "Going somewhere, Rafe?" he asked.

Rafe managed to catch hold of Chief, calmed him down with a few terse but reassuring words, and mounted. By God, if Emmeline *was* expecting a child, and she hadn't seen fit to tell him, he'd have a thing or two to say to her.

"You'd better hurry, if you're headed for town," Kade said, climbing back into the saddle himself. "Fine woman like Emmeline, why, she's probably got a waiting list of men wanting to court her as soon as she takes your ring off. Past or no past, baby or no baby."

Rafe's belly churned at the images taking shape in his mind. He wheeled the horse around, without another word to his brother, intent on only one thing—confronting Emmeline.

Emmeline's bags were packed, and stacked on the sidewalk outside the general store. The stagecoach had just rolled in, disgorging an interesting flock of passengers, and the air was roiling with dust. Becky stood next to Emmeline, a handkerchief pressed to her nose and mouth. John Lewis was there, too, as unsettled as Becky was.

Neither of them wanted Emmeline to make the trip to San Francisco, especially alone, but she'd made up her mind. She needed some time away, to think matters through. Especially since Minnie, who managed the post office in the back of the general store, had confided, two days ago, that Rafe was "up to his old tricks again."

Emmeline, there to pick up Becky's mail, most of it forwarded from Kansas City, had not been able to resist asking what those "old tricks" might be, and Minnie had told her, with feigned reluctance, about Rafe's *new* letter to the Happy Home Matrimonial Service, in Kansas City. She'd heard tell, Minnie said dolorously, that Rafe was fixing to try married life again, with a brand-new bride. Emmeline, seething, wouldn't have been surprised if the old snoop had steamed the envelope open and read Rafe's letter for herself, but at that moment, and in the furious and anguished minutes, hours, and days following, the other woman's perfidy was hardly her foremost concern.

Emmeline could barely eat or sleep, and she found it impossible to concentrate on any task more complicated than peeling potatoes for Stockard. The *nerve* of Rafe McKettrick. Why, she must have meant nothing at all to him—by now, her name had surely been crossed out of the fat family Bible, under "Marriages," to make room for the next, the *real*, Mrs. Rafe McKettrick.

"I've always wanted to go to San Francisco," she told Becky and the marshal calmly, as she waited to board the coach. She kissed Becky's cheek. "You've been feeling much better, and now that Clive and Mandy are properly trained, and John here is overseeing things, I don't have to worry—at least, not quite so much—that you'll overwork yourself and fall ill."

"But—" Becky protested. She'd already tried all her best arguments, it seemed, and now she was fresh out.

Emmeline forced a smile. The driver was loading her things into the boot of the stage. "I won't be gone long," she said. "I'll order the new furniture we need for the hotel, take a week or so to see the sights and do some shopping, and then I'll be back."

"Ready, Mrs. McKettrick?" the driver asked. She flinched at the use of the name that had never been rightfully hers. Apparently, she was the only departing passenger.

She nodded numbly.

"We could order everything we need from the catalog!" Becky protested, not ready to give up, even though she'd used that suggestion before, several times.

The driver opened the door of the stagecoach, pulled down the folding step, and extended a hand to Emmeline.

Emmeline shook her head at Becky. "I wouldn't think of making such an investment without looking at the merchandise in person," she said, almost convincing herself that business was the real reason for this journey. "We want the very best for the Arizona Hotel."

"I want the very best for you," Becky said. "I don't give a damn about the Arizona Hotel!"

"Take care of her," Emmeline said to John in a soft but stern voice. Then she kissed Becky once more, offering a silent prayer for the other woman's well-being as she did so, said one more goodbye, and boarded the stage. She waved through the window, and Becky waved back with the handkerchief, before pressing it to her eyes.

It was well after dark when Rafe finally reached the Arizona Hotel, Chief having thrown a shoe on the way to town, and subsequently come up lame. He'd had to walk for the better part of five miles, before Kade came meandering along in a buckboard, acting surprised to find his brother on foot in the middle of nowhere, leading a horse. "Need a ride?" he'd asked.

If he hadn't been so desperate to get to Emmeline, Rafe would have told Kade what he could do with the wagon *and* the team and kept walking. Instead, he took the necessary gear from the bed of the buckboard, replacing Chief's bridle with a rope and halter, and hitched him to the tailgate. The seat creaked as Rafe climbed up into the box beside Kade.

They couldn't travel fast, leading a gimpy horse, but riding was better than walking. Kade didn't try to strike up a conversation, but he was a burr in Rafe's side all the same, because he kept on grinning to himself, and whistling under his breath.

When they got to Indian Rock, Kade drove right to the hotel without even asking if that was Rafe's destination.

"I'll take Chief over to the livery stable," Kade said, with a wry grin and a tip of his hat. "Say hello to Emmeline for me."

Rafe didn't spare his brother a reply, but simply stalked into the lobby.

Becky was behind the registration desk, and she didn't just look startled to see him, she looked downright horrified.

"Rafe!" she said, running her gaze over the length of him, from his hat to his boots and finally back to his face.

He approached the desk, leaned against it, bracing himself with his hands. It didn't occur to him until then that he was dirty, and still wearing his work clothes—trousers, barn boots, the top to a pair of old long johns, and suspenders. He gave the matter of his appearance a cursory consideration, then decided he didn't give a damn what he looked like. "Is Emmeline here?" he asked.

"Are you all right, Rafe?" Becky came around the end of the desk to take his arm. "You look as though you walked all the way from the Triple M."

He felt as if he had done precisely that, and without his boots, but it didn't matter now how he'd gotten there. He had arrived, blistered feet, smarting pride, and all, and now he could have a word or two with Emmeline, find out what was what. "My wife?" he pressed.

Becky did not question his use of the word *wife*. She winced slightly, though, or so it seemed to Rafe. The movement was subtle, and quickly gone, so he couldn't be sure. "Oh, dear," she said in a trilling voice, steering him toward one of the lobby chairs. "You'd better sit down."

He sat. "Where is she?" he ground out, bending forward, resting his elbows on his knees. There was another potted palm next to his chair, and he swatted at it when the damn thing tried to grab him.

"She's gone," Becky said.

"Gone?" Rafe felt dazed, as if he'd just knocked back three shots of bad whiskey without taking a breath in between.

"Well, yes," Becky went on, straightening her spine and folding her hands in her lap. "She left on this afternoon's stagecoach, headed for San Francisco."

Even though Kade had prepared him for this possibility, out there by the creek, Rafe still felt as though he'd been run down by a loaded freight wagon, then backed over for good measure. "San Francisco?" he asked, as if he'd never heard of the place, though he recollected, vaguely, that Kade had mentioned it.

Becky made a game attempt at a smile, probably trying to appease him. "Yes," she said. "We're building on to the hotel, so we'll be needing proper furnishings. You know, beds, chairs, bureaus, carpets—"

Rafe thought he'd shoot right through the ceiling if he had to listen to any more prattle about household goods. "When will she be back?" he asked, rising slowly to his feet.

Becky caught hold of his hand, urged him, with a few small tugs at his fingers and a plea in her eyes, to sit down again. He did, but only because his knees had gone soft all of a sudden. "I imagine it will take a month or so," she said gently, as if she were soothing some great, steam-snorting beast fixing to run amok in her lobby. "San Francisco is quite a distance from here, you know. And

Emmeline wanted to buy some new clothes, see the sights, have a rest—"

"A month," Rafe breathed. A month was forever.

"It'll go by in no time," Becky said brightly, just as John Lewis strolled in from the street.

"Well," he said, clearly less inclined toward hospitality than Becky was, "if it isn't Happy Home's best customer."

Rafe was too tired, and far too discouraged, to lose his temper just then, but there was always later. "I've got to go after her," he said, getting to his feet.

Lewis laid a hand on his shoulder. It was an affectionate gesture, maybe a little more forceful than it ought to have been. "Come on over to the Bloody Basin," he said. "I'll buy you a drink."

"I don't want a drink."

"Yes," Lewis said, unruffled, "I believe you do."

The first stop on the route to San Francisco was at a little waystation in the middle of the desert, a wide spot in the road with the unprepossessing name of Rattlesnake Bend. There were rooms to be had for fifty cents a night, an exorbitant price for such rude accommodations, and Emmeline took one, though she wasn't sure she'd dare to close her eyes before morning. The man running the place was a seedy drunk, with breath so foul it nearly knocked her over, and there were outlaw types in the common room, which doubled as an eatery and a saloon, swilling whiskey and sizing her up with their eyes.

Emmeline was glad she'd brought some of Stockard's

meatloaf sandwiches and a bottle of lemonade for the journey. She was hungry, but she wouldn't have sat with those dreadful men or sampled the fare in that establishment to save herself from starvation.

Her room, at the back of a short hallway, offered no comfort. The walls were framed in, but not finished, and there were spiders. The mattress ticking was bare, and the print seemed to be moving. The basin on the rickety washstand was half full of grimy water, left behind by the last tenant, and the pitcher was rusted.

Emmeline shuddered. She'd stayed in some economical establishments on her way from Kansas City to Indian Rock when she'd first come to the territory, but none of them had been this bad. She wondered if a person could sleep standing up, the way horses did, and figured she'd try it that night and find out.

She was perched on the edge of the only chair in the room, a wooden one with a rung missing from the back, trying to eat her sandwich, when a brisk knock at the door nearly startled her out of her skin.

"Who's there?" she asked, trying to sound imperious. Becky had offered her a pearl-handled derringer before she left; now, she was beginning to wish she'd accepted it.

"Name's Lucy," called a cheerful voice. "Come to make up your room. Zeb shouldn't have hired it out before I got a chance to ready the place, but there you have it. Hasn't been sober a day since before I took up with him, old Zeb."

Emmeline carefully rewrapped her sandwich in the

napkin Stockard had packed it in, set it on top of her largest trunk, and went to the door. She opened it a crack and peered around the edge, relieved to see a woman standing there, smiling a gap-toothed smile and holding an armful of bedding.

"It's all right," Lucy said kindly. "Nobody out here but me."

Emmeline stepped back to admit the woman, then closed the door hastily behind her. She'd read of ruffians forcing their way into the rooms of travelers in broad daylight, let alone when it was dark out, like now, to commit robbery and mayhem.

Lucy made up the bed with threadbare but clean sheets, and tattered blankets bearing the legend U.S. CAVALRY. She clucked and shook her head when she saw the basin and pitcher.

"This place ain't fit for a sow bear, let alone a fine lady like yourself," she said, with an expansive sigh.

Emmeline certainly agreed, for her part, anyway; she wouldn't have presumed to speak for the bear. And it wasn't as if there were a great many alternatives, when it came to accommodations. Rattlesnake Bend was no Indian Rock, after all; she couldn't expect to find a room and a dining hall like the ones at the Arizona Hotel in a little outpost out in the middle of the desert. "Have you lived here very long?" she asked, trying to make conversation. Lucy's presence, such as it was, was comforting.

Lucy collected the basin and pitcher, still *tsk-tsk*ing. "Me and Zeb put up this place about ten years back," she said, headed for the door. "I'll fetch you my own china wash set, don't you worry, and be back before you can say 'Mary Todd Lincoln.' Mind you put the latch down, and don't open up to anyone but me."

Emmeline nodded anxiously, and fixed the latch as soon as Lucy had gone. She crept over to the bed and inspected the newly supplied sheets and blankets, which looked passably clean, and decided she might be able to lie down to sleep if she didn't take off any of her clothes.

In a short while, Lucy returned with a chipped basin and matching pitcher, obviously personal treasures, and Emmeline was touched that she was willing to share them. There was a towel, too, but no soap, which didn't matter, because Emmeline had brought her own.

"Thank you," Emmeline said, ridiculously grateful.

"You'd better put the chair back under the doorknob if you're ready to settle in for the night. Latch or no latch, some of these fellows out here are a mite on the rough side. You been to the outhouse?"

Emmeline reddened. She suspected there was a chamber pot under the bed, but she'd been afraid to look. And she'd rather pass the night with a full bladder than venture out into the dark alone.

Lucy smiled. "Here, now, don't be fretting. I'll walk out there with you, and wait while you do your business. You travelin' far, hon'?"

Having no other choice, Emmeline put on her cloak and slipped her drawstring bag over one wrist, for safe-keeping. Her tickets and traveling money were in that purse, and she wasn't about to leave it unattended in her room. "San Francisco," she said.

Lucy took a lantern from a hook on the wall, next to the back door, lit it, and led the way to the privy, a narrow, lopsided structure looming ahead like a ruin from some ancient and dissolute civilization. "Never been any further west than right here," she replied.

They reached the outhouse, and Emmeline went in, holding her breath, trying not to retch. She felt spiderwebs touch her hair, and heard something scurry away into a corner.

"Can't say as we get that many women through here traveling by themselves," Lucy called companionably from her post outside. "You runnin' away from the law or a man or something?"

Emmeline did what she had to do and dived for the door. Outside, in the relatively fresh air, she gulped for breath. "No," she said, though that was only a partial truth. The law wasn't after her. She was running away from Rafe McKettrick and his new mail-order bride, though. She hadn't admitted to herself, until that moment outside Lucy and Zeb's horrendous toilet, that she might never go back. Now, she knew that had been in her mind all along; Becky had known it, too. That was why she'd tried so hard to persuade her to stay.

Lucy held the lantern high. "All right, now?" she asked, with another smile.

Emmeline nodded, and followed her back inside.

It was the middle of the night, and Emmeline was

lying on that reprehensible bed, wearing all her clothes, including her bonnet and shoes, and only half asleep, when a thunderous knock sounded at her door. This time, she knew it wasn't Lucy who'd come calling.

She bolted out of bed and rushed over to the door, where she had not only put the latch in place but propped the chair back underneath the knob, as Lucy had suggested. Again, she yearned for Becky's derringer. If she'd had it, she might have fired right through the door, no questions asked.

"Go away!" she called. "I've got a gun!"

"I'm not going anywhere!" Rafe yelled back. It *was* his voice, wasn't it? She wasn't dreaming? "Dammit, Emmeline, let me in!"

A surge of joyous chagrin brought her wide awake. "It *is* you!" she cried, tossing the chair aside, lifting the latch, flinging open the door with such force that it clattered against the inside wall. She flung herself into his arms. "Thank God you came, Rafe! Thank God!"

He held her away, but not far. His blue eyes, their color discernible even in the deep shadows, searched her face. "You're *glad* to see me?"

She thought about it. "Yes," she decided. "Yes, I suppose I am."

"You're not going to San Francisco and have my baby alone," he said. "And that's final!"

She pulled him into the room. "What are you talking about?" she demanded in a whisper. Now that she was recovering from the shock of finding Rafe outside her door in the middle of the longest and most miserable night she'd ever spent, she was more conscious of listening ears.

Rafe stood with his back to the door. He was wearing work clothes, and he looked as though he'd been dragged behind a horse, at least part of the way. He needed a bath, and a shave, but he still looked as though he ought to have a place on Mount Olympus, he was so handsome. "I was wrong," he said. "I was wrong about everything, Emmeline. I love you, and I want you to come home with me. Marry me, right and proper."

She stared at him, her heart picking up speed with every beat. She couldn't allow herself any false hopes, though—the fall, when reality caught up to her, would be too long and too hard. He thought she was pregnant. That was why he was declaring himself now, after all this time, when he'd never done it before. "You mentioned a child," she said carefully. "There's no baby, Rafe."

"I don't care," he said, and he looked so anxious that he had to be speaking the truth. "I don't care what went on Kansas City, either."

"*Nothing* went on in Kansas City," she said fiercely.

He gathered her into his arms. "I love you, Emmeline," he repeated.

She pulled back, her head clearing a little. "What about that new bride you ordered?" she wanted to know.

His grin was boyish. "I'm sure Kade or Jeb will take her off my hands, if she shows up at all," he said. "Emmeline, did you hear me before? I said I love you."

She let her forehead rest against his strong shoulder.

"And I love you," she admitted. "Against my better judgment, Rafe McKettrick, I do love you."

"Then let's go home, right now, tonight. There's something I want to show you."

She laughed up at him, and there were tears of joy gathering in her eyes. "Rafe," she said reasonably, "we can leave in the morning."

His grin turned into a blinding smile. "You've changed your mind about San Francisco, then?"

"For now, anyway," she said, with a little shrug and a tilted smile. "The hotel furniture can wait."

# CHAPTER

## ❧ 19 ❧

As TOWNS WENT, Rattlesnake Bend did not have much to recommend it, but it did have a preacher of sorts. It took a dousing with bucket of cold well water to arouse the Reverend Horace P. Deever, who was passed out under the card table in the common room of the inn, but he was able to produce credentials when Rafe asked to see them.

After he'd been helped to his feet, the reverend patted various pockets until he located what he sought, and brought out a soggy document proclaiming him to be a graduate of a Bible college somewhere down south.

Rafe read it over carefully, with Emmeline peering around his arm all the while, determined not to enter into another bogus marriage.

"Looks all right to me," Rafe said.

"The reverend preaches a right fiery sermon when he's

sober," Lucy put in, with enthusiasm. This, apparently, was meant as a recommendation.

"Well, then, we're in luck," Rafe said. "The last thing we want right now is a sermon." He brought a five-dollar gold piece out of his vest pocket—Emmeline's eyes widened at the sight of it, and so did the reverend's—and held it between two fingers. "We want to get married." He paused, glanced uncertainly down at Emmeline. "At least, I do. Do you?"

She nodded, and then frowned a little. "There are a couple of conditions—"

Rafe looked worried, and none too patient. "Emmeline," he said, "we talked about this most of the night. *What conditions?*" It was true that they'd talked for hours in her seedy waystation room; they'd agreed that they both wanted children as soon as possible, and that there would be no more running away from a fight, for either of them. No lying, either by word or omission, and no secrets.

She took his arm, pulled him aside. Reverend Deever, mustache quavering, watched the retreat of the five-dollar gold piece with longing. "I want to help Becky at the hotel," she said. "We—well, we want to go into business together."

Rafe narrowed his eyes. "What *kind* of business?" he demanded.

Emmeline supposed he could be forgiven for asking such question, given past history, but she was a bit incensed, all the same. "The *hotel* business," she huffed, folding her arms.

"I'm looking for a wife, here, Emmeline," Rafe said carefully, "not somebody who passes through every once in a while, like a circuit preacher."

Emmeline linked her arm through his, shook her head, and looked up at him. "I promise," she said sweetly, "not to lapse in my wifely duties. That's going to have to be good enough."

"Suppose I refuse?"

"The wedding's off," Emmeline said. She spoke lightly, but her heart had come to a lurching stop in her chest.

He stared down at her for a long moment, his expression unreadable, and then laughed. "All right," he said. "We're bound to butt heads a few times, but we'll figure something out."

"Good," she said. And then she stood on tiptoe to kiss his cheek. The concessions he'd made were enormous ones for him; proof to Emmeline that he truly loved her. "Thank you, Rafe."

He gestured toward the bleary-eyed Reverend Deever, still pining visibly for the five-dollar gold piece. "Shall we get ourselves hitched?" he asked. "This time, for real?"

"This time, for real," Emmeline agreed. "And forever."

"It isn't going to be easy, you know," Rafe warned. "We're both going to make lots of mistakes."

She smiled. "Are you trying to back out on me, Rafe McKettrick?"

He kissed her nose. "Not me," he said.

They both turned to Reverend Deever then, and the man repeated his search-and-pat process until he came up with a small black book. Wetting his finger on the tip of his tongue, he turned delicate pages until he found his place. Then he cleared his throat and began.

"Dearly beloved . . ."

Emmeline could see the new house across the creek just as clearly as if it had already been built. Riding sidesaddle in front of Rafe, she lifted her feet slightly as Chief splashed into the water to make the crossing. The sweet grass whispered in a soft summer breeze as they climbed the low bank on the opposite side.

Once there, Rafe swung a leg over Chief's neck, and jumped nimbly to the ground, turning immediately to lift Emmeline down after him. Her body brushed his as he set her on her feet, and she was, for a few delicious moments, pinned between him and the horse.

"Our house will stand right here, Mrs. McKettrick," he said, in a low rumble. They'd been making love almost nonstop since their return from Rattlesnake Bend by wagon, and Emmeline was ready, to her private consternation, to go back to their bed right that minute. They had the main house to themselves, a rare event, since Kade and Angus were on the range with the rest of the cowboys, and Concepcion had gone to visit an ailing neighbor.

Emmeline smiled mischievously, but a memory touched her heart, soft as the brush of a tiny wing, and sadness flickered inside her. "Are you planning to burn this one down, as well, *Mr.* McKettrick?"

He tried to look stern, and failed resoundingly, since he was already grinning. There was a glint of tenderness in his eyes. "Before I answer that, maybe you'd better tell me if you've got any more secrets tucked away."

She laughed. "None at all," she said, resting her hands on his chest. It was, she thought, too bad they were in full sight of the house and barn on the other side of the creek. She wouldn't have minded making love right there in the grass, with the water singing its busy summer song nearby, but there were always ranch hands around.

"I love you," he said. He looked so solemn that she stood on tiptoe to kiss him.

"And I love you," she replied. She frowned, straightening his collar.

"But you still plan to be in town quite a bit, helping Becky get the hotel to where it's turning a profit."

She caressed his cheek. "And that's not all," she said.

"No?" he asked, arching an eyebrow.

"No," she replied. "I want us to go to San Francisco on that buying trip together. It can be a sort of honeymoon. And I want a real wedding, too, the kind that makes a person feel married, one with all our friends and family right there to help celebrate."

He leered at her, used the fact that the horse was blocking the view of anyone who might be looking on from across the creek as an opportunity to take one of her breasts in his hand. "Actually," he said, "I feel pretty married right now. But I'll agree to your demands."

She moaned involuntarily as he chafed a calico-covered

nipple with the side of his thumb. "Oh, Rafe," she whispered.

He chuckled and continued his nefarious work, bending his head, nibbling at her neck. "Yes?" The word was throaty, an intimate caress in its own right.

"We can't—not here—and I want to so much!"

He laughed, cocked a thumb over his shoulder. "How about back there, then? Behind those trees?"

She looked past his shoulder, assessing the stand of oak trees a hundred yards away. "I don't know," she said, feeling shy. "It might not be private enough."

He took her hand, led her away from the horse and toward the trees. "Let's find out," he said.

She scrambled to keep up with his long strides. "Rafe—" she protested, but without significant conviction.

The trees grew in a nearly perfect circle, and the center was like a little valley, tucked away under a canopy of green, chattering leaves. Emmeline looked back and saw only grass, rocks, and the faint sparkle of the creek. They might have been alone, the two of them, in a new Garden of Eden.

Rafe kissed Emmeline thoroughly now, his hands on her hips, and both of them dropped to their knees on the soft ground. This, Emmeline knew, would be the time, the magical time when they would conceive a child together.

She tilted her head back, gazing up at blue shards of sky, framed in oak leaves, as Rafe buried his face in her neck, at the same time unfastening the buttons of her shirtwaist, opening the camisole beneath. She gave herself up to pleasure, and to complete happiness, as he weighed her bare breasts in his hands, preparing them for his enjoyment, and for hers.

She whimpered softly as he lowered her into the delicious grass, prickly against her back, which was naked except for the thin cloth of the camisole, and plunged her fingers into his hair, guiding him to her. As he suckled, first at one breast, and then at the other, he lifted her skirts, and gave a small chuckle of delighted surprise when he realized she wasn't wearing any pantaloons.

"Mrs. McKettrick," he demanded, trying for a dour expression, "where are your britches?"

She laughed, though her flesh was hot and her nipples were hard and she needed Rafe's full and concentrated attentions in the worst way. "I got tired of always having to take them off, put them on, and take them off again. So I just left them behind when I got dressed this morning."

"Wench," he said, grinning, and went back to what he'd been doing.

Rafe was not a man to be hurried, no matter how urgent the pleas she uttered, and he had roused every part of Emmeline's body and soul to a dangerous pitch before he finally parted her legs, opened his trousers, and pushed inside of her in a single, sky-splitting thrust.

She cried out, clutching at his back, his shoulders, his hips, by turns, wanting to drag him deeper inside her, and then still deeper. When she raised her head to nip at his earlobe, he lost control, at long last, and began to move in earnest.

They strained together, flesh slick with perspiration, breaths shallow, hearts thrumming like horses' hooves in the heat of a desperate race. They reached the arch of their passion at the same time, clinging as their bodies flexed in violent response, one to the other.

Then they fell to the ground, still joined, both of them gasping, and waited for the world, thrown off its axis, to right itself. When it did, Rafe was the first to recover. He fixed his own clothes, and then Emmeline's, before hauling her to her feet.

"Do we look presentable?" she asked, still befogged with the echoes of all she and Rafe had just done together.

He laughed, plucked a blade of grass from her hair, which was surely disheveled, since Rafe had been running his hands through it. "We look," he said, glancing down at his rumpled shirt and trousers, "as if we've been making love on the ground."

"Oh, Lord," Emmeline fussed, trying to straighten her hair.

Rafe stopped her, drawing her back into his arms, and kissing her soundly. Things were already stirring inside her again when he drew back. "You're especially beautiful at this moment," he teased, "in a wanton sort of way."

She swatted at him. "You'd better get to work on that house," she informed him, touching her abdomen with one hand. "I want this child we just conceived to be born in a proper bed."

His blue eyes widened, and the full impact of the love she bore him bludgeoned him from within, the way it so often did. "You really think there's a baby?" he whispered, sounding awed.

"I'd bet anything," she told him, and slipped her arms around his neck.

Emmeline wore Georgia McKettrick's simple ivory wedding dress, altered to fit her, and a veil Becky had ordered all the way from Boston, the day she and Rafe were formally married. It was September, the leaves were just beginning to fall from the oak trees that had sheltered them while they made love, not just that once, but many times, within their circle. The house, though not completely finished, was fit to live in, and furnished with a bed, a shiny copper bathtub, and a kitchen table. The rest of the rooms would stand empty for a while, pending their honeymoon trip to California in the spring, but neither of them minded that. They had all they needed.

The ceremony, performed by the circuit preacher, a somber-looking man dressed all in black, took place in the afternoon, with the sparkling creek for a backdrop. Angus and Concepcion were there, of course, as were Becky and John, and the enigmatic Holt, now mended good as new. The staff from the hotel attended, including Sister Mandy and Clive, an unlikely pair for a celebration if ever there was one. Kade was best man, handsome in his Sunday suit, but Jeb didn't show up, even though the word had been put out weeks before that it was time he made his way home and let bygones be bygones.

If the informal invitation had reached him, he'd chosen to stay away, and Emmeline knew that everyone was disappointed, most especially Angus. He hadn't said anything to her, but Concepcion had confided that he walked the floor most nights, worrying that something had happened to his youngest son and blaming himself. He'd lost weight, and he spent an inordinate amount of time up on the hill, at Georgia's gravesite.

After the wedding, there was a reception at the main house, complete with cake and punch and a special surprise arranged by Becky and John. They'd sent for a photographer, and he'd come all the way from Tucson to take pictures of the bride and groom and all the guests. While they were celebrating, everybody talking at once, he'd gone out to his wagon to turn the plates into tintypes, by means of some mysterious chemical magic.

Kade, his back especially straight, his countenance solemn, approached Emmeline while Rafe was being congratulated by all the cowboys, who took special delight in the cake and punch and other refreshments. "May I kiss the bride?" he asked quietly.

She smiled. "Of course," she said.

He kissed her lightly, in the expected brotherly fashion, and then glanced over at Rafe. Holt looked on solemnly as the bridegroom enjoyed another round of congratulations, but he winked at Emmeline when she met his gaze. She laughed, and blushed a little.

"I'll be riding out soon," Kade said, gaining her full attention. "Look after my brother, will you? And Pa, too, though I think Concepcion does a pretty good job of that."

"You're leaving?" Emmeline whispered. "Why?"

Kade sighed. "It isn't like Jeb to hold a grudge this long," he said. "I'm going looking for him." He scowled, a McKettrick through and through. "And when I find him, I'm going to take a strip out of his hide, first thing."

Emmeline bit her lower lip. "We'll miss you," she said in all sincerity, but she knew Kade was doing the right thing. Angus was showing the strain, and the rest of them were feeling it, too. Something was very wrong where Jeb was concerned. "Do you have any idea where to start looking?"

"I thought I'd check out that rumor about him and the widow woman first," he allowed. "If that doesn't pay off, I reckon I'll make my way over to San Francisco. It would be just like my little brother to go over there and get himself shanghaied to China or some damn fool thing like that."

"Would you follow him that far?" Emmeline asked, with a little shudder, her eyes wide. "Even to China?"

"Yes," Kade answered without hesitation. "He's my brother." He smiled and kissed her forehead. "I've already congratulated Rafe on being the luckiest man in the world," he said, "so I'll be going now."

Emmeline embraced her brother-in-law. "Be careful,"

she said, "and don't stay away too long, no matter what. Angus doesn't need to be fretting himself about *both* you and Jeb."

Kade squeezed her hand. "Pa knows I'm leaving," he said. "Unlike Jeb, I'll be sending a letter whenever I get the chance."

"Goodbye," Emmeline said.

He merely smiled again, sadly this time, and walked away, disappearing through the doorway into the dining room. The kitchen was beyond, and the back door.

Rafe came over to Emmeline and slipped an arm around her waist. He was frowning, and she knew he'd watched the exchange with Kade. "Where's he off to?" he asked.

Emmeline was almost afraid to answer, lest Rafe take it into his head to join the search for Jeb and ride out after Kade. Alas, she and Rafe had agreed to keep no secrets from each other, and it was a bargain she meant to keep.

"He means to find Jeb and bring him home," she said.

Rafe nodded thoughtfully, watching Kade out of sight. Holt, standing nearby, with a cup of punch in his hand, did the same.

"I hope he finds him," Rafe mused, "and soon. Pa's fit to be tied, he's so worried."

Emmeline nodded, looking after Kade, and Rafe took her hand. "Come along, Mrs. McKettrick," he said. "I believe Concepcion is about to set out our wedding supper in the dining room, and I'm starved." He wriggled his eyebrows and spoke low and close to her ear. "I'll be needing my strength," he added. Then, taking her hand, he pulled her into the center of the celebration.

It was after nightfall, and the stars were almost within reach, it seemed to Emmeline, when she and Rafe got into a buckboard and crossed the stream, headed for their first night in the new house.

Outside the door, Rafe brought the team to a stop, lifted Emmeline down from the wagon seat, and carried her over the threshold. He set her on her feet in front of the large stone fireplace, where a nice blaze was crackling, and kissed her. Then, beaming, he reached into his coat pocket.

"I've got something for you," he said. He handed her a photographic likeness, taken that afternoon, in Angus's parlor, of her and Rafe in their wedding clothes. Although the photographer had instructed them to present a sober countenance, they were both smiling, Rafe seated in a chair, Emmeline standing beside him, with one hand resting on his shoulder.

She felt tears sting her eyes. "Oh, Rafe," she whispered, caressing the image with the tip of one finger, touching first his face, and then her own.

He reached up to the mantel, and took down the album he'd given her long since. "I reckon that's just the picture to start it off with," he said.

She took the album, with OUR FAMILY inscribed on the front cover in gold, and opened it, placing the picture carefully inside, with the flower he'd picked up at the other house, on the mountaintop, in what was to be their bedroom.

Indeed, they were a family now, she and Rafe.

He reclaimed the album gently, and set it aside, back in its place on the mantel. Then he held out his arms to Emmeline, and she went into them without hesitation.

This was home, not the fine new house rising around them, not the ranch reaching for miles in every direction, but Rafe's embrace. This was where she belonged, where she rejoiced in being, where she was most truly herself.

# ❧ Epilogue ❧

## Two weeks later

Emmeline stood in front of the Arizona Hotel with Sister Mandy at her side. Both of them watched, with a hand shading their eyes from the late afternoon sun, as two women got off the stagecoach. Even from that distance, Emmeline could tell they were at odds with each other, and she felt a funny little quiver of anticipation in the pit of her stomach.

"Who do you suppose they are?" asked Sister Mandy, who was wary of strangers. "Their clothes are pretty fancy."

Indeed, both the new arrivals were well and fashionably dressed, if a mite dusty from the trip.

"I think we're about to find out," Emmeline said as the women started toward the hotel, walking carefully apart. In the middle of the street, they stopped and fussed at each other, but they were still too far away for her to hear them clearly. "Looks like they mean to take rooms right here at the hotel."

Sister Mandy let out a low and very un-nunlike whistle through the small gap between her front teeth. "Loaded for bear," she said. "I hope they don't carry guns."

Emmeline spared her friend a brief, curious look, then turned her attention back to the approaching customers.

"How do you do, ladies?" she said, smiling, as the women drew near. One snapped open a fan and fluttered it fussily beneath her chin. Both were quite pretty, though their temperaments were less appealing.

"How do you do?" replied the taller one in an unfriendly tone. "Can you please tell me where to find Mr. Kade McKettrick?" she asked. "I've come all the way from Philadelphia. He and I are to be married."

A joyous giggle bubbled up into Emmeline's throat and she swallowed it, though just in time.

"That," said the other woman, rummaging in the depths of her reticule, "is what *you* think, Sue Ellen Carruthers! I have letters to prove that *I* am Mr. McKettrick's bride!"

Emmeline and Sister Mandy exchanged glances, Emmeline's amused, Sister Mandy's—well—*not* amused. In fact, Emmeline would have sworn she saw a glimmer of tears in the young woman's eyes.

Sue Ellen Carruthers looked as though she would swing her handbag at her traveling companion's head. "Nonsense!" she cried. "Kade McKettrick is *marrying* me!"

"Oh, my," Emmeline said, smiling. She could hardly wait to tell Rafe about this, and she'd have her chance soon enough. He'd be driving in from the ranch to collect her at any minute. "Brides to spare."